Captive Dreams

ANGELA KNIGHT

DIANE WHITESIDE

BERKLEY SENSATION, NEW YORK

THE BERKLEY PUBLISHING GROUP
Published by the Penguin Group
Penguin Group (USA) Inc.
375 Hudson Street, New York, New York 10014, USA
Penguin Group (Canada), 90 Eglinton Avenue East, Suite 700, Toronto, Ontario M4P 2Y3, Canada
(a division of Pearson Penguin Canada Inc.)
Penguin Books Ltd., 80 Strand, London WC2R 0RL, England
Penguin Group Ireland, 25 St. Stephen's Green, Dublin 2, Ireland (a division of Penguin Books Ltd.)
Penguin Group (Australia), 250 Camberwell Road, Camberwell, Victoria 3124, Australia
(a division of Pearson Australia Group Pty. Ltd.)
Penguin Books India Pvt. Ltd., 11 Community Centre, Panchsheel Park, New Delhi—110 017, India
Penguin Group (NZ), Cnr. Airborne and Rosedale Roads, Albany, Auckland 1310, New Zealand
(a division of Pearson New Zealand Ltd.)
Penguin Books (South Africa) (Pty.) Ltd., 24 Sturdee Avenue, Rosebank, Johannesburg 2196, South Africa

Penguin Books Ltd., Registered Offices: 80 Strand, London WC2R 0RL, England

Captive Dreams **was originally published in e-book format.**

PRINTING HISTORY
Ellora's Cave Electronic Publication / 2002
Berkley Sensation trade paperback edition / September 2006

Library of Congress Cataloging-in-Publication Data

Knight, Angela.
  Captive dreams / Angela Knight, Diane Whiteside.
    p. cm.
  ISBN 0-425-20775-7
  1. Occult fiction, American. 2. Erotic stories, American.   I. Whiteside, Diane.   II. Title.

PS3611.N557C37   2006
  813'.6—dc22

                                                                        2006017370

PRINTED IN THE UNITED STATES OF AMERICA

10 9 8 7 6 5 4 3 2 1

PROLOGUE

Jarred Varrain was no stranger to fear. He'd tasted its metallic tang staring down the muzzle of an ion pistol held in a scaly hand. He'd smelled its sickening stench as a prisoner on an alien moon, so deep underground he'd thought he'd never see the stars again. He'd even felt it drain away into hopelessness as his life's blood pumped from gaping wounds he somehow always survived.

And he'd seen the sheen of fear in his enemies' eyes as he'd killed, with pistol or blade or bare hands. So many times he no longer kept count.

He'd killed to protect. Killed to avenge. Killed because there'd been no other choice. Killed until he'd become an object of fear himself, even to the aliens and androids who didn't feel that emotion as humans did.

But he'd never known this kind of icy, helpless terror, even bound and beaten at the mercy of a merciless enemy. He'd been too busy plotting then, trying to find a way to escape and win. And he had. Jarred always won.

But not this time. He knew from bitter experience there'd be no last-minute victory for him now. Not if Mykhayl failed.

Because Celeste Carson was tired of him.

"I mean it, I'm killing the son of a bitch off," she said, as he stared at her with clenched fists. Oblivious as she always was to his invisible presence, Celeste sprawled across a white love seat in her primitive twenty-first century living room. Irritation pulled her full lips into a tight line and narrowed her cat-green eyes. Yet even in her anger, there was a lush sensuality to that delicately angular face. Dressed in a confection of black lace and red silk that hugged every alluring curve, she looked more like a Kyristari sexsub than the implacable enemy who'd tortured him for a decade. "I just have to come up with a suitably heroic way to cash in his chips."

Her sister looked up from the pile of whisper-thin fabric on her lap, blue eyes rounding with scandalized horror under her smooth cap of platinum hair. "You can't do that. The fans . . ."

"This is science fiction, Corinne. Nobody promised them a happy ending."

"But look how many people love Jarred! Take the convention yesterday. Hundreds lined up for your autograph."

Celeste rolled her eyes. "Most of whom wanted to be extras in *your* movie."

"But . . . kill Varrain? I love that character!" Jarred wanted to kiss her elfin face. "*You* love that character!"

"And I've been writing about him for ten long years. Ten long *books*. I want to do something different." Celeste rose and began to pace. Her lovely breasts swayed seductively under the thin black lace that barely covered them as her long, muscled legs scissored with her stride. Jarred watched with resentful hunger. God, he ached to turn the tables on her. If Mykhayl came through with that spell . . .

But without the spell, Jarred couldn't touch her. He was trapped in this limbo, able to see and hear his tormentor, but unable to take the revenge he craved.

"You don't have to kill Jarred to do something different, Celeste," Corinne said. "Just give him a desk job and write about one of his subordinates." *Management?* "Or make him an instructor at that agency star academy. Or . . ."

"He'd hate that worse than dying." Celeste glowered, nibbling a thumbnail. "That character is so damned infuriating. No matter what I plot out, he insists on doing the opposite."

Usually because whatever she planned was going to get someone killed. Like Garr.

The memory of his friend's bloody, broken body rose up in Jarred's mind until he had to fight the need to strike out in pointless rage.

"And if I try to force it, the characters just turn into cardboard," his enemy said, pacing by. Reluctantly compelled, he opened his eyes to admire the way her luscious ass rolled with every long-legged, seductive stride. "It's driving me nuts."

"Tell me about it," Corinne muttered, picking up the bit of lace draped across her lap to study it dubiously. "Mykhayl's been making me crazy for years. Now I can't even get him to pick a wife. And since he's sterile, God knows who he's going to name as his heir . . . Do I really have to wear this?"

Celeste propped her hands on her curving hips. Jarred stared, his attention caught by the golden shimmer of all that hair tumbling to her waist. He imagined wrapping his fist in gleaming curls as he rode her, taking a slow, sweet revenge while he taught her to crave every minute of her punishment. "Oh, come *on,* Corinne," she said. "It's just us girls. Everything you've got, I've got. Besides, considering what that slip cost, I'd think you'd want to try it on."

"Yeah, well, I only bought it because you insisted."

Full lips curled into a teasing smile. "I only insisted because you dress like a bag lady. Who can write sexy romance in sweat pants?"

"Me," Corinne retorted, sticking out a long leg covered in baggy gray fabric. "And I've got seven books to prove it."

"True, but the sweats obviously aren't working for you this time. Why else are you having so much trouble deciding who Mykh's going to marry?"

"Sheer numbers." Corinne balled up the silk and threw it against the wall. "The man's got a hundred women in his harem. Why should he fall in love with anybody when he's got the entire Rockettes chorus line waiting at home?"

Celeste rolled her eyes. "That's just sex, 'Reeny. Any guy will screw a hundred women if they're handy, whether he's shooting blanks or not. What Mykh needs is somebody who'll drive him so insane with desire, he's just got to have her."

"Exactly. But who?" Corinne retrieved the black lace. "I'm thinking of returning the advance."

"What?" Celeste gaped. "A million dollars? Are you nuts?"

Her sister turned to face Celeste, biting her lip. "Maybe if I didn't have that kind of pressure I could think of something. After all, if two weeks spent in daily kung fu practice didn't break the block loose, then I don't have anything else left to try. That's always worked before when I got stuck."

"Honey, it's not that bad, honestly." Celeste hugged her sister. Corinne returned the embrace then slipped free, eyes damp as she tried to smile. She began to wander the room, tossing the cloth from hand to hand.

Celeste flopped onto the couch, one shapely leg curled over the arm, the other stretched to one side. Jarred's eyes were drawn to the thin red fabric molded lovingly over the lips of her vulva. He thought about plunging his cock into her, burying himself in slick cream and heat. "Look, I think you're just having a hard time getting into his head as a romantic hero, instead of just the guy who comes to the rescue," she said, lacing her long fingers together over her taut little belly. "So turn it around and focus on the heroine instead. Any ideas on the kind of character you really want to do?"

"None. I even made a list of all the archetypes I could think of. The only tingle I got was for a sorceress," Corinne said glumly.

Celeste nibbled that fingernail again. Jarred imagined how she'd look with his cock in her mouth instead. "And all the female mages are all dead."

Corinne nodded. "Every last one of them, thanks to Mykhayl and his brothers-in-law."

"Okay, so that's out." She grimaced. "We'll just have to try something else. Which brings me back to my original point: nothing puts me in the mood to dream up something fantastic like wearing really expensive silk. If you need to create someone sexy and hot, dress like someone sexy and hot. Works every time."

"Maybe for you. You *are* sexy and hot. Me, I'm flannel and sweatpants." But she didn't put the lacy scrap aside.

"You only think that because you married an abusive creep." Celeste's voice dropped into a coaxing purr that went straight to Jarred's crotch. "Go on, put on the slip and we'll brainstorm. You can help me figure out how to kill off Jarred."

Her sister frowned, eying her. "You're really serious."

"Hell, yes! And you're going to marry Mykh off and finish your series. Get dressed and let's get started."

"Yeahhhh." Corinne nodded slowly. "We've always been able to help each other over rough spots before." She sighed. "Unfortunately, I don't know how much good it's going to do this time. Writing an erotic romance around Mykhayl feels kind of like French kissing your brother." Grumbling, she turned to march down the hall to the bedroom.

Jarred barely noticed, his attention locked on his deliciously sprawled foe. "Bitch," he growled at her. Celeste didn't hear him, of course. She never had, not even in the beginning when he'd roared at her like a madman for the way she tortured him.

For a decade he'd shuttled back and forth between his own universe and this limbo between their worlds, listening to her plan his torment, then going home to try to outmaneuver her. His attempts always failed. Even when he blocked one plot, she'd come up with something else that landed him in the same agonizing situation she'd originally intended. Yet she always made sure he survived.

Bloodied, broken, surrounded by the bodies of those he loved, he always survived.

But if Celeste had really decided to kill him, this time he would die. It was incredibly frustrating. The cybernetic implants scattered throughout his body allowed him to call up superhuman bursts of strength that made him a match for the toughest, most vicious alien warriors the galaxy could produce. Yet tiny, delicious Celeste could torment and destroy him at her whim, and there was nothing he could do about it.

But if he ever got his hands on her . . .

Suddenly he felt a familiar presence—a sense of simmering, formidable power. "Mykhayl?"

"Aye," rumbled a deep voice. Not for the first time, Jarred wondered if his friend looked anything like he did on the covers of Corinne's romance novels. As many years as they'd shared this half-existence, neither had ever seen the other. They remained as mutually invisible as they were to their creators, though at least the two men could communicate. Sometimes that had been all that had kept Jarred from going mad.

"Did you get it?" he demanded.

"Aye. I had to pay that thrice-damned wizard in dragon's blood. Now the blood-soaked amulet and the spell are mine to use."

But would it work? Mykhayl lived in a realm of sorcery where dragons were as common as the star cruisers of Jarred's universe. But that was no guarantee the enchanted amulet he'd fought to obtain would function here. And if it didn't . . .

"What are the little witches plotting now?" Mykh asked.

Jarred clenched his fists. "Celeste's going to kill me off."

There was a short, stunned silence. "Then we must act quickly. If you have a god, my brother, pray to him."

"What are you going to do?"

"Work a spell." The warrior king sounded grim. "A very dangerous spell that the hellspawn wizard had never performed and would not guarantee."

"Just do it," Jarred snarled.

Mykhayl's deep voice dropped even more as he began to chant, incomprehensible phrases streaming off his tongue in twisting, guttural syllables. As he spoke, Jarred felt threads of power shimmer into being, lines of force that quickly wove together in a net around them both. Energies so dark and strange, his skin crawled and his mind howled in instinctive disbelief, *There is no such thing as magic!*

And yet there was. The proof came in a blaze of pain as his nervous system protested the forces building around him. For a moment it seemed something massively alien ground against his body like a prowling dragon. Light exploded behind his eyes . . .

Suddenly there was a floor beneath Jarred's booted feet. He staggered forward, barely catching himself in time to keep from falling on his face. As he looked up, a man appeared beside him—even taller than he was, red hair brushing the small of a broad back, tight green trousers clinging to powerful thighs as a fringed vest hugged his muscled chest.

And yes, Mykhayl looked just as he had on all those romance covers.

Jarred's head snapped around. Celeste was staring up at them, her lush mouth rounded in a perfect O, green cat eyes huge in a face as bloodless as paper.

She could see them. It had worked.

Glancing back at his ally, Jarred felt a demonic grin of pure anticipation spread across his face. Mykhayl returned it with one just as nasty.

At last, the moment they'd dreamed of was at hand.

Impossible!

Celeste's jaw dropped as she stared up at the two enormous men towering over her.

One minute she'd been the only one in the living room. The next, everything had seemed to . . . stretch somehow, like a rubber sheet or a movie special effect. Then she'd heard a thunderous *CLAP*, a kind of mini-sonic boom.

Now Rambo and Conan the Barbarian were standing in her living room, looking as if they'd teamed up to kick somebody's ass. And since both were staring at her with identical expressions of pure menace, she had an ugly feeling whose ass they were planning to kick.

But what really spooked her was her own sense of recognition. The redhead was damn near seven feet tall, with the same handsome, hawkish face she knew from the covers of Corinne's books.

He looked just like Mykhayl, protective older brother of her sister's clan of romance heroines—except for the terrifying smile on his face. It was an axe-wielding-Jack-Nicholson-in-*The-Shining* kind of grin, and she didn't like it one bit.

The other man she'd seen only in her dreams. No artist had ever managed to capture Jarred Varrain's hard, lupine face with its broad cheekbones, narrow nose and cruelly sensuous mouth framed in that neat dark goatee. Yet here he was, just as she'd always imagined him, dressed in the gleaming black armor that looked and moved exactly like leather.

Celeste gaped helplessly, her eyes locked with his, feeling as though the planet had suddenly rocketed out from under her feet. "How did you do that?" she managed at last. "Who are you?"

The redhead touched a green gem that hung on a thick gold chain around his neck. "I built a doorway to this world, a portal of magic dearly bought with dragon's blood." The redhead's handsome jaw took on a grim cast, as if he were remembering something nasty. "And not a little of my own."

She licked dry lips, finding herself almost believing him. "But . . . who *are* you?"

The Jarred clone gave her a deliberately insulting head-to-toe scan that lingered at her cleavage. "Exactly who you think we are."

Before she could insist otherwise, high heels clattered in the hallway. Corinne burst in, just barely dressed in that stretch lace slip. "Celeste, what the *hell* exploded . . . ?"

"By the dragon's breath," the Mykhayl lookalike said, his eyes lighting as he rocked back on his heels to look her up and down. "There was a woman's body under all that baggy fabric after all."

Corinne's brows snapped down. "Oh no, not again. Look,

buddy, I have nothing to do with casting that damn movie, so you're wasting your . . ."

"I don't think they're actors," Celeste said hoarsely. For one thing, their costumes were far from cheesy, unlike the outfit the last would-be Mykh had worn during a futile bid to convince her sister to get him an audition. And while Corinne's *The Leopard and the Lily* was scheduled to start shooting next month, Celeste didn't have a movie deal. There was no reason for the dark-haired man to dress up like Jarred.

Besides, what kind of wannabe actor could produce a sonic boom at his audition?

"Of course they're actors." Corinne propped her fists on her lace-covered hips and scowled at the Mykhayl-alike, who started toward her with a long, lazy stride. "And they're going to be actors in jail if they don't get their leather-clad backsides out that door *now*." She broke off and blinked as the redhead loomed over her, grinning evilly. More than a foot taller than she was, he looked as wide across the chest as Arnold Schwarzenegger. "Damn, you're big."

"And getting bigger by the moment," the Mykhayl-alike rumbled. "What call you that bit of lace you wear? 'Tis intriguing." With a taunting grin, he reached out and cupped her left breast in long, bold fingers.

In one smooth blur, Corinne plucked the redhead's hand from her body, twisted his arm, pivoted, kicked his feet out from under him, and sent him tumbling across the floor like an astonished bowling ball. She struck a combat stance and glared. "Who the hell do you think you are? Get out before I get nasty."

"That's my girl!" Celeste cheered. A third-degree black belt in kung fu had done wonders for Corinne's self-esteem after that wretched marriage. It was also great for discouraging would-be Lotharios with fast hands.

But then the redhead looked up from the carpet. Celeste felt the temperature drop in her opulent apartment just from the ice in his eyes. He rolled into a feral battle crouch—Conan, ready to kick some kung-fu ass.

A soft chuckle sounded behind her back. "This should be good," the Jarred-alike said. "Too bad it won't last long."

Corinne studied the redhead's stance and frowned in wary recognition. She shifted her own position as her hands wove delicate patterns designed to confuse and intimidate.

Which had absolutely no effect on her opponent. He leaped for her as though intent on rolling over her like a masculine tidal wave. She met him with a flurry of blocks and blows. For an instant they seemed evenly matched, but then the redhead picked Corinne's wrist out of the air and spun her around, waltzed her three steps forward, and bent her over the arm of the couch.

Celeste gaped in horror. Her sister had finally met a faster opponent—and it couldn't have happened at a worse time.

"For these ten years, you tormented me as a child pokes a chained dragon with a stick," he snarled, whipping a length of rope from a pocket of his trousers. Before Corinne could rear out of his hold, he twisted it around her wrists in several neat, tight turns. Ignoring her frantic kicks, he knotted the ends, leaving her wrists thoroughly secured. "But now the dragon has slipped his leash, and you will pay for every poke." He rolled his hips against her butt in a gesture that spoke volumes about just how he intended to collect.

Corinne had a phobia about being bound. Any minute now, she was going to go nuts. "Let her go!" Celeste lunged for the big man, but before she took more than a single step, a powerful forearm coiled around her waist. One jerk slammed her backwards against a hard male body. Frightened and furious, she shrieked like an opera star trying to shatter a wine glass.

The Jarred-alike clamped a hand over her mouth, his hand so big it practically engulfed the lower half of her face. "Shhhh," he crooned. "I haven't given you a reason to scream. Yet."

Dammit, she would not be terrorized by him, no matter who he was. Baring her teeth, Celeste sank them right into his palm. He simply tightened his grip until it seemed the bones of her jaw creaked. Desperately, she stomped one high-heel down onto his foot, but it glanced off the hard, slick material of his boot.

A material that felt way too much like the armor she'd always imagined Jarred wearing.

Celeste forgot her fright at that comparison when he bent her forward and forced her down onto the carpeted floor. She went wild, kicking and punching at him as she spat a stream of acid curses, but she couldn't get in a solid blow with him behind her.

Fear surged through her veins, cold as a river of dry ice. *Oh, God. They're going to rape us . . .*

He ignored her frantic struggles and flattened her ruthlessly on the pretty white carpeting. The smooth, slick surface of his armored jacket pressed against her back as he covered her body with his, then caught her right wrist with his free hand and released her jaw. She writhed, but it felt as though he'd blanketed her in solid steel. "Let me go, you son of a bitch!" *This can't be happening!*

"Not until I'm done with you," he told her in a low, threatening rumble. Deliberately, he let his weight settle onto her, trapping her so thoroughly under two-hundred pounds of very large male that all she could do was squirm. "And considering everything I have in mind, I won't be done with you for a long, long time."

Oh, God, a small voice prayed at the back of her mind. *Get me out of this, please! I swear I'll never write another space opera as long as I live!*

The man reared off her just far enough to pull something metallic from a pocket. In seconds, he had the thin cable wrapped around her wrist, then grabbed the other hand. Despite her attempts to jerk away, he gathered both her wrists behind her back and finished coiling the cable around them. The minute he released it, the flexible metal line snapped tight and rigid.

Celeste's eyes widened. The fictional Jarred used something just like that to handcuff captives in her books, but there was no such thing in real life. Which meant . . .

Oh, no. The ice in her veins chilled still more. Could he really be . . . ? She thrust the idea away. *That's ridiculous. He's an actor. Or a nutcase with really cool toys. Or . . . something else. Anything else.*

Her captor stood, pulling her up with him as though she weighed no more than a cat. She cursed him futilely, since there was absolutely nothing else she could do. When he turned her lose, she almost fell on her face, off balance from her bound wrists. He caught and steadied her with a hand on her bare shoulder. His fingers felt very warm.

Shrugging off her kidnapper's grip, Celeste saw the big redhead still had Corinne bent over the couch, his hips plastered against her fanny. He whispered something in her ear that made her blue eyes go the size of dinner plates.

Celeste bit her lip. Corinne couldn't even stand to watch cop shows on TV because she was so phobic about handcuffs. How long could she take being bound like that?

"Dungeon? That's . . . that's not necessary," Corinne stammered, apparently replying to something the big brute had said. "Look, dammit, I'm sure if we all just *sit* down and *talk* . . ."

"If we sit, it will not be to talk." Mykhayl-alike smiled with chilling anticipation. "It will be so I can slide my rod into some tight orifice of yours." He pulled an amber pendant from his pocket and dropped it around her neck.

Corinne gasped and reared up, her feet flailing as if he'd done something much worse than put a piece of jewelry on her. One swinging high heel caught her captor between the legs. Cursing, he whipped another rope around her ankles. She wriggled under him frantically and hurled a string of locker room names at him. He squeezed her hip, growling a warning.

Terrified for her sister, Celeste twisted to stare up at her own captor. "He's hurting her! Make him stop!"

He lifted a taunting brow. "Why? He deserves a little revenge after what she's done to him."

"You don't understand! Corinne was abused by her ex-husband. She can't stand being tied up. Please!"

She threw a quick glance at her sister. Corinne stood stock still as the big redhead fondled her breast possessively and whispered in her ear. Fine tremors ran through her slender body, but she seemed to be hanging on to her self-control and her tongue.

In fact, she looked almost . . . intrigued?

"Just me?" Corinne whispered. Her voice strengthened as she drew herself to her full height and tossed her head in dismissal. "No, you're only an actor. And you're exaggerating anyway. Even in Hollywood, there can't be that many horny bimbos."

"I do not exaggerate," the big man said, his eyes narrowing in offense at her skepticism. The embroidered green dragon on his chest seemed to sneer. "All the women of the Seven Kingdoms consider it a great honor to warm the High King's bed. 'Tis why I often take more than one to my furs—Juli and Daio last night, Mhari and Treva the night before. I . . ."

"How did you get those names?" Corinne interrupted, staring at him in startled shock. "I've never even told Celeste who the concubines are."

The redhead arched a brow. "How could I not know who serves my lust?"

"Well, I'm still not buying any of this," she told him defiantly. "For one thing, if you *were* him, why would you give up all those beautiful women to concentrate on me?"

" 'Tis simple, wench." Lowering his head, he explained with silken menace, "The thought of listening to your pleas for mercy night after night makes my rod hard as a sword."

As both women stared at Corinne's captor in shock, Jarred shifted. "There'll be time enough for that when you're back in your own universe, Mykhayl. Why don't you work your spell, so we can both get started on our revenge?"

"Revenge?" Celeste squeaked.

"Revenge for what? I didn't do anything to you!" Corinne protested, as the big redhead chuckled and stepped back. A thoroughly impressive erection strained the fabric of his tight green pants. She stared down at it, her eyes widening even more. She whispered, "Well, except for *that* . . ."

"You also fed me to a thirty-foot ice serpent," the redhead told her grimly. "Not only did the cursed beast near kill me, the enchanted venom of its fangs rendered me as sterile as a gelded bull." His lips curled back from his teeth. "A palace full of concubines, and I cannot get a son on any of them no matter how many I fuck."

The acid in his tone made Celeste's heart skip a beat. As angry as he was, what would he do to her sister once he had her alone?

"Don't even bother asking what you did," the Jarred-alike hissed in Celeste's ear.

The reminder that she was in just as much danger as Corinne made the bottom drop out of her stomach. "Stop it," she ordered in a voice that shook. "I will not believe this. You are *not* him!"

"But I am—and it's time I proved it." He looked over her head. "Mykhayl?"

The big man nodded and swung his captive up over his shoulder as he began to chant something alien and guttural.

"Dragonese? Nobody else speaks that! I made it up!" Corinne's voice rose, taking on a note of true hysteria. She broke off in a screech as Mykhayl smacked her rump without interrupting his chant.

They're fiction, Celeste thought frantically as her skin began to tingle from the rise of dark energies. *None of it really happened. Oh God, I hope none of it happened. Garr . . . If he thinks I killed Garr . . .* Her heart lurched with a sudden, horrible suspicion. *Did I kill Garr?*

Rainbow bands of energy appeared and began to swirl right in front of Celeste's living room couch. The colors swirled tighter and faster, until it seemed they were boring like a giant drill bit, right through the wall into . . . somewhere else. Somewhere almost visible through the dark, man-size opening the energy drill created. Staring inside, Celeste could make out wavering shapes that looked at once alien and yet naggingly familiar. As she fought to make out more, wind poured through the shimmering hole to lift her hair, cool and smelling faintly metallic.

"Jump, my brother," Mykhayl said, his voice urgent and strained. "I know not how long I can hold the connection to your world. It . . . fights me."

"No!" Celeste gasped, jolted out of her unwilling fascination with the energy doorway. She whirled to run. With a soft, grim curse, Jarred bent and swept her into his arms. She screamed in pure terror as he turned and leaped right into the glowing maelstrom.

"NO! Celeeessste!" Looking over her captor's shoulder, she saw Corinne fighting Mykhayl's iron grip, an expression of panic and hopelessness on her pretty face. "Don't leave me!"

Her heart twisted, but for the first time in her life, she knew there was nothing she could do for Corinne. Or for herself.

Bound
by the Dragon

DIANE WHITESIDE

ONE

"Damn you, bring her back!" Corinne screamed at the leather-clad jerk disappearing into the gate's swirling maw with her sister. A dull thud sounded, like a drum skin snapping back into place—and then the gate was gone, leaving only Celeste's prized artworks on an expensively painted wall.

She twisted farther around on her own captor's shoulder, hoping for one last glimpse of Celeste. But no strange cauldron of frothing colors above endless depths returned her protective older sister. She swallowed a last sob and turned her back on the unresponsive paintings.

"I'll hunt you down, no matter who you are. Or where you are," she growled. She'd have to rescue Celeste somehow. And fast. That dark male looked pissed as hell and capable of anything.

The big man holding her chanted again in Dragonese but Corinne barely listened, too worried about her sister to think of her own predicament. Even the ropes rasping against her wrists and ankles were less nerve-wracking than Celeste's plight. And the amber pendant that clutched her neck like an unseen hand was only a minor irritant now.

Maybe—maybe the police could help if she yelled loud enough to overcome the soundproofing that Celeste was so proud of. *I should be able to do it; screaming for the cops shouldn't be too hard . . .*

She opened her mouth to try.

A last rasping masculine phrase snapped another gate open in front of them, its energies whirling with all the colors of the spectrum. He settled her more securely on his shoulder and leaped into the void beyond.

Shock clamped her throat shut.

They fell endlessly through darkness, brightened by cascading plumes of light that burned her eyes, even as the winds slashed her bare shoulders. They spun as they dropped, until the only reality was his iron grasp on her hip and his long red hair whipping across her face, borne by the vortex's chill, dry wind.

She tried to tell herself that this was only an illusion or fancy movie stunt. But George Lucas couldn't pull off an effect like this.

I swear I'll never write another cross-genre book, if I can just wake up in my bungalow again . . .

The lights formed into spirals, then icy nets of power that threatened to carve her flesh from her bones. Every energy path in Corinne's body wakened to agonized life, as her *ch'i* flowed in a hundred different directions. She screamed, but the vortex carried her voice away before she could hear herself.

She flung her head from side to side, searching for somewhere solid to take refuge against, and found her captor's head and neck. His warm strength flowed into her and his grasp tightened on her hip. The energy lines pulsed then quickly aligned into a cleaner flow than she'd ever found in a kung fu class.

Suddenly the vortex burst into a world of air and matter, not energy. Far below, she could see a forest of polished marble columns rising above a bright floor. She squeezed her eyes shut and screeched, as they plummeted downward. But he merely grunted and gripped her more tightly. Somehow he landed on his feet, maintaining his hold on her behind. Corinne gagged when his hard shoulder slammed into her belly.

Her eyes cracked open warily. She hung upside down over the stranger's shoulder, staring at a complex mosaic of a dragon and a tiger. Pulling herself upright, she looked away from the all too accurate replica of Torhtremer's Great Seal and tried to ignore the massive hands gripping her ass.

"What the hell," she moaned and swallowed hard. The sudden change to a stable universe irked her stomach, while her *ch'i* was taking its own sweet time returning to normal patterns.

"By the gods, I did it," he groaned. His chest heaved as he fought for breath, but he managed a weak whoop of triumph.

"Oh damn." She looked around for help. With any luck she'd be on a sound stage and could complain to the director. But if she wasn't lucky, and the big body builder with a grand master's speed really was Mykhayl . . .

The enormous room didn't look like any set she'd been shown in New Zealand, not with its frame of green and white marble pillars, marching in pairs along each side. More marble covered the floor in patterns as intricately wrought as any oriental carpet. Murals washed the walls and ceiling in celebration of the green dragon and the white tiger, Torhtremer's emblems. A rainbow of banners fluttered high above, gradually recovering from the vortex's winds. Long windows opened one wall to a view of the harbor beyond and the gentle southern hills, curling into a phoenix's fluid outline under the first rays of sunset.

No cameras, no lights, no scaffolding to support lights or a wall, no hairstylist fussing about the big guy's tousled locks . . . Thousands of nicks in the floor looked like the result of centuries of boots, not a set decorator's polishing.

"Oh damn," Corinne said again, rather more forcefully. Panic welled up until she shivered, but she fought it back down. She knew better than to lose control in front of a man.

Great sconces circled the room, each holding aloft a round golden globe backed by a silver shell. The globes glowed softly now, the traditional sign that a Dragonheart was present. Mykhayl Tibronson, High King of Torhtremer, was the only living Dragonheart: he could summon the Imperial Dragon to life at any time. Still, any lighting designer who'd read all six of her books would know that much.

"Welcome to Torhtremer," the big redhead announced hoarsely as he set her down, sliding her over his front as if he didn't trust his grip. The bilious green of his skin was so unflattering that no actor would tolerate it for a minute. Looking up at him, she fought the increasing conviction that everything was just as genuine as it appeared.

Corinne swayed, off-balance from shock and the shoe she'd lost. She tried to widen her stance and recover, but her bound ankles couldn't obey. She squeaked and wobbled helplessly, her hands tugging futilely against their ropes.

He caught her easily, his strength and size making her feel even more defenseless.

"Let me go, you bastard!" she snarled instinctively. The amber pendant immediately flared into life, shooting hot stabs of fury into her lungs. She gasped in pain and the pendant cooled instantly.

"The more you curse me, the greater will be your punishment," the big redhead remarked, sounding entirely too pleased.

"What are you talking about?" She angrily kicked off the useless shoe, and he steadied her carefully until she could stand on her own. Even then, he kept a viselike grip on her elbow. Stubbornly she refused to wince.

"Dragon's blood and mine thrice soaked the amber. It will magnify any harm you wish on me threefold and turn it back against you." His skin was losing its unhealthy tint, while his mouth twitched. Damn him, he looked like he enjoyed fencing her in.

"Oh, come on! Don't give me that bullshit," Corinne blustered, finally shaking free of his clutch. "Why would you waste all that effort on a nobody like me?"

"You're a sorceress, are you not?" he snorted and swept his hair back from his face, making the huge emerald in his heavy signet ring catch fire. "I'd give a sweeter welcome to a colony of Zemlayan fire ants."

"I don't do magic! I'm just a romance author." Corinne took a deep breath, trying to ignore the ropes cutting into her skin, and edged farther away from him. His broad chest was swirled with auburn hair and strained the embroidered vest with every breath. Her five feet ten felt fragile next to him until she tried not to shiver. The marble floor was entirely too cold for comfort, her skin was producing goose bumps faster than her lack of clothing could account for, and her stomach was tossing as if to evict that last expense-account dinner.

"Pray tell, how did an *author* compel the northern ice fortresses to surrender to a company of women? Or bring a fleet of Amazons from the lost islands to save the Goddess's shrine from burning? Or . . ." He raised a mocking eyebrow as he eyed her retreat.

She stayed put to face his unspoken challenge and glared at him. "Those were just stories! They didn't happen." But her voice lacked conviction even to her own ears.

Any casting director would have killed to put that face on the silver screen: golden eyes under winged eyebrows and a broad forehead, high slanted cheekbones, straight nose and hard chin framing a mouth designed for endless kisses, a thick fall of auburn hair that touched his waist. Any actor who looked like him would have been a star years ago, not an unknown trying for a secondary part in a movie.

"What you name yourself matters not, only the pleasures you'll bring me. Now where shall I begin . . ." He began to circle her slowly and she took a quick step back, choking for breath. Maybe reasoning with him would work.

"It's a lovely set you've got here," she began, trying to sound as rational as a woman could while wearing only a stretch lace slip that barely covered her behind. Maybe if she didn't think about what she wasn't wearing, he wouldn't, either. Maybe she could still regain the initiative. Yeah, and maybe that cow really did jump over the moon.

"Truly magnificent and so accurate down to the last detail," she continued hastily. "I'll be glad to recommend Peter and Janet hire you for the next movie. Now, if you'll just untie me and let me go, then we can both forget that this happened." She smiled at him, as charmingly as she could.

To her horror, he lifted an eyebrow and began to laugh.

"Hire me, the High King, to be a traveling player? But perhaps I would, if I could return to you each night." He eyed the cleavage displayed above her slip's black lace, while his forefinger traced a lazy path between her breasts.

"Keep your hands to yourself!" Corinne took a hasty step backwards, which was too much for her hobbled ankles to manage. She tumbled to the floor and automatically rolled to avoid bruising. She wound up facing the dais and its two thrones.

The smaller throne was silver and carved in the shape of a great white tiger—powerful, elegant and emphatically female, its sapphire eyes lifeless. A great halberd hung on the wall behind it, its curved blade on the long iron staff strangely reminiscent of an outstretched cat's claw.

The larger throne offered a seat between the two forepaws of a great green dragon; the dragon's body supported the seat with the tail coiled neatly behind. The head loomed over the seat, looking both powerful and omniscient. Its eyes met hers, ancient and inscrutable, filled with an alien curiosity more terrifying than the ropes binding her wrists or the fall through the vortex.

Three months in New Zealand polishing *The Leopard and the Lily*'s script had taught Corinne the limits of modern movie making. Nothing in Hollywood's bag of tricks could make a piece of furniture seem alive while you looked at it. Modern magic added the life later, in an effects shop after the actors had gone home.

All her earlier nausea rushed back and hit her in the stomach like a bullet train. That was Khyber, the Imperial Dragon, manifesting himself as a throne. She truly was lying in Torhtremer's throne room, eyeing a beast who could swallow her whole, just as he'd used the sorcerer Hardradda's bones for toothpicks.

Which meant she really had caused an ice serpent to emasculate the man standing next to her. To say nothing of the other torments she'd caused him, like that time with the Gray Sorceress. *Damn, damn, damn.*

Suddenly her brain was very far removed from the ice-cold body that couldn't catch a breath of air. Her pulse speeded up and she nearly fainted.

Then she caught a glimpse of the Great Seal with its dragon and tiger from the corner of her eye, the tiger ready to leap on any enemy.

The dizziness receded slightly and she fumbled for her *sifu*'s proverbs before a kung fu tournament. Her heart slowed to deep thuds that seemed as loud as a rock concert. A single breath rasped her lungs, then another and another. She came up on her knees very carefully, still trembling, her eyes never leaving the enigmatic intelligence before her, her brain still barely connected to her body. She had to directly confront the only magic she'd written of but never understood.

"Khyber, are you frightening my captive?" Mykhayl's voice, low and rumbling with suppressed laughter, was as infinitely welcome as the marble floor's increasing warmth.

The dragon yawned, displaying rows of knife-sharp white teeth. "Merely inspecting what you took so long to retrieve." His voice was calm and precise with a faint hint of Scotland, like Sean Connery playing a very haughty dragon. Definitely Khyber. Why hadn't she realized before just how big a thirty-foot long dragon really was?

Corinne bit her lip and tried not to shiver more. Either male would pounce at any sign of weakness.

"If you'd carried me to her as I asked, I would have returned in a candle's span." Mykhayl lifted her upright against him. She gathered her feet under her, desperate for some independence, but reluctantly thankful for his body heat and the support of his strong arm. Her hands were trapped between her back and that iron ridge inside his trousers. She didn't dare move them.

"You learned more by performing the spell yourself," Khyber returned calmly. "And it gave you the freedom to send the other man back to his world with his woman."

"But mine is more beautiful, is she not?" Mykhayl bragged as he wrapped his arm around her and lazily stroked her hip. She quivered under the possessive touch and her treacherous nipples beaded. The hair on the nape of her neck lifted, a slow warmth building where her naked neck and shoulders brushed against his satin skin.

She started to protest but stopped. She'd disappear in a moment down that scaly throat if Mykhayl didn't protect her.

"Perhaps she is comely only because you captured her," Khyber snorted, swirling the banners with a gust of sulfur-laden air. His massive head lifted from the throne and uncoiled to inspect her closely, his reflections rippling through column after column, until she felt surrounded by dragons. Ice stormed through her veins again and she shuddered, her mouth too dry to speak. Her only comfort was the big body behind her, towering over her, while his hand slid over her stomach.

"Nonsense! You're simply envious that a mage will grace my bed tonight and not yours," Mykhayl retorted, still fondling her. Heat followed every slow smooth glide of his fingers over the lace, until she thought she might collapse. Her silk slip and his leather trousers didn't stop his truly impressive erection from nestling into the crack of her ass. He rolled his hips so that his balls stroked her bound hands. Heat flooded her blood and bones everywhere he touched. She was helpless to stop him, open to anything he wanted, and worse yet, melting in anticipation of his next move.

"No!" Corinne gasped at the sudden realization of how much self-control she'd lost and tried to jerk away. Her hobbled feet stumbled and she'd have fallen under the dragon's nose if Mykhayl hadn't caught her.

"Foolish wench," he chuckled, settling her back against him, both hands coming up to hold and tease her in a way that felt totally different from anything that jerk Dylan had ever done. She shuddered when he began to rub against her hands again, her breasts tightening with every wicked touch.

The silver sconces nearby started to glow, until the three stood in a pool of light as bright as high noon.

"Mortals." Khyber sniffed and swung his massive head to consider the two humans from first one side, then the other. His golden eyes were damn near the size of her torso. She refused to consider the size of his teeth. He could swallow her whole.

"Please," she got out, wishing her mouth wasn't so damn dry. "Please untie me!"

"Indeed? Why should I release my little captive?" Mykhayl plucked her nipples through the silk. A jolt of sheer lust ran down to her core in response.

Corinne shook, overwhelmed by proximity to a dragon, anxiety over Mykhayl's intentions, and old nightmares. He probably wouldn't kill her, but she remembered other times when she'd have welcomed death rather than bondage at a man's hands.

Sweat beaded on her forehead as she tried to think. Three enemies in this room: Mykhayl, Khyber, and the ropes. Which one could she dispose of first? How could she escape at least one?

"Do you really need me bound like a Christmas roast?" Corinne stammered, uncomfortably aware of the blazing brand that ran from Mykhayl's hand to her breast and straight to her vulva. She tried to think, which was difficult when column after column showed her half-swooning against Mykhayl's hard body. "Is this how you always persuade a woman to sleep with you?"

"Your consent isn't needed, sorceress, only your body." His voice was idle, but his touch and that blazingly hot bar against her ass were anything but relaxed.

The Tiger Throne shimmered in the silver sconces, as Mykhayl nuzzled her shoulder. Corinne shuddered in response and made up her mind. If she couldn't control him or the dragon, then she'd settle for not being helpless.

"Please take these ropes off me," she begged, then added, "Your Majesty."

"A pitiful plea, sorceress, hardly worth the mention. Perhaps you have something you can offer in exchange for a boon," he half-growled, half-sighed, pressing himself against her hands.

Corinne closed her eyes, his fat balls behind their leather veil rolling into her palms until her fingers instinctively, involuntarily stroked them. If she was very lucky, none of the dew between her thighs showed underneath her incredibly short slip.

"Wouldn't you prefer a complaisant, willing woman, Your Majesty?" she managed, forcing herself to look up at him. This was not how she'd ever written a seduction scene. "Not one who would weep and wail every time you came near?"

Mykhayl smiled down at her, hunger and excitement boldly apparent. "Your words begin to excite me, sorceress. Perhaps I'll lash you to my bed that I may hear you beg more."

The evidence that he spoke the truth was unmistakable. Corinne gulped, uncomfortably aware of how her nipples had grown under his greedy gaze. "Look, I swear that I will do anything you want while I'm here, as long as you don't tie me. Please!"

Mykhayl threw back his head and laughed. "My rod leaps at the sound of your pleas, sorceress. And you have yet to learn the full measure of my revenge."

If she didn't get free soon, she was going to beg him to take her. What else could she try?

"Does raping a helpless woman make you hard?"

His golden eyes flickered at that.

"Wouldn't you prefer to hear me beg for more?" She wet her lips, wishing that her nipples weren't such hard buds. This had to work. "I swear that I'll be an eager bed partner if you'll untie me."

"An oath is binding on a sorceress who gives it freely," Khyber remarked, resting his chin on a forepaw to study her better.

Corinne stared at the enormous green dragon. Why on earth was he helping her win this argument? She kept silent.

"She has earned any punishment that I care to mete out," Mykhayl reminded Khyber. Damn, some of his fingers had found her slip's hem. Her pulse pounded harder and she prayed for escape.

"Her magic is servant to her words, so long as she commands it or gives oath. You can always bind her, if you want to hear her pleas again." Khyber yawned, showing some viciously sharp teeth and setting Corinne's hair to fluttering. Her stomach clenched. "Do you mean to take her hence or use her here where I can watch?"

Mykhayl frowned at the dragon, then shrugged.

"I accept your given word, sorceress. You'll moan in my bed soon enough." He stepped away from her and cut her wrists and ankles free with a slender dirk.

Corinne shook the circulation back into her hands and managed to keep her balance without assistance from Mykhayl.

A surreptitious glance showed her that the Dragon Throne now looked like just an ordinary piece of furniture, while the Tiger Throne's silver shone as bright as the sconces. She frowned, not comforted at all. She was in Torhtremer at the mercy of a justifiably furious High King. Hopefully, he'd never find out exactly why she'd made the ice serpent bite him.

Mykhayl swatted her ass and she jumped with a small shriek. Nobody'd ever dared to do that before, not even Dylan. "What the hell!" She swung at him, but he caught her wrist and pulled her close.

"Spitting at your master, already?" he purred, boldly running his hand up her hip under the slip. She gasped and glared at him.

"No more words for me? Do you think to avoid swearing another oath by keeping your lips sealed?" He laughed at her outrage and bent his head to hers. The masses of auburn hair tumbled down like a veil when his lips touched her temple.

Corinne started to jerk away but caught herself. She froze, fighting the tremors of nervous anticipation, while his warm mouth traveled down her cheek.

His hand caught her chin, tilting it up to meet him. "You little minx, I wish to taste what my strength and cunning has captured. Show me the delights of a willing sorceress."

Her tongue ran out over her lips and then retreated. She closed her eyes against the lust in his and waited, not quite daring to breathe. But his long callused fingers stroked her face slowly, tracing the muscles and tendons and pushing back her hair. She forgot to worry about his mouth, while she wondered which pulse he would set on fire next.

He stroked his tongue over her lips softly, like the first scout of an advancing army. Her body stilled in anticipation.

The kiss, when it finally came, seized her like springtime's rush into the Arctic tundra. His lips covered hers and his tongue surged into her fiercely. Her sigh opened her mouth even more to his assault. She moaned and clutched at his shoulders as he ravaged her mouth, sending heat flooding down to her toes.

One last thought flashed past before her wits vanished: he didn't kiss like an older brother.

Corinne took several long breaths afterwards before she tried to open her eyes. Her breasts' tightness was mildly revenged by the glazed look in his eyes and the tic in his jaw. But he had the advantage with that big paw slowly stroking her back. Under the black lace.

Damn.

He smiled at her with the wicked anticipation of a gambler

who knows he holds the winning hand. "Your kiss shows some womanly skills, sorceress. Let us go hence and see what more you offer."

Mykh watched his captive closely, admiring what his blood and courage had gained him. By the Goddess, she was a beauty with her silvery hair and blue eyes. What trick of fate had kept that body hidden from others under leagues of cloth? She was fierce and fast when she fought, skilled enough to cost him a moment's caution. Would she love as hotly?

He would have to be careful not to lower his guard around her. A sorceress could turn a man's will into meltwater in an instant. Perhaps this night's pleasures would bring sound sleep without old nightmares.

She flushed but didn't resist when he towed her along beside him. A few quick strides brought them over the dais and past the two thrones. He raised an eyebrow at the Tiger Throne's glow but didn't pause. It had to be a trick of the light, since almost a thousand years had passed since a tigerheart had ruled beside a Dragonheart. Although a tigerheart was always a sorceress . . .

He pulled open a small door, cunningly hidden in the rich carvings behind the thrones. "Come in," he welcomed the men who stood beyond it and Corinne stiffened beside him.

His mouth quirked. He never shared women until he was bored, which was usually all too soon. But he had a great many plans for the long-legged beauty beside him.

Two men entered quickly and closed the door behind them. Yevgheniy, retired *primus pilus*, or first spear, of the High King's personal guard and now Guardian of the Dragon's Hoard, the traditional reward for decades of loyal service. His weather-beaten face was as incongruous as ever above the Guardian's rich scarlet robes.

Mykh lifted an eyebrow at the two beakers and goblets Yevgheniy bore on a silver tray but said nothing. He'd no need now of Bhorizh's latest potion, even if it could freeze a sorceress in place. He'd learn soon enough what the other beaker held.

The other man was a welcome surprise. He'd told Yevgheniy to keep watch with no hope that his oldest friend would return in time to help. But Ghryghoriy doted on his wife, more than enough reason to make a hasty return for the Goddess's Dance. He'd been back for some time, since he wore the immaculate black uniform of the Dragon's Claw instead of muddy courier's leathers.

The little sorceress paled before blushing scarlet at the sight of Ghryghoriy. Mykh wondered how much she knew of the man's bloody past, then shrugged. Answers could be found later, after settling his innards back to a more landlocked pace.

"Yevgheniy, Ghryghoriy," he greeted them each with a strong hug, noting how she edged off to one side.

"Welcome home, Mykh." Ghryghoriy's answering embrace lasted a hair too long to be casual, while Yevgheniy rapidly blinked away tears. "The bonds you requested . . ." He held them out ready for use, as Mykh had ordered before departing. Izmir's Curse, the only ties capable of holding a magic-wielder against his will.

The little sorceress shook but didn't run away, her eyes widening like a deer caught in the hunter's snare as she stared at the heavy golden cuffs. Her sister had mentioned abuse, which must have been fearsome to inspire such dread in a sorceress.

Mykh brushed the cuffs and their connecting chain aside. "No need for that. She's bound to serve willingly in my bed."

Both men stared at her then relaxed when she nodded jerkily. The gold disappeared from sight and Corinne openly fought for calm, while Yevgheniy filled a goblet after one last survey of her.

The door eased open and a huge black leopard flashed in. He leaped up at Mykh, braced his forepaws on Mykh's shoulders, and lavished kisses on his face.

"Down, Mazur!" Mykh laughed, cupping his friend's head in his hands. "You have known me gone before to see the sorceress. Did you fear that I would never return?"

A long swipe of rough leopard tongue from chin to forehead was the answer, then Mazur butted his head against Mykh's cheek. He reassured the big cat with a quick hug.

"You've been gone two days and a night, Mykhayl," Ghryghoriy observed quietly.

"So long?" He cursed the demons who haunted the void between worlds.

Sensitive to his master's mood, Mazur dropped to the floor and began to wind himself around Mykh's legs. Mykh rubbed the plush head distractedly and accepted a goblet from Yevgheniy.

"Give her a drink of the same, Yevgheniy, not the potion." He waited to ask for reports until Corinne held the other goblet. "How quiet is the city? Did anyone notice that I was gone?" He took a deep swig of his ice-cold ginger beer, savoring the demons' departure from his guts.

"It's been silent as my maiden aunt's bedroom," Yevgheniy snorted. "What did you expect for the first day of the Hunter's Watch?"

"City's full of pilgrims. There should be some unrest," Mykh observed, his senses coming alert at the strange tidings.

"Hell, the whole province is full of pilgrims. Temples are calling it the greatest pilgrimage in five hundred years. And everyone's keeping watch, like the priests told 'em to. Just so they can give all their strength in the Goddess's Dance."

"By the gods!" Mykh's fist tightened around the goblet's stem and Mazur hissed in agreement. "Must they all believe that I need their help?"

He hurled the goblet into the throne room's shadows and Mazur roared his own battle cry in support. Khyber's long dragon snout and neck flashed forward. He caught the goblet in his teeth then set it neatly down on Yevgheniy's tray. Ghryghoriy raised an eyebrow and the little sorceress flinched at the byplay.

"Are you telling me that every sailor in Bhaikhal, Torhtremer's greatest port, is meekly obeying a handful of saffron robes?" Mykh snarled.

"Aye," Yevgheniy answered, unimpressed as ever by Mykh's temper. "No drinking, no fighting, no coupling between a man and a woman. Even the whores have sworn celibacy for the next three nights."

"What did they preach to cause such a display?" When neither man responded, Mykh snarled. "Tell me, Ghryghoriy."

"All of Torhtremer must labor together that the High King might be healed," Ghryghoriy answered carefully.

"Does everyone in the Seven Kingdoms know that I can't breed a woman?"

Corinne bit her lip at the naked agony in his voice and hid her face in her goblet.

"Not easy to hide that with the size of your harem and the hard use you make of those girls," Yevgheniy remarked, brutally frank as always.

Mykh cursed again, damning all meddlesome folk who would not leave a man to solve his own problems. Mazur stropped himself on Mykh's shins, while the little sorceress shook violently.

"We've put out word that you began fasting yesterday, so no one's looking for you," Ghryghoriy reported, turning the subject.

"Even the girls aren't anxious," Yevgheniy added, stoppering the beaker. "Told 'em you attended private services here at the palace."

"Tides are rising hard and fast for the Goddess's Dance. All shipping cleared harbor yesterday," Ghryghoriy assured Mykh, answering an old fear.

"Priests promised the greatest dance in a thousand years. Looks like they're right about that much at least," Yevgheniy commented, before falling wisely silent at Mykh's glare.

"Borders are quiet. No word from the sentries watching the northern mountains, either," Ghryghoriy finished. That was one piece of good news, that the Dark Warrior was still trying to recover his strength before challenging Mykh and the Seven Kingdoms again.

The little sorceress gently petted the big cat's head with her free hand, rubbing his ears through her fingers until he butted against her legs for more.

"Damn watch," Mykh muttered. "No purpose in it when the priests' magic can't give me a son." He pulled Corinne against him and fondled her hip possessively. She was a battle trophy worthy of a High King and a far better treat than the priests' useless chants. He was finally free to fulfill all the promises he'd made himself, while slaving for the Gray Sorceress.

He dropped a kiss on top of her head. "Keep the priests away from me until the morrow, Ghryghoriy."

The Dragon's Claw bowed in response, his face politely blank.

"And you, Yevgheniy, I've a sorceress to taste tonight. Make the usual preparations then get yourself gone. I presume the Tasting Room is ready for use."

"Yes, Your Majesty."

"Very well then." He left the room with a firm stride, his attention fixed on the slender woman at his side and the rare treats to be found between those long, beautifully muscled legs.

Corinne trotted down the corridors at Mykhayl's side, barely able to keep up with the pace he and Mazur set. Her mind reeled from seeing Yevgheniy and Ghryghoriy in person. Yevgheniy, with his ancient soldier's eyes that had seen everything at least twice and done it at least once. He truly was the spitting image of the longest serving Navy SEAL.

But seeing Ghryghoriy was worse, since he was the secondary hero of *The Raven and the Rose*. One look at him and she'd immediately recalled his inventive sexual tastes, including an anal sex scene that had made even Celeste blush. He looked much more like Jarred Varrain than she'd imagined, now that she'd seen them both in the flesh.

In the flesh. Oh dear God, then Celeste really must be in that far future world with its terrible devices . . .

She yanked her mind away from the tortures Jarred had endured—and could visit on Celeste—to the scenery around her. She'd never thought much about Mykhayl's living quarters, only the romantic advantages and disadvantages of the women who visited him there.

Mykhayl gave her no time to study the riches they passed, other than to gain an impression of still more murals featuring the dragon and the tiger, above beautiful marble wainscoting and polished marble floors. She stayed close, having learned in the throne room that the floor was nicely warm near him.

He turned into a quieter section, nodding at the two sentries who snapped to attention as he passed. They wore the green and gold uniform, with black breeches and boots, of the High King's personal guard, with weapons far more functional than ceremonial. Their cold eyes warmed at seeing Mykhayl but measured her with a steely calmness that named her as a threat.

The floor and wainscoting changed to rare woods in intricate marquetry, echoing elegant tapestries of the green dragon flying above the great eastern woods. She swallowed, recognizing the signs of the High King's private quarters. She'd plotted many scenes in the throne room, including a wedding. But never anything in his bedroom. She shivered at the thought, wishing that he didn't make her so damn hot.

And what was he going to do to her? He kept calling her a sorceress, which didn't bode well for her future. Ever since his captivity by the Gray Sorceress, he'd treated all sorceresses suspiciously, ready to strike and kill before they could hurt him. They were admittedly some of the Dark Warrior's nastiest servants, more than deserving the deaths that Mykhayl and his brothers-in-law had meted out. But Mykhayl had always watched them more apprehensively than any other enemies.

What exactly had the Gray Sorceress done to him? Back then, Corinne had been so interested in writing Lily's romance that she'd considered Mykhayl mostly as a plot convenience. Now she reached out to learn what had happened during his months of slavery and ran up against a blank wall. The same unyielding barrier that had given her months of writer's block. The same total inability to see Mykhayl's thoughts and emotions from the inside.

Corinne cursed silently and refocused her eyes on her surroundings. Mykhayl was striding straight toward a simple door set between richly patterned tapestries showing mating dragons.

Its vigilant sentry quickly snapped to attention as they approached, her eyes widening at the High King's companion. She saluted and opened the door behind her, then shut it silently after Mykhayl and Corinne entered. Mazur stayed outside, uttering a disconsolate *mrow*.

The room was fashioned entirely of crystal, curving around a raised platform in the center, and almost as enticing as a hidden spring in the woods. Corinne surveyed it warily.

"The Tasting Room, sorceress," Mykhayl purred, his deep voice suggestive of triumphs yet to come.

"What the hell do you taste here?" Corinne spun around to quiz him.

"I savor women here, Corinne. The heat of them pouring up from their core like the taste of life itself."

Savor women? She frowned at how his rumbling voice seemed to burn from her ears to her gut. And those fierce golden eyes that heated her even more. But didn't monarchs let the concubines do all the work? "That's crazy. What happened to sprawling on the bed and letting the girl slither up to you?"

He chuckled and picked her up. "Ridiculous. Why should I permit you to set the pace? Or choose what to do first?"

"I didn't mean that," Corinne lied, stiff as a brass statue in his arms. There was something about being handled as if she weighed nothing that scared her, no matter what she knew of him personally. But being surrounded by a massive chest and arms set her pulse pounding, while the slip might as well not be there for all the protection it gave from his iron-hard sinews under hot satiny skin. "But don't you want me to prove just how much I'm willing to do for you?" *And maybe distract you until you're doing what I want?*

"The first step of my revenge is to eat you until you beg me to cease, unable to endure any more."

Her brows snapped together. "You're joking, right?"

"Hardly." He settled her into a sling that had appeared in the exact center of the room. It was made of fine white silk webbing, more comfortable than any hammock she'd ever enjoyed in a backyard. Instinctively her hands reached up to trace the two bands that secured it above her head, while her feet settled into the perfect little hollows at the other end. She was safe, supported—and hanging in midair before a set of mirrors that showed every inch of her.

"Uh, shouldn't I be kneeling at your feet, saying how unworthy I am and promising to do better next time?" She tried to sit up so she could scramble free. Instantly his hands clamped around her wrists, forcing her into the sling. She trembled, praying he wouldn't realize how wet she was between her legs.

"You are attempting to divert me," he whispered into her ear.

"No! Just suggesting some options . . ." Her words trailed away as he nuzzled her cheek. He licked her ear delicately and she jumped at the echo in her womb. "You've got to let me do something, not just lie here!"

"But you plead so well when you're lying still." He smiled down at her, gliding his fingertip along her collarbone. "Perhaps I should keep you exactly like this, just to hear you beg."

She went bright red in an instant. "Isn't there something else you want?"

"Your woman's jewel will glow like the dawn sky when my tongue polishes you." He smiled at her, his hand playing with the lace over her breast.

She choked as her nipples hardened under his casual attentions. "Conquerors are supposed to be fat-assed men lolling around on pillows," she snarled.

"Thinking only with their man-parts?" He chuckled. She stiffened under the truth in his words. "Is that what you desire, little sorceress, a man you can lead by his rod? You'll not have me that way." He stroked her cheek with victor's certainty and she closed her eyes, bitterly determined not to give him any more insight.

But his touch burned into her faster without distractions from her eyes, as he fondled her cheeks and forehead, then smoothed her eyes before delicately stroking her mouth. His rough hands, hardened by decades of swordplay, triggered sensual waves through her nerves and veins until she tossed her head, arching her body toward him.

"Beautiful," he murmured. She would have run, if she'd thought past the caress in his voice.

He stepped between her legs, widening them easily. The sling adapted readily to the new position and kept her spread. Before she could say anything, he covered her mouth with his own. She sighed and opened for that insidious tongue, sliding her hands into his wonderful silken hair to pull him closer.

Corinne blinked when he finally lifted his head. Her tongue ran over her lips and he smiled. Damn, her lips were just as swollen as she'd been afraid of. He chuckled wickedly at the look on her face. Then she realized that his strong hands were steadily stroking the inside of her thighs—all too close to her thong.

"Hey, where'd you get the stool from?" she demanded, seizing on the least important change in the room. Fiona, the mother-in-law from hell, always said that interior decorating was a safe gambit in the most difficult situations.

"Magic: it appears when I need it. Now take hold of the sling, little sorceress," he rumbled.

"I read a pillow book once that said the pasha should always . . ." Corinne tried to come up with something more enticing for that finger of his to do.

He raised an eyebrow at her. "More pleading, sorceress? Pray continue that my rod may grow even further. No? In that case, your hands and feet must be well seated."

"I really don't think . . ."

"Then don't."

She gulped and obeyed him but screamed as the sling vanished from sight. She could feel its support and her body's happy comfort in it. But she lay suspended in the room's center, like a ballerina poised in an erotic music box, while he sat between her legs. "What the hell!"

"I told you I would savor your woman's jewel," he chuckled wickedly. "The sling disappears from sight so that my eyes can enjoy you as much as my tongue. Or my hands." One blunt finger traced her through the thong.

"Oh shit," she muttered, feeling the gush of cream that leaped in response. This was starting to look like the beginning of a very long night.

He pressed the thong's silk against her clit and she whimpered. He rubbed it over her, circling the little nub until she writhed under him. "There really are things I should do to you," she muttered, resenting her body's ready response to him.

"I am quite sure there are," Mykhayl agreed easily. "Such as wrapping my rod with your throat."

"You really are such an arrogant sexist jerk," she bit out, as her thighs clenched around his hand. "But I can think of other games to play."

"Some which you'd not like the pendant to learn," he remarked. She didn't answer him and his hand never stilled. She tried to find someplace to look that didn't show either of them.

If I get out of this, I swear I'll only write sweet inspirationals . . .

He spoke again after a few minutes.

"You have the makings of a tasty meal, sorceress." His eyes were heavy-lidded, half-concealing the fires in the gold. "Open wide for me that my eyes may feast."

She started to shake her head, denying her body's willingness, and he raised an eyebrow. "Does your oath mean so little?"

"As you wish," she gritted and slowly widened her legs.

He took his time looking her over, the bulge strengthening inside his leather breeches. The crystal displayed him from every conceivable angle: strong, graceful, masculine beyond belief, and eager.

She cursed again when she felt her pulse pound heavily and her core tighten in eagerness to hold him. *Don't let him see how much of an effect he's having on you . . .*

His eyes met hers and he licked his lips deliberately. "Excellent beginning," he purred and slid a finger under the silk. Her eyes closed and her head fell back at the answering jolt that rocked her.

His teeth traced the thong's edge and then his tongue. She twisted under him, ready for more.

"A woman's honey is the water of life," he rumbled and she quivered. A big hand palmed her breast, then gently kneaded her. A meridian leapt into life, anchored by his hand and his mouth.

"Mykhayl," she moaned and shuddered when he set another energy line into being.

"Open your eyes and watch," he purred against her mound.

She shook her head silently.

"See yourself, as I command. Or I will stop." The wicked hands lifted from her breasts.

"As you wish." She dragged in a steadying breath and opened her eyes.

Corinne could see every inch of herself, breasts flushed and skin

beaded with passion's sweat. Her own musk scented the air and the
shuddering breaths that her lungs fought for echoed across the
chamber. She'd never dreamed that the sight of her own excitement
could be such a turn-on.

Mykhayl sat between her legs, attentive and hungry, with his
mouth glazed from her juices. And somehow the look on his face,
when his two big hands cupped and lifted her ass for his next taste,
was the most arousing sight of all.

He tossed his hair over one shoulder to free his mouth. The long
strands poured over her leg like a firefall of living silk and she
moaned. He blew on her through the thong as delicately as if he
was coaxing a flame from a handful of twigs. He licked her, following her folds until her very being seemed centered on his
mouth. Her thighs desperately clenched in response to every touch
of his mouth.

"Please, I beg of you," she moaned, too far gone to care about
anything except her need for more.

A finger entered her at the words. "Ask again, sorceress," he
growled.

"Please! Damn you, please finish it!" she gasped, trying to place
herself so that arrogant finger of his would satisfy her ache. The
ever building, fiery ache that demanded him.

Two fingers stretched her wide, while his mouth found her clit.
She groaned and finally rolled into her climax's pounding beat.

And while she surfed those waves, his mouth and hands set to
work again.

Two hours passed in the Tasting Room before Corinne had a
chance to think again, let alone wonder why his touch felt so damn
right.

TWO

The latest tremors were still shaking Corinne's lithe body when Mykh reluctantly straightened up. He desperately needed to stop tasting her, stop drinking her sexual nectars as if they were the food of the gods. He was more than familiar with the rush of *ch'i* that every woman's ecstasy created, but the little sorceress's excitement lifted him higher than an eagle soaring above the dragon peaks.

A ripple of moisture highlighted her wet thigh, like a stream flowing across stone under the roots of the world. He'd spent nearly a year in those dark realms, treasuring any glimpse of the life far above. He'd watched for salamanders in the little stream that bordered his dungeon, tossed rocks into the quiet waters, and tried to escape through it. Such quests were futile in the Gray Sorceress's domain.

His fingers traced Corinne's nectar's path, as his thoughts slipped back to those endless days.

*   *   *

*The gray raiders hit on a moonless night, cutting through his com-
pany of mercenaries like an ice storm through cherry blossoms, as
the little sorceress had planned. They were so contemptuous of op-
position that they didn't bother to kill the fallen, simply rode onward until they reached him.*

*He fought them like a trapped timbercat but to no avail. They
laughed at his struggles then dropped rope after rope around his
neck and arms. He was helpless as his sword dropped out of his
nerveless fingers. He could see and hear, but not speak or fight, as
they carried him off. He watched Ghryghoriy and Mazur struggle
to their feet and try to follow. He begged the Horned Goddess, pa-
tron of fertility and healing, that his old friends and the few remaining mercenaries would live, as the little sorceress had said.*

*The Maiden's moon hung low on the horizon when they
reached the ironbound portal in the mountainside. Its fat silvery
orb was as far distant from the Hunter's moon as his hopes of rescue. He prayed to the five gods as they entered the mountain,
promising them a lifetime's service if his people were safe and he
was rescued. He pleaded for guidance from his totem animal.*

*Days later, as time was reckoned below the roots of the world,
he stood before the Gray Sorceress in her council chamber. Warriors ringed the room, hungry and ready for battle, while a dozen
naked men crouched below her throne, watching her avidly. Another drooled as he stood beside her, eyes half-closed and scarlet
beads dripping down his chest, while she fondled his iron-hard rod.*

*She rose without a word, leaving the naked men behind, and
came to Mykhayl. She was more beautiful than the bards had whispered with her night-black hair and raven eyes. Her dress was alive
with small spiders etching intricate black webs into the gray velvet.*

She played with Mykhayl's man parts and chuckled at his lack of response.

"The Dark Warrior wishes you dead, pretty boy," she cooed. "But not yet. You still have much to amuse a woman with. Oh, you may speak if you want." She waved a hand then squeezed his rump as the ropes loosened. By the red god of war, he had learned to hate that casual flick of her hand that brought only agony and humiliation.

"Why would the Dark Warrior concern himself with a simple captain of mercenaries?" His words echoed through the vaulted hall and she laughed, while he fought to get a hand free.

"You truly don't know? It's such a delicious jest that I must share it. You're the High King's heir. His true-born son, no less." Her fingernail sent a crimson trail over his chest. Only her enchantments stopped him from heaving what little food still dwelt in his stomach.

"Impossible." He could talk but all his efforts to move left him sweating and fixed in place.

"Oh, quite, quite true, barbarian. Your mother spent the Goddess's Dance with a stranger, a tall, handsome young man with gray eyes and a slight limp. Correct?"

He nodded, thankful that she didn't seem to hear his thoughts.

"The stranger insisted that they forswear all other partners during that month, calling it a custom of his people. Entirely proper, that. Every imperial prince must do his utmost to breed a son from one, and only one, woman during the dance. Did your mother enjoy his efforts?"

"That is none of your affair!"

"Angry, little princeling?" the Gray Sorceress mocked, her scarlet mouth forming a perfect moue. "You are so amusing now and I'm sure you'll do better in the future!"

She swept up a drop from his chest with her finger and tasted it
consideringly. "Delicious! It's been so long since I played with an
imperial brat."

"Remove your hands from me!"

The ropes tightened until he began to faint from lack of air then
slowly eased.

"You'll be much happier, you know, if you just let me do what
I want," she remarked while she licked her finger clean. "Now,
what were we talking about? Ah, yes. The imperial court names
that oath, handfasting, which your mother and the stranger both
swore. A few words that make a valid marriage during the Goddess's Dance. And which lasts for a year and a day afterwards, if
the woman breeds."

She took another taste of his blood before continuing. He remained silent and appalled.

"The stranger was Prince Rhodyon, come east to seek counsel
from the Oracle of Clouds, and you are his true-born son."

She snapped her fingers and one of the naked men rushed to
bring her a goblet. She sipped from it while watching Mykhayl.
"He was so very young and foolish, don't you think? Not to guard
your mother closely lest she quicken with his heir. A mistake he
never repeated, although he gained only daughters for his efforts."

"You are a spinner of lies," Mykhayl said hoarsely. His mother
had always mentioned Mykhayl's father with affection, though
she'd had little to relate. She'd spoken only of the Spring Ren-
dezvous and the tall, kind stranger. They'd parted amicably after
the dance, but before she'd learned of her pregnancy. Mykhayl had
been accepted readily by Iskander, the smith that she married before his first birthday.

"Your doubts wound me," the Gray Sorceress sniffed, her eyes
bright with anticipation. "How can I convince you? Perhaps a de-

scription of your totem? A very long, green animal with teeth? And wings and a tail? Who breathes fire on your enemies?"

He went pale. "No!" he roared. "My dragon has nothing to do with this!"

"Poor ignorant boy! Only a male of the true line can see the dragon during his dreams. And you're the very last one who'll do so."

"Impossible!"

She snickered. "All true-born males can summon the Imperial Dragon, little mercenary, using the great sword and words of power, thus earning the title of Dragonheart. Or would you prefer to take your rightful place on the Dragon Throne as High King of the Seven Kingdoms?"

"I will never kill King Rhodyon! The dragon will . . ."

"The Dark Warrior wants you dead but he's promised me a year to play with you first. You'll be far too busy to summon the Imperial Dragon, even if you could find where I've hidden the sword."

"I'll kill you," he vowed. "I'll tear your heart out and burn it. I'll . . ."

She threw her head back and sent peals of laughter ringing through the chamber. "Foolish, foolish brat! You're going to be sprawled across my bed, trying to build your strength for another try at satisfying me. You'll be one of my bed slaves, another toy to amuse me. Another worm crawling for a taste of me. And when I tire of you, I'll toss you away like all the other fools who begged me to let them stay."

"Never. I will never serve you like that."

Her hand seized his rod suddenly and cruelly. He bit his tongue until the blood ran but didn't scream. "You'll be less than dust before I leave here," he vowed hoarsely.

*"You will do as I please," she hissed, glaring at him. "Your rod
will rise at my command. Like this!" She snapped her fingers and
he was instantly hard, aching to mount her as if he'd never ridden
a woman before.*

*He could not persuade his rod to soften, either by force of will
or the exercises he'd learned as a youngling to ease lust's hard edge.
Even as a child, he hadn't felt so helpless, so unable to act against
what disturbed him. His flesh was as far removed from him and his
control as if he'd been castrated.*

*"Exactly so, slave!" She kissed his unresponsive lips, while her
palm smeared crimson over his chest. Finally she stepped back,
only to laugh at him again.*

*"Is it not the most splendid joke that you're here, now, with
me?" she trilled. "And in a year, the Dark Warrior will tear you
into shreds. Should I give you a taste of my carnal liquors so you'll
grovel to me? Or should I enjoy your silly obstinacy? What a sweet
choice, with delights on either side!" She wrapped her hands
around his throat, painting a crimson collar over his veins. "Perhaps I'll know later after I become bored," she mused.*

Mykhayl gritted his teeth against the memory of her voice. He relaxed slowly, letting himself relive how it had ended.

It had begun as the Gray Sorceress had decreed, months spent
cursing her while she used his rod. She'd command his flesh to
obey her will then grind herself against him like a mortar and pes-
tle, all the while laughing at his promises of revenge.

His only hope had been the little sorceress and her plans, overheard as she chatted to her sister. The little sorceress had insisted
he wouldn't die: he had to live to slay the Gray Sorceress and rescue his younger sister Lily and her lover. She'd also diverted the

Gray Sorceress time and again from demanding that he set his mouth between the Gray Sorceress's legs. He'd watched and listened endlessly for the sword that the Gray Sorceress feared.

Then one day the little sorceress had suddenly yanked him back to that mist-filled realm where he'd listened to her and her sister. She'd spoken of hidden clues in the Gray Sorceress's words and guards' watch pattern. He'd understood immediately and he'd fought to reach the sword, where it was hidden behind the throne in the vaulted council chamber. It'd been a bloody fight but he'd stood free long enough for one sweep of the sword to turn the Gray Sorceress to ashes, then summoned the dragon to blaze a path through the sorceress's vengeful armies.

Mykhayl cocked his head, remembering how dragonfire had lanced across that room, destroying all who stood before it. His hair swept up Corinne's thighs before pooling between her legs, setting off long pulses of ecstasy through her body. Her scent was heady and rich, overwhelming his senses like a sorceress's spell.

He forced himself to remember other lessons about women's powers. What had he really learned in those deep caverns, where life was measured in the slow trickle of water?

He'd sneered at the Gray Sorceress's slaves who'd traded all honor and duty to their clans, so that their tongues could delve between her legs. He'd insisted that his service as a slave held some remnants of manly virtue because he always fought against yielding to her. They'd laughed at him in the beginning, named him ignorant and foolish because he'd never tasted a sorceress's nectar, then attacked him when he destroyed the woman who kept them enthralled.

He hadn't understood them at the time but he did now. He'd kill anyone who took the little sorceress's pleasure from him. Her *ch'i* poured into him and increased his own, while every taste of her honey built his hunger for more.

Had he come to this, that he'd forswear his revenge to gain another minute between her long white legs? Those strong thighs that locked around his head so that she could better hurl herself onto his tongue? Or her woman's pearl, once hidden behind layers of ugly cloth, but now bold and beautiful? And what of her yoni's petals, now scarlet and cream like the finest peony as they pouted for more attention?

His hand reached out for another touch. Three fingers had dwelt within her. Would she lunge as eagerly when four fingers drummed her inner points of delight?

He jerked back. No! He would not behave like those magicked half men. He was a High King who walked with the Imperial Dragon. The little sorceress should be desperate for him, stamped by his strength and hungry for his essence. Pleading for him to return to her . . .

He stood up and lifted her out of the hammock abruptly. His furs were a better place for tumbling a woman than the Tasting Room.

"Whazzat?" she mumbled.

Another aftershock traveled her body when he brought her up against his chest. She stiffened, eyes heavy-lidded as she savored the little crest of delight, then blinked lazily and licked her lips. She turned her head against his shoulder and relaxed into his hold. "Damn, you're good," she mumbled and his stupid heart missed a beat.

"By the gods," he cursed, recovering himself quickly. He needed more from her than this.

Mykh carried her through the door and short corridor that led to his bedroom with more haste than majesty. No sentries here to see him, not this deep in the Dragon's Lair.

One wall of his enormous bedroom was taken by a balcony that overlooked Dragon Mountains' high peaks to the east and the wide river carrying its burden of fertile soil below. He could glimpse the Phoenix Hills to the south, if he leaned out during daylight, but not the northern mountains' brutal ice-capped peaks or the western mountains' ridges that had turned back more than one invading army over the centuries. The Hunter, its seven-year quest almost at an end, cast its pale golden light through the curtains, while the Maiden's silver orb hung just beyond its reach.

The room's furnishings reflected his tastes, not a High King's pomp and ceremony. A huge platform took up the center, covered with furs, silks, and pillows to provide ample ground for bedsport. A single lamp cast a soft glow over the floor's thick covering of scattered rugs, another excellent place for tossing a woman or two. Roses and lilies hidden between those rugs yielded their perfume under his feet, echoed by the lamp oil's fragrance. More silk covered the ceiling and walls in a cunning likeness of the tents he'd known in his childhood.

He loved to stretch a woman across that bed, stand between her legs to impale her, and watch her breasts bounce as she screamed for more of his plowing . . .

By the Horned Goddess, he'd yet to have his fill of Corinne's nipples.

Mykh set her down on the bed and began to strip, eyeing them hungrily.

At some point, he'd ripped off the silken rope that traced her hips and yoni, so that his tongue could lash her harder. Another instant had seen him tear that scrap of lace away from her chest so he could find her sweet spots without any distraction. Now the ridiculous black cloth was reduced to little more than a belt.

She had beautiful breasts, high and firm, elegantly shaped to fill a man's mouth and hands, while he suckled on her equally perfect

pink nipples. They weren't as blatant as her sister's pair, which
Jarred so admired. But Mykh had always preferred females whose
delicate frame belied their internal fires, like a tigress's refined fe-
rocity. The Tasting Room had taught him that Corinne's passions
ran hot and wild under that fragile exterior.

His clothes couldn't come off fast enough.

Corinne flung an arm up over her head and opened one eye
slowly. "Mykhayl," she began and stopped. Both eyes opened wide
to stare at his rod, freed now from his breeches and throbbing with
eagerness. She swallowed and her tongue traced her lips as her eyes
clung to him.

"What think you, sorceress?" His rod grew larger yet under her
gaze. He stroked it slowly, lengthening and polishing it with the
dew that rose eagerly from the tip. A pulse beat madly in her throat
and her breasts grew rosier still. "Will it satisfy you tonight?"

"Yes," she breathed and shivered. Her eyes shot to his face,
then away. He growled happily.

"I, ah, Mykhayl," she tried again.

"Sorceress," he answered and knelt between her legs. He spread
them wide and considered her for a moment, then rubbed his
thumb through her yoni's petals.

She gasped and jerked as another crest glided across her. She
was so swollen and sensitive now that the slightest touch triggered
rapture.

He sniffed his thumb, started to taste it, then stopped. A High
King did not depend upon a sorceress's nectar. Instead he painted
her mouth with her musk.

"Mykhayl!" She jerked away in shock.

"Taste yourself, sorceress. Swirl your tongue and find the elixir
of life," he rumbled. She shivered and hesitated, her lips clamped
shut. "Must I invoke your oath, sorceress?"

"No," she snarled and obeyed him, her eyes closed. He watched her little pink tongue creep out and delicately trace her mouth, then retire behind her pearly teeth. She swallowed, eyes lowered so she could focus more on the task he demanded.

He fondled her breast, admiring how it swelled to fit his hand. "Again," he growled. "Do it again that I may reward your breasts for your obedience."

"Okay," she said softly and licked her lower lip. His two hands echoed the movement and she arched into the caress.

"Again." She obeyed him more quickly this time and he rewarded her promptly, admiring how the answering jolt ran from her breasts to her core. "Again—and bring your knees up that I may see you more clearly."

"Again?" But she did as he asked. He savored the sight of the dew flowing from her petals onto her thighs and how her hips writhed.

"Wrap your arms around your legs to keep them spread," he said hoarsely and plucked her nipples. She gasped and jerked, then moaned again when he repeated the caress, building her hunger even as her nipples lengthened and swelled. She rocked from side to side against the soft ebony furs, her hips circling restlessly while she fought to keep her knees raised.

Mykh pushed her breasts up and dropped his head to meet them. He took her nipples into the hot cavern of his mouth and suckled them hard. She screamed and arched under him, pleasing him by her speedy tumble into ecstasy.

He spent considerable time exploring her delight at that path. Suckling, laving, squeezing all sent her into rapture. She writhed under him but rose to meet every pull, sobbing his name repeatedly. "Mykhayl, please, oh no, Mykhayl . . ."

He brushed his rod's fat tip against her, testing how much control he still held over himself. She moaned and pushed herself against it. "Please Mykhayl, fill me."

Discipline's last vestiges fled at the sound of her hoarse plea. He set his rod against her and she shifted to meet him. He sank into her like a great sword entering the scabbard built for it.

"By the Horned Goddess!" Mykh shouted and caught her by the shoulders. He locked his arms around her so that he was buried to the hilt. He growled and ground his pelvis against her, enjoying how her nipples caressed his chest and her woman's pelt rubbed his loins. He gasped for breath and his sweat glided onto her satin skin.

Then he froze when Corinne wrapped her legs around him and pulled him deeper yet. "Oh yes, Mykhayl," she moaned, arching under him. And his body slammed against her in response.

He rode her hard, fighting to stave off his ecstasy. She battled him desperately with muscles clenched around him, inside and out. She keened her hunger and he grunted his need, while the sound of his fat balls pounding against her cleft measured their urgency.

"Now, sorceress, now!" he roared when he caught her jewel with a rough finger. She screamed and convulsed, sending him into rapture. His flood boiled out from the deepest wellspring in his body, sending tidal waves raging up his spine. It continued on and on out of his balls into his rod and her cavern, overflowing until the hot musky liquor coated both of their private pelts, while he was yet pumping into her.

He collapsed onto her, spent and shaking as his body shuddered again and again. Her little hand trembled as it pushed the damp locks of hair off his face, then slid up the nape of his neck to hold him. His rod twitched inside her.

By the gods, she was the hottest bed partner he'd known.

He took her thrice more, lashing them both into rapture, before he found sleep.

Corinne roused slowly, woken by the unfamiliar warmth of a large masculine body nearby. It took her a few moments to recognize the heat source occupying much of the bed as the cause of her aching muscles. When she did remember the evening's events, she hastily slid as far away as she could. Crazy as it sounded and felt, she was in the High King's bed, awaiting his next use of her. Heck, she'd even begged him for more.

She turned her head to see him better. Auburn hair spilled across his face, hiding his expression. His magnificent body was on full display as he slept, covers tossed carelessly aside. Broad shoulders, narrow hips, arms corded with muscles . . . Hell, even his ribs were plated with muscles.

Old scars shone silver under the single lamp. She recognized the slash across his thigh, the missing fingertip, and more. She'd experienced all of them with him while she wrote her books, those romantic fantasies that had turned all too real.

She turned her eyes away from the two deep scars on his upper arm, the lingering traces of the ice serpent's bite, and the Gray Sorceress's whip marks covering his back. What else had that bitch done to him? He'd seemed almost nervous a few times in the Tasting Room.

She had a lot to pay for, having sterilized him, and she wondered what he meant to do next. His treatment of her so far had been intense but not harmful, unlike her ex-husband Dylan, whose attentions were always risky and usually terrifying.

Would Jarred Varrain behave more like Mykhayl or Dylan? At least Celeste was a fighter, so hopefully she'd survive until Corinne found a way to rescue her. It'd have to be some kind of magical solution though.

Magic. Who'd have thought that magic really existed? Still, if there was one thing she knew for sure, it was that this world reeked of magic and it would take dragon magic to cross worlds. Corinne had understood and written about most of Torhtremer's magic, except dragon magic. Maybe she could learn and use that style well enough to help her sister.

Assuming she really could work magic. Crazy idea but it was that or somehow con Khyber into helping her, which had as much chance as persuading the sun to rise in the west.

She pondered the various forms of magic she'd learned while writing about this world. She knew all the major forms and most of the minor forms: the white sorcerers' magic, the Gray Sorceress's magic, and the wizards' magic. She could even provide a detailed description of the strengths and weaknesses of the Dark Warrior's magic.

But she'd only glimpsed dragon magic when it blazed onto her books' pages, bypassing her brain. How could she hope to wield it—or understand those who carried it inside them, like Mykhayl? And Mykhayl was so very much a Dragonheart, with all of a dragon's fire raging in his sexual appetite. She'd probably carry the marks of a night in his bed, spent satisfying that fire, for days or weeks.

She was bruised and sore but intensely aware of him. Her fingers itched to explore those magnificent muscles. Every breath he took sent a warm gust across her skin until her lungs rose and fell in unison with him.

A large hand abruptly clamped around her wrist. She squeaked and stared into his narrowed golden eyes.

"What are you thinking of, sorceress?" His voice was a low growl in the night's silence.

"Uh, nothing," Corinne managed. How could she tell him that she'd been wondering whether his buns would feel as tight as they looked?

"Liar," he remarked and pulled her closer. She went without protest, quivering as goose bumps rose on her skin and her breasts tightened and firmed in eager anticipation. Dammit, why was she letting him see what effect he had on her?

"Your thoughts, sorceress," he demanded softly. She gasped when he carelessly thumbed one nipple, watching her face the entire time.

"Nothing you'd be interested in," Corinne stammered. She had to learn how to think with her head, not her cunt, when he handled her like that. *Yeah, right.*

"You watch me too closely, sorceress. Do you think to cast a spell with your eyes?"

"Of course not!" Well, she had considered trying some of the Gray Sorceress's magic but that felt too unclean to be used, even if she could work magic.

"Hypocrite," he growled and she jumped. "Do you think I'd let you master me so easily?"

"No! Mykhayl, please listen to me: I don't do magic."

He snorted, clearly unimpressed. But it's hard to make a convincing argument when your heart starts drumming like a rock opera as soon a certain man touches you.

"Tell me exactly what you were pondering while you studied me." His hand left her aching breasts to glide over her belly. She sucked in a breath, shaken by the heat that leaped ahead of his touch to lance into her vagina. "Speak."

"It wasn't important. Truly." She shook with the need to feel his fingers travel lower.

He studied her dubiously then shrugged. "Perhaps not, but

there's no need to take the chance. Roll over that I may explore your backside and you cannot pierce me with a single glance."

Oh damn, now what does he have in mind? She rolled over onto her stomach, well aware that she dripped with eagerness to find out. *Perhaps there are some advantages to letting a sex scene go where it wants and not where your brain suggests.*

He skimmed his hands over her back, learning her quickly. She shuddered when he set his mouth to her in licks and little nips that mapped her trigger points, while building her arousal. She trembled and twisted under him, then turned her head to look at him.

"Mykhayl, please," she started to ask.

"No!" He smacked her rump smartly. She jumped in surprise, realizing that he'd just managed to turn her on more, and closed her eyes. He kissed the junction of her neck and shoulder, easily finding the spot where a single touch set her shuddering. She moaned long and low, while her nipples rubbed against the black bearskin.

"On your knees," he growled and lifted her hips. She obeyed willingly and he stuffed silk and brocade pillows under her hips to keep her ass high in the air. "Now drop your shoulders to the bed, but keep your face turned away from me."

She shook as she assumed the position demanded. Had the Gray Sorceress worked silent spells, using just her eyes? But that wasn't important now when his body dipped the bed, signaling his cock's approach. She'd consider later why he was so wary of her in the bedroom.

He knelt between her legs and gripped her hips hard.

"By the Horned Goddess, you look like a tigress ready to be mated." His hands shook slightly as he rubbed his cock against her. "My woman," he growled and thrust into her.

She cried out as her hips pushed back against him, his cock so deep in her that he seemed to touch her heart. She stared off to the side, wishing that she could see him. Suddenly a mirror sprang into place, small but perfectly positioned to show him.

Mykhayl's face was harsh with hunger and a fierce concentration as he knelt behind her. She shivered, watching his cock's immense length glide out until only the fat tip remained hidden.

Mist gathered deep within the mirror and condensed into a view of the throne room, both thrones somehow alive and alert. The Tiger Throne's blue eyes snapped open when Corinne whimpered in frustration.

"Mine," Mykhayl growled and thrust again, the mirror showing how his every magnificent muscle worked to carry him into her. "I will not gaze into your eyes," he groaned and rode her hard and fast, every motion matched by her body.

She stopped thinking altogether as her *ch'i* burst into blazing life along passion's meridians. He grunted and growled with every thrust and she answered him in the same language, as befitted the other half of the mating drive. She grew more and more excited, pushing herself back at him, but climax stayed just beyond reach as he pounded into her. She began to beg, desperate to feel his seed flood into her again.

Khyber's golden eyes longingly watched the Tiger Throne from deep within the mirror.

Still Mykhayl drove into Corinne. She circled her hips, trying to find the little difference that would bring release. Abruptly his cock found a new point deep inside her and she convulsed in ecstasy, while current after current rolled up her spine and through her body.

The Tiger Throne's eyes closed and the mirror disappeared.

"Mykhayl!" Corinne shrieked as she came again and again, shuddering. He yowled like a beast and climaxed as she reached her third peak. He was still pumping her full of his cream when she collapsed into unconsciousness.

Corinne's sleep became restless after Mykhayl left the bed, which was still damp from their usage. She flung out a hand then a leg in search of reassurance. She rolled into a ball, trying to find comfort, but instead found the old ordeal in her dreams.

She was in a bed. Her marriage bed.

Dylan stood above her, his blue eyes smiling as always. Black eyes watched from somewhere distant, stern and forbidding above a harsh nose and cruel mouth.

The Dark Warrior.

Oh no! She tried to wake up but the black eyes turned colder and the nightmare rolled on inexorably.

"Jes' relax, dahlin'," Dylan slurred. "I'll jes' pickup a lil' ol' bottle of bourbon an' be righ' back."

She shook her head violently and tried to object. But the damn gag choked her, even larger in the dream than it had been in real life.

"Yo'll be fine," Dylan insisted, clumsily patting her breast. She flinched away but the ropes held her immobile. "Yo' sure you don' wan' any bourbon? Or gin, p'haps?"

She shook her head again and her heart hammered against her ribs.

"Well, al'righ' then." Dylan stumbled out of the room. She heard his beloved Porsche roar into life then depart with a growl and splash of gravel. She could usually hear him reach the main road in that damn car and sometimes at the liquor store if the night

was quiet. If she was lucky, he wouldn't play a game of chase with the police on the road or meet up with friends at the store. Was it more or less frightening to be a passenger when he played with the police?

But luck had never favored her marriage much . . .

Hours later but an instant in the dream's logic, the sun peeped through the curtains. She gnawed the ropes, frantic to reach the phone. Just one finger free for speed dial and Celeste would rescue her. Celeste, the big sister, who'd looked after her from the beginning. Who'd explained that Daddy wasn't ever coming back and it really, truly wasn't Corinne's fault for being a bad girl. Who'd fixed dinner and helped with homework when Mama was too drunk to so much as crawl home. Who'd been maid of honor at the picture-perfect society wedding . . . and kept her mouth shut about Dylan after only once pungently expressing her opinion.

Celeste . . .

The black eyes came closer and the cruel mouth smiled triumphantly.

"Wake up!" The deep voice did not come from the dream.

She awoke screaming, pounding her fists against the man holding her. She stared up into Mykhayl's face then burst into tears.

"Hush now, little sorceress," he soothed, pulling her into his arms and rocking her. "Hush."

She buried her face against his broad chest and sobbed, sending a flood of saltwater down his torso. He continued to croon to her, nonsense syllables that combined with the steady heartbeat under her cheek to soothe her. She was ridiculously glad that Mykhayl had been well-trained by his mother and sisters to handle feminine hysterics.

The crying slowed and she hiccupped, trying to stop. Her lashes were stuck together so that she saw rainbows when she tried to open her eyes. Her hands gripped his shoulders as if he were the Rock of Gibraltar.

"Poor little sorceress," he murmured and kissed the top of her head. "Such a long time sporting with a dragon . . ."

She sniffled and tried to gather her wits so she could seize the excuse he offered. She'd rather blame tears on carnal games than a humiliating episode in a disastrous marriage. Blowing her nose was the first necessity for regaining control.

He closed her fingers around a small bit of silk. She gulped inelegantly but blew vigorously.

He nuzzled her hair and she froze when his mouth traveled toward her face. Even with dragonfire in his veins, it had to be almost dawn and an end to a very long night. Surely he couldn't still be interested?

The answer came soon enough when a finger gently lifted her chin. She opened her eyes cautiously and found his face inches away from hers. His eyes were molten gold, heavy lids veiling only some of his intensity. "Give me your lips that I might slake my thirst, Corinne."

He'd spoken her name for the first time and her pulse raced at the thought, despite her sniffles. She leaned up and very tentatively touched her mouth to his. He purred, a deep rumbling sound that spoke volumes of masculine satisfaction, and responded gently.

They kissed for a long time, sweetly and simply like high school sweethearts first exploring each other. His cheek was rough with beard as she caressed him, feeling the play of their tongues and teeth within his mouth. He held her face between his hands when his tongue moved to explore the hot, moist depths behind her teeth. She sighed and kneeled in front of him so she could better match him.

Her fingers glided into the heavy silken weight of his hair. It was cool and smelled of flowers, as if he'd stood outside in the last moonlight before dawn. She threaded her hands deeper until they curved around the back of his skull to pull him closer to her.

And still they kissed.

His hands fell away to stroke down her body, thumbs finding the sides of her breasts where they flattened against his chest. A caress there sent her moaning into his mouth and rubbing her nipples against him. She smirked when he shuddered at the touch. But that game forced too quick a pace and his hand moved to her back.

She rubbed his arms restlessly, too taken by his strong presence to stay still. Muscles there flowed over and around each other in ropes, built for battle but offering protection to a frightened female. She made a small sound at the back of her throat and pressed closer to him.

He quivered and his mouth traveled to her cheek and down her throat. She tilted her head eagerly and he nuzzled her until her pulse ran hot and true. He nipped her, setting her blood pounding stronger, then laved the small hurt until she moaned and clutched at him.

"Mykhayl." Her voice was a whisper of need.

"Mykh," he answered; she fell silent as she tried to think. "Call me Mykh."

"Mykh," she tried the name softly, shy of the intimacy that a nickname implied. He licked the sensitive point again and she shuddered. "Mykh," she groaned, pressing against him.

He growled softly and traced his path lower. She arched against him, opening herself to the caress. One night had taught him more about what her body preferred than Dylan had learned in three years of marriage. But now Mykh explored her breasts as if he'd never seen them before, mapping the veins with his tongue until her aureoles bloomed. He tugged on one aching, upthrust nipple very gently and she moaned in satisfaction, her fingers tossing the fiery silk of his hair.

"Mykh," she sighed when he suckled her and pulled him closer still. He stroked her back, fondling her spine until she writhed under his mouth. She felt safe and cherished in the circle of his arms. Her eyes closed to better focus on the pleasures he brought. Self-discipline be damned, she was going to enjoy this man.

Mykh shifted his position under her, kneeling with his feet tucked under him. She barely noticed, too caught up in what his very talented tongue was doing to her other nipple. His hands gathered her hips, lifted her up, and brought her down over him. His cock glided into her, stroking her clit with its every inch, and she gasped in shock. "What the hell? Mykh!"

"Easy now, Corinne." He rocked against her in the most delicate of movements. But every touch pressed the heated brand against that bundle of nerves and filled her core at the same time.

"Jesus Christ, Mykh," she groaned and tried to drive herself onto him. His grip tightened and she stopped.

"Gently, Corinne, gently. A morning's play after a long night."

"Doesn't feel like playtime," she grumbled and wriggled again.

"Corinne," he warned. His touch remained implacable and she finally yielded, her buttocks sinking into his hands while he did as he pleased. He controlled her now, although he could make only very little thrusts.

His hips circled and she shuddered. How could such small movements trigger such an overwhelming response in her? She licked his shoulder, enjoying the salty taste of his sweat and the shudder that her touch set off in him. At least he wasn't as calm as he'd like her to believe.

Ch'i rippled into life along her meridians, circling between the anchors of their mouths and groins. His *ch'i* was hot and urgent but felt blocked somehow, so it couldn't circle as freely as hers did.

"Sweet lady," he rumbled and she kissed his neck. They were almost equals in height when wrapped around each other like this. She stroked his shoulders and tried a little hip circling of her own. He groaned and she smiled. Two could play at this.

It wasn't a game that could be enjoyed for long, not when every breath sent one or the other of them shuddering. A climax was creeping closer, its slow burn gliding down to her toes where they pressed against the small of his back. She moaned and buried her face against the strong tendon under his ear.

He rocked again, more strongly. She bit down against a scream and her mouth closed onto his shoulder, finding the exact pulse point where a tigress marks her mate.

Mykh jerked, groaned her name and jammed her body down deeper onto his. He used his hands as well as his body after that, lifting and dropping her onto his hips until sanity fled. She clung to him, panting as she clenched around him. *Ch'i* burned brighter until her bones turned incandescent.

He arched his back to gain more contact and gasped. A hot jet caressed her core, then another and another until they became a flood. His *ch'i* reached to hers and she kissed his mouth, instinct demanding that the circuit be completed. He moaned into her mouth as he came, linking their *ch'i*. She burst into flame throughout her body, pummeled and overwhelmed by a climax more complete than she'd ever imagined.

They sprawled on the bed afterwards, still linked together as much by *ch'i* as his cock. But neither of them dared to speak. Corinne yawned and turned her face away from the rapidly increasing light outside. She was asleep before she could finish another breath.

Later she awoke slowly, disappointed but not quite surprised to find herself alone, and moved just enough to open one eye. She could observe Mykh through the half-open doors separating them, holding a conversation about the army's readiness during the month-long festival to come, while two men braided his hair and another paraded brocade robes for his approval.

To be precise, he was discussing whether or not the army could do battle against an unexpected attack. Damn. She'd have to tell him what she'd seen in her nightmare.

Mykh was nothing like Dylan, the husband who'd abused her. Mykh could have weighed her down with chains, tossed her into one of his many dungeons, and used her however and whenever he pleased. Instead he'd taken the bonds off in exchange for a promise, even though he was furious at her and had no reason to trust her. If he could give his word under those conditions and keep it, then she didn't have to be terrified of him.

At least not about him killing her.

The bedroom looked remarkably similar to his old campaign tent, where she'd first seen him. It had a comparable tumble of furs and silks and pillows, although these were the finest silks instead of a mercenary's well-worn collection. This room had opulent tapestries shielding its ceiling and walls, not the tent's carefully patched canopy. She'd first seen him leaning against its center post, worrying about his sisters' well-being, while his big black leopard, Mazur, slept curled up on the bed. Corinne had taken one look at him and known immediately that he was the family's protective leader.

She glimpsed Mazur pacing restlessly in the council room and pausing from time to time to nudge the doors leading to the bedroom. Finally the moment came when Mykh was too busy to pay attention and Mazur slipped into the bedroom. He padded softly over to the bed and considered Corinne.

She looked back at him gravely. Mazur had been Mykh's constant companion since they were adolescents. She could name his battle scars as easily as she could Mykh's, although she'd never been in his head. Her fingers itched to pet his velvety soft fur but she sensed this was a formal introduction, unlike the encounter in the throne room.

Mazur's nose twitched and his big pointed ears shifted forward as he studied her more carefully. She held her breath, uncertain of his reaction. Mazur was too feline to simply accept Mykh's judgment of her.

He sat down suddenly and his tail curled around his feet, as he assumed the imperious posture of all regal cats since before Egypt. He rumbled a deep throaty purr. "May the Celestial Guardians bring peace and prosperity to you and yours, Great Lady."

Corinne blinked as her mind fumbled through scraps of lore. A conversation with a cat? Well, white sorcerers had done so centuries ago, before the Dark Warrior destroyed them. She knew the Language of Beasts, thanks to *The Wizard and the Wisteria*, the second Torhtremer novel, but she'd never spoken it in public. Years of training to sing operas had produced some strange sounds from her voice, but that language was far harder. The white sorcerers had a point when they taught that the Language of Beasts required magic to shape human throats around feline sounds.

She coughed and tried to say the ritual response in English as gutturally as possible. "May the blessings of the Four shine upon you and yours, Great Hunter."

Mazur sniffed and gave her a disgusted look, as if she'd offered dry kibble for breakfast when he wanted cream. His tail twitched impatiently before he purred again. "Forgive me, Great Lady, I did not fully understand your meaning. Would you please repeat yourself that I may become enlightened?"

What now? She could pretend stupidity or inability, but Mazur clearly knew what she was capable of.

Oh, God. She couldn't do this. It was too strange, too frightening here.

"Mazur," she faltered. "I can't, I just can't."

He patted her knee softly in encouragement. "Great Lady, you smell like the high meadows in the western mountains where humans once walked with us. My mother and her mothers said such humans can speak with us. Please try again."

Tears pricked her eyes at his gentleness. "Okay. I'll try. But don't laugh at my accent."

"Never," he swore and resumed his formal pose.

She tried to remember the sounds she'd made while pacing her little office overlooking the lake. She'd tried for hours until she could purr like a cat or whinny like a horse with equal ease.

Corinne took several deep breaths to cleanse her lungs. Then she growled the ritual response, "May the blessings of the Four shine upon you and yours, Great Hunter."

At least it sounded like a cat talking. *Oh hell, what if she really was the sorceress Mykh called her?*

Mazur, of course, suffered from no such qualms. He grinned, his tongue sweeping over very sharp teeth, leaped up onto the bed with a delighted *mrow*, and began to lick her face. His rough tongue rasped her face and she giggled.

"Mazur!" she laughed, then switched to the Language of Beasts. It was much easier to speak it while in Torhtremer. "You're very exuberant this morning."

"Of course," Mazur rumbled. "Why not? We have waited long to speak again with a two-leg."

She chuckled and petted him, savoring his welcome.

"What are you doing, sorceress?" Mykh's cold voice shattered their romp.

Oh shit. Corinne looked up and found a High King frowning down at her. He was dressed in a pale green silk tunic, high necked and loose sleeved, with rich bands of gold embroidery around the neck, down the front, and circling his wrists. Matching silk trousers wrapped his hips and thighs in loose folds, before diving into high boots. A wide sash was folded in intricate pleats around his narrow waist. His hair was now plaited into dozens of small braids, every one touched with gold and amber until they seemed alive with tiny flames. A sleeveless brocade coat, worked in fabulous designs of flying dragons, emphasized his broad shoulders before it fell to the floor, while his great sword, Dragon's Breath, hung across his back.

The ensemble was calculated to evoke awe and majesty, yet the man within was more dangerous and impressive than his clothing. Her pulse began to thud at sight of the bulge rising behind the trousers' soft silk.

Why was he armed in his own bedchamber?

Corinne disengaged herself from Mazur and sat up, hastily pulling a silk quilt around herself. The big leopard felt no similar constraint. He leaped off the bed and wound himself around Mykh's ankles, purring wildly. "She's a friend! Come at last!" he mewed but Mykh didn't understand.

"Sit, Mazur."

Even a feline couldn't disregard that tone. He sat reluctantly, his tail twitching frantically as he watched the two humans.

"I was greeting Mazur," Corinne said slowly, sticking with the truth. "He said hello, so I answered him."

Mykh's face tightened with an emotion she couldn't quite read.

Fear? Regret? Was he remembering something from the Gray Sorceress? "Only sorcerers speak the beasts' tongue. You must dress so you can accompany me."

"You can't mean to keep me under your thumb all the time!" His anger was all the more frightening for being unexpected. Was he angry that he'd spent the night with her? But her *sifu* had taught that dragons always attacked from an unexpected direction.

"You are far too dangerous for a loose leash, sorceress. I will send Yevgheniy with clothes. Will you obey him in my absence or must I watch you every minute?"

"I think I can manage to get dressed without your help, thank you very much!" Corinne snapped. The contrast between last night's gentle passion and his cold ascendancy now shocked her.

"You will not find your punishment amusing if you injure him in any way," he warned.

"He's a goddamn *primus pilus*! What the hell can I do to him?" Corinne shot back. Was he so terrified of magic? Surely not, given his comfort with Khyber. Was it scars from the Gray Sorceress's imprisonment?

"Too much." The simple words echoed with a multitude of scars.

Mykh turned to leave, his robe shimmering around him like dragon's wings. Mazur dodged his boots, visibly uncertain about where to go.

"Mykh," she called out to him.

He spun back to her. "You will address me as Your Majesty."

"You jerk! Last night you weren't so formal," Corinne spat, too hurt by the change to watch herself.

"Last night I was a fool." A glacier would have been warmer than his voice.

"Asshole," Corinne muttered under her breath and the amber

pendant flared briefly. She took a deep breath and tried to recover. She wanted to throw something at his arrogant head, but she needed to warn him about the dream. She silently chanted a Daoist meditation, until she could speak without spitting at him.

"Your Majesty," she tried again. *Let's try playing it his way* . . .

He stopped just before the doorway, reluctance in every line. "Yes?"

"As a sorceress," she looked for phrases that would keep his attention. "I must warn you that the Dark Warrior stirs in the northern mountains."

He frowned. "My sentries have given me no warning of this."

"He woke very recently."

"Thanks to your presence, no doubt." Mykh shifted slightly, bringing Dragon's Breath closer to hand.

Oh shit, he was right but she couldn't bring herself to say so. The Dark Warrior had avoided Torhtremer for the year since *The Raven and the Rose* ended, while Mykh rebuilt the country and healed from his wounds. To awaken immediately after she arrived meant that the Dark Warrior hunted her, which his presence in her nightmare confirmed. Damn. At least she was in the palace's heart, where the Dark Warrior had never walked. "I had thought that he would return in five years, or maybe as little as two years. But now I sense . . ."

"How long?" The demand slashed the room like a sword swept from its scabbard.

Corinne reached out as she always had when plotting. The answer came quickly, which meant that it was true. "Weeks, I think. Or maybe even a few days. He's very close," she whispered and their eyes met.

All emotion vanished from Mykh's face before it assumed a mask of resolve, hiding any traces of his thoughts. "I will make inquiries and set guards as necessary. My thanks for the warning, if it is true," he added reluctantly. "If it is false, then Izmir's Curse will adorn your wrists."

Corinne flinched then nodded. She'd much rather wear those damn cuffs and not have the Dark Warrior attack Torhtremer. "Very well, Your Majesty."

Mykh studied her for a moment longer, measuring her acquiescence, before sweeping out of the room. Mazur hissed and started to follow. The door slammed in his face and he came back to the bed, swinging his tail dejectedly.

"He is a good man, Great Lady," Mazur chuffed softly, as he leaned his head against her leg. "He will change."

Corinne rubbed the leopard's ears but didn't dare speak.

THREE

Yevgheniy entered from the antechamber a few minutes later, wearing crimson brocade robes and carrying a leather-wrapped bundle. He approached warily, as if he expected furniture to start flying at any minute.

Corinne silently inventoried the spells she'd written for the Torhtremer romances, like lighting a fire, dumping a bucket of water, sending a rug flying. She knew some bigger spells, too, such as bringing rain. And greater magic yet, like making a life-size fleet from a set of models. But even if she really could work a spell, Mykh was the one who deserved to get hurt and not his obedient servants.

Yevgheniy stopped well back from the bed. "His Majesty sends these for you to wear."

"Fine. Just put 'em down and get out," Corinne snapped.

He tensed almost imperceptibly. "His Majesty insists that I remain in the Dragon's Lair while you dress."

"Then I'll get dressed in the bathroom."

"I'm afraid . . ." Yevgheniy began but never finished.

Mazur sprang from the bed, knocked the old warrior to the rugs, and pinned him there. He yawned, displaying a full set of very large teeth, and delicately took Yevgheniy's head into his mouth. The man's eyes closed but he made no move.

Corinne jumped off the bed and took a hasty step forward, then stopped as Yevgheniy slowly relaxed under the big cat. A fountain's lyrical song floated in from the garden beyond as counterpoint to Yevgheniy's harsh breathing and Mykh's curt voice in the other room. Her body ached from a multitude of bruises and muscles exhausted by a night's hedonistic exertions.

Finally Mazur opened his mouth, lifted his head, and looked at Corinne.

"Go," he chuffed. "You can splash in the water while I guard. It's very nice water. You will enjoy it. The other women never went there."

Corinne nodded, reassured about Mazur's attentions. But Yevgheniy might not be as relaxed. "Are you okay?" she asked the human nervously.

Yevgheniy shrugged very slightly. "Mazur has never hurt me before. I can wait for you."

She swallowed hard and tightened the silk quilt around herself. "Thank you very much, Mazur. Please be careful with Yevgheniy." Corinne picked up the discarded bundle and edged around the two sprawled across the rugs.

"Of course. We have played before." Mazur yawned again, sat up, and lay down, this time between Yevgheniy's legs. Any attempt to escape would place the man's private parts within inches of Mazur's splendid teeth.

Yevgheniy wisely didn't try any such thing. Instead, his eyes tracked from Mazur to Corinne where they lingered with an unreadable expression.

"I'll hurry," she assured him.

"His Majesty expects us to join him in a candlespan."

Corinne sent her mind back to what she knew of timekeeping in Torhtremer and translated hastily. A candlespan, or how long it took for a large candle to burn down, was approximately an hour. That should be long enough for a bath and getting dressed, plus some Tai Chi as exercise. She nodded at Yevgheniy and escaped, still clutching the silk quilt around her. She refused to limp in front of him.

The bathroom was bigger than she'd expected. It centered on a pool, which dwarfed any bathtub she'd seen in publicity tours or Celeste's sybaritic decor. The pool looked like a small mountain spring, surrounded on three sides by marble and granite crags. The polished rock looked more like shower stalls at an expensive resort than a backdrop for waterfalls. Other nooks and crannies held mirrors that swam in and out of the mist unless looked at directly. There were also sinks, toilet, and bidet, all carved from rock with brass fixtures and remarkably recognizable for an Iron Age world.

She tested the water by dipping her foot into it and frowned. It was barely lukewarm. Better than nothing but her abused muscles wanted more. Maybe she could try something similar to *The Leopard and the Lily*'s big bathing scene. She cleared her throat and spoke to the empty room.

"I would like some hot water."

No steam arose from the pool. Damn. Was there a magic word involved? She tried again.

"Please give me some hot water. Please."

Clouds of steam instantly floated above the pool. She tentatively touched her toe to the water's surface and jumped back with a yelp. "A little cooler, please!"

The clouds of steam immediately faded to a smooth haze. She tested it again and smiled. Perfect.

Was Celeste doing as well with basic technology in that far future world? Was she even alive to try? Corinne bit her lip and pulled her thoughts away from her sister's plight. Worry wouldn't help her to escape and rescue Celeste.

An hour later, Corinne considered her situation. The bruises had faded within minutes of entering the pool, while the aches had turned into a strong sense of well-being under the cascading water. Any spa on Earth would kill for that pool.

A simple breakfast had appeared when she finished drying herself, showing up on a ledge as soon as her stomach growled. Her taste buds welcomed the brown bread, goat cheese and oranges with all the enthusiasm to be expected after living off room service and airline food for three months. And displayed not a trace of nerves about being held captive on a world so far away from Earth that she had literally no idea of how to go home.

None of this helped her escape or find Celeste. Maybe she should have searched the room one more time for an escape hatch, instead of devouring breakfast. Maybe Celeste was choking down one of those dreadful meals in a tube, or hooked up to a machine that pumped things into her blood instead of feeding her. Maybe Celeste wasn't eating at all.

Corinne closed her eyes and stopped her breakfast from reappearing in her mouth. That done, she repeated a few more of her *sifu*'s proverbs before taking stock of her situation. The disadvantages were clear enough but there had to be some advantages. Maybe Mykh's lust was an advantage for her, uncomfortable though her response to him made her feel. Even so, she still didn't want to go naked.

Corinne tried one more time to persuade the silk quilt to become a toga but it slid off her shoulder rapidly again. It was much too slick and bulky to become clothing and she reluctantly picked up the leather-clad bundle. She just didn't want to find out what attire Mykh thought suitable for a dangerous sorceress. Perhaps a transparent shift that barely reached her thighs? No, that was a concubine's wardrobe. Sackcloth, with a ball and chain as accessories?

The heavy leather was scarred and stained almost black from age and hard use. It was tied with rawhide cords and looked like a man's luggage, not a palace ornament. At least the knots came undone easily.

Corinne folded back the leather only to gape at the contents. Gold and jewels blazed against brightly colored enamels. Neither sackcloth nor prisoner's garb and far too lavish for his concubines. She began to get dressed as quickly as possible in the skirt and top.

Finally she surveyed the result in the long mirror. The outfit was lightweight, a perfect fit, extremely comfortable and embarrassing as hell. The long skirt was made from dragon wing scales, long triangular pieces hanging from a broad leather band that rested on her hips. A single, very wide panel in the front was flanked by overlapping scales that encompassed her, like a strange cross between a kilt and a grass skirt, while mercifully reaching past her ankles. The result was entirely decent, especially if she stood still, but an open invitation for a man to slip his hand between the scales and fondle the woman underneath.

The upper half was much like a bikini top with narrow leather bands looping around her neck and back. Its cups were circular, each shaped like a dragon's claw with five sharp spikes holding a leather cord that spiraled to cover her nipple. Both skirt and top were enameled and gilded, then accented with jewels. Even the leather sandals shone with the same gilt and enamels.

Technically there was nothing to offend even a movie studio's censors but the reality was scandalous. It offered everything to invite and nothing to hinder a man's possessive touch. She looked like a combination of hula dancer and porn star.

Corinne whirled to see her back, but the movement sent the panels soaring up to her hips. She froze, blushing, just as Mazur yowled. "Great Lady, the man is growing restless. Will you join us or shall I play with him again?"

"Don't play with him!" Corinne answered hastily. "I'll be right there." She cast one last glance at herself in the mirror and headed out, trying to walk as smoothly as her drama instructor had taught. Maybe a glide that kept Victorian hoop skirts from bouncing around would keep her respectably covered in this rig.

She found Mazur stretched in front of the bathroom door, idly polishing a gleaming black claw, while Yevgheniy paced across the bedroom. He stopped when she entered and assessed her. His eyes flashed with appreciation, but he veiled his expression quickly then opened the double doors into the meeting room. "Come with me; His Majesty is waiting for us."

Corinne followed him hesitantly, her mouth dry at meeting her captor—and lover—again.

Mykh's eyes blazed with triumph and possessiveness when she entered the room. The handful of councillors there, all dressed in fine silks and brocades, watched closely as he strode toward her. They showed more interest in her than she'd expect a concubine to evoke.

"Perfect," Mykh pronounced. "Dressed for display as the High King's trophy. But you look cold as ice, sorceress. You are lacking only one element."

"How about a cloak? Or a long kimono?" Corinne suggested,

made restless by the greedy sweep of his eyes over her and the cool draft tickling the backs of her thighs.

"Hot blood pounding through your veins, sorceress. You must look eager to serve the Dragonheart."

"Eager?" Corinne squawked, nervousness forgotten.

His kiss silenced her retort and scorched her down to her bones. She brought her knee up sharply between his legs, but he dodged the attack easily. He captured her hands and held them together in one giant paw.

"I won't kiss you," she vowed. "I won't. No matter what you do."

He laughed down at her. "Such a fierce kitten, always fighting like a tigress," he purred and pulled her up against him. She twisted and fought like a wildcat but finally stood quiescent, growling at him in frustration.

He took her mouth with a conqueror's sureness, then lingered until she moaned and yielded to him. His fingers kneaded her ass and she forgot their audience, as she tried to move closer to him. She clutched him closer when he transferred his attentions to her breast. The room could have been full of kings and queens and their entourages but she didn't care, not when his mouth was sending jolts of fire from her nipples to her cunt. Her hips circled and pushed restlessly against his hard thighs.

She blinked when he finally lifted his head. Her eyes would barely focus.

"Much better, sorceress," Mykh purred as he touched her mouth assessingly. "You're swollen from my kisses and flushed from my teeth, while your hips sway eagerly to cradle me."

"You sexist jerk!" Corinne shouted and kicked him, a good solid sweep kick. The amber pendant burned her throat but she didn't care, not when he staggered as a result. "Asshole," she grumbled.

He recovered quickly and grabbed her by the shoulder. "Behave yourself or I'll mount you here and now."

"You wouldn't dare!" But her body tightened at the thought and she threw a wary glance at the nearby table. Two of his big strides could take them to it. He could sweep the maps off and bend her over it. A trickle of heat surfaced from her core and touched her thigh.

"And now, my sorceress, you also smell like a woman in heat," he whispered in her ear then released her. "We will proceed to the throne room now," he announced to the room at large. "Little sorceress, Mazur, you will follow me." He lifted an imperious eyebrow at them.

Corinne bridled but Mazur nudged her leg. "Must I?" Corinne muttered but she fell into step behind Mykh, Mazur on one side of her and Yevgheniy on the other. She sniffed her disgust as she followed him through the door. The councillors' voices blurred as they joined in.

Ghryghoriy waited outside with two of his men, gorgeous in his black and gold dress uniform with his hand resting on the hilt of his magical sword, White Fang. Corinne immediately remembered some of the clever ways his long fingers had driven his wife to ecstasy. She blushed and lowered her eyes, hoping that he couldn't read her expression.

Ghryghoriy bowed slightly and walked beside Mykh in response to an unspoken signal. His two men slid into place behind Corinne, assessing her with the cold clarity of undercover cops searching for illegal weapons. She tilted her nose higher in the air and stalked after Mykh, heedless of her revealing attire.

If they didn't stop treating her like a sorceress soon, she'd figure out how to act like one, just to teach them a lesson.

Sentries snapped to attention, while footmen hastened to fling
doors open, as the procession passed along the corridors. They
halted before two immense portals, while servants clucked over the
exact fit and hang of Mykh's garments.

One manservant moved toward Corinne but she glared at him.
"Touch me, buster," she hissed, "and I'll knock your teeth so far
down your throat that you'll see your creator before you find those
pearly whites again."

The man blanched and shrank back. Then he started forward
again but Mykh waved him off, chuckling. "Keeping yourself for
me alone, my sorceress?" he whispered.

"You wish!"

He laughed at her response and tucked an errant lock of hair behind her ear. "Such a ferocious tigress you'd make, my sorceress."

"Beast."

Mazur rumbled something suspiciously like laughter. She
glared down at him and he met her eyes. He couldn't have looked
less innocent if he'd been caught in the middle of the lily pond,
with a goldfish's tail hanging out of his mouth.

A ram's horn sounded, long and rich like spring coming to the
high mountains, and Mykh turned back to face the portals.
Corinne instinctively straightened her skirts.

Once, twice, thrice the great horn called out. Then trumpets
blew, long and sweet, before other trumpets answered them in a
triumphant paean of joy and rebirth. And the great doors opened
slowly, without a hand touching them.

Mykh strode into the throne room, looking both magnificent
and deadly, and the wall sconces burst into light as the trumpets

sang. The result was blinding, like standing in the middle of the Super Bowl at half-time. Most of the assembly fell prostrate as Mykh passed. But some froze, staring up at the great sconces blazing from both the round golden globes and the silver shell backings, before dropping to the floor.

Mazur's tail thumped Corinne's ankle and she quickly followed Mykh, as Ghryghoriy's two men and Yevgheniy stepped aside. The enormous room was full of people, more than double the number that had attended the Raven and the Rose's wedding. They ranged from uniformed soldiers with hard faces and hands made restless by lack of weapons, to cynical diplomats and bureaucrats in their silk uniforms, to black-robed scholars and peacock-vain courtiers watching and memorizing every one of Mykh's movements.

Wizards gathered at every corner in their white robes, each one made unique by shimmering threads in their specialty's colors. They worked low magic, casting spells that made life easier such as heating bath water or transferring food from the kitchens to where it was wanted.

Curved balconies lifted above them, meant for sorcerers but empty now since no sorcerers lived in Torhtremer. Sorcerers worked high magic that could do such wonders as moving armies or rivers, even steal a person's soul by looking into their eyes. And as different from low magic as an atom bomb is from a sledgehammer.

Representatives of Torhtremer's Seven Kingdoms stood closest to the dais, while diplomats from the world's other realms watched from farther back.

Simultaneously, another procession emerged from the matching portal on the opposite side of the room. Two sturdy women in pleated white dresses carried the great metal halberd that had previously hung behind the Tiger Throne. They were followed by three young girls, also dressed in white and carrying sheaves of flowers.

Mykh ascended to the dais and stood in front of the Dragon Throne, looking out over the throng. The throne's golden eyes opened as Khyber entered his wooden shell and began to watch the assembly. Mazur's tail tickled Corinne's leg and she obediently took a position next to Mykh, on the side closest to the Tiger Throne, while Mazur stood haughtily on his other side. The women brought the halberd onto the dais and up to a display stand behind the Tiger Throne, sweating a little as they carried the massive weapon up the stairs. The councillors filed into place on either side of the dais and tried to look important.

The ram's horn blew again three times when Mykh seated himself and the halberd thudded into its stand. The Dragon Throne immediately came alive, turning itself in an instant from stiff wood to softly breathing dragon scales. Khyber blew delicate gusts of sulfur-laden fire, lighting the ceremonial braziers at each of the dais' corners, and relaxed. His posture managed to convey great respect and affection for the man reclining against his forepaws. Corinne was simply glad that the Imperial Dragon was apparently paying no attention to her.

Mazur hissed softly as he dropped down, a second after Mykh. Corinne blinked but followed suit, only to find herself seated on a large and very comfortable cushion that had appeared out of thin air. She gulped and assumed the most decorous position possible, straightening her skirts to provide the maximum amount of coverage before looking out over the room.

A brass gong rang from beyond the great portal, sending shivers through Corinne. Its echoes died away slowly before it rang twice more.

A religious procession filed in, beginning with young acolytes waving small brass pots of incense to cleanse the room. Others carried garlands of scarlet and white roses, mixed with branches of sage. Priests and priestesses followed, beating on small drums and cymbals, while elderly ones carried the symbols of their deities. Their robes were wrapped like togas, echoing the style of Buddhist monks. The colors ranged from the pale yellow of sunshine, through dark gold, to a red deep enough to appear crimson. Most prominent of all were the followers of the Horned Goddess, their robes so pale as to be almost silver but bordered with the other gods' and goddesses' colors.

All of them marched down the central aisle, then broke into separate strands to curve around the outside, until a solid wall of priests ringed the throne room. Alert guardsmen stood behind them, spears in hand.

Last came the leaders of each deity's adherents, every one holding the symbol of their office. They stood shoulder to shoulder, facing Mykh.

A sigh ran through the gathered throng, as they humbled themselves deeper into the floor. Corinne frowned, trying to remember why they were so awestruck. Maybe it was because all the religious leaders only came together every seven years in Torhtremer for the Goddess's Dance. This was, after all, the first such dance since they'd defeated the Dark Warrior's armies at Tajzyk's Gorge and the first peacetime dance in more than a century.

The Horned Goddess's priestess, a mature, rounded woman whose mouth looked more suited to laughing than frowning, brought her staff of office down with a thud.

Mykh dropped to both knees before his throne and bowed his head. Corinne also bowed, thankful for her years of martial arts as she tried to bring her forehead as low as possible. Even proud

Mazur lowered his head when the priestess rapped for attention three times, every beat echoing through the room.

The last beat completely died away before Mykh lifted his head. He resumed his place on the Dragon Throne and the audience seated themselves, each on their own little cushion.

Corinne straightened up cautiously and wished that she'd plotted something set during the Goddess's Dance at the capitol, just so she'd understand it better. But she'd only considered that festival as it related to Mykh's conception, not as an event that she'd need to know in detail. She settled back to watch the proceedings with the happy anticipation of an author whose characters were now running the show, and surprising her during every minute.

"Welcome to Torhtremer, Holy One," Mykh greeted the priestess. "How may we serve the Mother of All Life?"

"We have come to bless the Dragonheart's Companion for the Goddess's Dance, that she may be fruitful and the realm rejoice."

A muscle ticked in Mykh's jaw but his voice stayed even. "Holy One, I am but a young man and newly come to the Dragon Throne. I have no wife to celebrate the dance with."

Shock ran through the throng and even the high priests and priestesses looked startled. "Not handfasted yet?" Corinne heard one shocked whisper.

She tilted her head, wondering why they were so surprised when Mykh spoke the truth about his unmarried status. *Did the people really honor the Companion as if she was married to the High King?* She'd thought they were only concerned about the child, not the mother.

Mykh's fingers tightened on Khyber's hard scales before he continued. "I wish to beg the guidance of your wisdom, as my ancestor King Rhodyon the First did. Will you guide me in selecting a jewel from the Dragon's Hoard that she may accompany me for the Goddess's Dance?"

The hall broke out into a chorus of gasps, mutters, and whispers as the audience absorbed this. The High Priestess's jaw frankly dropped, but she recovered faster than her fellows. "We are honored to assist the Dragonheart as the gods and goddesses lead us. Please bring forth the Dragon's Hoard that we may see."

"Certainly." Mykh raised his voice slightly to reach across the chamber. "Guardian, bring in the jewels."

Yevgheniy's scarlet robes blazed in the great portal. He bowed and clapped thrice. Two women appeared behind him, then more.

Yevgheniy stalked into the throne room, followed by Mykh's hundred concubines, walking two by two and looking like what they were: the most beautiful, intelligent, skilled young women in the Seven Kingdoms. Each one had been selected as the finest example of her province's womanhood during an annual competition that made the Miss America Pageant look like a game of tic-tac-toe.

Traditionally, a third of the finest jewels were set aside for the enjoyment of the High King and his personal guests. The remainder gave their favors to the kingdoms' bravest soldiers and diplomats. Magic ensured that the men, except for the High King and the Guardian, remembered these encounters only as a delightful dream never to be spoken of lest it vanish. Magical oaths kept the women silent after their time as jewels ended.

When not so engaged, all of the women studied the carnal arts to capture and hold the High King's attention, as well as the arts and sciences that best suited each one's taste.

Every woman, unless pregnant by the High King, departed after a year with a substantial dowry and the freedom to choose her own future. *A jewel knows its own setting*, said the ancient proverb, and imperial bureaucrats enforced that wisdom against any parent foolish enough to arrange a jewel's marriage without her consent. The jewels were eagerly sought as brides, and many of them married the fine soldiers or diplomats who'd caught their eye.

Corinne settled back to watch the women she'd thought so long and hard about. Mykh was secure enough on the throne so that he didn't need to seek a foreign alliance, leaving one of his beautiful concubines the obvious choice to become his true love. But none of them had struck sparks when she'd tried to plot a romance for him.

Still, maybe she'd been wrong and she could spot his mate during this parade.

The women streamed down the center aisle in a steady flood of beauty and elegance. Some were dressed to emphasize their suitability as queen while others focused on their womanly assets. Some wore beautiful gowns of embroidered silk or rich brocade, or the modest silk tunic and trousers of their native provinces. Still others wore sheer gauzes, with only a few bands of velvet or embroidery for decorum.

Someone in the audience recognized a hometown girl and shouted encouragement. Another clapped, while a third whistled. The air began to swell with sounds of the crowd's approval.

Corinne recognized Juli immediately and sighed. Tall, richly curved with lavish golden curls, she strode through the throne room like the trained fencer she was. She was also one of the very few women whose sexual appetites approached Mykh's for frequency and intensity. But Alekhsiy—Mykh's younger half brother and the image of his father, Iskander the Smith—had caught her eye on the journey to the capitol, a yearning unaffected by Mykh's exciting but irregular attentions.

True to form, Juli walked next to Wen-Chuan, her favorite

sparring partner. They made a striking pair, with Juli's height and lush golden beauty set off by Wen-Chuan's raven-haired delicacy. Even their clothes were different, with Juli wearing flamboyant blue chiffon with a low-cut bodice and high waist to frame her breasts and slit skirts to show off her beautiful legs. Wen-Chuan wore a scarlet silk tunic and trousers, outwardly modest but so soft and closely fitted that it highlighted every elegant curve. But both costumes allowed their wearers to move with the ease and precision of trained fighters.

Corinne smiled as she saw Vholodhya, Ghryghoriy's right-hand man, watch the oblivious Wen-Chuan. He'd met her when she first arrived at the palace and fallen hard for her wit and beauty. Since then, he'd plotted and contrived to deny other soldiers access to her. Now he prayed daily that she'd marry him after her service as a jewel ended.

By this time the throne room sounded like the beginning of the Super Bowl, as the spectators shouted, clapped, or thumped the marble floor. Their enthusiasm had spread to the crowd outside as additional cheers floated in from the balcony.

A gap appeared in the line behind Wen-Chuan. Then a single woman sashayed down the aisle, head-high and magnificent bosom prominently displayed. Corinne stretched up to see better then chuckled when she recognized the walk.

Only Mhari could strut her stuff like that. She'd fluffed up her red hair until it glowed and danced like a river of living fire. Her outfit was closer to the traditional harem outfit than that of any other woman, featuring a velvet bodice so short and low-cut that it was barely more than a band around the most generous breasts in the harem. A wide jeweled waistband above pleated, transparent silk trousers allowed glimpses of her other spectacular charms. She had a wicked sense of humor that kept the other women roaring with laughter, when they weren't threatening murder for her shameless attempts to eliminate any competition for Mykh's attentions.

Mhari moved to her own beat as usual and she rapidly closed the gap to Wen-Chuan, focusing totally on Mykh as she smiled and winked at him. Her attempts at flirtation blinded her to the women before her and she ran into Wen-Chuan's back, making the smaller woman stumble.

But Mhari's luck had run out this time. Wen-Chuan quickly recovered her balance and grabbed Mhari's hand. A few cunning twists of her fingers sent Mhari's fingers into unnatural directions and agonizing pain across her face. She bit her lip and Wen-Chuan released her. Mhari fell back into step beside her assigned partner, shaking the circulation back into her hand.

The altercation was over so quickly that few caught it. But Vholodhya, Wen-Chuan's beau, relaxed beside Ghryghoriy while Mykh coughed. Corinne settled back down on her cushion, trying to remember who she'd thought could keep Mhari happy and out of mischief.

Finally all hundred women stood before the dais, flanked by junior priests and priestesses. The crowd fell silent as Yevgheniy swiveled to face Mykh and bowed. "The Dragon's Hoard is assembled, Your Majesty."

"Thank you," Mykh acknowledged. "Holy One, I offer you the finest jewels in Torhtremer to choose from."

The high priests and priestesses immediately circulated among the women, occasionally asking a soft question.

Corinne leaned forward eagerly to watch. She caught sight of Mykh's hand, knuckles white with tension, clamped down on Khyber's paw. Mazur looked frankly bored while only Khyber's golden eyes moved as he studied the priests.

When the religious council huddled together before the southern windows, a single nod from Ghryghoriy sent the guardsman to clear a private space around them. Order reestablished, Ghryghoriy glanced up at a small balcony above the portal. Corinne followed his eyes and discovered a clump of archers standing watch . . . and Ghryghoriy's beloved wife, Amber. The two exchanged a look so full of love and understanding that Corinne's eyes burned.

Now that is what I want for Mykh, Corinne thought fiercely. *And maybe some day for myself, too.*

The priests and priestesses broke their huddle and returned to face Mykh. The room was so utterly silent that Corinne could hear the fire burning in the braziers and smell saltwater from the harbor beyond the windows.

"We have studied the jewels and truly they are splendid beyond belief. The Goddess is proud of all her daughters," the High Priestess pronounced. She stopped to clear her throat.

And . . . Corinne prompted silently when the silence stretched out.

"But no one of these beauties stands out beyond the others."

Mykh's fist beat on his leg then stopped abruptly. The crowd's tension was as palpable as the marble columns.

"There is another who may answer your question, Your Majesty," the High Priestess continued. "The Imperial Dragon has known every Companion of a Dragonheart. We ask him to share his wisdom in this matter."

That's passing the buck, Corinne sniffed to herself.

The throng gasped but no one spoke. Mykh became even stiffer while Mazur sat up, his ears pricked.

"Greetings, Holy One," Khyber answered. "It is gratifying to be remembered by the Goddess's servants." He nodded politely to the priests and priestesses, very much like Sean Connery reporting for duty as James Bond.

Many in the throng squeaked in awe and prostrated themselves. They stopped when they realized that none of the dignitaries had moved and sheepishly sat erect again.

"Only one woman in this room has the strength needed to heal the High King," he continued and paused for effect.

The crowd rustled but didn't dare interrupt him by so much as a whisper. Mykh's Adam's apple bobbed as he swallowed hard. Corinne glanced from him then back up to the huge dragon head looming overhead.

"She sits before you, beside the High King. Corinne, a sorceress from a far-off world and his battle trophy." Khyber's head swung down and around to look Corinne in the eye. She jumped to her feet and glared at him. She was glad that Khyber wasn't inclined to eat her, but forcing her to marry Mykh was almost as bad.

"Now just wait a minute, you big lizard!" she began but was cut off by Mykh's simultaneous snarl when he erupted from the throne.

"I will not be bound to a sorceress, Khyber, even for a month."

"Enough!" Khyber growled. His words reverberated oddly and Corinne quickly looked around.

Everyone else in the throne room was frozen in place, some with mouths open or hands lifted to gesticulate.

Mazur yowled triumphantly, "At last a friend on the Tiger Throne."

"What did you do to them, you green control freak?" Corinne demanded, shaking her finger at Khyber. Forcing her into marriage was just too much to be borne.

"Nothing much. They are frozen in time until you children come to your senses." He looked sternly from Corinne to Mykh.

"Any other woman but her," Mykh snarled.

"You are the one who permitted the religious council to select a Companion. Don't object now because their choice offends you. Or do you mean to prove that a High King is more changeable than spring weather?"

Mykh flushed and set his mouth hard.

"And you." Khyber's voice lowered to a gravelly purr as he considered Corinne. "All the *ch'i* of Torhtremer will be focused on the Dragonheart's Companion during the dance, more than enough to melt the ice serpent's poison and heal Mykh."

"But there's no remedy. I'm sure there isn't," Corinne protested.

"You don't know dragon magic, which can send fire through a person's meridians, or earth magic."

"Okay, I won't argue with you about that," Corinne said slowly. "But what does it have to do with me?"

"The people's *ch'i* will come first to the Dragonheart's Companion. Then she will circle it through her body and the High King's until it cures him."

Corinne snuck a glance sideways at Mykh. His mouth was set in a hard line as Khyber spoke.

"Only a sorceress can successfully channel this much power," Khyber continued. "You are the only sorceress alive today so you must do it."

She could see the muscle throbbing in Mykh's cheek.

"You know, I really don't think it's a good idea for me to do this. After all, I'm the one who caused this mess. Isn't it asking a lot for me to execute the fix properly?" Corinne demurred.

"Precisely why you must do it. You must balance the harm you did with the good of healing."

Corinne tried again to dissuade Khyber. "What happens if Mykh can't forget it's my fault and won't share the power with me?"

"The High King will do his duty. Unless he provides a true-born male heir, the Dark Warrior will destory Torhtremer." Khyber's tone permitted no argument.

Mykh growled something that sounded like a curse.

"Very well," Corinne agreed reluctantly. "I don't think this will work but I'll try." Her eyes met Mykh's. His earlier fury was now overlaid by icy resolve.

"Do you swear that you will be Mykhayl Rhodyonovich's wife, forsaking all others throughout the Goddess's Dance?" Khyber demanded.

"I do," Corinne answered cautiously. *A month of his kind of sex, why not?* she encouraged herself.

"Excellent," Mazur purred, happily kneading the pillow under him.

"And do you swear that you will be his wife for a year and a day thereafter, should the Goddess bless you with a child?" the dragon continued.

Corinne opened her mouth to object but thought better of it under Khyber's frosty glare. She consoled herself with the thought that if Mykh became fertile, he'd probably seek a child from any other woman in Torhtremer than her. "Okay, I'll agree to that, too."

Khyber nodded at Corinne, his expression saying that he'd noted her hesitation, then turned to Mykh.

"And do you swear that you will be a faithful husband to Corinne Carson throughout the Goddess's Dance? And for a year and a day thereafter if a child is granted to you?"

"I swear," Mykh gritted.

"Children, children," Khyber soothed, sounding lethally

amused. "You now have the Goddess's blessing to spend as much time as you can between the sheets."

Corinne and Mykh both flushed scarlet. "Hurrah! A great lady to ride the tiger again!" Mazur enthused, wildly rolling around on his back and purring as loudly as a drumroll. "Hurrah! Hurrah!" Khyber chuckled as he coiled himself into a throne again. Mazur somehow managed to slip into a very superior pose just before Khyber spoke again.

"Behold the Dragonheart's Companion!" he announced in a voice that made the room quake. "May the land rejoice and an heir be born!"

The crowd erupted to their feet, shaking the rafters with their cheers. The roar spread beyond the room and echoed back through the open windows from the courtyard beyond, sending pigeons circling through the sky. Even the guardsmen pounded their spears on the floor in approval. The concubines' faces showed a mixture of emotions: shock, disappointment, then relief. Finally they, too, joined the cheering.

Mykh took Corinne's hand and bowed, then straightened up to smile and nod at the throng. She copied his movements and expression, wondering what she'd gotten herself into.

At least this affair didn't look anything like her first wedding. That dress had encased her in white lace from throat to toe, with a ten-foot train for emphasis. Her current leather and jewels outfit was more remarkable for what it didn't cover than what it hid. And these witnesses were as raucous as any World Cup fans, unlike the stiff formality of that prestigious chapel and country club.

The High Priestess finally pounded her staff long and hard enough that the crowd quieted as Mykh ushered Corinne to the Tiger Throne. She glanced up at him quickly, he nodded curtly, and she sat down very, very slowly. The silver was surprisingly warm and comfortable, rather like a comforting fireplace seat at a ski lodge. She settled herself securely, making sure that the dragon scales covered all the important parts, while Mykh took his place on the Dragon Throne.

The High Priestess marched onto the dais and the other high priests and priestesses fanned across the steps behind her. Two young acolytes brought her crowns of roses and sage, with cedarwood points, then bowed their way back down the steps. The throne seemed softer to Corinne, as if it was decked with cushions.

"Blessed art thou, oh dragon, who brings the cloud and rain to quicken the earth," the High Priestess intoned and lifted a crown to Mykh. He kissed it quickly, mouth set, then lowered his proud head so she could set it on his red hair.

"And blessed art thou, oh tigress, who bears the fruit of the earth's fertility," she chanted and offered another crown to Corinne.

Corinne bit her lip, then kissed the thing and bent her head to don it. This was feeling entirely too real for comfort. *If that business about "bearing the fruit" actually comes true . . .*

The High Priestess began to chant, invoking the Horned Goddess's blessing on Mykh and Corinne.

Corinne lowered her eyes while she listened, her nose twitching at the crown's clean, sweet scent.

Welcome, little sister, a voice purred, sounding like Rene Russo.

Corinne's eyes darted from side to side. *Who on earth is that?*

I am Svetlhana, little sister. Her Russian accent was so thick that it sounded more like "leetle seestr." *The Imperial Tigress. We can chat together as friends now that you've been seated on the Tiger Throne.*

Where are you? Corinne demanded, lifting her head to search.

Don't look around! The Dark Warrior watches us, even here.

Corinne closed her eyes and took a deep breath. She'd known about the Imperial Tigress, just as she understood all four of the celestial animals who walked in Torhtremer from time to time. They took shape whenever a catalyst lived, someone like Mykh who could summon them. A Dragonheart, as the people of Torhtremer called him.

But a tigress's catalyst, or Tigerheart, was the rarest and most unpredictable of all. Corinne had briefly considered one as Mykh's wife, then rejected the idea as too difficult to manipulate.

Da, you are my little sister. Thanks to you, I can roll in Torhtremer's mint fields again, Svetlhana purred.

Why don't you show yourself as Khyber does? The silver under her was now as soft and yielding as an old leather sofa.

Why should we tell the Dark Warrior everything? Let him wonder for as long as possible whether you truly are my little sister. Perhaps it will buy us a little time.

Okay, Corinne said slowly, trying to grasp the implications.

Now we must talk quickly before I depart. Understand, above all, that the great halberd is the key to summoning me, as the sword is for Khyber.

Corinne grimaced. It was a very big halberd, twice the size of anything at the *kwoon* where she'd studied kung fu.

Da, it is as impressive as my claws, Svetlhana agreed smugly. *Relax; it will be as light as a feather in your hands.*

Thank you, Corinne said dryly. *But what about . . .*

I must go now before I am discovered, Svetlhana hissed urgently. *Enjoy yourself, little sister.*

Corinne settled back into the throne, which had become a very agreeable place to sit. If only she'd been able to ask Svetlhana who Mykh's true love was.

The High Priestess finished her chant, and the other high priests and priestesses came up onto the dais where they gathered in a circle around Mykh and Corinne. They raised their hands over the two and sang in a variety of languages, some magical but most not, about how the land's fertility reflected the High King's. The musicians joined in, adding a sweet counterpoint to the priests' melody. Corinne listened politely, more interested in the harmonies than the words.

Then power welled up in her from her feet to her throat. It brushed her face like perfume before diving back to the floor. Her face flushed and her breath came faster.

The power looped through her again as the crowd joined in the song. It gained strength as more people sang and sent sparks along her meridians. Her nipples swelled against the leather and liquid heat rose from her core.

Mykh's dragon coat lay neatly against his strong neck, reminding her of the man underneath the costume. A glance sideways showed her his cock rising hard and proud inside the trousers, with a small wet spot in the silk marking its tip. She remembered how it had looked when he displayed it for her . . . and how completely it had filled her. She wanted to touch him, kiss him, taste him immediately.

Ch'i drummed through her bones until she swayed with the glory of it. She needed that cock inside her now. She shifted restlessly on the throne.

Mykh shuddered with each breath. He looked like a man straining to reach shore, given how his shoulders rose and fell. His cock strengthened until the silk barely contained it. She bit her lip against the temptation it offered.

The song finally finished in a crash of cymbals and flourish of trumpets and Corinne staggered at the ebbing energy flow. A rose landed on her hair and another brushed her shoulder, as all the priests and priestesses showered them with flowers. Her *ch'i* stabilized, but she still ached for the man beside her.

"Guard her well that she may dance with joy on the third day," the High Priestess intoned as she raised her hands in a final blessing. Corinne had just enough wit to follow Mykh's lead and nod politely.

Then the priests and priestesses stepped aside, opening a path to the great portal. Mykh came to his feet in a rush and grabbed Corinne's hand. She jumped when a spark flew between them and all but flew at his side when they marched down the aisle.

The audience cheered and cheered again. Rose petals and sage leaves, plus bits of cedarwood bark rained down on Mykh and Corinne. Too much to brush off, the potpourri gathered in their hair and clothing, its aroma filling their nostrils. Every breath swelled her lungs and sent blood pounding through her. She was more intensely aware of the man beside her than ever before.

Outside the portals, Mykh turned sharply down a short corridor. Sentries held open the doors at the end, their faces beaming. Mykh and Corinne emerged onto a balcony above a great courtyard, overflowing with a chanting crowd, which Mykh saluted.

Beyond the palace wall, the streets were full of more cheering people as far as she could see. Even the piers jutting out into the harbor were covered with leaping figures.

Instinctively Corinne waved at them and the applause redoubled.

"Dragonheart! Dragonheart!" they roared, while a few voices rose in counterpoint, "Tigerheart! Tigerheart!"

Mykh wrapped his arm around her waist and pulled Corinne close. Hidden by the railing from the crowd, his fingers slid inside her skirt and fondled her. Her breath caught as her insides turned liquid with longing. He delved farther and her knees nearly failed her.

Corinne gritted her teeth. *If he doesn't stop handling me soon, I'm going to grab him . . .*

FOUR

Somehow Corinne smiled and waved at the crowd again. Mykh's big hand cupped her and she arched, her head lolling back helplessly. He jerked away from her.

"Come now," he said abruptly and dragged her back inside the palace. He strode through the corridors at a conqueror's pace, leaving sentries and servants in their wake. She could hear the crowd celebrating in the distance.

He slammed open a door, shoved her through it, and snarled at the guards who tried to follow.

Corinne found herself on a balcony with marble walls and columns, overlooking a horse paddock. A large black stallion looked up quickly, ears pricked to identify the intrusion. Battle scars on his flank marked him as Nightflyer, Mykh's warhorse.

A shadow loomed up behind her. Nightflyer relaxed and returned to grazing.

Two big hands spun her around and tossed her up against a column. Mykh crowded her against it before she could slide down, his legs ruthlessly spreading her thighs.

"Wife," he growled, a universe of possessiveness in the single word. Then his mouth covered hers and rational thought fled.

She was sandwiched between marble and hot masculine muscle. His tongue slipped down her throat so quickly it was a wonder she didn't strangle instead of moan. Her hands dug into his arms and found slick silk, instead of a man's satin skin.

She moaned again, frustrated. Nothing mattered, not the setting where servants could appear at any moment, not his opinion of her, not her vulnerability to him, nothing. Only being immediately filled by him meant a damn.

His hand moved urgently somewhere below and then his cock's fat head finally branded her nether lips. She lifted her legs to wrap them around his hips in welcome. Mykh simultaneously shoved into her hard and fast, buried to the balls with his first thrust.

Corinne screamed into his mouth as she promptly climaxed.

Pinning her against the stone, he rode her with the hard, mindless rhythm of a stallion in rut. His ruthlessness allowed her no time to recover but sent her spiraling into another climax. She was still pulsing when he tore his mouth away from hers to bellow his release, as jet after fiery jet filled her.

He leaned against her afterwards, gasping for breath but still hard deep within her. She doubted she could stand up if he freed her, given how her legs were trembling.

A polite knock sounded on the door. Mykh disregarded it and circled his hips against her.

"Shouldn't we answer that?" Corinne said faintly, trying to ignore how her body melted to welcome him. If he touched her again like that, she'd melt and say to hell with ingrained pride and wariness. A grunt was his only response. Then his fingers bit into her hips as he adjusted her against the column.

She paid no attention to the second knock, since it came just as he started riding her again. Long, deep thrusts this time that sent her sliding up and down the marble, twisting and pulling her top in different directions. Her body burned in welcome, nipples hard against their leather cages as his brocade coat rasped against her over-sensitive breasts and shoulders. His silk tunic brushed her bare midriff while his trousers rubbed against the inside of her thighs.

And still he pounded into her time after time, stretching her to the limit around his magnificent cock as his crisp pubic hair teased her.

He finally came in a tumultuous flood that caused him to scream in satisfaction. The harsh sound triggered something equally primal inside her and she yielded to her own climax. Waves pounded up through her spine and her head banged against the stone.

"Report." Mykh's voice was a rough bark in her ears as he let her slide down, then stepped away from her to fasten up his trousers. She caught the railing for support and managed not to sit down.

"I have the wizard's report you requested, Your Majesty." Ghryghoriy's voice was muffled and completely neutral as if he hadn't heard any of the noise they'd made.

Corinne's face burned as she pulled herself fully erect and tugged her bikini top back into place. Obviously this marble column wasn't perfectly smooth, given the smears of blood on it from where Mykh had pumped her up and down. She flexed her shoulders experimentally. It didn't feel too bad, especially if she could just get back into that magic pool of water.

Bodice rippers never mentioned that you could feel a man's impact down to your bones.

"Very well," Mykh answered Ghryghoriy, half sorry to be diverted.

He took a deep breath before he spoke to Corinne. His wife, the sorceress, a woman who could probably destroy him with a single glance. Duty had never seemed harder than when he handfasted her, nor sweeter than when he rode her. "Ready?" he asked without looking at her.

"Of course." Her voice was a little husky but that wasn't surprising after the way she'd screamed. Something masculine deep within him roared in triumph.

"Come then." She followed him meekly out the door, avoiding contact with him, which suited him well enough. His rod was already hinting its willingness to fill her again.

One quick look at Ghryghoriy's face made all thoughts of carnal amusements vanish. Thankfully, Yevgheniy and Mazur waited just beyond, the big leopard prowling restlessly through the corridor. They could guard Corinne while he spoke to Ghryghoriy.

Mazur broke off his fretting and bounded to Corinne, where he butted his head against her leg and purred wildly. She choked and stooped to hug him, a silver glint on her high cheekbones hinting of tears. Blood trickled down her shoulder blade.

Mykh froze. Even at his youngest and clumsiest, he'd never hurt a woman without her consent. His mouth tightened when he saw how stiffly Corinne caressed Mazur, showing the after-effects of his rough handling.

"Yevgheniy, take Her Excellency to the Tiger's Den. She'll need healers and food." She'd be more at ease in the palace's feminine heart.

"Now you're showing some sense, putting her in there," Yevgheniy approved. "Don't worry. She'll be ready for you in no time."

"I don't need special handling," Corinne protested, color staining her cheeks.

"The Tiger's Den is the Companion's chambers, Corinne," Mykh reassured her.

She stared at him then nodded grudgingly. Her evident surprise at his courtesy twisted his heart.

"Really? Okay then," she acquiesced. "But can Mazur come with me, please?"

"Of course," Mykh agreed. She'd need a friend to comfort her after his rough handling. Goddess only knew how she'd charmed Mazur, who'd always before alternated between ignoring and hissing at Mykh's bed partners.

He watched her bloodstained back move proudly down the corridor behind Yevgheniy, every step twisting a dart in his side.

"Did you treat the Gray Sorceress as harshly as that before you killed her?" Ghryghoriy murmured.

Silence stretched between them for a moment, longer than when he'd faced that pestilence for the last time.

"No," Mykh said finally. "It was over very quickly."

"Then why do you treat this one so poorly?"

Mykh whirled to face his friend. "She's a sorceress and she took my manhood," he hurled back.

Ghryghoriy shrugged, undaunted by Mykh's temper. "She saved your six sisters time and again from your enemies, then found them strong husbands and rich lands. She gave you a kingdom more easily than anyone thought possible, given the civil wars after the old king died. You'd have traded your manhood a dozen times over for the peace found today in Torhtremer." He studied

Mykh for a moment before going on. "So what is different between her and the Gray Sorceress?"

"I don't know," Mykh admitted slowly. "I will offer her some recompense for my discourtesy."

Ghryghoriy's mouth quirked. "Fair enough that you, too, should do penance to a woman. Amber claims it often enough from me, especially if I am less than courteous to a woman."

Mykh's eyebrow lifted at the unexpected insight into his friend's marriage. Ghryghoriy never chattered unless he wished to build calm to receive some unsettling news. "Penance?" Mykh questioned, curious to learn more and willing to allow the diversion.

"She calls it that," Ghryghoriy shrugged. "She chooses the feat and I must perform it. She searches long and hard in the old scrolls to find those deeds. But I confess that I've found much to enjoy, including acts that I'd never thought arousing."

Mykh snorted at his friend's besotted smile but tucked away the advice for later consideration. Such penance would balance his ill treatment of Corinne. His voice strengthened. "Enough of that. What news makes you hide in talk of my women?"

"Ice storms in the northern mountains," Ghryghoriy answered, all soldier now. "Too late in the season to be natural and too strong for any wizard to peek through."

"The Dark Warrior has returned and hides his preparations from us." Mykh voiced the only explanation, as the all too familiar taste of fear dried his mouth.

"Just as she warned you," Ghryghoriy agreed.

At the other end of the corridor, Corinne's long skirt whisked around a corner while Mazur playfully tried to pounce on its hem. Surely she wasn't in league with the Dark Warrior, if she warned of his coming. But who else could he ask for word of the Dark Warrior? Who might be able to tell him more than she had?

"Damn wizards!" Mykh cursed, as he had so many times before. They could manage a bit of rain on a summer day or baffle a hundred soldiers before an attack. But they were no use for great magic and hopeless at facing the Dark Warrior. "You'll send in someone on foot then." He spoke the obvious while mulling over alternatives.

"Aye. But a week or more must pass before we can learn anything."

Mykh grunted agreement then gave the only comfort he could offer. "At least he hasn't regained his strength since losing his army, else he'd have visited us with a snowstorm before now. What preparations have you made?"

He headed toward his private office, Ghryghoriy falling into step beside him.

A few minutes turned into hours as Mykhayl and Ghryghoriy made what plans they could for defense against the Dark Warrior. Finally Mykh caught Ghryghoriy stifling a yawn.

"Go home, old friend," he urged. "We've done enough here for the day. Anything more would mean disturbing the Goddess's Dance, something no man wishes to do. Go occupy yourself with your wife."

Ghryghoriy snorted as he straightened up and stretched openly. "More like she'll amuse herself with me. She's determined that we'll make our first child during the Dance."

"Solemnly observing the Hunter's Watch, is she?" Mykh raised an eyebrow. "Well, she is a priest's daughter."

"Aye, but I hadn't thought before that she was this devout! She insists that we observe every detail of the rituals. Worship at the temples during every high tide, sanctified food for both of us, celibacy for me during the month before. All the while I build her woman's *ch'i* with my hands and mouth, so that it can be offered

in sacrifice." He shook his head ruefully. "I swear that I'm count-
ing the hours until the White Horses sweep in."

"So is every other man in Torhtremer, if the priests have any
say," Mykh reminded him. At least Ghryghoriy didn't sound envious of Mykh's role as High King and Dragonheart during the
Hunter's Watch and Goddess's Dance.

The priests emphasized that his first responsibility was ensuring
that his Companion would be an enthusiastic partner during the
dance. That could mean either frequent bedsport with her when
both spent themselves or focusing solely on the Companion's pleasure, as all other men did for theirs. The priests did suggest that the
High King remain celibate on the Watch's last night, the lightest
amount of fasting mentioned in the sacred texts.

Mykh was simply pleased that no one insisted that he abstain
from his Companion's bed. Avoiding Corinne was something his
rod strenuously objected to, especially now when it tented his
breeches at the thought of her.

Ghryghoriy's eyes met Mykh's, suddenly entirely serious. "The
wizards say they've never seen anything like the strength of the *ch'i*
in Torhtremer now. They promise that it will be far greater during
the Advent of the White Horses."

"Not enough to cure an ice serpent's bite," Mykh answered,
feeling a return of the old despair.

"They say any power can be focused, if there be a lens strong
enough. And that puissance gained from a woman's pleasure is the
mightiest."

Mykh forebore mentioning how often wizards' interpretation
of great magic went amiss.

"Two days more to stoke her fires," Ghryghoriy mused. "Two
days . . ."

Mykh chuckled at the helpless longing in his friend's voice and slapped him on the shoulder. "Enough of that! Take your plaintive cries home where you might find some comfort," he half-teased. "As for me, I'm off to see what mischief my little sorceress has created in the Tiger's Den."

Ghryghoriy swept him a full court bow. "As you command, Your Majesty."

Mykh slapped him on the shoulder and the two men went their separate ways. Mykh took the stairs three at a time, worried more than he'd admit about Corinne's back. His nod set the sentries posted outside the Tiger's Den into a quick salute, followed by a hasty—and silent—opening of the door. He'd left the ceremonial coat behind but still wore his great sword, too wary of potential threats to set it out of reach.

He'd only seen these rooms once before, when he surveyed the palace after he claimed the throne. The Tiger's Den had seemed formal and cold then, guarded by generations of priestesses and the ghosts of women who'd lived within.

The Dragonheart's Companion dwelled here throughout the Hunter's Watch and the Goddess's Dance, so that she might be blessed and protected in the palace's feminine heart. If the High King set a child in her, then she remained for the year and a day that she was his Companion. But queens, created by dynastic marriages that emphasized masculine concerns with land or gold or armies, had no rights in these rooms unless they were also the Dragonheart's Companion for the Goddess's Dance.

Five generations of High Kings had bred sons only during the Goddess's Dance. Five generations had seen no woman live here longer than a year and a day before fleeing the rooms that whispered of the white tigress' power.

But this time Mykh could hear splashing and laughter, mixed with snorts and light growls. He followed the sounds into the great bathroom, where he found Corinne and Mazur playing in the enormous pool. He'd considered it a tedious room before, with its enormous pool and surrounding colonnade that looked out to walled gardens on the west. It had felt flat and open, unguarded and defenseless, compared to the crags seen from his bathroom.

Now it seemed like paradise as Corinne ducked under a floating rose to wrestle with Mazur. She laughed as they came up for breath, Mazur playfully tapping her cheek with the soft side of one great paw. Clouds of steam rose around them, scented with roses. She grabbed the big cat by the ears and tried to pull his head forward. But he chose to dive under with his predator's suppleness.

Suddenly Corinne was sucked down, shouting, "Dammit, Mazur. Let go of my ankle!" She went under rapidly, slapping the water but leaving only bubbles behind.

Mykh ran forward hastily, ready to dive in after her.

But Corinne came up laughing with one arm draped over Mazur's shoulders. "You are a silly beast!" she chuckled before switching to a series of soft purrs and chuffs that Mazur answered in kind. He tapped the water lightly, sending a ripple to caress her shoulders. She patted Mazur's cheek and laughed again, looking as innocent as a kitten playing with a weaver's yarns. Mykh found himself needing to apologize somehow for shredding the skin on her back.

Corinne caught sight of him and stilled, her hand still resting on Mazur. Then she smiled at him and slid down until only her neck and head showed, leaving scant evidence of her enticing blushes.

He took a half-step toward her then caught himself, hungry for control lest she somehow prove to be a sorceress.

"Good evening. Would you care to join me for supper?" he offered, feeling like a thrice-dammed coward for taking refuge in politeness.

She tilted her head and surveyed him, blue eyes lingering on the ridge behind his ornate trousers. "If you'll turn your back so I can get out," she countered, color burning her cheeks.

He pivoted immediately and fought the temptation to peek. The marble columns here had too many flowering vines, roses and jasmine mostly, to be mirrors for watching her. The sounds of water splashing and falling goaded his imagination, raising memories of feasting on her in the Tasting Room.

"You can turn around now." He found her completely covered in a white robe with her hair wrapped up in a turban, both embroidered with red roses. Neither robe nor turban looked like they'd slip any time soon. Damn.

Her hand flew up to cover her smile.

"Corinne," he got out, needing to start talking. He had to create balance before he could tumble her again.

"Yes?"

"Pray forgive me for hurting you on the balcony this afternoon."

Her jaw dropped. Whatever she'd expected, it wasn't this.

"I have never before caused harm to a woman during bedsport. I swear it won't happen again."

"Please, Mykh, don't worry about it. It's already healed, thanks to the pool." Roses swept across her cheeks in a blush.

"As my lady wishes." He bowed politely, relaxing slightly at her quick forgiveness. She raised an eyebrow at him but didn't challenge the formal phrase.

Mazur snorted his opinion of their flirtation, then stalked toward the food with his back arched and tail high.

A small table was set for two under the colonnade, offering an excellent view of the pool and gardens beyond. It was flanked by two other tables, each containing an array of tempting dishes.

Corinne studied them closely, making Mykh immediately remember how she'd stared at him in the Tasting Room.

"It looks like they brought fresh food for me and separate food for you, Mykh." She said the last word hesitantly with a quick peep up at him through her lashes. He swallowed hard before he could speak.

"Very proper," he remarked, relieved for once by social chitchat. How could he consider leaping on her so soon after the pool's healing? "Men and women have separate needs for the Goddess's Dance and must prepare differently."

She studied him curiously, open and unguarded for the first time. "Really? You'll have to tell me more while we're eating."

The following silence was comfortable as each filled their plates and poured tall mugs of tea before sitting down and starting in on the delicious repast. Mazur crouched next to a side table, neatly consuming a large saucer of milk and diced rabbit that had appeared for him.

After a few minutes of silent consumption, Corinne propped her elbows on the table and studied the food before them. Mykh lifted an eyebrow but didn't stop eating, trained by too many years as a mercenary to value every meal the gods granted.

"Looks like you've got red meat there with a hefty dose of pine nuts, too. Plus lots of fruits and vegetables: carrots, asparagus, bananas. Are those berries?" Corinne asked.

"Juniper berries." He nodded, pleased that she was chatting. "Tasty sauce for the elk meat."

"Okay. Red meat for masculine strength and some phallic symbols in the fruits and veggies. But why is that flatbread made with oats?"

His mouth quirked at her description of his meal. "The priests demand that men consume much of it during the Watch. I demand that it appear as oatcakes, in the fashion that my mother prepared it."

"Probably tastes better like that." Corinne took up her fork again and dug into her food, then smiled tentatively at him. "How long do we eat like this?"

"Throughout the Hunter's Watch and the Goddess's Dance."

"What's the Hunter's Watch?" Corinne blurted then shrugged. "I never tried to understand it back home on Earth so it's all new to me."

Mykh blinked at her ignorance but answered her easily, pleased that there was something she didn't know. "We celebrate the Hunter's Watch for three nights and three days before the Goddess's Dance begins. Most folks spend it purifying themselves for the Dance. But it is also the time when all shipping must leave port."

"Why?" She watched him as she chewed. He immediately thought of a dozen ways her mouth could wrap around his rod, which predictably hardened.

"The Hunter's Watch here in Bhaikhal is different from elsewhere, thanks to the harbor. The Advent of the White Horses, marking the end of the Hunter's Watch and the beginning of the Goddess's Dance, is truly a monumental tide in these waters and not just a poet's pretty turn of phrase."

She waited, hanging on his words.

"You know that we have two moons, the Hunter and the Maiden. The Maiden is silver and follows a predictable path, its great orb at its fullest once every month."

"Equatorial orbit," Corinne agreed.

"As you wish," Mykh nodded, unwilling to admit his unfamiliarity with the term. "But the Hunter is golden and travels the far reaches of the sky in search of his mate."

"Polar orbit."

"Indeed," Mykh said neutrally. Perhaps one of the wizards could explain her words. "They come together once every seven years and shine as one for a month, which marks the Goddess's Dance. At the same time, the tides here increase until the high tide covers many cliffs, while the low tide leaves mud where ships once floated. No ship can withstand these changes, so all must leave during the Hunter's Watch."

"And the biggest port in the world is celibate, in the commercial sphere at least. It must be impressive." She pursed her lips as she considered.

Mykh damned his unruly pulse, pounding like a youngling before his first battle, and hastened into speech. "Precisely. Pilgrims come from around the world to celebrate with us. The other planets, as the wizards call them, sometimes stretch themselves across the sky in a single line to join the Hunter and the Maiden in worshipping the sun. When the Goddess's Necklace is strung thusly, as it is this year, then the Advent of the White Horses is larger yet."

"Wow," she breathed. "And we'll be right there to watch it."

Mykh nodded, startled by how soft she looked now, changed from the angry fighter he'd met in that distant world. Now was the time to seek equilibrium and pray that she wouldn't transform into a greedy witch if he yielded to her.

"Corinne, I must make amends for shedding your blood this afternoon."

"You really don't have to, Mykh," she demurred and poured herself another cup of tea. She added honey, as if the sweet was a necessity for creating a worthwhile drink of the dark brew.

"It is necessary that there might be balance between us." His mouth firmed. If she passed this test, perhaps he needn't fear her as a sorceress.

"Mykh . . ."

"It is best that this is accomplished where the symmetry was upset. In bed."

"Now, why did I think that you were leading up to something sexual?" She carefully stirred her tea until the honey dissolved. "So what do you have in mind?"

"Corinne, how would you like to sport?"

"Excuse me?" She lifted the cup and took a deep swallow.

"Bedsport. How would you prefer it?"

Corinne coughed and spluttered tea across the table. "Mykh, what the hell are you talking about?" she demanded when she could speak again. "Are you honestly asking me to decide what we're going to do next in bed?"

He nodded steadily, despite the way his blood roared into his rod. "I will do whatever you wish."

"What if I tell you to strip, lie down on the bed, and let me do whatever I want?" she asked slowly.

"As you wish." *What if she wants to handle me as the Gray Sorceress did with all her slaves, squatting astride their prone bodies? An act I've found intolerable with any other woman since?*

Balance must be rebuilt, a little voice reminded him, *lest the Goddess's Dance fail.*

And the Goddess blessed her as my companion, Mykh reassured himself. *I can do no less than play my part in serving the Goddess, as the High Priestess dedicated me. At the very least, I can worship the Goddess in her, as other men do with their ladies on this night.*

But unlike other men, the voice reminded him, *you can give your seed.*

If she asks it, Mykh answered silently, slipping into the pattern of the Goddess's service.

He stood up and took off Dragon's Breath, propping the great sword against the wall. Then he began to unfasten his cuffs.

"You're really going to do it, aren't you?" Corinne breathed, tea cup drooping from her fingers.

"Yes." He finished undoing the cuffs and started on the ornate knots that held the tunic closed.

Corinne blew out a breath raggedly. "Dear God in heaven," she murmured as he shrugged the tunic off, "you really are such a fine-looking stud. And you're going to let me explore you."

He smiled privately as he folded the silk and placed it on his chair. Maybe this would work.

Mazur chuckled, an odd cross between snort and purr that startled Corinne. "Until tomorrow, Great Lady," he purred as he stood up and stretched. "May the Celestial Guardians grant you joy tonight."

"And may the Four keep you safe," she answered, giving the ritual response. Mazur gave her hand one long, rasping lick before he glided from the room, as bent on his own amusements as any other cat.

Corinne tried to sit still as she watched Mykh slowly, oh so slowly, remove his clothing. If he'd been mouth-watering in the silk tunic and trousers that clung to every magnificent muscle, his bare skin made him damn near irresistible. Those plates of muscle that covered his broad chest, the hard arcs of muscle that wrapped his shoulders, the beautiful rippling abs, the sweep of biceps and triceps, his big hands . . .

She wriggled in her chair and clamped her legs shut as heat trickled onto her thigh. The heavy silk robe that had once felt so protective was now busily irritating her stiff nipples as she tried to breathe. And if she could only persuade her pulse to calm down and beat steadily . . .

She closed her eyes and tried to think about dragon magic or another intellectually challenging subject. Anything to buy herself time until she regained her discipline and wouldn't lunge at him.

Something thudded to the floor. She looked over quickly and found Mykh setting his high boots neatly aside. His soft trousers stretched over his tight ass, emphasizing its clean, strong lines. Her mouth dried immediately and she ogled him.

He stood up and turned so quickly that their eyes met. She blushed at his swift understanding of what she'd been doing but defiantly refused to look away, letting him see her hunger. He smiled at her, a pleased masculine quirk of the lips that gave her hope a man wouldn't hurt her if she showed her emotions.

Then Mykh began to unlace his trousers. His cock was a solid ridge behind the lacings, but so engorged that it peeped above the green silk. More and more of its scarlet strength was exposed by each cross lacing tugged free, leaving it shining from the trickles of moisture flowing down from the tip. Her pulse raced faster and she shivered, trying to adapt to the bursts of hunger that raced between her breasts and her clit.

He caressed himself boldly as he had in his bedroom, polishing his cock and stretching it. Corinne squirmed and tugged the turban off her head, shaking her hair free with a careless snap.

"Is that stripping and lying down on the bed? Or did you change your mind about doing penance?" Corinne asked, pleased that her voice didn't sound as shaky as her legs felt.

Mykh's hand hesitated then fell away, leaving his cock standing free like a living definition of masculine beauty. It was perfectly matched to his splendid body and would have seemed unbearably huge on another man, blessed as it was with an elegant mushroom tip and thick enough at its base that even his massive hand could barely wrap around it.

Any carver of male nudity would have knelt to worship it. A virgin would have run screaming away from it. Corinne simply wondered how she was going to avoid it long enough to make him sweat a little.

He tossed his head to straighten his hair, setting the jewels in his braids clattering. The plaits covered his chest and shoulder blades in a silken tide accented by flashes of light from the jewels and beads. Heavens, she wanted to play with them. *Well, why not?*

"Stand still," she ordered just as he turned toward the bedroom.

Mykh frowned at her. "We decided that I'd lie down on the bed."

"We agreed that you're going to do what I want, which might mean lying down on the bed. But I want you to keep your ass exactly where it is. So just do it, buster." Corinne's heart thudded nervously while her fingers flexed, longing to sink into the long strands.

Mykh's eyebrows rose, he started to speak, then came to attention like a man who wasn't quite certain of the next step.

Corinne smiled in anticipation, a look that Svetlhana would have understood and approved of. *Playtime.*

She rose and strolled over to him, enjoying how his eyes followed the sway of her hips. She ran her fingers lightly down the braids, fascinated by how soft his hair was. Then she glided her fingers across the plaited strands, exploring how the various jewels and beads rippled. It was such a unique feeling that she did it again and again.

"By all the gods of war, what are you doing?" Mykh demanded.

"Having fun." Corinne slanted a teasing glance up at him. "Got a problem with that, big guy? Thinking about backing out?"

"Certainly not." His heart thudded under her hand.

She lifted a single braid with her finger and let it fall back to his chest. It settled into place with only the slightest whoosh. She lifted a handful of braids and brushed them over his skin. His small male nipple exhibited a very strong reaction, stiffening like a diamond in a jeweler's showcase.

Corinne purred happily and repeated the caress on the other nipple, with equally gratifying results. "Very nice indeed."

She threaded her fingers through the braids. They tugged lightly on the sensitive webbing between her fingers, a most intriguing sensation. She lifted a strand to her nose and inhaled the spicy, musky odor of him.

Corinne ran her hand up his shoulder from his nipple, savoring how his breath caught at the simple caress. But what did he look like from the other side? She'd never really studied his ass, which should be a magnificent sight.

She walked around him, trailing her hand over his arm to his shoulder blade, then stopped to stare at the view. Gorgeous. In fact, absolutely fabulous with that hard compact ass above two strong pillars of leg and below a cascade of fiery hair that any Paris model would have killed for. She kissed his back, nuzzling between the braids until she found bare skin. Hot and sweaty skin, too.

Corinne peeled off her robe, desperate to feel as much of him as she could, and tossed it aside. Then she rubbed herself against his back like a cat, letting her hip and arm and shoulder and head ride up and down his spine, curving around his buttocks on the way down and nestling her cheek between his shoulder blades at the summit.

"Yummy," she murmured and did it again. She thought he moaned when her hair rippled over his ass on the way up but, frankly, she wasn't paying much attention. She was far too busy enjoying the play of skin against skin in a very feline fashion.

She stopped finally and rested her head against his back, trying to recover some shred of self-control. Her breasts were tight and aching, while her cunt itched with the need to hold him again. She wrapped her arms around him so that her hands could smooth the inside of his thighs, while her breasts nuzzled his back.

"You're shaking," she observed softly. "Are you afraid of me? Or just sexually aroused?"

"Dammit, Corinne, why do you ask me such things?"

She kissed his back until he relaxed. "I'm an author so I'm always curious. To put it another way, was the Gray Sorceress so dreadful that she scared you away from all sorceresses?"

"Yes." His voice was scarcely any louder than the ripples in the pool. Corinne flinched guiltily as she realized how much pain she'd caused this man.

"But she doesn't matter now." He grabbed her hands and wrapped them around his cock. "This does."

Corinne jumped and involuntarily tightened her grip on him. He groaned and arched into her hold. "Yes, like that!" he growled and thrust again.

"Mykh!" Her hands curled to hold him, all the hot, hard length of him filling her hands with motion and power. His hips rocked back and forth between her belly and her hands, sending shockwaves through her body until she could barely stand. Her hips matched his rhythm, while her thighs clenched in eagerness.

He stopped suddenly and broke away from her. Corinne stared at him, dazed. Her eyes dropped and found his cock rising enormous and urgent. She licked her lips.

"By the gods, you are bewitching," he growled. "But I made a promise and will keep it." Suddenly he dropped onto the bed, stretching himself in invitation. "Take me fast and hard, woman, if you dare."

She shook her head, trying to recover herself.

"Dammit, Corinne," he roared. "Finish this!"

Corinne knelt astride his waist on unsteady legs and took a deep breath. He shuddered with every breath, making his abs press against her thighs. It built her need for him rather than helping her concentration.

Desperate, she seized his cock with one hand and hurled herself down on it, sheathing him in a single stroke. He flexed inside her and his hips rose up to meet her.

"Corinne," he gasped. His golden eyes flew wide open to watch her. "Corinne," he demanded again. "Dammit. Hurry."

"Yes." She lifted up and swooped down on him again, moaning as he filled her. That magnificent cock of his caressed her aching clit with every stroke, so she repeated the movement. His hips lifted as he pushed himself into her harder and harder. She rode him strongly, groaning when his cock thrust toward her heart. The pace of their lovemaking grew faster and more frantic as she drove them both onward.

Then climax burst through her, setting off fireworks behind her eyes while freight trains roared through her blood and bones. She keened her pleasure, only distantly conscious of his roars as he poured himself into her.

Afterwards she lay sprawled across him, enjoying the feel of all that delicious masculine strength and heat. Her head lay pillowed on his chest and her hair whispered with every breath he took. His big hand rubbed her back idly, making her eyelids almost too heavy to lift.

She was exhausted but she needed to say this while she had the courage.

"I'm sorry," she said finally.

"For what?"

She turned her head to look at him. Tears trickled down her cheeks and through her voice. "For having the ice serpent bite you. I shouldn't have done that and I'm so sorry it happened."

She managed to meet his eyes as he studied her. Finally he nodded and kissed her lightly on the mouth. "You are forgiven. Besides, you stopped her from killing me a hundred times."

"The Gray Sorceress? That was easy," she disclaimed.

"Easy? For you, perhaps, but no one else in Torhtremer."

She sniffled inelegantly as she tried to smile, then laid her head back down.

"Can you play me like a fish, as you did her?"

Corinne's head shot up. "Oh no! You have always been the most obstinate, impossible character in the world to write! You've always gone your own way, doing your own thing." She snorted at the memory of how often she'd cursed his uncooperative hide, while she was on deadline to finish a book.

"Good," he purred, sounding very well pleased. Then he asked more sharply, "Is there anyone else you can't twist?"

"The Dark Warrior," Corinne admitted, biting her lip. "I can see *what* he's doing most of the time. But I can't make him do anything and I've no idea *why* he does a lot of things."

"Damn. Ah well, the gods must play their little games so it's unlikely they'd let us rig the results." His next question caught her completely off-guard. "Why did you do it?"

She didn't pretend to misunderstand as she cringed. Writer's convenience was not good cause to emasculate a warrior. She gave him the truth with an effort. "I was afraid that you'd get some girl pregnant right away and marry her, before I could find your true love. So I bought time with the ice serpent." She finished her apology in a rush. "I didn't know then that it would be this bad."

"An honest reason," he rumbled.

He sounded pleased somehow, but Corinne could only find the energy for relief that he wasn't angry. Sleep claimed her before she could find something more to say.

FIVE

Mykh lay in the great bed, listening to Corinne sleep. Above him, the four silver pillars at the bed's corners met in a silver and gold canopy resembling an orchard, with blossoms, leaves, and fruit seeming almost real in dawn's first light. Almost as real as the sight of Corinne rising over him, her blue eyes blazing and head thrown back in ecstasy, while her sheath gloved him hot and close. The memory of her nectar pouring over him washed away the last traces of the Gray Sorceress's evil from his body, if not his mind.

Corinne slept as she did everything else, totally abandoned to the moment: one arm flung over his chest and her face buried against his ribs. Her silver hair tickled him with every breath he took, while her warm breath comforted his heart.

He shifted slightly to adjust a strand of hair teasing his nipple. She stirred, grumbled . . . and tightened her grip on him. He went quite still at the touch.

His little sorceress was possessive of him. Had always been, else why would she have sabotaged so many proposed alliances with foreign princesses? Or with the daughters of great nobles, whose fathers had promised armies to help him take the throne if he'd only marry their child? To say nothing of the concubines who'd developed unsightly rashes or twisted ankles at inopportune times, which kept them from his furs before they could intrigue him.

Possessive enough that she'd finally set the great ice serpent on him, rather than lose him to a female she couldn't control. He would have killed her for that once, done so slowly and with great relish. Now he found himself oddly warmed by the thought of how fiercely she'd fight for him, no matter what the cost.

She mumbled again, the sound felt more than heard. He kissed the top of her head and she wriggled. Almost time for her to wake up and start the second day of the Hunter's Watch.

Perhaps Khyber was correct and she could heal the harm she'd caused. Mykh had never heard of such a thing, either from the bards or the ancient scrolls he enjoyed in his rare private moments. But even if Khyber was wrong for the first time in a very long life, it wouldn't come amiss to teach her the other skills of the Dragonheart's Companion. They were highly enjoyable in the bedroom, whether or not they helped her master the Advent of the White Horses.

Mykh leaned up on one elbow and gently uncovered her face from its veil of silvery hair. He kissed her forehead lightly and nuzzled her cheeks, waking her slowly. His unruly mane, long since freed of its formal braids, fell around them like a curtain.

Corinne began to return his kiss before she was fully awake. He hummed approval of her willingness and tickled her ribs.

"Whazzat?" she mumbled as her eyes opened. An odd word but he understood perfectly.

"Good morning," he whispered into her ear, then licked her earlobe delicately.

"What are you up to now?" she inquired, sounding more intrigued than irritated.

"Playing," he answered and tickled her again.

She squirmed and giggled. "Just playing?"

"Fun playing," he clarified and chuckled when her fingers teased his ribs.

"Which means that you're going to wind up between my legs again," Corinne said dryly.

"Perchance."

Corinne snorted. "You're going to have to try harder than that, big boy, if you want me to believe that you're not interested in nookie." She jumped and laughed at another tickle.

"We should practice our lessons before tomorrow," Mykh announced a little breathlessly. Her slender fingers were frolicking with his balls, without once touching his rod directly.

"Lessons? I'm not interested in schoolwork," Corinne pronounced, a lofty effect spoiled by her gasp when he tweaked one of her plump nipples. "But then again," she sighed as his tongue teased her breast, "a little homework never hurt anyone."

"Hmmm," Mykh agreed. She sent the most amazing dances down his spine when she took his head close and played with his hair, giving a scalp massage like no other. He did his best to return the favor, kneading her breast lightly along the paths she favored. After taking the time to ensure that both nipples stood as firm and proud as fireberries, he sat up reluctantly.

Corinne opened first one eye and then the other. "I was never much good at homework," she remarked. "Perhaps we should go back to what you were just doing."

Mykh laughed at her request. "These lessons are very simple. You only have to breathe."

"I do that all the time," she protested. "What's to practice?"

"It is how we will absorb the land's energy tomorrow, by circling it through our bodies like clouds of incense through a temple. Or so the priests say." He stroked her thigh, enjoying the satiny skin above strong muscle.

Corinne cocked her head while she considered his words. Her hand glided idly up and down his arm, sending prickles of awareness through his skin. "It sounds like some of my *sifu*'s lessons for gathering and projecting *ch'i*."

"Aye, it's close to some of my arms training as well. But . . ."

"There's always a but," Corinne grumbled, sotto voce.

He raised an eyebrow at the interruption but finished. "We pass the energy back and forth between us."

"By breathing?" Corinne queried.

"And where we are one in body as well." His heart skipped a beat at how long he would be inside her.

"Ah, I knew there was some nookie involved!" Corinne laughed. She tucked her hand over his thigh, one slender finger not quite touching his balls. "So how do we start?"

"More playtime first, until we are one."

"Yummy," Corinne purred and slid her hand up his chest. Mykh laughed a little hoarsely and bent his head to hers again. Her delicate skin glowed under his touch, blushes showing where she'd caught fire from his passion. He encouraged her with mouth and fingers, chuckling when she arched off the bed and rumbling with pleasure at her sighs.

He played with her woman's portal, strumming the little bud and painting her lower lips with her nectar. One climax, then another swelled through her.

"I don't know about homework," Corinne groaned as he slipped three fingers inside to stretch her, "but I'm definitely fond of playtime."

Mykh mumbled agreement. He'd have agreed to almost anything then, while she rippled and pulsed around him. His rod's eagerness was an insistent voice but one to be ignored for the present.

He lay down on his side and lifted Corinne's leg over his hip, then guided his rod to her portal. A supple twist of his hips and he entered her.

"Damn, Mykh, that's inventive!" Corinne gasped. She wriggled slightly but her spine rested flat and comfortable on the bed.

"An ancient practice," he disclaimed, pleased nonetheless at her appreciation. He slid her other leg between his thighs, then rested his hand over her lower belly. His thumb delved and played with her bud lightly. He groaned softly when another climax rippled through her, his rod alive to her slightest pulse.

"Okay, I can get used to doing homework like this," Corinne announced a little breathlessly. "What now?"

"We must learn to breathe as one," Mykh answered raggedly, "then move as one."

"Of course," she agreed dubiously.

He kissed her hand and played with it until she giggled and relaxed her touch. Their hands glided and swooped as they learned to work together in this simple fashion.

"Breathe in when I breathe out," Mykh said softly, watching the sunlight gild their fingers.

Corinne promptly exhaled as he breathed out. She broke out laughing but didn't let go of his hand. Nor move away from where his rod flexed within her. "Sorry!" she gasped. "I'll do better next time." And she did.

When their chests rose and fell in unison, Mykh took the next step. "Now send the energy through your body. Down to your woman's portal and up to . . ."

He broke off as she rolled to face him while keeping her hips flat on the bed. His rod swelled at her womb's spiraling caress. "By the Horned Goddess, woman!" he growled, fighting to keep their breathing in rhythm. He had no words, only groans, when she returned to her prior position and her sheath screwed him in a different direction.

Her blue eyes danced wickedly. "You were saying?" she prompted demurely. "Perhaps the energy should come up to my head?"

"Exactly." Mykh took a more relaxed breath when her gaze turned inward. He reached inside himself to find his own meridians, then sent his *ch'i* down to his rod and back up to his head. He welcomed its warmth, especially against the chill at the base of his spine where his seed should have been forming.

"Lovely," Corinne murmured, wriggling closer to him and resting her hand on his above her bud. "Lovely way to do homework."

"Aye," Mykh murmured and began to rock against her, chuckling as different tempos caught her off-balance and groaning when she quickly matched him. By the gods, she caught his rhythm faster than any other woman ever had. Even the temple priestess who'd trained him hadn't been as smooth, and she'd known hundreds of partners.

Ecstasy built in his groin and through his rod with every breath, like a campfire on a winter's night. His balls tucked up hard against him, trying to get closer to the *ch'i*'s warmth. But just as if he was standing at that campsite, he felt no urgency, only a steady growth of intensity.

"Do you want to come first? Or should I?" Corinne asked, twisting from one side to the other gently.

"Whenever you wish," he murmured, sliding into that realm proclaimed by the priestesses where the woman's pleasure was the source of life.

"Then I'm coming now," she said emphatically. "Ah, Mykh!" Her sheath fluttered and caressed his rod as she climaxed. He permitted himself a small climax, releasing his muscles but not his seed. Practice of this sort was necessary, that he might control himself for as long as tomorrow's ceremonies would demand.

She raised her head slowly from where it had fallen back in rapture. One blue eye blinked, causing the other to open so both could start focusing. He flexed inside her, setting his continuing hardness against her swollen flesh.

"Hot damn," she moaned as sweet pulses traveled through her. He smiled broadly, feeling her pleasure warm him to the bone. Then he set himself to see how many times he could trigger her ecstasy before a finger's breadth of his cock left her feminine caverns. He allowed more of the little raptures to travel his body. But he denied himself full release, that he might remain hard and capable of drawing shudders of delight from her.

At last she groaned against his shoulder. "Mykh, please . . . Oh God, if you don't stop . . ."

He circled his hips and her head swayed as she climaxed again.

"Mykh." Her voice was a bare thread. "If this is about my pleasure, then I want you now."

He tilted his head back until he could see her face. She blinked until she could meet his gaze. She was dazed and breathless but clearly determined.

"Mykh, next time . . . Damn, I can't believe there's a man that I can expect another time like this with." She stopped, blushing. He kissed her forehead, smiling.

She tried again. "Next time I climax, I damn well insist that you climax, too. Full climax, full ejaculation, full . . . Oh hell, just fill me with your cock and your seed!"

Mykh threw back his head and laughed in triumph.

She chuckled but turned her attention to his nipples, now achingly sensitive from their bedsport. "You're not getting away that easily, big guy," she muttered and started suckling.

He gasped in surprise but yielded to the demanding rhythm Corinne set. His finger sought her woman's jewel as his cock swelled further than he'd thought possible. Her head fell back in rapture and he groaned as he followed her into ecstasy. Wave after wave shook him, while his balls pumped seed as if he was a youngling again.

Mykh's limbs straggled across the bed afterwards like rice fields after a thunderstorm. He rubbed his belly slowly, instinctively storing the *ch'i* they'd generated as his breathing and pulse slowly returned to normal. He'd matched rhythms with other women before, including a handful of priestesses. None had affected him like his little sorceress.

A sorceress. Damn.

Corinne sat patiently as the maids fussed one more time over her hair. They were going to a lot of trouble, considering that she was wearing it down. And a good haircut can bounce back from almost anything, including travel between worlds and two days and nights with a sex maniac.

Celeste had always called Jarred a sex maniac. Could she be enjoying her time with him? Perhaps . . . but what if she wasn't?

Corinne reviewed again what she knew of high magic. Most of it came from writing the long prologue to *The Raven and the Rose*, about the last white sorcerers. But their magic didn't tell her how to travel between worlds, as Celeste's rescue would demand.

"Your Excellency," one of the girls pleaded. "Please don't frown. It is very bad luck if you're unhappy today."

"Sorry. I was just thinking, not offended." Corinne plastered on the patient but still interested expression that her ex-mother-in-law wore during long church services and went back to considering how to rescue Celeste. But her thoughts kept straying to Mykh and how he growled her name when he was excited.

The maids finally finished arranging her hair and clothing to their satisfaction and brought a long mirror for her to inspect the results. She wore a long high-waisted dress, composed of layers and layers of fragile white silk bordered with silver ribbons. The layers increased in length until they touched the floor, beginning with one reaching just below her hips. The sleeves were long but slashed many times from shoulder to wrist, every edge trimmed with silver ribbon. The neckline, as could be expected during a fertility festival, was so low that it was a miracle her breasts didn't fall out. Chiffon bordered with silver covered her hair and a short train, also edged in silver, spilled behind her feet. The combination of white silk with silver ribbons reminded her of a white tiger's stripes.

All of it was embroidered with tiny diamonds, while more jewels dangled from her ears and danced around her throat. Silver slippers, also embroidered with diamonds, gloved her feet.

She wore a wreath of red and white roses to indicate that she wished a child by the man she would dine with. Mykh's mother had also worn roses when he was conceived, yellow in her case.

Corinne Carson was wearing a white dress to a formal banquet. If she was very lucky—unlike any other time she'd worn white—they'd never heard of spaghetti sauce and she wouldn't stain the dress before the night was out.

"Beautiful. Thank you for dressing me so well," she complimented them, praying silently that Celeste was at least warm and dry. The maids twittered and preened as they accepted her praise.

They also continued to fuss worse than any fancy stylist she'd ever met.

A loud knock sounded before she lost her temper at them. Two maids rushed to answer it and Yevgheniy entered. His all-encompassing sergeant's eye measured her. Corinne was surprisingly relieved when he nodded and relaxed.

"It is time to leave for dinner, Your Excellency," he announced.

"Very well." She swallowed hard and followed him out the door. Ten minutes later, she stood outside the magnificent set of doors that marked the banquet hall, waiting yet again.

But Mykh arrived very quickly, looking splendid in gold brocade that shimmered with every movement and a rose crown. His great sword hung at his back, the one thing he always kept close to hand. He smiled at Corinne and kissed her hand, making her blush.

Mazur paced at Mykh's side, ears pricked and tail swishing. He wore a ruby and gold collar with a matching leash that Mykh held. As soon as Mykh looked away from him, Mazur immediately sat down, hooked his front foot in the collar, and tried to lift it over his head.

The ram's horn rang out, trumpets blared, the doors swung open, and Mykh yanked Mazur to his feet with the ease of long experience. They entered the banquet hall to a roar of applause, Mazur as demure now as a child in a church choir.

The hall faced south, opening on to a wide terrace and beyond that to the great courtyard. Long tables ringed the banquet hall with men and women closely packed along them. A wide red carpet led from the doors to the dais across the great central space. The maids had chattered endlessly about the entertainers that would perform here during the banquet.

The terrace and courtyard were covered with white-clad tables, all filled with couples wearing rose crowns. The streets beyond were packed with watchers, like a Times Square crowd waiting for the ball to drop on New Year's Eve.

Mykh and Corinne proceeded down the red carpet between the tables, nodding graciously as they went while his hand gently rubbed the small of her back. It felt good enough that she began to consider ways to sneak off with him.

She recognized many of the concubines and grinned when she saw Vholodhya seated next to Wen-Chuan. Her jaw dropped when she saw the priest next to Mhari. She'd never considered a religious man for the rollicking girl, although few orders in Torhtremer were celibate. And this fellow had been one of Mykh's mercenaries . . .

The guests clapped wildly, the rhythm quickly settling into the steady pulsing beat of winning fans at a World Cup match. The women clapped, too, Juli's arm frequently brushing Alekhsiy's.

Mykh yanked her attention back when his hand slid low enough to fondle her ass. She jumped and glared at him. He tilted his head infinitesimally and she realized that they were now standing at their seats, waiting for the High Priestess to speak. Corinne shrugged slightly, apologetically, then painted a suitably devout expression on her face.

When the High Priestess finished invoking the Horned Goddess's blessings, Mykh lifted Corinne's hand to his lips and kissed it. Her breath stopped and she gazed at him foolishly. She was still a little dazed when she settled into her seat.

Perhaps he could stop thinking of her as a sorceress.

Five minutes later, Corinne was looking at combination of milk, eggs, and rabbit on her plate, with a side dish of rice and chopped dried apricots—the same foods that she'd eaten in the Tiger's Den. A page offered her a bowl of gorgeous fresh apricots;

she accepted one and bit into it, careful not to get the juice on her dress. Another page hovered with a beaker, ready to instantly refill her goblet of herbal tea. She strongly suspected this tea was brewed from more fertility enhancers.

Beside her, Mykh was happily eating red meat again with a juniper berry sauce and his beloved oatcakes. His tea was probably also some sort of male fertility enhancer. An entire cookbook could be written about the fertility boosters being consumed at this banquet. You had to admit that when Torhtremers chefs decided something was important, they went all out to get every last detail right.

Musicians filled the central space, performing various folk tunes. Three tenors sang of marriage's delights, alternating with three sopranos who celebrated the joys of a man's loving. They were loud enough that the diners could focus on eating, rather than making polite conversation.

Corinne had just taken her first bite of rice pudding, which used a different combination of spices than she'd encountered before, when a loud boom broke through the music. A large black smoke cloud appeared in the center of the hall, blocking her sight of the musicians and the terrace. A tenor and the balalaika player crawled away from the smoke but froze in mid-step.

Mykh came quickly to his feet, drawing his great sword, Dragon's Breath, in the same instant. Corinne stood up more slowly. No one else moved in the hall and the only sounds came from outside. Even Mazur's tail lay still.

"The Dark Warrior," Mykh hissed then vaulted the table, Dragon's Breath at the ready. "Show yourself, coward." He crouched at the dais' edge, ready to respond to an attack from any direction.

A low chuckle from within the smoke answered him, cold as a

northern blizzard. "Remember me, Dragonheart? We met once before in a banquet hall. It was hosted by your mistress, the Gray Sorceress."

Oh shit. How would Mykh respond to those memories?

His face was white and tense but his concentration never wavered. "You left rather abruptly on that occasion, as I recall, after a reminder of other concerns. I'm certain you'll leave here, too, after you're prompted." Mykh even managed a fairly credible sneer. Its effect was somewhat lessened by the tic in his cheek.

"Oh, I'll leave here—with the sorceress. She needs some education, you see, before she can serve me as the Gray Sorceress did so well." The smoke shimmered then started to move sluggishly toward the dais.

"She is not yours to claim," Mykh asserted boldly. Suddenly he lifted Dragon's Breath over his shoulder like a javelin and hurled it at the smoke. The noisome pillar jerked to one side, avoiding the sword, then returned to its previous path.

"Tsk, tsk," the Dark Warrior chided. "So childish of you to use a physical weapon on something that does not exist as flesh and blood."

Mykh held up his hand, eyes never leaving the smoke. Dragon's Breath circled the hall swiftly then settled neatly into his grasp. What could he try next?

Corinne looked around for help. Ghryghoriy stood motionless at the corner of the performance area, sweat running down his face as he tried to move. The other guards were similarly immobile, as were the wizards. She wished that enormous halberd was here, instead of the throne room, so that she could summon the Imperial Tigress.

She had to do something. Magic might help, if she could pull it off. Shaking, she tried one of the white sorcerers' spells.

"By the five elements, show me all guests in this hall," Corinne called. *Ch'i* crept into her meridians at the words. The smoke stirred, its shape mutating from a slender column into a lumpy block, before coalescing back into the column. But it continued to jerk and shudder, as if fighting off a wind.

She'd worked a spell that had an effect. She gulped. What would happen if she used a stronger spell? Would acting as a sorceress make her vulnerable to the Dark Warrior, so that he could subvert her?

Mykh half-turned to face her. "Don't do this, Corinne," he warned. "This danger is for me to face."

"That would risk your life." She moved to one side of the table so she'd have a clear path at the smoke. Serious spellcasting was aided by hand gestures.

"By all the gods, Corinne, don't prove yourself a sorceress."

She shivered at the deadly warning in his voice then set her chin stubbornly. "I have to try, Mykh."

Corinne took a deep breath and used the strongest invocation she could think of, one that had worked for white sorcerers but not the wizards who served them.

"By red fire, green wood, white metal, black water, and yellow earth, I command all guests in this hall to show themselves." The smoke spun, its edges fraying.

Corinne repeated the invocation twice more, her hands pushing out as if removing a veil. The smoke hissed and snarled, becoming more and more transparent, as she chanted. Her last syllable still hung in the air as the smoke snapped angrily, then funneled into one of the tenors.

The tenor sat up stiffly, his eyes changed from merry brown to cold black as the Dark Warrior possessed his body. They fixed on Corinne with the cold concentration of a murderer.

"Ah, the voice of power!" the Dark Warrior called, his voice rough with the effort he was making to appear in the palace's banquet hall. "I greet you, sorceress, as you come into your own. Join me and we can rule the world."

Corinne trembled. She'd successfully worked a spell. Now the Dark Warrior had become flesh and blood and could be dealt with as such. But Mykh's eyes avoided her as if she really was spawned in hell.

Ice sliced Mykh's veins at the Dark Warrior's greeting. Two voices, both carrying magic. The last time he'd heard a man and a woman chant had been in the Gray Sorceress's chambers, where she had competed with the Dark Warrior to see who could make more men tear themselves apart.

Mykh had rolled in the blood and worse that covered the floors, his cock stiff from the Gray Sorceress's commands, while she rode him and laughed, then laughed again with the Dark Warrior before ensorcelling another slave to destroy himself. Mykh had thought he'd never be clean again.

Now everything came flashing back as if he stood in that thrice-dammed chamber again. He staggered as the smells of blood and death leaped into him and his skin crawled as if the foul waste covered it again. He barely retained enough control to remember that he needed to fight the Dark Warrior here and now.

Mykh shook his head to clear it. He must contest his enemy. But the sorceress present spoke first, every syllable pounding spikes of old anguish into his skull. He began to chant Khyber's summons silently, forming the phrases clumsily.

"Begone! By red fire, green wood, white metal, black water, and yellow earth, I command you to leave!" Corinne demanded.

The tenor's ponderous frame swayed like a tree in a hurricane then steadied. The voice that emerged from his throat had all the warmth of a glacier grinding rock into dust. "No," it said hoarsely, then more strongly, "No. You may only force what is physically present in this hall, not my spirit, which controls this man. I will do what I came for."

The tenor began to stand, propping itself on the balalaika player for balance. Mykh smiled tightly, recognizing a threat that he could remove. He lifted Dragon's Breath over his shoulder once again then threw it. The long golden sword sliced through the tenor, who instantly became a handful of ash. Then it fell to the floor and landed against one of the sopranos.

Mykh extended his hand toward the sword, his palm open in invitation, while his golden eyes never left the small ash heap. Dragon's Breath lifted into the air and flew back to him as Ghryghoriy stumbled toward the musicians.

"No!" Mykh shouted. "Stay back, Ghryghoriy. It's a trap." He caught Dragon's Breath just as the balalaika player lurched upward, his slender body quickly mastered by the Dark Warrior. Ghryghoriy froze although Corinne could see his fingers twitching.

The musician laughed in the same voice that had possessed the tenor. "You cannot stop me so easily, Dragonheart. You dare not take the time to summon Khyber lest I destroy someone else in the meantime." He started walking toward the dais in a zigzag path, always touching one of the diners. Mykh could see their horrified eyes as his hand fell on each one in turn.

"How many of your guests will you destroy before you learn that you cannot kill me?" The Dark Warrior laughed again, making Mykh remember how the Gray Sorceress's cackles had blended with his, and reached for Ghryghoriy. "Now I will take your Companion and you will die childless. Never again will a Dragonheart stop me."

Mykh swung Dragon's Breath and beheaded the Dark Warrior's puppet, just as he brushed Ghryghoriy. Ashes floated to the floor as Ghryghoriy's expression changed from desperate rigidity to evil gloating.

"Nooo," he screamed, starting in his own voice but finishing in the Dark Warrior's. Mykh could see Amber just beyond him, tears trickling down her face.

"Oh yes," the Dark Warrior mocked. "Now, Dragonheart, what will you do? Will you kill your dearest friend? Or shall I take the sorceress and leave him unharmed?"

Mykh's mouth was set so hard that his lips were nearly bloodless. He settled into a fighting stance, ready to strike a blow at Ghryghoriy. He returned to summoning Khyber, the syllables running through his mind like a chain of signal fires.

"By Mars's . . ." Corinne began then stopped to clear her throat.

"I can win this battle, Corinne," Mykh hissed. He only needed to gain some time, no matter how high the cost.

"I can't let you kill Ghryghoriy," she answered, a slight tremor running through her voice. She filled her lungs with the agonizing precision of someone ready to leap off a precipice.

"By Mars' fire, Jupiter's wood, Saturn's earth, Venus's metal, and Mercury's water," Corinne chanted, her voice effortlessly filling the room with a sorceress's mastery. "I command you to leave that man's body. Now!"

An unearthly shriek came from Ghryghoriy's throat. Mykh froze, recognizing a puissance that he couldn't hope to defeat.

Corinne repeated the spell twice more until black smoke poured from every inch of Ghryghoriy. It hung in a cloud above him, then formed into the shape of a short, barrel-chested man facing Corinne.

"Damn you!" the Dark Warrior screamed. He moved toward her, but Mykh took a quick step to block him. At least he was fast enough to counter the enemy.

The man shook with rage but steadied before speaking again.

"You have grown into your powers faster than I expected, foreigner," the Dark Warrior sneered. Old memories welled up in Mykh, of hearing that evil voice discuss the death of everything Mykh loved. "I will not underestimate you the next time."

He vanished in a clap of thunder, leaving only the stench of dank rot behind.

Ghryghoriy staggered before collapsing to the floor. Amber screamed and rushed to him. Pandemonium swept the banquet hall as some screamed, some fainted, some bolted out, and others began to talk far too loudly and quickly.

Mykh stared at Corinne across the tumult, reliving his helplessness before the Gray Sorceress's evil. He identified her with one word. "Sorceress."

"Dammit, Mykh, don't you realize what could have happened . . ." She flinched at the look in his eyes.

He had to remove her now before he took Dragon's Breath to her, as he'd destroyed the Gray Sorceress.

"Leave me now while I remember that you can do good, before I consider the harm you have done before and may do again in the future. Begone before I wrap Izmir's Curse around your wrists!"

"You ungrateful brute!"

Mykh cursed as he reached for Corinne's wrists. Didn't she realize how desperate he was? That this was the only way to protect her from himself?

Mazur sprang between them, his teeth bared and tail lashing.

Corinne lunged for Mazur's collar, but the leopard snarled deep in his throat and showed his fangs. Mykh took a step closer and Mazur crouched to spring at him.

Even that didn't sway Mykh's decision to send her away. He'd kill as often as needed to ensure her safety and Torhtremer's.

But the gods of war were kind to him in this much, when they removed that need. Mykh set Dragon's Breath's point down and rested his hands on the pommel as he watched his wife turn and run away from him. Mazur growled again at Mykh, then loped after her.

And if they were more merciful, they'd send him death before he saw that look on her face again.

It was the last watch before dawn when Mykh entered the throne room, still wearing his formal attire. He settled on the Dragon Throne with a bone-deep sigh, after removing his sword, then leaned back against the warm dragon scales. He could see reflections of Khyber's golden eyes staring straight ahead in the marble columns.

"Are you done playing your mortal games yet?" Khyber inquired acidly.

"Yes, we've taken all the necessary steps." Mykh wondered why he'd come here when he knew Khyber would lecture him. He rubbed his aching head and wished that he'd eaten since that thrice-damned banquet. "We've signaled the army and navy, we've issued warnings to the diplomats, we . . ."

"Was it also necessary to terrorize and dismiss the only person who can help you?"

"She's a sorceress! Dammit, you know they can never be trusted," Mykh defended himself, unwilling to admit being trapped in the old nightmare. He'd never told anyone all that had happened in the Gray Sorceress's realm, not even Khyber.

"Would you care to describe what would have happened if she hadn't acted? You can begin by reckoning the number most likely to die. A hundred? Or every guest in the hall, perhaps five hundred?"

"Or more, if he'd gotten into the people outside," Mykh agreed quietly.

There was a short silence.

"Well, you've learned that much at least," Khyber said grudgingly. "What do you want from me?"

"How do I defeat him? It took every man and woman in the Seven Kingdoms capable of bearing arms to destroy his army once. Yet he lives on."

Khyber stretched then coiled his long neck so he could look at Mykh easily, with his chin resting on the floor. Mykh adjusted his posture for the long lecture to come.

"What do you know of him?"

"He is the Terrapinheart. Ever since he stole immortality's secret from the last white sorcerers, he has ruled the North like a ravaging beast."

"Continue."

"What else is there to tell? The ice storms are bad and grow worse with every year. Winter lasts longer, while summer is cooler and shorter than the old scrolls say. All the seasons are out of balance with each other."

Khyber considered one very long claw. "Do you see any patterns there?"

Mykh flogged his tired brain. "Balance?" he suggested. "The Terrapinheart has upset the harmony between the four directions?"

"Precisely. An excellent description of the current situation."

Khyber studied another claw. "Knowing that, how would you suggest achieving equilibrium again?"

"If I, as Dragonheart, attack him personally . . ."

"Do you really believe that Dragonheart fighting alone against Terrapinheart can reset the scales?"

"No," Mykh admitted.

"Correct. Try again." Khyber polished his claws on his scales, glowing eyes resting on Mykh.

"Can you kill him?"

"Much as I would like to, no. Every celestial beast is forbidden to kill one another or their catalyst. Otherwise the Imperial Terrapin would have attacked me long before now."

Mykh grunted unhappily but didn't argue.

"You may remember from Tajzyk's Gorge that he can summon Azherbhai, as you can bring me into existence when you're away from this throne. Difficult and time-consuming for you because you're not a sorcerer. Easy for him, because he is a sorcerer."

"You're saying that I have to kill the Dark Warrior, while holding off the Imperial Terrapin."

"Impossible. One catalyst against the other strike an equal balance, even with their celestial beasts present. But two facing one makes change possible."

"Tigerheart or Phoenixheart must be my ally then."

"Unless you mean to wait until your true-born son, another Dragonheart, stands beside you."

"There is no time for that. The Dark Warrior will attack again within days or hours." Mykh fell silent, considering his options. Inviting the Phoenixheart meant risking that the great southern deserts would increase to the north, toward or perhaps into Torhtremer. The other choice was the Tigerheart, that rarest catalyst of all.

"Corinne is the Tigerheart," he said slowly. "The lights shine for her and the Tiger Throne's eyes glow."

"Correct analysis. Yes, she is the one who can help you defeat the Dark Warrior."

"She's a sorceress!"

"You keep bleating that as if she carried Zemlayan fire ants in her robes," Khyber complained. "Are you saying that you'd prefer to see the Imperial Terrapin seize the Seven Kingdoms, rather than charm a woman?"

"No, of course not," Mykh snapped back.

"Then will you act the High King and do your duty?" the dragon inquired.

"I have to, mustn't I?" Mykh snarled. He stared into the shadows, his heart bleak.

Corinne crept into the throne room just before dawn, when the great chamber was at its darkest and shadows lurked behind every column and in every corner. Her long silver robe with its charcoal gray embroidery made her look and feel like a ghost. As if sensing her loneliness, the silver shells held mere traces of light.

Mazur glided silently beside her, his ears pricked for the least sound.

She sank down on the Tiger Throne with a sigh, tucking her feet up under her and wrapping her arms around her knees. The throne quickly warmed and softened under her, reminding her of sleeping next to her neighbor's Maine coon cat as a child. Mazur settled on the floor next to her in a sphinx's posture, ready to defend her.

Svetlhana? Corinne whispered.

Da, little sister, I am here. Svetlhana's voice was very gentle. *Men are selfish pigs sometimes but we must forgive them.*

It'd be more fun to kill him, Corinne tried for some humor. *In some gory fashion, like a bad horror movie.*

Boiling in oil might teach him a lesson, Svetlhana agreed.

Silence stretched between them before Svetlhana spoke again. *What will you do now?*

What I must. I will be his Companion and do my best to heal him.

You are very generous.

I love Torhtremer. I have spent ten years dreaming of it and seven years writing of its greatest hours. I can't let anything happen to my friends now, not when I can help them.

Do not underestimate tomorrow's obstacles, Svetlhana warned. *The Advent of the White Horses will be very difficult, even if you two were at ease with each other.*

I figure I must focus solely on being the best Companion possible and not think of anything else. I'll have to stop worrying about Celeste. She had to let her sister go, trusting that she'd survive somehow. Any distraction tomorrow would ruin her chances of pulling this off.

And all I ever wanted was to make a good marriage, she mused. *Now here I am, married to a king no less. But I'd rather be married to a mechanic who loved me.*

Svetlhana was wisely silent, although the throne warmed against Corinne's cheek in a sympathetic gesture.

Her throat was tight but she'd long since run out of tears. She had to succeed in healing Mykh. Maybe then he'd find somebody else to give him a son and she could go explore the rest of Torhtremer. She didn't think she could stand to be pregnant, knowing that he hated her.

She turned away from her personal agony to Svetlhana's future. *Maybe when this is over, we can find some mint fields. I'll summon you and you can play there.*

And Khyber, too, Svetlhana agreed. *The big lizard can be so silly when he rolls around like a cub. It is vast fun to see him like that and very different from flying with him, when he is so thrilling.* She lingered over the last word until it sounded like a description of untold delights. *What a male he is,* she purred in a tone that confirmed the carnal direction of her thoughts.

Corinne sat bolt upright, Celeste's plight totally forgotten in her surprise. Her author's instincts had never taken her in this romantic direction before. *Is Khyber your mate?* she demanded.

But of course he is, little sister. Svetlhana sounded surprised. *Didn't you know? The green dragon is the only true mate for the white tiger. And if we are ever summoned at the same time,* her voice lowered suggestively, *then we are free to live in Torhtremer. Unconfined to these thrones or the weapons that can call us. We can play in the sunshine, we can fly.* Her voice deepened. *We can love. Oh, such loving!*

Forever? Corinne squeaked, her mind boggling at the thought of Khyber and Svetlhana making love.

For as long as Dragonheart and Tigerheart live, we can love one another in the flesh.

Both fell silent, considering that image.

I wish, Corinne murmured, *I wish that Mykh and I could love each other that much.*

SIX

Corinne tapped Mazur's nose with the condor feather and laughed when he spluttered. He sneezed and batted at the long feather, but she still tickled his cheek with it. His head twisted away from it as his paw tried to catch it. He hopped when she bounced it against his chest and finally dived playfully after the torment as she dragged it along the path before him. They laughed together when the feather escaped his pounce in the early morning light.

Mazur mock growled and attacked again. Corinne knew that he'd play with the feather like a kitten for as long as she was interested, especially since her status as Tigerheart somehow made her fast enough to keep up with him. He'd played with a red ball while she ate her breakfast, his antics distracting her from another round of rice pudding and tea. At least the tea had been a lovely iced, sweetened version that tasted better than anything she'd ever found in a Georgia diner.

Mazur was such a good friend, never speaking of why she was

so quiet. The perfect companion, he'd play if she wanted amusement or snuggle next to her when she wanted company. It wasn't his fault that she longed for a tall, red-haired warrior with a rotten temper.

The maids were just as protective, treating her as if she were made of glass. They'd pampered her with a relaxing bath and massage the night before without once hinting, by so much as a stray glance, how odd it was that the Companion slept without the High King. In fact, she'd overheard some of them grumbling about what selfish wretches men were. Now the maids assembled inside, allowing her privacy in the few remaining moments before the day's first ceremonies.

Eyes half-shut, Mazur sat erect on the path, pretending he didn't notice the feather tickling his paw, although one eye was looking stealthily down. Suddenly his ears pricked and his eyes opened. He stared straight ahead then hissed and sprang to his feet.

"Mazur?" Corinne questioned. "What is it?" The leopard ran past her, his tail bottling in indignation. She spun around to see what had disturbed him.

Mykh stood under the portico at the top of the steps leading down into the great rose garden, looking as he had when she first saw him. He was dressed in the simple black leathers of a mercenary captain—long black vest laced neatly down the front, black trousers, high black boots, wide cuffs at his wrists. His beautiful hair hung loose, tamed only by a small braid at each temple. He carried no visible weapon, not even his sword, Dragon's Breath. He looked like a man and not a High King to be feared.

He stepped away from the column when he saw her looking at him. "Corinne," he said quietly.

Suddenly a black shadow flew up the steps and nipped the man's ankle. "You thrice-damned furball!" Mykh cursed, trying to jerk his leg free. His hasty movement combined with Mazur's momentum to send him stumbling backwards. Corinne ran forwards, shouting at Mazur to stop.

A huge splash erupted from the pool, sending water flying upwards and out between the columns. Corinne dodged the spray and leaped up the stairs, still calling to Mazur. The sight that greeted her eyes at the top stopped her in her tracks.

Mykh stood chest-deep in the pool with water running off him. He ran a hand over his face, sweeping his sodden mane clear and sending scarlet rose petals down his back. Mazur paced beside the steps leading into the pool, closely watching Mykh's movements and Corinne's reactions.

Corinne giggled. Mykh glared at her. "Oh Mykh, if you could only see yourself," she gulped then chuckled. Her maids arrived in a twittering flock and watched from the doorway, hands hiding their mouths and eyes bright with surprise.

"Damn furball will be a rug before sunset," Mykh grumbled and started to walk toward the edge, his black leather clothing billowing in the water. Corinne chuckled again at how far removed he was from the all-powerful High King. Her amusement built until she was laughing helplessly but quietly as she came to help him out.

Mykh easily lifted himself out of the pool then hesitated. He dropped to his knees and bowed to Corinne, until his forehead touched the paving.

Corinne froze, her laughter forgotten. The little maids were silent. Even Mazur stopped his pacing to watch.

"I have come to beg your forgiveness, wife," Mykh spoke softly in a rough tone that reeked of truth. "You battled as mightily as any warrior out of legend. Yet I permitted my shame, that I could not defend my people, to overcome me and dismissed you. Pray accept my honest contrition and let us begin again."

Corinne's heartbeat hammered in her ears. Ten years of studying Mykh had shown him to be arrogant and clever and proud, never as one to apologize. She remembered how he had looked in the banquet hall, angry and determined. A total contrast to his playfulness when he'd taught her to breathe with him. Which man was he now? Could she trust him again? She tried to think of something to say.

Mazur sat down and started to groom himself, ears pricked.

Mykh spoke again when she remained silent, his voice still harsh. "I acknowledge that I have proven myself to be unworthy of you. If you do not wish to have anything further to do with me, then I will accept your wishes in this. But I beseech you to consider the welfare of Torhtremer, especially those who will die in ice storms or starve from lost crops if the Dark Warrior wins. I implore you to labor with me that they and their children might have a future full of peace and hope."

"Ah . . ." She cleared her throat and tried again. She couldn't trust him with her heart, as she once might have, but she could work with him to save Torhtremer. Wistfully, she wished that he'd spoken of something more personal than a kingdom. But it was probably asking for the moon, to think that he could fall in love with a sorceress. "In the name of Torhtremer, I accept your apology. And I'll do whatever I can to save your people."

Mykh straightened up, his amber eyes somber as he studied her. Something bleak swept over his face before he schooled his expression. "Thank you for your gracious pardon, my lady. I vow that I will do my utmost to be worthy of your clemency."

"Yeah, okay, fine," Corinne agreed, nervous of his formality. What was he really thinking behind all that polite contrition? "Aren't we supposed to attend some sort of ceremony to kick off the third day?"

"Aye, the High Priestess will lead morning prayers." To her relief, Mykh dropped much of his formality as he rose to his feet. "We should depart now if we are to attend."

"Don't we have to?"

"No, it's understood that the Dragonheart and his Companion might prefer to say their devotions in private." Corinne blushed scarlet and Mykh went on quickly. "But all others who celebrate the Goddess's Dance gather for prayers at the last high tide before the Advent of the White Horses."

"If we're going out in public, you need some dry clothes," Corinne observed. A thought stirred about testing his reaction to her magic. There was one spell that the white sorcerers had used frequently. It should be easier than those she'd used in the banquet hall.

"Aye, I'll send for some."

"Is there time?" Corinne walked closer to him, raising an eyebrow.

He frowned at her. "Perhaps not. What are you considering?"

"How far can I trust you?" Corinne demanded. "I can dry your clothes but will you run?"

"I will not flee," he vowed and stiffened his shoulders like a man preparing for battle.

"I'll use high magic, not low," she warned him.

He nodded curtly and waited.

Corinne eyed him warily then lifted her hands. A few quiet phrases and Mykh stood as dry and polished as when he'd entered the Tiger's Den. His mouth twisted as he looked himself over. He shook himself out like a dog after a dust storm.

"Ready?" he asked and offered his arm.

"Sure," Corinne agreed and took it. He glanced at her, daring her to mention any shivers on his part, and took her outside. The

maids followed close behind, keeping their whispers to a minimum. Mazur ambled as far as the portico, yawned, and curled up
to nap.

The morning prayers were recited at a watchtower rising above
the inner harbor, nestled underneath the citadel. Waves lapped at
the great walls, showing no signs of the piers underneath. The main
harbor lay to the west, free of shipping with its bordering ware-
houses now marked by white and green banners and pavilions.
Hundreds, perhaps thousands, of people watched from every available space. Corinne could see no sign of piers there, either.

A small island rose in the center of the main channel, a wide terrace below its crest blazing with reflected light from the sun.

The parapet was covered with soldiers, servants, and their families, many of them leaning out to look at the water. They beamed
as Mykh and Corinne approached and bowed happily, pleasing
Corinne that she and Mykh had publicly reconciled.

The High Priestess also smiled and raised her hand in blessing
when the royal couple reached the balcony at the watchtower's
top. "Make haste," she hissed. "It is almost time."

"Yes, Holy One," Mykh answered and steered Corinne into position by the high priestess, a location blessed by a spectacular view
of the water. A ram's horn blew as soon as they stood still. Another
answered from the main harbor, then three more blew one by one,
each more distant. The watchers bowed and waited.

"Mother Goddess who we recognize by the symbolic moon, the
horns that wax and wane as thou dost change thy aspect over time,
we . . ." the High Priestess prayed, her hands lifted up to invoke
the gods.

As Mykh had promised, the prayers were brief but heartfelt,
basically asking the gods to sanctify the day and the worshipers
who would be celebrating the Goddess's Dance with their bodies,

echoing the Earth's dance of praise. The High Priestess tossed flowers into the water afterwards, a gesture that Mykh and Corinne copied. In fact, all the watchers threw blossoms into the harbor, so many that the water close to shore looked like a living carpet.

The High Prestess blessed Mykh and Corinne afterwards in a simple invocation of the five elements. "Now go," she urged them, making shooing motions, "the Companion must be prepared. Go, go!"

Corinne blushed at the High Priestess's earthy enthusiasm and glanced up at Mykh. He smiled at her, caught her hand, and strode away from the crowd.

"Ready for your bath?" he asked, looking down at her.

Corinne nodded. "Yes, of course." Duty. He was discussing duty again, the tasks that would prepare her for that long boat trip around the harbor and whatever happened on board. She could handle that, even as her hand learned every nuance of his fingers wrapped around it.

"Do you wish to use the small bath tub or the large pool?"

Corinne shrugged. "The small one, I guess. It's quieter." Why was he asking? Maybe he planned to give the maids some instructions before he disappeared again.

Mykh gone. She shivered at the hollow sound of those words then steeled her heart. She'd better get used to his absence as soon as possible, since that was what the future held.

She pulled the rose coronet off her head as soon as they entered the Tiger's Den and shook her hair free. "Thanks, Mykh, for escorting me," she said without looking at him. "See you later at the boat."

"I am serving the bath to you, my lady."

She stopped dead in her tracks. "Excuse me?"

"I am the one responsible for bathing you."

"What the hell are you talking about?"

"I will also anoint you with sacred oils so that *ch'i* may more readily leap between us. Then I will dress you in the Maiden's robes before I escort you to the royal galley."

"You've got to be kidding. High Kings don't do the bath-slave thing, okay? They snap their fingers and flunkies come running." Corinne protested his words as much as the rapid pulse that they caused.

Mykh shook his head slowly, his eyes serious and possibly a bit nervous. "The Dragonheart and his Companion are to be together at all times on this day. It ensures that their dance is the culmination of their trust and eagerness for the other, without which no child can be conceived during the Goddess's Dance."

"You're honestly going to give me a bath?" She wished again that she'd set just one scene during the Goddess's Dance in Bhaikhal, so that she'd know what the heck was going to happen next. Her knowledge of Torhtremer was apparently limited to what she'd picked up during her writing and what she could persuade people to tell her in the here and now. But they kept assuming that she knew as much as they did, while instead she faced big gaps. And a lot of butterflies in her stomach.

"Aye." Now that single syllable sounded a lot more like the warrior she knew: curt, emphatic, decisive.

"Okay then, you're the man. Just let me get into the water before you come in."

"If that will make you more comfortable." She shivered at the sensual promise in his voice and walked quickly into the bath chamber. The small bath tub could only be called that in comparison to the great pool in the main quarters: it would have swallowed Celeste's hot tub with room to spare. It was nestled in a corner of the Tiger's Den, ringed by windows on three sides and a fireplace on the fourth. The tub had felt cozy before, but now the waters seemed to bubble in anticipation of Mykh's arrival.

Corinne stripped rapidly and tossed the white and silver crepe tunic and trousers onto a pile with her sandals. The royal palace's magic would ensure that they were removed and cleaned. Then she stepped into the tub and sat down, settling back until the foam reached to her shoulders. A simple "Tea, please" brought a goblet of iced tea onto the ledge next to her hand. She sipped it and tried not to wonder what Mykh planned to do.

Mykh's arrival brought an abrupt end to all such higher thoughts, even as it sent her blood rushing to her cheeks and breasts. A trickle of heat brushed her core, but she ignored that. He wore only a simple white loincloth that left his magnificent body open to any ravenous glance she cared to give.

She shivered and took a long pull on her tea. No man had a right to look as good as he did in so little clothing. It simply wasn't fair to womankind.

His mouth quirked, but he nodded and slid into the tub with a simple, "My lady."

Corinne's eyes narrowed, watching him wade over to her feet.

"May I?" he asked. He didn't wait for her answer before he'd cradled her ankle in one big hand.

She tilted her head, considered, and assented. What could he do to a foot?

Quite a lot as it turned out.

Corinne and Celeste had always had different definitions of true luxury. Celeste liked gadgets. Her apartment was both opulent and comfortable, full of high-priced items that made life easier. The kind of cutting-edge technology that costs a fortune but doesn't need a genius to operate, like that unbelievable espresso machine. Her boyfriends were equally functional: very good in bed but somehow never connecting with her heart.

Corinne, on the other hand, enjoyed simpler pleasures. She had a 1920s Sears & Roebuck house, lovingly restored with the minimum of twenty-first century gadgets. But it looked out onto an enormous flower garden and was only twenty minutes from the finest day spa in Savannah, whose profits she assiduously contributed to. She collected spas on her publicity tours, insisting that she visit one every week during those whirlwind combinations of no food, no sleep, and endless smiling. She could tell you exactly who provided the best aromatherapy massage, deep tissue massage, reflexology, Reiki . . .

But none of that compared to the feel of Mykh's long fingers wrapped around her toes. He cuddled her foot until she relaxed, before slowly stroking each tendon in turn. The combination of delicate touch and hard strength sent shimmers of awareness across her skin, even including the parts he hadn't touched.

And there was more, like how he stretched her foot and gently tugged her toes until they felt like taffy. And when those strong fingers turned to rubbing the knots away, including the ones in the back of her ankle and calf . . .

Corinne melted. She closed her eyes, slid down into the water and offered her foot up for the most sybaritic experience of her life.

He kissed her big toe. She cocked one eye at him, then both eyes when his tongue swirled over her. When he sucked it, she nearly arched out of the water. "Oh my God," she gasped.

He sucked again and she bucked. He smiled wickedly, knowingly. "Am I the first to pleasure you in this fashion?"

"I, ah, yes!" She stared at him, ruefully conscious that her eyes truly must be as large as saucers.

"Excellent," he purred and moved to the next toe.

She moaned as he worked it over, her thighs clenching in rhythm with his pulls. The connection grew stronger every time he touched her until his lips seemed to be drawing on her core, although his hands hadn't reached above her calves.

She lolled back against the tub's rim, legs spread wide to ease his access. Cream trickled from her core in heated anticipation of his next step.

Mykh moved closer to her until he was almost alongside her knees. His palm glided up her leg and cupped her aching core under cover of the frothing water. Corinne sighed and pushed against it slightly; he felt so damn good. His finger stroked her clit as if considering its potential.

"Nice," Corinne murmured. "Very nice."

"But you'd like a climax better."

"Yes. Oh yes, please, Mykh . . ."

He took her big toe back into his mouth, while continuing to stroke her clit to reinforce the pull on her extremity. First one finger, then two in that wicked combination she'd found irresistible before. She groaned as a climax rose up and over her, awakening her body to the erotic potential of its most distant components. If this was the reward for putting a kingdom's welfare first, then more women ought to try it.

He worked on her hands and arms in a similar fashion until she was a puddle of sated, and anticipating, womanhood resting in the tub. She even forgave him the smile that flickered around his mouth. Instead she idly wondered what he'd do with her torso.

He eased her hand back into the water, then picked up the sponge. He washed her gently but thoroughly until the scent of frankincense, roses, and cedarwood wafted from her. The nicks and calluses embedded in his hands by years of warfare became satin smooth skin covering wickedly skillful strength. And the

tub's magic helped him, setting the bubbles to dance more pur-
posefully, so that the least trace of dirt or used soap disappeared.

Mykh murmured, "Pillows, please" and a soft mound appeared
on the tub's edge. "Can you kneel?"

"Sure," Corinne agreed. She'd have consented to almost anything by then. He guided her into position facing the rim, with her
head and most of her body resting on the pillows. She murmured
something about being cold and the air obligingly warmed up.

She was still mumbling her appreciation, when he delicately ran
the sponge over her nether lips. She squeaked and jerked, just a little. She relaxed again—only to feel him spread her legs wider.

She turned her head to look at him and found him tossing his
hair over one shoulder. Mykh raised an eyebrow at her and she
blushed but kept staring at him. He smiled at her and delicately
blew a puff of warm air over her clit.

Corinne gasped as that gentlest of all caresses made her core
clench in desire. He blew again and her thighs clenched, until she
trembled with the need to touch him. "Mykh, what are you
doing?" she choked out.

He answered her by gliding first the sponge then his tongue
over her folds. A second pass delved a little deeper, and a third sent
her twisting in anticipation. He explored every subtle nook and
curve, more and more with his mouth rather than the sponge. She
bucked against him eagerly, making him chuckle. He tossed the
sponge aside and set his tongue and teeth roaming over her, while
his hands gripped her hips firmly. She moaned, soft rumbles that
sang of pleasure, while her body surged and floated under his
mouth's coaxing.

She grinned at a stray thought. Had any other romance novel-
ist ever labored like this to save her characters?

Suddenly his teeth tugged lightly on her clit and a climax swept like a geyser from her toes to her scalp, leaving her sprawled half-in and half-out of the tub.

Corinne tried to catch both her breath and her wits in the aftermath. She knew she should be embarrassed by how exposed she was to him, but that seemed far too much effort. And rather silly, considering what he'd already done to her. She did manage to be mildly curious when he stood up. "Where are you going?"

"It's time for your massage now."

She swiveled her head around to look at him. Damn, he was gorgeous standing there in the water with clouds of steam caressing all those smooth planes of muscle. She could see every inch of him, even his cock standing crimson and erect now that the loincloth was so wet as to be invisible. But the scrap of linen did manage to annoy her anyway. "Mykh, would you please take off that damned loincloth? Or would that be sacrilegious?"

He threw his head back and roared, almost dropping the towels in his arms. Corinne blinked then blushed, as she tried to roll over and sit up. But her relaxed muscles wouldn't obey her, making her lurch and nearly fall back into the water. He caught her instantly and held her against his chest. He was still chuckling softly while he wrapped fresh dry towels around her.

"I didn't know loincloths were so funny," Corinne observed to his collarbone.

"Very seldom," he answered, setting her down on the bench. It was cool but heated up nicely once she touched it. "I would be happy to obey you but . . ."

She snorted. Mykh was never going to obey anyone or anything but his own sense of right and wrong. Thankfully, that included caring for his family or she'd never have been able to get her heroines out of half their escapades.

His mouth twitched but he continued, "On the last day, my rod cannot touch a woman until we board the galley. The loincloth is a symbol of that fast."

"Damn." Corinne's disappointment was emphatic. She reviewed his behavior in the bath tub. "But it's okay for me to climax? Seems a little one-sided. We'll have to make up for that on the boat."

"Whatever my lady wishes," Mykh purred. He swooped down and scooped her up off the bench. He started walking toward the bedchamber.

"Yeah, right," Corinne commented a little brokenly. The tip of his magnificent cock was rubbing her hip through the layer of towels, which felt almost nonexistent at the moment. She tried to think of something clever to say, failed, and turned her face into the curve of his neck. He smelled of frankincense, cedar, and roses, as she did. But the strongest aroma was of himself, that satisfying masculine scent that spoke of hard work and hard loving.

She was still purring about his scent when they marched hand-in-hand through the castle an hour later.

The high priests and priestesses led the procession, together with all their attendant acolytes and lesser priests and priestesses. The acolytes waved censers, sending incense laden with frankincense through the air, while priests played flutes, trumpets, and other musical instruments.

Then came a handful of guardsmen, two men carrying Dragon's Breath and two women with the great halberd, Tiger's Paw, directly in front of Mykh and Corinne, while Mazur glided alongside.

They were both dressed now, if you could dignify their costumes with that role. He wore a finely pleated kilt, covering him from hip to knee, with a green and gold sash. She was garbed from armpit to mid-thigh in a strapless full-skirted dress, topped by a floor-length, intricately pleated robe, belted in silver tissue. Matching rose coronets, with cedarwood and frankincense, plus sandals, finished off their outfits.

Mykh's great emerald signet was the only jewelry he wore; not even a bead could be found in his thick coppery mane, now falling free down his back. She suspected that he missed his knives, judging by the way his fingers had twitched when they first left her rooms.

The tissue-thin silk was a total contrast to her beloved gray sweats. But the sweats' comfort faded next to the fire in Mykh's eyes when he first saw her in this outfit. That look promised enough excitement to make her forget modesty, the difficulties of healing him, even the threat of the Dark Warrior's return.

Still, her skin prickled every time she saw his eyes check Dragon's Breath. If the Dark Warrior attacked now, the only defense was Mykh's skill and speed with that great sword, until he managed to summon Khyber.

Corinne wondered again how she could call Svetlhana. She could grab the halberd fairly quickly since it was only two paces away; hopefully, it would be as light as the tigress had promised. But what did she say or do then to bring Svetlhana? A sorceress was supposed to accomplish that faster than the long chant Mykh used with Khyber. But she didn't know what they did differently.

She remembered the endless minutes at Tajzyk's Gorge, while the knife-edged beak of Azherbhai, the Imperial Terrapin, had torn apart Torhtremer's armies faster than a man could run. But no one had fled the carnage. Instead, men and women died by the hundreds and thousands to keep the Dark Warrior away, while Mykh's voice rose and fell in the summons. And finally they roared in relief when Khyber appeared, his fiery breath ultimately reducing the enemy's forces to ashes.

Corinne had wept when writing that scene and she'd never rewritten it, not even to polish it while correcting the galleys.

Ghryghoriy, with his hidden scars gained during that desperate battle, and his wife, Amber, followed Mykh and Corinne. Behind them came Alekhsiy and Juli, then another handful of guardsmen. Yevgheniy and one of the jewels, then the remaining jewels and their escorts appeared next, followed by the royal musicians and palace servants. More musicians and servants joined at every turn until Corinne couldn't calculate how big the procession was. It was certainly longer than any Fourth of July parade she'd seen back on Earth.

All of them, including the priests and priestesses, fell silent as they approached a pair of towering gold and silver doors. A ram's horn sounded in the distance, then another and another. A gong answered three times from within the palace, sending echoes through the walls and into Corinne's bones. Two guards, a man and a woman, flung open the doors and the throng flowed into the central courtyard.

The enormous space was filled to overflowing with people— standing on the intricate paving, waving from the encircling balconies, or watching from the parapets above. They cheered for the religious community leading the procession, but they went wild when Mykh and Corinne appeared.

Mykh halted at the top of the stairs, bringing Corinne to a stop with him. The crowd's boisterous approval swelled the air and flowed into her, lifting her spirits higher than any applause she'd ever heard after a college concert. "Dragonheart, Tigerheart!" they cheered.

Mykh smiled down at her and lifted her hand to his lips. She blushed when he kissed the inside of her wrist, his warm lips sending shivers up her arm. His molten gold eyes promised more, just as the priests' drums started up again.

A path opened through the crowd wide enough for two people

to walk side by side. Roses and other flowers rained down in a soft, scented cloud. Corinne was torn between laughing and crying at all the love reaching toward her from everyone. She glanced up at Mykh and caught a glimpse of tears in his eyes before he blinked.

The high priests and priestesses abruptly turned and entered a passage set into the outer wall. The great sword and halberd followed the high priests, as did Mykh and Corinne, Mazur, Ghryghoriy and Amber, and a few trailing guardsmen. Everyone else marched down the avenue in a loud haze of music and laughter.

Corinne looked an inquiry at Mykh.

"We'll depart from the inner harbor but they'll participate from the watchtowers," he answered quietly.

"Will they be able to see everything?"

"Certainly. They wouldn't miss a jot of the festival."

"Ah." What was going to happen on the boat? She had planned to ask the maids while they prepared her, but Mykh's arrival had put all such thoughts out of her head. She chewed her lip, wanting to question him further but not daring to do so, given the clergy and soldiers close at hand.

The galley's appearance didn't answer any questions. It lay peacefully moored to the now visible stone pier in the inner harbor, looking almost innocent except for the dragon rearing up at its prow like a Viking longboat. It had a central cabin with a canopy on its roof enclosing a second level. Musicians occupied the cabin, visible through doors folded back against each corner. Sails and rowers stood ready to propel it, its shallow draft making it usable no matter how low the water level fell. It looked both fast and stable, almost like a CEO's fancy yacht.

The parapets above the small inner harbor were lined with

more cheering throngs. They continued to applaud as the party boarded, priests and priestesses heading for the bow and guardsmen moving to the stern. Dragon's Breath and Tiger's Paw were mounted in stands beside the canopy, before their escorts disappeared into the lower deck. Ghryghoriy and Amber seated themselves on an enormous cushioned bench near the musicians.

Mazur hesitated on the pier, his tail lashing. "Great Lady," he rumbled. "Great Lady, I cannot go farther. This boat is forbidden to all but humans."

Corinne stooped down to Mazur. "I'm sorry. We will miss you, friend."

He rubbed against her legs, his tail curving around them. "Great Lady, I will miss you, too."

"Tell him that we both wish he could accompany us," Mykh interrupted.

Corinne gaped at him. It was the first time he had acknowledged that Mazur could speak. His voice and expression were completely serious, so she probed a little. "Would you like to talk to him yourself? The effect would be permanent," she added quietly.

Mykh hesitated briefly before nodding. "Let me speak to my old friend."

Corinne cast the spell, a little surprised at how easily it came to her. Mykh blinked and shook his head, then cautiously tried a few simple words.

Mazur leaped up and put his paws on Mykh's shoulders. They stood like that for a few moments, growling softly together like a pair of lions. Finally the big leopard rubbed his jaw against Mykh's, ruffling the man's fiery mane while purring loudly enough to rival the crowd's noise. Then Mazur dropped onto all four paws and backed away. He sat down regally, only his pricked ears and twitching tail showing any inner tumult.

Mykh looked back at him for a long moment before leaving with Corinne. They were halfway up the gangplank before he spoke. "I promised him that I would guard you with my life."

Corinne paled. "Do you think that the Dark Warrior could strike here?"

"No, the galley is protected by ancient wards that Khyber swears cannot be breached. But I suspect that he is close."

Corinne shivered and Mykh drew her close against his side. "Enough of that talk. We should not waste our energy fretting about what we cannot change." He kissed the top of her head.

SEVEN

Corinne shivered again, thinking of everything that could go wrong. How on earth was she going to cure Mykh, defeat the Dark Warrior, eventually rescue Celeste . . .

Then she sniffed and threw her head back. It was show time, dammit, and she had things to do, no matter what they cost her personally. At least she could pray that Jarred was treating Celeste well.

She smiled up at Mykh, chin high. "We have nothing to fear but fear itself, as a wise man once said. So let's get this show on the road and kick some butt. Figuratively speaking, that is," she added hastily.

Mykh blinked then chortled. "As you wish, my lady." He swept her on board the galley with a flourish and escorted her carefully up the narrow stairs rising next to the cabin. The green and white canopy above it created the impression of a private room with filtered light and dancing shadows. Its only walls, if you could call them that, were the green and white silk panels flutter-

ing at each corner. Its deck was covered by fabulous rugs and cushions and edged by a short railing. The only other furnishing was a
small hanging table; it boasted no chairs, benches, sofas, or any
other rigid supports. Based on years of writing erotic romance,
Corinne judged it as competent to host any sexual act she'd ever
written, plus some she'd only heard of.

Mykh seated her on a large cushion much like the one she'd
used next to his throne. A ram's horn sounded as soon as Mykh sat
down and the watching throng quickly fell silent. The galley immediately backed away from the pier, oars moving with quiet precision through the still waters. It stopped in the center of the inner
harbor and the High Priestess lifted her voice in a speedy, liquid
melody, rather like a traditional Hawaiian chant.

When she paused, the cabin's drummer played a few notes in an
undulating rhythm, which the High Priestess answered, followed
by the drummer again.

Then the galley departed for the main harbor, slicing between
the enormous gates showing Torhtremer's Great Seal with its
dragon and tigress. The only sounds were the drumbeat and the
oars' whispered contact with the water, casting ripples and eddies
across the strong, steady waves of the great port. Roses and other
blossoms from the morning prayers swirled across the water.

The High Priestess began a new verse but the priestesses answered her this time, continuing the gentle rhythm of the drum by
clapping.

"Now we must kneel facing each other," Mykh said quietly, his
voice pitched so as not to carry. "Make certain that no cloth comes
between you and the cushions."

Corinne blinked, blushed, and thought of a question. "Who
faces forward?"

"It is tradition that the Dragonheart does."

"Okay." Corinne crawled into position on a velvet-covered pillow, glad that her robe was loose enough not to get caught. "What next?"

"Sit down thusly, making certain that all is comfortable."

Seems easy enough so far, Corinne thought nervously, as she tweaked her skirt out of the way and crossed her legs, settling into the familiar lotus position.

"Now we must close our eyes and look into ourselves, as we learn our bodies."

Learn our bodies? She slipped into the focused state smoothly, relieved not to think about that glorious male body so close to her. The boat rocked gently as it passed through the waves, making her nether lips brush against the velvet. It felt so good that she did it again and again, delighting in her core's first delicate warmth. She was glad that her full skirt hid her activities from the watching crowd, although surely they were far enough away that they couldn't really see anything.

Was this what he meant by "learning our bodies?" She peeked at Mykh from under her eyelids and caught him swinging his pelvis slowly back and forth. He was leaning back though, which must spread the cushions' caress across a wider area. Corinne copied his movement and enjoyed the sensations seeping into her backside as well. *Who would have ever thought that a boat and some cushions could be a sex toy?*

The High Priestess's song strengthened as more priestesses joined in from the shore, while all of the boat's passengers began to stamp their feet in unison with the drummer.

"Tighten your inner muscles now as we sway," Mykh purred. "And release them when you lean away from me. Tighten . . . and release."

Women were singing on both sides of the harbor, as Corinne

obeyed him and sighed. This was a lovely way to enjoy a boat ride.
Her breasts warmed, as her cunt's enjoyment of this new game
spread upwards. She unbelted the robe and tossed it aside, glad to
be free of even that little restriction.

The women's voices fell silent, allowing the song to be carried
by the drummer. The High Priestess chanted alone and was answered by a single man's voice, then a chorus of men. A flute in-
tertwined with the drum to carry the melody.

"Now we must look at each other," Mykh rumbled, sounding
oddly determined.

Corinne looked at him sharply. His eyes were closed and his jaw
set. "Mykh? What is it?"

"We must share with each other now," he said slowly and
opened his eyes. Their gaze meshed briefly then he glanced toward
the great fortress visible on the shore.

"Mykh, please . . ." Corinne reached out to him but he held up
his hand. She settled back onto the pillow, still maintaining the
steady, delicious rocking and clenching.

His eyes swept the harbor once more before returning to her.
"They say a sorceress can steal your soul if you look at her."

"I would never do that!"

"I hope that is true. But I know that I must open myself to you
in this way, if the rite is to be completed." He was grimly determined but his eyes kept tracing the harbor edges.

The High Priestess sang again to be answered by the men, and
Corinne peeled off her dress, letting it drop slowly onto a rug.
"Now I'm naked to you, too, Mykh. Does it help?"

Mykh stared at her, taking in everything she'd never offered to
him before of her own volition. Her nipples tightened under the
heat in his golden eyes while her breasts rapidly rose and fell.

"By the Horned Goddess, you're a beauty, Corinne," he said hoarsely and smiled at her.

She smiled back at him, tremulously at first then with more confidence as his eyes softened. *Ch'i* sparked deep inside.

"Let me equal your attire as our breathing becomes one," Mykh growled. A single tug and his sash disappeared, followed by his kilt. His cock rested heavy and throbbing between his legs, aroused but not yet erect, as his hips moved slowly backwards and forwards.

Corinne's tongue touched her lip, eager to taste his delights, then she smiled into his eyes. Better play this game to the end according to its rules, not her own urges.

It was easy now to synchronize breathing with him, even when he played games with how fast or how slow he filled his lungs. She began to believe that they were sharing a kiss, given the way his breath seemed to fill her lungs. Her cunt tingled and burned as moisture slipped down her thigh, while his cock filled further. Her meridians glowed with power as *ch'i* built higher.

The musicians began to play a simple tune, which continued the priests' chant. It was a merry tune that invited all listeners to share in the day's glory. The priestesses joined in while the watchers on shore sang and stomped in unison with the drum.

Mykh's hands started to move with the beat and Corinne's hands copied him. Their palms touched and frolicked together. Her arms moved with the rhythm, then her torso until soon her entire body was dancing with him. Her energy waltzed along its pathways, circling from her head down to her cunt.

"Let me touch you, Corinne," Mykh rumbled. He took a small flask from the table and poured oil into his hands, then rubbed it onto her arms.

Shivers ran across her skin and down to her toes at the familiar scent of roses, cedarwood and frankincense. The velvet rubbing her cunt wasn't reaching the true itch deep inside. Her head lolled back as he caressed her shoulders.

"Look at me, Corinne." It was the softest possible order.

"Yeah," she sighed and fought her heavy eyelids back open. His golden eyes were intent on hers, molten with lust. "Oh yeah," she agreed. "But I get to handle you, too."

"Yes," Mykh growled. "Yes, you may and you will." He watched hotly as she oiled him, tossing his hair back so she could reach every inch of his neck and shoulders. He was magnificent under her hand, plated muscles tensing and releasing as she stroked him. She massaged his feet and legs before she touched his cock, approaching it slowly as her hands worked up his thighs.

He quivered when she cupped his balls, letting her hands' warmth ease the fragrant seduction into his sac. He groaned when she gripped his cock for the first time, then again and again as she smoothed the oil into every frill and ruffle of his foreskin. He groaned once more when she worked the scented fluid into his cock, which stood proud and erect now. But he managed to keep moving to the song's beat.

"My turn," he gasped, catching her wrist. She smiled at him and yielded the flask willingly. He poured the oil slowly into his hand, then stroked it over her breasts. A single fingertip touched her first, then his palm smoothed over her, until she was writhing to follow his hand, still following the undulating rhythm of the dance.

She leaned backward to open herself to him. Mykh massaged her legs lightly then brought his knowing hands higher. He delved and played in her folds, smoothing the oil into her while exciting more cream from her. She felt molten and alive, like a volcanic hot pot bubbling heat and willingness to erupt. *Ch'i* sang through her, building with the people's song.

"Come astride me that we may join."

Corinne came to him eagerly, the dance's rhythm so deep in her bones now that it sang in her every movement. She knelt over him and their hands met on his cock.

"Mine, I think," Corinne muttered and drummed her fingers on his aching rod in time to the music. Mykh arched in pleasure, growling softly as his hand fell away. She was so aroused and wet that he slid into her easily, although she allowed herself the luxury of a few shimmies as she sank down onto him.

"By the Goddess," he muttered and did a little wriggling of his own. "Now wrap your legs around me. The cushions . . . oh, Goddess! . . . use cushions, if you please."

Corinne did and also added pillows to their nest, increasing their comfort and stability. She rested her head against his shoulder, letting his heartbeat's heavy thud ease her impatience. He rubbed her neck, as their breathing matched, and began to rock. She crooned happily at the familiar game and tightened around him rhythmically.

"By the Goddess," he muttered again and kissed her gently. She wrapped her arms around his neck and settled into the embrace, enjoying the men's song with its simple accompaniment of flute and drum.

Soon the kissing game had turned into an exchange of breath, one inhaling when the other exhaled. Corinne's *ch'i* was strong and urgent as it circled within her, almost scalding hot in its eagerness. She shared it with him in her breath, bringing it up from her cunt through her spine. She could feel his *ch'i*, the dragonfire at his core, fighting to rise up from his loins but something blocked it.

She began to move up and down on his cock, building his *ch'i*. His hunger increased and she sensed his energy racing along his pathways. But it always stopped just above the base of his spine.

Corinne fought to understand what was wrong. She stopped moving on him and tried to think what a white sorcerer would do.

"Mykh, can you focus your *ch'i* as if you were in battle? Make it follow the great circular pathway so it can be tapped?"

"By the gods, Corinne, do you ask me to stop now?"

"Please, Mykh, it's important."

He blew out his breath. "Aye, I'll do it for you." His hips bucked and he shuddered under her. "Goddess help me," he gasped. The High Priestess answered the men's chant with her own and Mykh steadied, his breath rasping as it slowly evened out.

Corinne looked at him with the eyes of sorcery that see power and not flesh, a trick that she'd learned from the white sorcerers and employed to write more than one battle.

Mykh's spirit burned fiery bright within him. But the central path up his spine that would let him share energy with her, or raise yang in his seed to fertilize a woman, was blocked. A cold wall sat across it, signed by the ice serpent's malevolence and her own guilt.

She focused her *ch'i* on the wall like a laser. It melted a bit around the edges but stayed firm. She reached for more energy and found a wellspring in the High Priestess's chant with its male chorus. The wall swayed under her increased strength but obstinately remained standing.

Corinne looked further and found the people of Torhtremer. Every one of them stood united on this day, wherever they were. And they brought the lifeblood of Torhtremer, from its deep roots in the earth, with them. She probed that cauldron cautiously and it blew her apart like a firestorm.

She went spinning, frightened and disoriented in that world where power dwells. She instinctively snapped her *ch'i* back into herself . . . and felt the ice wall grow twice as high and wide.

Corinne ground her teeth in fear and frustration. She had to accomplish this somehow, so she began to move up and down again on Mykh. He gripped her hips and started to do most of the work. But she quickly tapped his cheek and he looked at her.

"We must finish this," he grunted. "It's almost time for the fifth, and last, station."

"Then I must do the moving, so I can heal you," she snapped, then softened. "Trust me please, Mykh."

"Corinne, do you think you can succeed where all the priests and healers have failed? Must you prove to me that you are a sorceress who could give me gifts with one hand, while stealing my soul with the other?"

She flinched at the accusation, but continued to plead with him with her eyes.

He shoved his hair back from his face before speaking more gently. "Let us take what pleasure we may, while we may."

"Then give me the delight of doing this," she insisted.

"Corinne." He shook his head in frustration.

She deliberately rippled her muscles around him in a reminder of the ecstasy she could bring if she chose.

"Goddess!" he gasped. "Let it be as you wish," he rumbled in resignation and wrapped his arms around her. He bent his head to hers for another kiss and she shared breath with him. Mercifully, he knew how to ease out of the tension that leads to orgasm. His pulse slowed as his muscles relaxed.

She remembered the fall through the void and how fractured her *ch'i* had been until she had meshed it with his. She wrapped her arms around his shoulders and gave herself up to the kiss, anchoring her energy in his and rebuilding her meridians as she had in the void.

When she was confident that the pattern was stable, she reached out for the priests' store of *ch'i* and wove that in. Mykh's chest rose and fell against hers, imprinting her with his passion.

Then she cautiously opened herself to the people's *ch'i*. It stormed at her portals but she added it bit by bit, always matching Mykh's rhythm. She was drunk with energy, stuffed to overflowing with it. But that meant nothing if she couldn't focus it.

Now Corinne started to ride Mykh, lifting up and plunging down on his cock. Every wave of sensation passing through him blazed across her sorceress's vision until she could see exactly where and how to attack the ice wall. She took his cock deep within her until they were as united as possible.

She narrowed her vision to the ice wall, keeping a tight focus despite the ice serpent's ghostly mockeries and the torrent of *ch'i* stored in her pathways. Mykh growled in agony as his body rocked under her.

"Relax," Corinne muttered. "Relax."

"You make demands that no other woman would dare voice," Mykh gasped, but his heartbeat steadied and his hips stilled.

She sent the full force of *ch'i* against the ice, cutting into it like a ruby laser. It glowed sullenly but melted into a silvery mist that vanished into his *ch'i*'s dragonfire.

"Thank God," Corinne murmured. She rubbed her cheek against his and he patted her back. Now they could drive toward orgasm.

She tightened herself around his cock. Only the High Priestess was chanting now, aided by a single drummer.

"By the Goddess, Corinne, you have your ways!" Mykh shuddered, so she did it again and again. Nothing in the world existed for her in this moment except Mykh and their union, with the song rising around them. She squeezed him faster or slower, harder or softer, always looking to the chant for guidance.

His chest hair rasped her aching breasts, while her core melted around him. His breath possessed her mouth, moving in and out in agonizing pulses. His *ch'i* swelled up his core, building up in his spine as it ached to erupt. She moaned at its eagerness but postponed the climax, as she watched his yang power build his fertility. Everything in her that was female, everything that was yin, demanded this man.

She rocked against him, trying to remember why she was delaying satisfaction for both of them. Her womb fluttered as the steady pulse designed to caress became one intent solely on its own purposes. Another pulse rippled.

She erupted into climax. She shrieked her satisfaction, while her body clamped down on him like the keys to heaven. He jerked, arched, and bellowed as he pumped himself into her, hands gripping her so hard that she felt him in her bones. She saw fireworks before she went blind and deaf from sheer wonder, waves ripping through her like a hurricane making landfall.

It was a very long time before she could think again, let alone consider moving.

Corinne rubbed her cheek against Mykh's as she slowly floated back to earth. He nuzzled her hair, his pulse heavy and slow beneath their sweat-soaked bodies.

"You can sire children now," she murmured, sighing as another ecstatic pulse rippled through her. "Any time you want, any woman you want."

His arms tightened around her. "Are you certain?"

"Oh, yes. Didn't you feel it, too? That moment when your hot energy poured into me without a hitch?"

"Thanks be to the Horned Goddess! I'll sacrifice a thousand baskets of western roses to her when we return," Mykh vowed.

"Amen." Corinne was too mellow to worry about theology right now. She buried her face against Mykh's neck and breathed in the wonderful scent of him, male sweat with a dash of incense for excitement.

But why am I not pregnant? He was healed before he ejaculated, her heart fussed.

Because you didn't want to bear a child to a man who hates what you are, a little voice answered. *And the Goddess's Dance grants children only when both partners yearn for the gift.*

Damn.

"Corinne, it's time to disembark," Mykh said softly and tilted her chin up to look in her eyes.

She blinked, reluctant to face reality again. "Can't be. We haven't been on the boat long enough to go anywhere."

Mykh chuckled and kissed the top of her head. "Drink this."

He held an iced goblet for her, its sides dripping with condensation and the most wonderful aroma of fruit and honey rising from it. She sipped, reluctant to move from her cozy nest in his arms, and felt a slow surge of well-being rise through her.

"Good lass," Mykh praised. "Now lift your arms so I can slip this over your head."

"Clothing?" Corinne sighed but she obeyed him. Moments later, she found herself in a long white silk dress, embroidered with dozens of red roses. Mykh dropped a long silver tabard over her head and tied it under her breasts with a white sash. A white tiger was embroidered on the left side, head resting over Corinne's heart, its body climbing up her back and its tail wrapping around her hip.

Corinne touched it gently, testing her sorceress's awareness, and felt a hint of warmth coming from the tiger's blue eyes. A surge of warmth lifted, like a tigress's friendly breath, when she petted the exquisitely detailed features.

Mykh spoke softly, making her glance up at him. "I can sense Khyber when I touch this corselet."

Corinne looked at him closely for the first time. He was clad in a green corselet made of overlapping green dragon scales edged with gold, which looked remarkably like a close-fitting muscle shirt with its simple neckline, sleeveless cut, and snug fit. A green and gold dragon emblem draped over his left shoulder, matching Corinne's tigress. Jade armbands, snug green leather pants, and high boots completed the ensemble. Her breasts firmed, as if it had been months instead of minutes, since she'd experienced her warrior's touch. "Gorgeous," she breathed.

Mykh swooped down and claimed her in a hard kiss that promised a repeat later. "We've landed and must climb to the dance floor. And do it speedily so the galley can reach the harbor, while there's yet water to float it," he warned.

That reasoning sounded so strange to Corinne that she moved away from him and looked around. A mountain of wet rock rose along one side of the galley. Ahead, she could see water but behind them was mud. *Mud?* "What happened to all the water?"

"It departed the harbor and waits in the open sea. It will bear the White Horses back to land."

Corinne allowed Mykh to help her disembark while she figured this out. "Are you saying that the harbor is going to refill with all the missing water? When a big wave comes in?"

"Exactly so."

This was beginning to sound suspicious. "Just how large is that wave going to be?" Corinne demanded.

"The priests say the White Horses will reach the dance floor or just below."

She followed his gaze upward and paled. "It's at least ten stories high. You're telling me that a damn tsunami is coming in, while we hang around and wait for it?"

"Not wait precisely," he murmured. A handful of priests and priestesses, plus guards carrying the sword and halberd, its sharply curved blade flashing in the afternoon sun, started up a flight of steps carved from the living rock.

"What do you mean, not wait? Are you saying that we'll be doing something?"

He smiled but didn't look directly at her.

"You're crazy! I would never screw anybody on an island during a tidal wave!" She propped her hands on her hips and glared at him.

Mykh lifted her hand to his mouth and kissed the inside of her wrist. Then he bit precisely on the spot under her thumb that made her knees buckle, while moisture gathered between her legs.

"And you're telling me that you can get me to do just about anything in bed," Corinne grumbled. Her feet automatically fell into step with his. "Goddamn arrogant jerk, you don't have to be right all the time."

She was still complaining quietly when they reached the dance floor, after passing other, smaller terraces on the way up. It was a wide marble terrace circling the island's crest, with a heavy stone balustrade marking the edge of a very long, very steep drop to the water below. Any opera company could have staged the Ring Cycle's spectacular pageantry twice over on that terrace.

Priests and priestesses had left the climb at each smaller terrace until only the High Priestess and the weapons' guards accompanied them now. She was slightly flushed as she smiled at Mykh and Corinne.

She began the invocation with a heartfelt, "My children," and went on to beg long life, health, prosperity, and many children for Mykh and Corinne in remarkably few words. Then she smiled at them, signed a blessing over their bent heads, and departed, taking the steps much faster on the way down than she had on the way up.

The guards mounted Dragon's Breath and Tiger's Paw, so the

weapons formed an arch over the narrow path leaping up to the island's craggy summit. Then the men bowed to the Dragonheart and his Companion and headed downhill at a quick trot.

Corinne yawned, feeling ready to collapse into bed, since the drink's effects had worn off during the climb.

"If you wish, the High King's pavilion is pitched on the far side. We can wait there for the Advent of the White Horses," Mykh offered.

"Sounds good," Corinne agreed. "Are you ready for a nap, too?"

"Nay, I am duty bound to stand guard until the Hunter's Watch ends."

She bit her lip at the reminder of why Mykh was her lover.

"Corinne." His voice was softer, catching her attention. "It is how we reenact the Hunter's quest for the Maiden, not the actions of a nervous jailer. I greatly anticipate sharing the Goddess's Dance with you."

His eyes were intent on hers, willing her to understand something. But what? Well, he'd never been a very cooperative character in her books; he'd always kept his thoughts hidden from her.

She smiled up at him tremulously and patted his hand. "Thanks." Another yawn surprised her and she covered it quickly.

"Rest now, Corinne. I will wake you when the time comes."

"Sure." She was asleep within seconds of reaching the lavish pile of quilts inside, yet another spectacular example of how well Torhtremer treated its royalty. She slept dreamlessly and well, with her arms wrapped around a pillow, hugging it close like the man she longed for.

She woke easily, becoming fully awake within instants. She considered her empty bed with a sigh and wandered out to find Mykh.

He was looking out by the cliff's edge, one hand shielding his eyes as he studied the skies. Dragon's Breath was less than three steps away from him.

"What is it?" Corinne joined him. The harbor floor was pure mud as far as she could see, with cliffs marking the land's edges and trees high above. Bhaikhal, Torhtremer's capitol and greatest harbor, looked more like a cliff dwelling than a seaport. Nothing moved.

"No seagulls are flying." He turned to face her. "It is far too quiet."

"What do the priests say?"

"That it is always thus before the White Horses appear." He shrugged. "Enough of what we cannot change. Let us go to the arch, that we may be ready for the Advent of the White Horses."

They took up position under the arched weapons, Corinne underneath the halberd with her back to the west and facing Mykh. A stance that meant she couldn't see directly where that tsunami would come from.

A ram's horn sounded in the distance and Mykh kissed her left hand.

Another horn blew, closer this time, and he kissed her right hand. She shivered in anticipation.

A third horn call rose closer yet. "My lady," he murmured and kissed her gently on the forehead. Corinne slid her hands up his chest, savoring all that hot male strength underneath the leather.

The fourth horn sounded and he kissed her mouth. She sighed happily and yielded to his tongue's delicate strokes.

The fifth horn sounded . . . and rose to a shriek of alarm. Mykh released her immediately and thrust her away as he whirled. Corinne stumbled back and ended braced against the sword's empty stand, staring at Mykh's back. He waited in a battle crouch, Dragon's Breath drawn and ready.

Beyond him loomed masses of angry water, boiling as they rose to form a mighty wall before the setting sun. The tsunami roared louder than a jet engine on final approach. It drew itself up higher yet until its pinnacle, marked by the White Horses' foam, was as high as the island's peak.

A black mass shadowed the wave's crest, swinging in and out of the swirling mass like a surfer. It was as large as a boat but flat and massive, rather than tall with masts reaching for the stars. Corinne frowned as she peeked around Mykh, trying to see better.

"Up the stairs! Quickly!" Mykh commanded and she instinctively obeyed. But she halted after a dozen steps and turned to watch.

The tsunami crashed against the island in a storm of salt spray. The land shuddered at the impact, knocking Corinne off her feet. She grabbed a boulder and slowly hauled herself erect.

Below, water raged over the terrace, sending Mykh leaping back. He snarled in rage as the wave uprooted balustrades and paving with loud cracks like a freight train derailment. The pavilion was gone in the first instant, disappearing in a cloud of green and gold amongst tumbling rocks and marble slabs. Fish and seaweed tossed across the marble before sliding off into the water.

Mykh flung his hair back, spun Dragon's Breath in a circle, and crouched again, ready to meet his attackers.

The water disgorged its rider and Corinne screamed.

The great Imperial Terrapin, Azherbhai, loomed over Mykh, more frightening at this distance than she'd ever imagined. But this thirty-foot long version of an alligator snapping turtle was far meaner and faster than its Earth-born relative. Its head had haunted her nightmares for years, uglier than sin and equipped with a knife-edged beak that could swallow a man whole whenever it chose. Fighting this would be comparable to a single infantryman, equipped only with a bayonet, taking on a tank with the fastest, nastiest gun turret around.

"Begone! You disturb the harmony here," Mykh ordered.

Azherbhai lunged at him and missed by a fraction of an inch. Mykh lashed out but Dragon's Breath also missed its target. Corinne's heart stopped beating.

An evil chuckle grated on her ears and the Dark Warrior jumped down from Azherbhai's back. He was slightly taller than Corinne but noticeably shorter than Mykh, and more barrel-chested in the flesh than he'd been as a spirit visiting Mykh's palace. He wore a long chainmail tunic that reached his elbows and knees, made of a dark metal that repelled the light, over black shirt and leggings.

He leaned on a long black staff and laughed again. "Foolish mortal, your feeble efforts have no chance against Azherbhai."

"Begone," Mykh repeated calmly.

The Dark Warrior snorted and straightened up, spinning his staff in deceptive patterns. "Why would I do that? All we need do is hold you prisoner until you rot. You have no magic to stop us."

Corinne's toe silently found the step below her.

"Balance will be achieved," Mykh insisted. He flung Dragon's Breath suddenly with a backhand motion like a frisbee. The Dark Warrior jumped aside at the last moment so that the sword took only the edge of his tunic.

Another wave broke over the island and sent a coat of glistening water over the terrace. Fish and bits of seaweed remained to mark its passing. More rock tore free and Corinne thought she saw marble statues from the lower terraces. Neither of the combatants paid any attention to the water's surge, while the sword returned to Mykh's hand.

Azherbhai clacked its beak and lunged for Mykh. He dodged successfully and Dragon's Breath nicked the turtle's shell.

"Damn you, puny human," Azherbhai cursed. "What care I for your ideas of equilibrium? The land should be mine all the year, not just for a few winter months. This one will give me that after you are gone."

Mykh lashed out at the Dark Warrior, Dragon's Breath catching the staff with a resounding crack. Sparks flew and the Dark Warrior staggered. He recovered quickly, brought the staff back up, and lunged at Mykh. Mykh countered and the battle was on.

The two men fought with a cold precision that their lightning speed only emphasized. Sword met staff, man spun or man lunged, men circled each other. The pattern repeated again and again as neither gained any ground, nor enough time to work a spell . . . or summon Khyber. The third wave broke just below the terrace while Azherbhai hissed in frustration.

Suddenly the Dark Warrior flattened himself to the paving. Azherbhai took instant advantage of the opening and lashed out with his tail, sending Mykh tumbling toward the parapet. The Dark Warrior sprang to his feet and raised his hand for the spell.

Tiger's Paw sang through the air, reaching for the Dark Warrior's leg. He cursed and spun to face his new enemy.

Corinne showed her teeth in a snarl. "You have to face me now, windbag."

He cursed again and feinted with his staff. She matched him neatly and smiled, grateful that Tiger's Paw was as light as Svetlhana had promised. "I'm a sorceress, remember? We're evenly matched."

The Dark Warrior stared at her and the first traces of understanding crept into his eyes. "Why do you fight for him? He uses you like a brood mare, while I could make you queen of the world."

"Talk, talk, talk," Corinne mocked. She attacked and a complicated pattern of attacks and feints ended when Tiger's Paw nicked the Dark Warrior's cheek.

Azherbhai roared and attacked her from behind. His beak ripped a piece out of her skirt and she leaped away. *Oh shit, some cavalry would be really useful about now. Svetlhana, come please!*

A feline growl split the air and Azherbhai snarled. Corinne came out of her roll and saw a great white tigress snarling at the turtle. Svetlhana was double the size of the largest tiger Corinne had ever seen in a zoo, but only two-thirds the size of Azherbhai. She growled again, showing her fangs, and attacked with a swipe of her paw. Her claws ripped though the air, drawing a trickle of blood from the turtle.

"Remember me? Remember how we fought before? And how you hid in your shell like a coward while I danced on your back?" Svetlhana mocked Azherbhai. She leaped at his head and they fell into battle, hurling insults at each other.

Instinct sounded the alarm, and Corinne spun to counter the Dark Warrior's strike at her knees. The halberd and the staff pressed against each other, while the two sorcerers glared.

"You can't win," the Dark Warrior warned. "Catalyst against catalyst, neither wins."

Corinne smiled mirthlessly. "No," she agreed. "But neither can you."

"He won't come for you. He doesn't need you, now that he's healed."

"Do you honestly think that you can defeat an author with words?" she drawled. There was no point in arguing a truth she'd known for a long time: Mykh would never find a happy ending with a sorceress. But if she stayed here fighting till doomsday, it would be worth it, just to ensure Mykh's well-being. Out of the corner of her eye, she saw Svetlhana rake her claws across Azher-bhai's throat then leap away, leaving his beak to snap shut on empty air.

"Silly man," Corinne taunted. "You can just talk forever and I'll keep on listening. Sounds like a Mexican standoff to me."

Growling dire threats, the Dark Warrior attacked again but his staff was just a little too high. Thanking the gods for her *sifu*'s lessons, Corinne lunged.

Her foot skidded on a bit of seaweed, sending her flat. Her enemy quickly brought the staff down for the death blow, as she tried to scramble out of position.

EIGHT

A black blur streaked across the terrace and the Dark Warrior screamed, a high piercing cry like tortured metal in a crash. He jumped back and spun around, limping on one leg.

Mazur snarled at him and crouched deeper, ready to spring again. He was wet and muddy . . . and his fangs dripped blood, matching that flowing down the Dark Warrior's leg. Corinne had never seen anyone quite so beautiful in fur before.

Behind him, Svetlhana danced along the damaged balustrade to avoid Azherbhai's raging beak, knocking chunks of stone into the harbor in his attempts to kill her.

Eyeing Mazur, the Dark Warrior lifted his hand to cast a spell. Corinne sprang to her feet and threw Tiger's Paw. He jerked away and it missed. He began the spell, staring at Corinne, before the halberd returned to her hand. She prepared shielding wards, frantically trying to protect both Mazur and herself.

Suddenly a line of flames blossomed between Svetlhana and

Azherbhai. The immense head immediately retreated into its shell. The Dark Warrior chanted faster, his eyes sweeping the skies for Khyber.

Then Dragon's Breath sliced through the Dark Warrior like a chain saw through kindling. His remains drifted to the terrace as ashes, destroyed by the same dragon magic that had claimed the Gray Sorceress and the banquet musicians. As Corinne's *sifu* had taught, *the dragon always attacks from an unexpected direction.*

Mazur roared his approval.

Mykh had come to rescue them. He didn't have to: it would have been safer for him and Torhtremer if he'd saved himself. But he was here. Corinne's throat went tight as she blotted away tears with her sleeve.

Khyber dived out of the sky and blazed a fiery trail from the Dark Warrior's remains to Azherbhai. He circled then returned to etch a blazing noose around the turtle, who hissed in frustration from within his shell's protection.

The Imperial Dragon finally landed on the terrace, wings held high and trumpeting victory. Svetlhana sat down and started cleaning her whiskers, rather like a society matron repairing her makeup before a party.

"How dare you kill my catalyst?" Azherbhai erupted. "He has served me well for three centuries!"

Svetlhana yawned, displaying a magnificent set of teeth, and inspected her claws. Corinne rested the halberd on the paving and leaned against it, catching her breath but ready to move again in an instant. *He came back, he came back, he came back,* her heart chortled.

Mykh joined her quietly, Dragon's Breath still drawn and Mazur at his heels.

"You knew you upset the equilibrium when you let him learn

immortality," Khyber answered calmly. "Do not begin weeping now that balance is restored."

"It will be years before I have another catalyst!"

"At least a century, by my calculations."

Azherbhai whipped his head around in a fury, missing Khyber but knocking out a section of balustrade. Corinne winced as she heard it tumble down the cliff and into the water. "I will return," he vowed hoarsely.

"As will we," Khyber agreed. "As will the Imperial Phoenix, if it comes to that. Be glad that you still have wintertime and the north."

The Imperial Terrapin lifted his snout to the sky in a storm of angry clacking and dived abruptly off the terrace, setting off a froth of water that washed away all traces of the Dark Warrior. Mykh cleaned Dragon's Breath with a scrap of silk and sheathed it.

Svetlhana leaped onto the balustrade to avoid the wet floor then sauntered over to Khyber. "Miss me, big boy?" she purred and tilted her head suggestively. She was an enormous tigress but she looked delicate and feminine next to the big dragon.

To Corinne's astonishment, Khyber flushed, traces of red rising under his scales. "Indeed I did. Many times, in fact."

Svetlhana patted his snout with her paw. "Poor darling, do you need a kiss to make it better? Or would you rather," her voice deepened, "fly with me?"

"Need you ask?" Khyber returned dryly.

Corinne shook her head, their love twisting a knife in her heart. She returned Tiger's Paw to its stand, before she could start crying over what she'd never find with Mykh.

"Perhaps not, but it is such fun to tease you." Svetlhana rubbed her cheek against his. Khyber's eyes closed in bliss as she purred loudly. "You are a wicked lizard with such lovely scales to scratch me. Let us go now before I remember how to be good."

She sprang aboard Khyber's back who crooked his head to watch her, a wicked smirk touching his mouth. She circled carefully and lay down with her chin tucked into the crook of his neck. She began to knead his shoulders and he rumbled approval, then leaped off the balustrade. He pulled out after a shallow dive that ended a hair's breadth above the harbor and climbed, his immense wings flapping as he gained height. A gleeful yowl floated back to the island. Cheers echoed from the crowds ringing the harbor.

"Victory is ours," Mykh said softly.

Corinne turned and found him standing just behind her. A trickle of blood on his arm showed where he'd tumbled against the balustrade, but he looked well otherwise. And entirely too sexy for a girl's peace of mind.

"Yes, we did win," she agreed slowly, trying to think of how to get away before she lunged at him. She edged slightly away from him. Mazur's ears twitched and he cocked his head to watch them.

"And if you ever do that again, I'll wring your neck!" His heart stuttered as she sidled away from him.

"What?" Corinne gaped at him.

"Attack the Terrapinheart, of a certainty! I died a thousand deaths when he lifted his staff above you."

"I'll fight the Terrapinheart any time I need to, especially when you're not available," she blustered.

Time to set some rules, three thousand years of kings told him.

"No, you will not. You will be my wife and my love and far too busy in my bed to so much as dream of fighting."

Mazur snorted and began the lengthy task of cleaning himself.

"Love?" Corinne stammered. A smile teased the corners of her mouth.

"Love," he insisted. "That is, if you care for me and will remain here, far from that strange world."

"Oh yes!" She hurled herself into his arms, buried her face against his corselet, and began to cry. He hugged her close and patted her back, her warmth starting to convince him that she truly was alive and his. His stepfather, Iskander, had always said it was ever a woman's way to sob for happiness.

Then an alternate explanation occurred to him. "Are you afraid that I would hurt you, as that other one did who put such dread of bracelets into you?"

"No! I'm sure you'd never hurt me the way Dylan did. You took the ropes off me the first night when you were furious. So I'm sure you'd never hurt me, no matter how angry you became."

"We had a bargain," Mykh reminded her.

She shrugged. "Bargains never mattered to Dylan, only his own pleasure. You're not Dylan."

"What the hell did he do to you?" Mykh glared. He would return through the void and destroy this lout.

"Mykh, are you feeling violent?" Corinne stared at him.

He nodded curtly. "Even so strange a world would be well rid of such vermin."

"Oh Mykh, that's so sweet! But you don't have to. He's doing a hundred years hard time for postal fraud. There's lots of big bad boys in that prison who'll either teach him manners or kill him. Let's talk about us instead." She ran a fingertip over his lip and he stroked it with his tongue. She shivered and went on hastily as he began to smile. "I've been obsessed with you for years, even when I didn't know it. I'd be glad to be your wife. And your love."

"Beloved," he rumbled and kissed her, hot and sweet like the obsession for her raging inside him. The leather breeches confined his rod too closely, as it yearned for her sweet sheath. A long time passed before he lifted his head. *Women always want to hear the words.*

"You'll be my queen and my consort," he promised.

"Forever? You'd pledge that to a sorceress?"

"You are my sorceress who gives me fertility, who does not steal my soul as an evil sorceress would, when I look into your eyes. I trust you with my heart and my people."

"Oh Mykh, that's so sweet! And I do love you, too. And we can visit your sisters and their families . . ."

He stopped her mouth with a kiss. She answered him passionately until he broke it off to throw his head back. He roared his triumph to the sky and hugged her. She laughed, then giggled as he picked her up and spun her around, setting her skirts flying. He lifted her higher and she stretched her arms over him, like a sheltering dragon. He grinned up at her and whirled again, his hair wrapping around them.

A faint whiff of sulfur warned them and he turned, still holding her. Khyber swooped out of the sky in a steep dive that would make a peregrine proud. Svetlhana clung to his back, her eyes closed in bliss and her nose pointed to catch the wind.

A rumbled "Again, darling," drifted back to the island.

"Yes, again," Mykh growled and turned for the stairs leading up. "I will have you again. Now, my little sorceress."

Corinne blushed and clung to him. He had almost reached the first step when she stopped him. "Mazur! Oh Mykh, please stop. We've got to help Mazur."

Mykh halted immediately and set her down. They turned back to the black leopard, who lowered the hind foot that he'd been cleaning and stared back at them, refusing to admit any embarrassment at the posture.

"Are you hurt?" Mykh asked.

"No, of course not," Mazur chuffed. "Dirty and a foul taste in my mouth from that wretched beast. But nothing more."

Corinne knelt to hug him, while Mykh dropped to a squat beside her. Mazur accepted it as his due then stiffened, signaling that he was ready to move onto other things.

"Thank you for saving me, Mazur," Corinne said sincerely as she straightened up.

He shrugged, looking as reluctantly proper as only a cat can. "My pleasure, Great Lady. Now go; it is almost high tide. Sport with him in the Goddess's Dance."

"Will you be okay?"

Mykh caressed the small of Corinne's back as he watched. The old tales spoke of the white sorcerers, who were allies of the Imperial Dragon and Tigress and always did good. She was his white sorceress, protecting him and his people with her magic. She had ridden him in joy, thereby casting out the evil memory of the Gray Sorceress rising above him. She had looked into his eyes and healed him, not stolen his soul. She cast spells that would assist, like the gift of Mazur's language. She was a cunning warrior who had taken him by surprise, as no other had done in years. And she had battled the Dark Warrior to a standstill.

She moved into his touch, making his heart sing. He would never again let her stray far from his protection. His heart had stopped beating while she fought the Dark Warrior, worse agony than he'd felt at Tajzyk's Gorge. Every syllable of Khyber's summons had been pulled from aching lungs, while his fingers gripped Dragon's Breath until they burned.

"A good bath and a few fish to clean my mouth are all I wish," Mazur admitted.

"May I help with the bath?" Corinne offered.

Mazur immediately sat at attention, his tail twitching eagerly.

A few words and the flick of her fingers turned Mazur's fur immaculate. He looked down at himself, checked his whiskers scrupulously, and started to purr.

"Good enough?"

"My thanks, Great Lady. Now I have fish to catch." His eyes slid toward a very large bass flopping on the marble but snapped back to the humans.

Mykh laughed with Corinne. "As you wish, friend." He slipped his arm around her waist and took her up the stairs to the crest. She gaped at the structure rising there.

"It's your tent," she stammered. "Your old tent from your mercenary days. Why? How did it get here?"

"The wizards fetched it over while you slept. As for why . . ." He looked for the right words. "It is the tent of Mykhayl Rhodyonovich, not the High King's. Among my mother's people, a man and a woman are married when they enter his tent together. Concubines," his mouth twisted but she needed to know, "are toys best kept elsewhere."

"It's where I first saw you," she murmured. "You were standing inside, worrying about Lily. And I had to know you better so I wrote about you."

"Beloved." He claimed her mouth in a long kiss, sweet as the passion he felt for her. Then he swept her up in his arms and carried her inside.

Everything there was as he had commanded it to be, exactly as he had last used it. The bed platform with its furs and silks, the thick rugs underfoot, a few broad cushions for seating, a low table offering a beaker of ale and goblets for drinking, the hanging lamps—all were the comfortable, and blessedly magic-free, possessions of a successful mercenary captain.

Mykh set Corinne down on the bed platform and kissed her again. Her slender hands fisted in his hair, pulling him closer. His tongue twined with hers like the life they would live together. She sighed into his mouth, sharing her breath, and he gave his back to her.

He stroked her hips and thighs, remembering how tightly they'd wrapped around him. Desire singed his fingertips when he slipped his hand under the silk and fondled her strong limbs. When his hand finally rose to her woman's bud, she moaned louder and her hips pushed against his touch. He played with her yoni in all the ways that she liked best and taught her a few more that pleased her well.

Then her thighs tightened on his wrist and her hips danced merrily as rapture overcame her and her hot liquor washed his hand. He lifted his fingers to his mouth and sniffed, filling himself with her unique scent.

"Corinne, beloved, look at me."

"Yes, Mykh?" she mumbled, her blue eyes blinking up at him

"Do you see this, your woman's nectar?"

She blushed fiery red but nodded.

"Every sorceress can bind a man to her with one taste of her nectar," he said slowly, turning his hand over slowly. "I knew that when I seized you. Yet I took you to the Tasting Room and drank deep and long. I must have loved you even then, the woman whom I had agonized over for years. Why else would I have done so much to claim you then tied myself to you for life, by drinking your nectar?"

He licked his hand in a single long sweep from wrist to palm to fingertip, before throwing his head back to savor the magic rising through his veins in response. When he looked at her again, her eyes were enormous blue pools while her breasts rose and fell in passion's ragged rhythm. He offered her his hand and she licked it delicately as he shivered.

"Mine," she whispered, "as I am yours."

Mykh swooped down on her and claimed her mouth. She responded fiercely like the tigress she was, and soon had her hands under his corselet. He growled his approval but quickly sat up. A few moments saw the corselet thrown into a corner, followed quickly by his boots and trousers.

To his delight, she was peeling her dress over her head when he turned back to the bed. She balled up the silk and threw it aside, then looked at him fiercely. Her voice burned into him. "Come to me, my dragon, and make a child."

She lay down on the bed, her eyes wild and eager. Mykh crawled up between her legs and leaned over her. She reached up and pulled him down to her, his hair spilling over them both. He held himself a little aloof and rubbed himself over her breasts, teasing her tender skin with his chest fur. Her nipples peaked into hard rubies and his own were as tight. His eyes closed and his rod leaped, as he repeated the caress again and again while she writhed under him.

"My woman," he growled and lifted her legs up over his arms. "My little sorceress," he insisted.

Her sapphire eyes widened as he opened her for his taking, a position that increased her vulnerability even as it prepared her to take him deeply within her. His rod swelled at her closeness and his balls ached in readiness.

"Mine," he said again and dared her to deny it.

"Yours," she agreed and stretched her legs farther over his

arms. "Damn it, will you just get down here and give me a baby!" she snarled.

He threw back his head and roared with laughter. Then he watched her as he placed his shaft at the center of her woman's flower and thrust into her, memorizing every nuance of her joy at being filled. She wriggled and tilted her hips until his rod slid home the last fraction into her, resting so deeply within her that their intimate hairs twined together.

Mykh's breath rasped his lungs as he tried to regain his discipline. The boredom that had always threatened him, when sporting with the jewels, was long gone. Now he felt like a youngling, more full of burning seed than cool wisdom. Corinne's hot sweet sheath fluttered around him and the last bit of deliberation fled.

Dragonfire boiled up in him as he thrust into her in the staccato rhythm of a male in rut. She gasped under him while her hips fought to pull him in and her nails racked his back, leaving a burning trail that incited him more. "Mine," he grunted and thrust. "Mine!"

She shrieked as she climaxed, her blue eyes flying wide open as her back arched and her arms flung up and over her head. She was totally abandoned to the moment, entirely his. Her sheath tightened around him and pulsed.

Mykh's yang power erupted up from the base of his spine, flooded his balls, and then rushed up his rod into her fiery cavern, finding her yin power. He roared like a bull as he filled her, blind and deaf to everything else in that moment. He collapsed onto her afterwards, ecstasy's final waves rippling through him.

They tumbled into sleep together, entwined in a single sweaty knot of skin and tangled hair.

It was almost midnight when Mykh and Corinne emerged from the tent, ready to consider the world beyond its shelter. Water filled the harbor, its quiet waves a gentle counterpoint to the day's tumult. Khyber and Svetlhana still flew, their path marked by the fireworks he tossed into the air.

Corinne settled on Mykh's lap, her head leaning against his shoulder as they watched the skies. He'd created a nest of pillows and rugs on the stairs, then brought food and wine. Mazur slept by the fire Mykh had built by the tent, too well-fed to move. Bonfires on the shoreline showed other couples watching the spectacle.

Khyber circled back over the island and blew a set of enormous rings, outlined in fire, not smoke. Then he glided through them, with Svetlhana stretched along his spine on her back and a paw lifted in bliss. "Magnificent, darling" drifted back on the breeze.

"The priests say," Mykh murmured, "that if a man and woman, who truly want a child, see the Imperial Dragon and Tigress mate during the Goddess's Dance, then their child will be blessed by the gods with health, happiness, and prosperity."

"Health, happiness, and prosperity? Sounds good to me." She kissed his hand, then the amber pendant around her neck.

"Aye. Many of my people shall be favored with such children this night." He kissed her head.

"Like this one?" Corinne caught his hand and placed it over her stomach.

He froze. "A babe?" he managed, joy blazing through him.

"I can see *his* lifespark clearly," Corinne assured him.

"A son," Mykh breathed as tears welled up. He felt as high in the sky as Khyber's flight.

"Another Dragonheart." Corinne smiled.

"I hope he's a sorcerer," Mykh mused. High magic would be very useful for Torhtremer's High King, if only to summon Khyber more speedily.

Corinne gasped then pulled his head down for a kiss. They were panting in passion's aftermath before either of them tried to form another sentence.

The three victors dined on the terrace under the early morning sun. The tide had turned with another dramatic tsunami, albeit smaller than that which had brought the White Horses. Mazur lapped his milk from an ornate silver bowl, studiously ignoring the giggles and murmurs coming from his humans.

"Will you grant me a boon, sweeting?" Mykh rumbled, nuzzling her hair.

"Of course, darling," Corinne purred, tilting her head into his caress.

"If you see a way to make Alekhsiy happy with your author's magic, please take it. He has earned some joy in his life."

"I'd be glad to, darling." She leaned up to kiss him, pleased that he accepted the author side of her magic. "Might as well exercise my plotting talents here. And you can relax about Junior's future: nobody back on Earth can write anything about Torhtremer if I'm gone, according to my will. So nobody's going to be jerking our son around to get a good book."

Mykh chuckled and kissed her back. " 'Tis a mercy that no one can try to change our world. I would have torn out the guts of anyone who tried."

Khyber glided in for a landing on the terrace, neatly folding his wings and tail. Svetlhana yawned and slid off his back, then began a series of stretches.

"Good morrow, friends," Mykh greeted them.

"A good morrow to you. And congratulations on your coming son," Khyber responded, sounding very pleased.

"Thank you," Mykh accepted.

Corinne glanced up at him and wondered if all fathers-to-be looked as if they'd created the baby by themselves. And would he still be half as smug during his son's birth?

Svetlhana prowled across the terrace and settled into a square of sunlight. "Darling," she purred.

"Yes, dear?" Khyber sounded even more besotted than he had the night before.

"Take our catalysts to see her sister."

"What!" Corinne sprang to her feet, Mykh just behind her. He wrapped an arm around her protectively.

"Can you do that safely?" Mykh demanded.

"Yes, of course," Khyber answered, sparing him a glance. "It would be easy enough to protect both of you and the baby from any harm." He looked back at the white tigress. "But will my dearest be well in my absence?"

Svetlhana shrugged. "Of course. Young cousin here can tell me all the gossip while we wait. If we exhaust that diversion, I may go south for a few games with the red phoenix. It's been centuries since I tweaked his feathers."

"Svetlhana," Khyber rumbled warningly. "You wouldn't dare cause trouble."

She gave him a disgusted look. "I would indeed dare, but you will never give me the chance. You will probably return within five minutes, after becoming a hero by rescuing her sister. And I will have to forgive you for having adventures without me," she sniffed.

"Thank you!" Corinne diverted them quickly. She hugged Khyber and Svetlhana, then stooped to kiss Mazur.

"Ready, sweeting?" Mykh asked, settling Dragon's Breath into its sheath on his back. He looked exactly as he had in Corinne's fancy living room.

She smiled at him. "Always, beloved."

Bound by the Dream

ANGELA KNIGHT

ONE

It seemed every atom in Celeste's body was torn apart and ground up with those of her impossible captor, then sent shooting into the darkness in a molten stream of light.

Until something caught the light, ruthlessly shredded it into atoms and molecules, and jammed them together again into two separate, quivering bodies. Her own howl of agony was the first sound she heard.

She took a mental inventory and found everything was there— arms and legs, head and body, Jarred Varrain's massive arms clamped around her with desperate strength. She felt him stumble as his feet hit something solid. Powerful hands lost their grip, and he dropped her.

Celeste slammed against something hard. She didn't even have time to yelp before her stomach went into violent spasms of rebellion. Fighting to keep its heaving contents, she saw Jarred reel away from her to brace against the nearest wall. He looked as green as she felt.

When she thought she could speak without losing control of the evening's pizza, she gasped, "What the flaming hell was that? Where are we?"

"Dimensional gate," he grunted. "Mykhayl's magic created it. We jumped through to my universe."

Well, they definitely weren't in Celeste's apartment anymore. Around them lay a long, narrow room built of three brushed-steel bulkheads that met overhead in a curving ceiling. The fourth wall was a transparent viewport awash in stars, which the ship's speed blurred into smears. In the middle of the chamber sat a recliner-style chair surrounded by a semicircular workstation studded with sleek, strange controls.

Yet the alien environment was as familiar to Celeste as her own living room. They stood on the bridge of Jarred's ship, *Garr's Vengeance*.

She squeezed both eyes shut and denied everything. "There is no such thing. There's no such thing as dimensional gates, or magic—or Mykhayl, for that matter. And I know damn well I made *you* up. None of this is real."

"Oh, but it is." Celeste opened her eyes again as he straightened away from the bulkhead, the greenish tint fading from his skin with a rapidity that she, fighting her own stomach, could only envy.

Of course, she thought, with the automatic logic of a writer who'd been treating her character as real for years. *He probably had his computer bring it under control.* With all those microscopic cyber-implants in his brain and studded throughout his body, there wasn't much that could keep Jarred down for long.

Oh, God. The truth hit Celeste with all the force of a runaway bus. She shot a horrified stare at the viewport and its streaming stars. *This is real,* she thought numbly. *This is really happening.*

Somehow, as impossible as it was to believe, she'd been transported into a universe where Jarred Varrain actually existed. It was the only explanation. *Besides, if I'd been crazy enough to have hallucinations this detailed, I'd have been hearing voices or talking to little pink rabbits long before now . . .*

"Oh, it's real," Jarred told her in a menacing growl. "And so am I." He started toward her with the long, fluid stride that reminded her uncomfortably of his cyborg strength. Hastily, she struggled to her feet, though it wasn't easy with her hands bound.

"What . . ." The word came out as an embarrassing squeak that forced Celeste to clear her throat. "What are you going to do to me?"

"I think you already know the answer to that." His grin held absolutely no humor. "But just to clarify the point, you spent the past ten years making my life a living hell. Now I'm going to return the favor."

Her mind flashed to *Varrain's Curse*. Not to mention *Varrain's War, Varrain's Vengeance, Varrain's Quest*, and all the other books she'd written about Jarred over the past decade. She remembered his suffering when he'd been captured and tortured by the reptilian Zyris, his rage when the woman he loved had betrayed him— and his agonized grief when he'd found his best friend's broken body after a Rekan general had murdered Garr for revenge.

Celeste's mouth went completely dry. Hastily, she scuttled back from his menacing approach. "Was there . . ." She licked her fear-parched lips as she looked up into those dark, furious eyes. "Was there a Garr?"

A muscle worked in his sculpted jaw. "Yes. There was a Garr."

She wanted to throw up again. "You think I made it happen."

"I know you made it happen." His handsome face went cold and rigid with an expression she'd described a dozen times.

It was his executioner's face.

"That's impossible," she whispered, feeling a scream of hopeless terror building deep in her mind. With his superhuman strength, he could literally tear her apart with his bare hands. "How could I influence events in another universe? Okay, maybe I . . . saw it somehow, but that doesn't mean . . ."

"You planned it before it happened, Celeste," he growled, stalking her. "I heard you discuss it all with that sister of yours. I listened to you lay out his death in detail. And when I tried to keep it from happening, you made sure it did anyway. *You helped that bastard K'charit torture him to death.*"

Oh, God. I'm dead, she thought, as her knees threatened to buckle. He was going to kill her just as he had his murderous Rekan enemy.

A particularly vivid passage from *Varrain's Vengeance* flashed through her mind. Jarred had forced General K'charit into the airlock, then coldly blown him into space. She remembered the book's description of the villain's death as he drowned in his own freezing blood, lungs and eyeballs bursting in the pitiless vacuum.

Celeste stared hopelessly at Jarred. He was a good ten times stronger than an ordinary human male his size—and given just how big he was, that was saying something. She didn't have a prayer in hell of fighting him off, especially with her hands bound. "I didn't know," she whispered, backing away again. "I thought I was making it up. I never would have . . . I liked Garr, I . . ."

"Shut up." His big hands closed around her shoulders and pulled her against his hard, armored body. Instinctively she writhed in his hold, but his grip tightened until she had no choice except surrender.

Panting with fear, Celeste went still as she stared up into his face, desperate pleas for mercy gathering on her tongue. She bit them back. Begging always disgusted him. Besides, she didn't want to die a coward.

"Your pistol," she said hoarsely, blinking hard against the tears of pure terror she could feel gathering behind her lids. "If you're going to . . . do it, please use the pistol. I had nightmares about that airlock scene for weeks after I wrote it."

"Airlock?" He looked confused, then stiffened as he realized what she meant. Discomfort flickered in his eyes, but it quickly vanished into the hard, implacable mask he always wore with his enemies. "I have no intention of killing you. You won't pay your debt to me that quickly—or that easily."

She sagged against him in stunned relief before convulsively jerking herself upright again. "But if you're not going to execute me, what do you . . ."

His mouth crushed down over hers.

It was a rapacious kiss, hungry, predatory, his tongue thrusting into her mouth as he released her shoulders to slide an arm around her waist. He tasted of masculinity and some sweet, alien spice. One big hand found the tight curve of her rump as the other claimed her breast—long fingers squeezing, roughly at first, then more gently as if he reined in his lust and set himself to seduce.

Celeste froze. As impossible was it was to believe, she was being manhandled by Jarred Varrain, the dark hero of her dreams.

She giggled against his mouth.

It was a giddy, nervous reaction as much as anything else, but it made him jerk back to glare down at her. His black eyes narrowed. "Am I *amusing* you?"

"Varrain, did you bring me here to have sex?" She couldn't seem to control her grin. Judging from his offended frown, he didn't realize it was largely a product of relief.

"I brought you here to pay," Jarred snapped, shoving her back, bending over and effortlessly jerking her across his shoulder in a fireman's carry. "Would you prefer to do it by sailing out the airlock?"

Head down, she eyed his muscled butt as he carried her from the *Vengeance*'s bridge and down the corridor she knew led to his quarters. The hero of her fantasies was carrying her off for hot sex. "No, this is fine." She giggled again. "Feel free to punish me as much as you want."

"The way De'Lar and I punished that little Rekan spy?" he asked in a silky rumble, one hand coming to rest possessively on her butt.

Celeste blinked, jolted out of her relief by shock. "I didn't publish that!" The words emerged as an embarrassingly high squeak. "That really happened?"

"Every single thrust." He laughed, the sound masculine and just slightly sinister. Long fingers traced the cleft of her rump suggestively.

She swallowed. The books being science fiction, she'd never written a sex scene with Jarred. But after finishing *Varrain's Betrayal* last year, she'd decided to try her hand at erotica with a short story about what he did to Ayla, the story's treacherous love interest. She'd never intended for that story to see the light of day.

Yet it seemed it had, at least in Jarred's universe.

Licking her lips, she looked up from her head-down position over his shoulder just in time to see an open doorway as he strode past. She got a glimpse of a broad fluidmat bed she recognized from her books, but he didn't stop.

"Wasn't that your quarters?" Celeste asked, shifting as she tried to relieve the pressure of his hard shoulder digging into her belly.

"Yes." Jarred's tone was mocking. "You don't really think I'd put you in my cabin, do you?"

But then he strode past the ship's two guest quarters, too, along with the one that had been Garr's. Celeste frowned. This particular real-life fantasy was rapidly taking on a sinister edge. "Then where are you taking me?"

"Where do I usually take prisoners?"

As she jerked around and craned her neck to see where they were going, he stepped through a doorway into the huge, echoing chamber that was the *Vengeance*'s brig.

Varrain was an enforcement agent of the Stellar Compact's government, and he often had to transport the criminals he captured to the nearest Compact law center for processing and trial. The ship's brig, accordingly, held several cells, each equipped with morphbeds that could change shape and size to accommodate any alien Jarred took prisoner.

But he veered away from the cells, too, instead heading for the big central holding tank he used for interrogations.

I definitely don't like the way this is going, Celeste thought.

She liked it even less when she saw what stood in the middle of the enormous transparent tube. At first she thought the huge, tongue-shaped mass was an animal because of the way it stirred when they stepped into the tank with it. Then she realized it was something much worse. The fear that had dissipated when he'd told her he wasn't going to space her came flooding back.

"Jarred, what are you doing?" Celeste demanded as he put her down and spun her so her back was to him. She was facing the thing now, and as she watched it stretch and flex its jet-black length, her heart began pounding in panicked lunges.

It was a Rekan torment rack, built of an alien material that was almost alive. Jarred had been locked in one in *Varrain's War*, and it had damn near flayed the skin off him.

"Relax," he said as she cringed against him, barely aware he was uncoiling the restraint cable from her bound wrists. "That's not what it looks like. Oh, it's the same basic design, but it's actually the Kyristari version." He tossed the cable aside, snatched her up, turned her around, and fed her to the thing.

That was what it felt like anyway. The rack extended black pseudopods to seize each of her dangling ankles in a surprisingly gentle grip, then reached up to cup the rest of her body.

"No! I don't know what you've got in mind, but forget it!" Instinctively, she swung a wild right cross at him. A pseudopod wrapped around her wrist in mid-punch, stopping her cold. Then it settled back, stretching out under her, carrying her along for the ride as it arranged her body at an incline, wrists crossed behind her head, legs spread.

"A little more," Jarred told it, and the rack obediently pulled her legs farther apart—giving him complete access to her sex. Celeste licked her lips.

She'd expected the alien device to feel cold and hard. Instead it was warm to the touch, like something alive, and it seemed to cuddle her body. Its matte black surface yielded under her weight, soft and silken against her skin. Wide-eyed, she starred up at Jarred. "Okay, this is really kinky."

He laughed. "Darling, we haven't even started yet." Taking a step back, he propped his fists on his hips and eyed her. The hot anticipation in his eyes made her stop worrying about what the rack might do.

Jarred was a much bigger threat.

The device picked that moment to tighten on the cheeks of her rump, kneading them through the fabric of her teddy. She yelped at its possessive grip.

Jarred grinned at her. "You have no idea how long I've waited for this moment." Reaching for the seal of his collar, he thumbed it open, then shrugged off the armored jacket. He wore nothing under it. Tanned skin gleamed like tight satin over the powerful pecs and abdominal muscles of his chest. When he tossed the jacket across the table that stood on one side of the cell, his biceps looked the size of her head. "It's been a very long decade, and I spent most of it dreaming about this moment."

Celeste was damned if she'd let him know how thoroughly he'd unnerved her. She managed a flippant smile. "Should I be flattered?"

The grin vanished from his handsome mouth. "Actually, I think terror would be more appropriate." Eyes narrowing, he moved closer like a tiger stalking a staked goat. Watching the muscles ripple in his arm as he leaned down to brace a hand against the rack's headrest, Celeste swallowed.

When his handsome face was inches from hers, he purred, "I'm going to enjoy this even more than the time De'Lar and I gave Ayla her . . . punishment for trying to kill me. She looked so deliciously helpless, all tied up in that neat little bundle, ready to be fucked."

She swallowed, reminded of the scene from that never-published story. The two big men had sandwiched the little spy between them, De'Lar using her cunt while Varrian screwed her helpless ass. Together they'd brought Ayla to a mind-blowing climax.

As her nipples drew into tight points of shamed excitement, Celeste focused her eyes on Jarred's sensuous mouth. She tried to think of some clever retort, but her arousal-addled brain just wasn't up to it.

"Her anus was so tiny. And my cock"—his white teeth flashed in a wicked grin—"isn't. I had to work it in a little at a time. Short thrusts, just millimeters." One big masculine hand came up, and his thumb brushed the tip of Celeste's aching breast. At the same instant, the rack reminded her of its presence, gripping her back-side and spreading her cheeks suggestively wide. Something that felt like fingers pressed into the crease of her butt through the silk of her teddy, then retreated. Celeste gasped and squirmed.

Jarred's smile flashed knowingly as he continued in that dark, velvet rumble, "Finally I was all the way in. My sensors told me being impaled on my cock was painful for her, but I also knew she was so hot, she burned. Besides, after everything she'd done to me, I really didn't mind making her suffer."

"You always were a little sadistic," Celeste managed.

"When the situation calls for it." Long fingers took possession of one of her desperately erect nipples. Stroked. Twisted. Tugged. All with such exquisite tenderness, pleasure streamed directly from the tormented peaks right to her creaming sex. His grin was definitely sinister now. "Finally De'Lar and I started fucking her. Slowly. And it didn't take her long to start loving every thrust."

Celeste licked her lips. "Yeah, well—" She stopped to clear her throat as arousal made her voice rasp. "Personally I'm not into pain."

Jarred leaned closer until his lips almost brushed hers. "Oh, yes, you are," he said in a low, taunting murmur. "Just not your own."

She stiffened, stung. "I didn't know what I wrote about was real!"

"But it was," he breathed against her lips. "Now, me, I'm almost as good at inflicting suffering as you are. But I don't mind admitting I enjoy it." His caressing hand suddenly dropped to cup her sex through the thin fabric of her teddy. "At least, when my target is . . . deserving." One long forefinger slipped under the damp silk and slid into her core. The sensation was so intense she couldn't hold back a gasp. Jarred chuckled wickedly. "And willing."

She gritted her teeth in outrage—though he was right, damn him. "Don't flatter yourself."

A second finger joined the one in her sex and screwed deep. Despite her determination to fight him, her eyes slipped closed.

Jarred suddenly wrapped a big hand in the bodice of her teddy and jerked. Silk ripped. Eyes snapping wide, Celeste looked down to see her own pale, bare breasts bobbing with the violence of his pull. Her nipples were hard and pink as pencil erasers against the red backdrop of the shreds of her teddy.

"Now," he purred, his eyes dark and hot as he stared hungrily down at her, "it's time you found out just how sadistic I can be."

Celeste's breasts were full, creamy mounds topped by tight pink tips that reminded Jarred of some exotic dessert. He'd seen them bare only once before, when she'd called Corinne up on the phone to plot while reclining in a bubble bath. The frustration of looking at all that gorgeous nudity and not being able to touch had nearly driven him out of his mind.

Now, after ten years of watching her prance around in bits of silk and lace, he finally had his hands on her. And damned if she wasn't even more lusciously tempting than he'd dreamed.

She lay helpless in the cradle of the pleasure rack, her green eyes dazed, her full mouth wet and swollen from his last famished kiss. Blond hair gleamed like strands of gold against the soft black surface of the rack, while her skin shone white through the rips in the red silk that clung stubbornly to her body. Looking at her, he felt his already hard cock lengthen even more.

Grabbing a fistful of what was left of the teddy, Jarred shredded it ruthlessly with a single hard tug. At last, he had her naked.

"Jarred!"

He ignored her protesting yelp and stared hungrily. Her long, finely muscled thighs were spread wide, revealing soft pink lips gilded with gold curls. The arch of her spine in the rack thrust those luscious breasts upward. He thought of everything he'd ever fantasized about doing to them. His dick jerked in lust.

"Oh, great," Celeste said, though the tough words were spoiled by the quaver in her voice. "Now what am I supposed to wear?"

"Nothing," he growled, his own voice rasping with arousal. "I'm going to keep you just like this. Ready for my pleasure whenever I want it."

It was a good thing his computer implants gave him such iron control over his body, or he'd never be able to last. Hell, he felt as though he could come just looking at her. And wouldn't that be humiliating? He'd hate to let the little bitch realize how much power she had over him, even bound and naked in the grip of that rack.

Especially bound and naked in the grip of that rack.

God, he had to get out of the rest of his armor. The seam was digging painfully into the shaft of his aching erection.

Jarred released her, though his hands hated to leave all that tempting silken flesh. Stepping back, he reached for the seal of his trousers. Celeste's eyes widened and flew to watch his fingers. He grinned and slowed his impatient hands.

If she wanted a show, he'd give her one.

Celeste watched with helpless hunger as the gleaming pseudo-leather parted, releasing Jarred's thick shaft to spill free. She stared at it in hypnotized fascination. His erection looked almost as thick as her wrist, with a beautiful, velvet-rose head and a long, veined shaft that jutted over a pair of furry balls. "My, Grandma, what a big cock you have." She winced, instantly longing to call the words back. She'd intended them as mocking, but they'd emerged as flirtatious.

"All the better to fuck you with, my dear," he said, grinning wickedly. Leaving his pants on so that only his cock was bared, he stepped up to her again.

And with a big bad wolf like you, Celeste thought, *this Red Riding Hood doesn't mind getting eaten.* Which was a good thing, since she was completely at his mercy. And God help her, there was something darkly titillating about that thought.

All God-sculpted muscle and long, granite cock, Jarred leaned over her, his feral stare reminding her of that fairy-tale wolf about to sit down to Red Riding Hood tartare. Celeste actually felt cream flood her cunt.

"For ten years," he murmured, "I thought about what I would do to you if you ever fell into my hands. I imagined making you beg. I imagined making you pay." His mouth drew into a hard, hungry grin. "And I promise you, you will. But first you're going to come until you scream. I want you to know how very good I can make it—when I choose to." The smile became a sneer. "So you can remember what it was like when I decide it's time for you to suffer."

TWO

Jarred lowered his head slowly to take one of her eager nipples into his mouth. Celeste caught her breath as he began to suck. Even as the luscious sensations sent more arousal flooding between her thighs, strong fingers slid deep. She whimpered, unable to suppress the sound.

"Oh, yeah," he growled against her breast, turning that dark lupine stare up to her eyes. "I'm going to love this. Cream and heat and tight, tight pussy. All mine. I'm going to make you beg, Celeste."

She was close to begging right now, but she was damned if she'd let him know it. "I never realized you had this much ego," she managed, though it was all she could do to make her dry lips form words.

"Not ego," he corrected, pulling back to brace a hand on the headrest and stare into her eyes. "Justifiable confidence. After all, which one of us is all tied up—and which of us is a superhuman cyborg with a very hard, very big dick?"

Her heart, already pounding, picked up speed. His grin flashed again as he looked down into her eyes. "Don't worry, though. I'll work it in a little at a time. Give that tight little pussy a chance to . . . stretch."

Celeste stared up at him, wide-eyed, her lips moist and parted in a stunned O of nervousness. But the hint of fear Jarred could see in her green gaze was mixed with a generous portion of sensuality, and he knew her sense of being at his mercy only made her hotter.

He much preferred that expression to the mask of stark, cold terror she'd worn earlier, when she'd feared he was going to space her. Once, right after Garr's death, he'd dreamed of seeing that look on her face. Yet despite all those fantasies of revenge, he knew he'd never be able to hurt her. After all, she was right; she'd had no way of knowing the adventures she imagined were actually happening.

Though it did cross his mind to wonder whether she could still bend his universe to her will, now that she was in it with him. He'd gambled she would be powerless here, but it would be the height of irony if she instead incinerated him with an instinctive burst of psychic energy. Fortunately, she hadn't thrown any lightning bolts yet, so it seemed he was safe. He could indulge his hunger at will.

But first he wanted to make sure she shared it. He wanted her to taste the frustrated lust he'd known all these years. He wanted her to know what it felt like to look without being able to touch.

Straightening, Jarred reached down to take hold of his thick cock. Celeste's eyes locked on his hand as he slowly stroked himself. Her throat worked as she swallowed.

"That's right," he purred. "Watch me. Watch me the way I watched you while you wrote that story about me and De'Lar and

Ayla. The way I kept right on watching you when you had to break off halfway through." Her eyes shot wide, color flooding her high cheekbones as she realized what he was about to say. He grinned slowly, letting her see his lecherous enjoyment of the memory. "And yes, I did see you lie down on that big bed of yours and slide your hand into your panties."

"Did it ever occur to you to give me a little privacy?" she said, stiffening with outrage.

"Why? You never gave me any. Besides, no man worth his cock could walk away from the sight of your long fingers busy between those pretty thighs."

She curled her lip and sneered at him. "Peeping tom."

Jarred barked out a laugh. "That's rich, coming from the woman who got off imagining me and De'Lar forcing Ayla."

Her blush darkened. "It wasn't force. She was as hot as you were. You'd never rape anybody."

She was right, but he had no intention of admitting it. "I wouldn't be too sure about that. We certainly didn't give her much choice—and I'm about to give you even less." He rocked back on his heels and watched her eyes drop helplessly to his massive hard-on. "But this time I want you to know I'm watching. Rack, play with those little pink nipples."

Celeste jerked in startled shock as the rack's surface extruded what looked like two long, flexible tubes that curled around her sides. The ends of both cylinders closed over the aching tips of her breasts.

And began to suck.

To her astonishment, it felt as if she'd been seized by a pair of wickedly skilled male mouths. Soft velvet lips suckled as two wet tongues flicked at her flesh while something she could have sworn were teeth scraped and nibbled. Her gaze flew to Jarred, who watched with taunting heat. She realized he was controlling the rack with his computer implant. "You brought me all the way here just to fuck me by remote control?" she demanded, trying not to squirm at the pleasure those lecherous tubes inflicted.

He laughed, a rumble of amusement. "Be patient, darling—this is only foreplay. We'll get to the main event soon enough." His dark eyes flicked to her wide-spread thighs. As if obeying a silent command, something immediately spread her lips. For an instant, Celeste felt cool air on wet flesh before a faux tongue gave her sex one long, hot lick. She gasped. He chuckled wickedly. "I just want to make sure you're . . . ready."

All around her, she glimpsed movement as the rack suddenly sprouted a dozen more seductive tubes, which immediately snaked their way over and around her body.

Then it started.

She felt as though she was at the mercy of a squadron of lusty, deliciously skilled ghosts. The rack moved under her like some huge animal, sprouting mouths and fingers that sucked, nibbled, squeezed, and caressed. All the while, Jarred stood between her thighs, lazily stroking his cock as it protruded from the open V of his fly.

"This has got to be illegal somewhere," Celeste gasped, squirming helplessly at the darkly erotic stimulation. It was wildly arousing and more than a little humiliating, all at the same time.

"Oh, I'd get locked up on half a dozen worlds at least," Jarred told her casually, his eyes hot as they flicked from her tormented breasts to her wet, spread cunt. "My superiors wouldn't be very happy, either, but frankly . . ."

". . . You don't give a damn."

"Exactly." He looked up from her sex as the rack tasted it with multiple tongues, simultaneously flicking her clit and wet, sensitive lips. "Ready for some penetration, darling?"

Celeste shot a glance at his massive cock, imagining how it would feel driving into her. Swallowing, she nodded.

He smiled. "Rack . . ."

"Damn you, Varrain! That's *not* what I have in . . ."

Something long and thin slid into her cunt and began to thrust. It wasn't enough. "Jarred . . ." she moaned, as her body clamored for something much, much thicker—like her captor's massively beautiful cock. But he only watched with possessive eyes as the rack played with her until she could feel an orgasm throbbing just out of her reach.

Finally frustration drove Celeste to recklessness. "Did you bring me all this way just to watch?" she snarled, staring hungrily at the tempting erection he slowly stroked. "If that was all you wanted, you should have told me. I could have found some guy back home, and you could have played invisible pervert all you wanted."

Jarred's eyes snapped up to hers. "Nobody else gets you," he growled. "You're mine." He stepped even closer until the thick thatch covering his balls brushed the curls on her cunt. His shaft jutted just over her belly, and her heart leaped with the hope that now, finally, he'd take her.

Instead one big hand began pumping his cock ferociously as the other caressed his tight testicles. "And I *am* going to fuck you, Celeste. Deep and hard. You're going to pay for every instant of pain you ever gave me with any kind of pleasure I want."

The tube inside her thrust in short, fierce digs, keeping pace with Jarred's big hand as he jacked himself off. She clenched her teeth and shut her eyes, feeling her hovering orgasm about to break wide as the rack fucked her while her hero . . .

"Look at me, dammit!"

Celeste's eyes flew wide just as his rod began to jet. White cream struck her belly and breasts, pooling there as he threw back his head and arched his brawny chest with a groan. Every muscle in his body stood out in relief. She drew in a breath to scream as her own climax broke . . .

And everything stopped. The rack released her nipples, withdrew from her sex, and went still beneath her body. As her climax died into a stillborn whimper, Celeste stared at Jarred in openmouthed shock. A drop of his semen rolled down one nipple. More of it pooled in her belly button. "You son of a bitch," she breathed.

But she could tell he hadn't even heard the insult. The pleasure on his handsome face was too stark as his muscled body shuddered through the last of his orgasm.

Jarred reeled against the rack as if his legs had gone weak. He leaned there a moment before pulling himself upright. The dazed sensuality on his face faded as he looked down at the rage she knew must be visible in her eyes.

"Frustrated, sweetheart?" Smirking, he fastened his trousers. "Now you know how I've felt for the past decade."

"I didn't realize I was doing a damn thing to anybody, and you know it!"

"True, but the effect was the same." Jarred's gaze flicked to his own semen as it rolled down her breasts and belly. He grinned. "But I'd say I've made a good start on my revenge—and started proving something I've suspected all along."

Simmering, she thought of everything she'd like to do to him, do once she got her hands free. "What—that you're a sadistic bastard? I could have told you that."

"No." He leaned forward and braced a hand against the rack's headrest so his breath gusted warm and spicy against her face. "That you're a sexsub."

She recoiled in shock. "I am not!"

"You can't lie to a man with sensor implants, Celeste. It aroused you to be bound and naked for me. And I knew it would. I realized you were a sexsub months ago when I saw your reaction to that kinky little story you wrote about De'Lar and me."

"I am not a submissive!" Celeste ground between her teeth. "I have no desire to be anyone's slave, even yours." Catching the implied admission, she added hastily, "Especially yours!"

"Now that is an out-and-out lie." He straightened and ran a hand through his hair, smoothing it. "Not that it matters. You *are* going to be someone's slave. Not mine, but someone's. Gag."

That last word had been directed at the rack, which instantly slid a broad pseudopod across her mouth, muffling her outraged curse.

Jarred looked over his shoulder. "Glad you could join us, De'Lar."

De'Lar? she thought in horror. *Oh, God! No, don't call him with me lying here naked and covered in come!*

Gagged, still in the grip of the now-frozen rack, Celeste watched as a tall, muscular blond faded into view near the doorway of the holding tank. She knew the figure was only a three-dimensional image of the real man, who stood in his planetary palace God knew how many light years away.

The com image's handsome face broke into a grin as his eyes focused on her spread and helpless nudity. "When you first messaged me, I planned to tell you what I thought about being used as a dumping ground for all the inconvenient women you can't bring yourself to kill," De'Lar said. "But I think instead I'll just be grateful. She's luscious, Jarred. Who is she, where did you get her—and did you mean it when you said you were going to give her to me?"

Give me to . . . ? Celeste thought, her shame turning to outrage. *What the hell is Jarred planning now?*

"She's the bane of my existence," her captor told De'Lar curtly, "and I'm giving her to you because I want her somewhere she can't cause me any more grief. As to where she came from—you wouldn't believe me if I told you."

Oh, God, she thought in horror. *Jarred's going to turn me over to that kinky alien dominant the way he did Ayla!*

"Somehow it sounds as if you're not doing me a favor." The lord of the Kyristari system frowned, his thick brows lowering over his brilliant green eyes. He was a remarkably handsome man, with a muscular, athletic build, set off to perfection by the elaborately embroidered silk robe that hung open across his massive chest. But then, she'd modeled the character on Mykhayl, so it stood to reason he'd be gorgeous. "I will not take a bitch into my cloister, Jarred. I have my hands full mediating between my sexsubs as it is."

Jarred grinned. "And I'll bet you work your . . . fingers to the bone keeping them all happy." He looked back over his shoulder at her, his dark eyes hardening in warning. "But I can safely promise Celeste will make no trouble. Here, at least, she doesn't have the power."

Don't bet on it, you big 'borg jerk, she thought, fuming. *I'll think of something.*

De'Lar made an impatient gesture, the sleeve of his midnight blue robe sliding down to reveal a powerful forearm. "Be that as it may, I won't take her at all if you can't prove she's a submissive. And judging from the fury snapping in those green eyes, I rather doubt it."

Jarred laughed, but it was a dark sound. "Oh, she's a submissive. She just doesn't know it yet."

A blond brow lifted. "You expect me to tame her?" De'Lar's

eyes flicked to her breasts. "Intriguing idea, but I don't think Kyristari law is quite flexible enough to allow me to make the attempt."

"Which is why I'm going to do it for you," Jarred said, as she tried to will him into dropping dead. "It will take two weeks for us to arrive at Kyristari. By then, I'll have convinced Celeste to embrace her nature—and compiled more than enough evidence to prove she's a sexsub under the laws of your world."

In your dreams, you son of a bitch.

"But are you sure you'll want to give her up once you arrive?" De'Lar asked, his image strolling over to look down at her. She was acutely aware of the drying semen that covered her body.

Jarred snorted. "After fourteen days of screwing, I'll be more than happy to see the back of her."

"Really?" De'Lar looked up at him, raising a brow. "Forgive me, my friend, but you seem to be sending mixed messages. On the one hand, you say you're going to give me this lovely prize of yours, but before you call, you shoot your seed all over her like an alpha bloodwolf marking its territory. If that doesn't scream '*Mine mine mine!*' I don't know what does."

Jarred stiffened as if someone had goosed him with a laser torch. When he spoke, his voice was icy with dignity. "Don't make more of this than she deserves. It's taken me a decade to get my hands on her, that's all. I just have to rid myself of the obsession."

De'Lar turned a calculating gaze on her. "Some obsessions don't die that easily, Jarred."

"This one will."

The king looked up at him for a long moment. "Well, she is lovely. I wouldn't mind having her . . . assuming you let me. I suppose we'll both have an answer to that question in a couple of weeks."

His image winked out.

His big body rigid, Jarred turned to glare down into her eyes. "De'Lar's a romantic," he said roughly. "I doubt it'll even take that long to fuck you out of my system."

He reached for the seal of his trousers.

She made a furious sound behind her gag. Jarred's hands hesitated in mid-motion before he said, "All right, rack, let her talk."

As soon as the muffling pseudopod left her lips, Celeste exploded. "You think you can just announce that you're going to use me like a Kleenex and throw me away, then expect me to go along with it? I don't think so, you 'borg bastard!"

"I hate to mention this," Jarred said, giving her a slow, nasty smile that was somehow far more threatening than anything he'd aimed at her before, "but you are literally in no position to refuse."

His shaft spilled out at her as he unsealed his fly. Given his computer implants, he didn't have the normal human male's lag time between erections. He stepped between her thighs.

"Use your sensors, cyborg," she snapped, refusing to be intimidated. "I'm not willing. Or are you going to rape me the way that civie raped your mother?"

Jarred froze. For an instant something anguished moved behind his eyes. Then they hardened. "There's the bitch goddess I know so well. Right for the jugular. I should have left on the gag."

"Well, excuse me if I don't want to be your human blow-up doll," she grumbled, cursing herself mentally for the ridiculous spurt of guilt she felt. Jarred didn't have many vulnerable spots; that he was conceived during a violent crime against his mother was one of the few.

His eyes flicked down her naked, semen-flecked body to her wide-spread thighs. Though her arousal had segued into outrage, she knew her sex was still wet. He focused his attention there, his expression speculative and slightly predatory. "I'll make you a deal, goddess," he said suddenly. "I won't fuck you until you say yes."

"Now, wait a minute . . ." she began, alarmed.

But he'd already gone to one knee. Before Celeste could even finish her protest, Jarred buried his face against her sex and began feasting like a lecherous version of Red Riding Hood's wolf.

Her spine arched in shock at the hot sensation of his clever tongue playing between her lips, swirling around her clit, stabbing into her opening. As she twisted in the rack's grip, he reached up her torso with both hands to capture her breasts. Long fingers kneaded the soft flesh while his thumbs flicked pink nipples that hardened with humiliating speed.

In minutes, the sensations he so skillfully created quickly overwhelmed her outrage. It was as though he licked and sucked the fury right out of her body.

Dizzily, Celeste stared down at the dark head between her thighs. She could feel the short, soft hair of his goatee tickling her bottom even as the silken black mop on his head caressed her inner thighs.

And his tongue . . . *Oh, God, his tongue!* He knew just how to use it to make her writhe, now flicking, now long, slow licks. At the same time, lips suckled and teeth nibbled as he worked the most sensitive part of her body with such skill it felt as if she was drowning in pleasure. In minutes he made her even hotter than the rack had with all its skillful pseudo-mouths and stroking probes.

But as much as she hated to admit it, it wasn't just his talented eroticism that got to her, mind-blowing though it was. What really lit her fuse was the knowledge that she was being seduced by Jarred Varrain, the handsome fantasy hero of a decade's worth of dreams, the sum total of everything she'd ever wanted in a man.

And something in her loved him, dark and tortured though he was. Despite his arrogance, despite his hunger for revenge and streak of cruelty, she wanted him.

So when he finally lifted his cream-smeared face and asked, "Do you want me?" she gasped, "Yes!"

And ignored the warning voice in the back of her head that howled "No!"

Saliva flooded Jarred's mouth as he stood, took his erection in one hand and parted Celeste's soft, slick lips with the other. He hoped she didn't notice his hands were shaking.

Pausing, he savored the sight of her delicate pink sex with the big head of his cock poised at its fragile opening. His heart hammered in his chest. How many times had he jerked off, imagining her like this—bound and spread and wet? How many times had he imagined all the erotic ways he'd punish her?

Now he could do each and every one of them. He could make her beg. He could make her come. He could make her dance to his tune as he'd had to dance to hers.

Then he'd forget her.

"Wait!" she said suddenly.

He snarled. "I don't think so."

"Don't . . . please don't get me pregnant." Her eyes seemed to take up her entire face. "I know you want your revenge, but don't do that."

Jarred sneered. "And leave a child of mine in your tender care? I don't think so." He made the comment mostly for effect. Thanks to his computer implant, there were no sperm in his semen anyway. He could change that if he ever decided to become a father, but now he wanted to leave no unintended children to suffer as he had.

Slowly Jarred eased forward, sliding the big head between Celeste's still-creamy lips and into her tight opening. He heard her breath catch at the sensation and looked up, wanting to watch her face as he impaled her for the first time. The sight was even more arousing than his fantasies as her pretty green eyes widened with delicious shock.

"Oh God," she breathed.

Jarred laughed. "Darling, you haven't seen anything yet. Just wait." He worked in a little deeper, loving the sensation of forcing her hot, slick silken walls to spread around his aching shaft. "I've been planning my revenge a very long time." Settling against her soft body, he slid in even farther, savoring the give of her breasts and belly, the smooth, satin texture of her thighs. As he drove the final inch, he slipped his hands under her butt and pulled her close.

She blinked rapidly in discomfort. He scanned her with his internal sensors, and smiled just slightly at the readout that flashed into his brain. "Does it hurt?" he asked tenderly.

Celeste licked her rosy lips. "A little."

"Good," he said, and began, very slowly, to thrust.

She'd always known that just beneath Jarred's heroism and hunger for justice lay a streak of creative cruelty. Since he only indulged it with his collection of sadistic enemies, he must count her among the people he could torment with a clear conscience.

Not that he hurt her beyond the discomfort of that first slow entry. He was more wickedly subtle than that.

Thoroughly trapped and helpless in the rack's grip, Celeste felt his massive cock possessing her in deceptively gentle digs that stroked and teased her slick tissues. Each clever thrust sent spasms of pleasure jolting through her body . . . and awakened some dark female need to submit.

What stung, though, was the way he watched her, the curl of triumphant pleasure in the corner of his sensual mouth, the gleam of conquest in his narrowed black eyes. Releasing her butt, he reached up to stroke each of her breasts in turn, thumbing her nipples until they sent sharp little zings of delight up her spine.

Somehow the sensations he created as he rode her felt so much hotter than anything she'd ever felt with another man. And much as it galled her to admit it, she knew that was because the pleasure came from Jarred's hands, Jarred's cock, Jarred's body.

Jarred.

"Remember the time you had me locked up on Zyris?" he purred, circling his hips so that his cock seemed to bore into her like a corkscrew. "There was that one guard there—you remember, the big reptile with the pink stripe. He loved kicking me right in that one broken rib. Fractured three more of them that way. I thought he was going to puncture a lung."

She gasped as he ground his pelvis against her clit, setting off a dark starburst of pleasure. "Yeah, well, you got your revenge when you garroted him with your restraint cable."

He grinned darkly. "I always get my revenge. Remember that." Deliberately Jarred arched his spine, probing the mouth of her cervix hard enough to make her writhe at the blend of pain and pleasure. He relaxed the pressure and lowered himself over her until his goatee tickled her jaw. "You know, I thought about you the whole time they had me chained, there in the dark." His breath puffed hot against her ear as he spoke. "Imagined putting *you* in chains. Stripping you. Fucking you. Making you beg the way I was too proud to."

With each word, he picked up the pace until he was shafting her in long, driving strokes. Every time he entered, he twisted his hips in some magical way that probed spots deep inside her she'd never known about, bundles of hidden nerves that triggered searing pleasure. Evidently his cyborg sensors told him where those sensations were most intense, because he applied the knowledge ruthlessly, building her heat, escalating pleasure toward ecstasy.

But just as she was about to shoot right over the edge into a boiling orgasm, he stopped.

"Noooo," she moaned. "Not again!"

He grinned demonically. "Ready to beg?"

His taunting tone jolted her to her senses, reawakening her sense of being misused. "Go to hell!"

"Already been," he said, and began thrusting again, slowly, silk and heat. "This time it's your turn."

But it didn't feel like hell. More like searing arousal that made her hunger mindlessly for the climax he dangled just out of reach. So close, so close, she began grinding against him, trying to force that last little bit of stimulation she needed. And he allowed it . . . until, just as she was about to tip over, he jerked from her body.

"Damn you!" she snarled, glaring as he crouched over her, his massive chest rising and falling in deep pants, his cock slick and violently red. "Let me finish!"

"Beg me," he growled, his black eyes wild, his nostrils flaring like a runaway stallion's.

"Fine," she gritted, staring at his violently hard shaft. "Fuck me."

He took his organ in hand, started to press it back into her opening. Stopped. Met her eyes with a sneer. "Not good enough."

"Please!" she wailed, unable to stand it anymore, needing him too much for pride.

With a triumphant snarl, he drove forward, ramming to the balls in one hard, hot thrust. Furiously he worked in and out, giving her no mercy, even as she, wanting none, drove up at him. Fighting each other and themselves, they writhed together until a single hot explosion took them simultaneously. Celeste screamed as the climax thudded through her body in endless hot jolts while he bellowed in triumph in her ear.

She didn't have another coherent thought until after the pleasure had faded and she lay under his heaving, sweat slicked body. *Oh, hell,* she thought, staring up at the ceiling of her cell. *I'm in deep trouble.*

THREE

Celeste lay pinned beneath Jarred's muscled strength and tried to think of something suitably annihilating to say. Before she could come up with a decent insult, her stomach rumbled loudly. As a blush heated her face, a warm, masculine chuckle gusted against her ear. "I guess that's my cue to feed my captive," he said, and levered himself off her with an effortless brawny surge.

She watched resentfully as Jarred sealed his fly with a brisk movement of one big hand. "Release her," he told the rack. It promptly obeyed, tilting upward as it uncurled its warm grip from her wrists and ankles.

Celeste struggled onto her feet, biting back a groan as her abused muscles protested. He turned his back on her glower. "Come on, I'll get you something to eat."

Longing to defy him, but afraid she'd be left in the holding tank if she did, Celeste hurried after him. When she was past the tank's doors, she heaved a silent sigh of relief. "I'd like a bath," she told his back with all the icy dignity she could muster. She wiped at the drying semen on her stomach. "I'm . . . sticky. And I need something to wear."

"You'll get the bath after we eat," Jarred said without looking back as he walked down the *Vengeance*'s corridor. "As to the clothes, no."

"Jarred . . . !"

Now he did glance over his shoulder, his smile mocking. "There's nobody here to see you but me, and I like the view."

Celeste tightened her lips. "Why are you doing this to me?"

"I think we've already covered that." He turned left into the galley.

"You are not this damn unfair." Clenching her fists, she wrestled with an urge to pop him in the back of the head. She wasn't sure he wouldn't pop her back—and given his strength, she might not get up for a while. "Not only did I have no reason whatsoever to think anything I wrote was real, I would have had to have been crazy as hell to think it was. I can't believe *you* believe I deserve to be sold into slavery for that."

"Actually, I'm giving you away." He moved over to a panel set into one wall and said to it, "Ambrosia snake with dressing and chiwka, a plate of Ga'q, and two glasses of seva."

Celeste had always thought seva sounded delicious, but she wasn't sure about the ambrosia snake or the Ga'q. Picking her battles, she decided not to protest.

While Jarred leaned against the wall waiting for the comp to send the food from the hold down the ship's internal transport system, Celeste stalked to a wide basin set in a counter and stuck her hands down inside it. Just as they would have in one of her books, a dozen tiny inset nozzles sprayed her hands with a thick blue cleaning solution that gradually went clear as water was added.

Pleased with that small victory over futuristic technology, she turned to eye her captor. "Why kidnap me, Jarred? You could have just appeared in my living room and said, 'I'm real, cut it out.' I would have left you alone."

"Or killed me." He lifted a dark brow as he moved past her to the basin to wash his own hands. "Given your history—not to mention the fact that you were already talking about 'cashing my chips'—I didn't care to take the risk."

Celeste winced. Despite her anger at him, the idea that she could have caused his death made her feel sick. "I wouldn't have actually killed you. I was just blowing off steam." She had no intention of admitting that she'd only considered it because he'd come to haunt her, obsess her, in a way nobody should be obsessed with a fictional character. She'd wanted to free herself. "If I'd known you were real, I would never have—"

"—Played God?" he interrupted, turning toward her, his dark gaze intensely cynical. "Oh, come on. Let's say I did appear in your living room and manage to convince you I'm real. Assuming you didn't kill me, you'd have tried to arrange some nauseatingly happy ending with some little"—his lip curled—"*romance heroine* like the ones Corinne creates."

Stung, she snapped, "Well, that's better than being tortured by aliens."

A hiss and thunk announced the arrival of their meal. Automatically, she walked over to key open the big wall panel with a touch of her finger. A pair of long flat boxes and sealed glasses sat inside. She took one of the boxes and a glass and handed it to him, then grabbed her own.

"The point is, I don't want you controlling my life." He strode to the gleaming blue dining table that sat in the center of the room and threw himself into a chair. With an easy flex of a muscular arm, he ripped the lid off his food, which instantly emitted a puff of steam as it flash-heated.

Celeste sat down opposite him and tore off her own lid more cautiously. "Well, we're even then," she said, cautiously eyeing the contents and trying to figure out if she'd ended up with the ambrosia snake. "I don't want you controlling mine, either. Particularly when it comes to giving me to some kinky alien dominant."

He slid a thumb along the lid of his seva to open it, then downed a deep swallow. "I've got to do *something* with you. Turning you loose to fend for yourself would be tantamount to that death sentence you were so worried about."

"So let me go home." Celeste copied his gesture to open her own cup. It instantly chilled in her hand. Warily, she took an ice-cold sip. The seva's taste seemed to explode in her mouth, vivid and sweetly sharp and completely unlike anything she'd ever tasted before. She tried to remember what it was made from. Some kind of alien root . . .

He lifted a brow at her. "How? I searched for years trying to figure out a way to get access to your dimension, without success. It took Mykhayl's spell and the blood of a dragon to get you here—neither of which are available in this universe."

Celeste put down her glass and stared at him in horror. If he was right, she was trapped. "Can't you communicate with Mykh somehow? Ask him to send me home?"

Jarred shook his head. "The only way we were ever able to speak is when both of you drew us into your universe. And even then, we were stuck in a kind of limbo between the dimensions."

Celeste frowned. "Why did Mykh do that?"

"Do what?"

"Transport you both into limbo?"

He forked a bite of something unidentifiable from his plate. "He didn't. I told you, you did that."

"That's impossible." She waved a dismissive hand and took another sip of seva.

"The same way it was impossible for you to kill Garr?" Jarred swallowed his mouthful of whatever and shook his head. "Look, I don't understand the physics of it, either. All I know is, whenever you worked on one of your books, I would be dragged into your universe. I could see and hear what you were doing, but I couldn't communicate with you. Mykhayl and I could talk if he happened to show up in limbo at the same time, but otherwise, we were completely cut off."

Celeste rubbed her forehead, feeling a tension headache gathering behind her eyebrows. "There has to be a way back."

"There's not," he said bluntly. "And even if there was, I wouldn't let you go. You'd kill me."

Stung, she glared at him. "I would not!"

"You would." His tone was as cold and hard as frozen steel. "And for the exact same reason I'm not letting you leave. You couldn't afford to take the chance I'd eventually figure out a way to get to you again—and decide to kill you."

She swallowed as her mouth went dry. "You wouldn't do that."

"You were pretty convinced I would when we got here," he pointed out. "In fact, you thought I was going to space you."

"Because you were deliberately trying to terrify me!"

"You should have been terrified. There have been times I *would* have killed you."

A chill snaked up her spine. She was suddenly very glad Mykhayl hadn't known how to work that spell when Garr was murdered. Tilting her chin at him, she hoped the fear didn't show in her eyes. "So why not let me fend for myself in your universe?"

"You wouldn't last a day," Jarred told her with a snort. "It would be like turning a medieval peasant loose in your time. Assuming he didn't get hit by a cargo transport . . ."

She frowned, then realized he meant a truck.

". . . he'd have no skills, no way to make a living. He'd starve. *You'd* starve."

"What do you care?" Celeste demanded, staring at him with narrowed eyes. "I'm the bitch who killed Garr, remember?"

He shrugged. "But as you've pointed out, you had no way of knowing what you were doing. I've decided you don't deserve to die—"

"That's big of you."

"And since I brought you here," he continued, ignoring the sarcasm, "I have some responsibility for you. With De'Lar, you could learn what you need to know while earning your keep—"

"On my back." Celeste glanced up sharply from her plate as she stabbed her fork into the dark lump that was apparently the entree. "Sorry, I really don't like the idea of being anybody's whore."

"Well, fucking *is* about the only marketable skill you have," Jarred retorted with deliberate crudity. After pausing long enough to calmly fork a bite into his mouth and chew, he swallowed and said, "The way I look at it, it's either De'Lar or it's the Sons of God."

Her own fork halfway to her lips, Celeste froze and stared across the table at him. The Sons of God were a fanatic religious cult that made the Pennsylvania Amish of her own time look like secular humanists. "Forget that! Those jerks don't even think women have souls. They're like a Christian version of the Taliban!"

"Taliban?" He lifted a brow as if he didn't recognize the name, then shrugged. "The point is, all they require of a woman is fertility. You can manage that much."

She put down her fork and said with careful control, "You are not abandoning me on some dirtball with a bunch of misogynist zealots who believe women are the source of all sin. I'd rather be De'Lar's sex toy."

He smiled slightly. "In that case, I suggest you help me prove you're a submissive. Because if you don't pass De'Lar's test, I'm dropping you off at Christ Colony."

Celeste stared at him as her heart sank. Jarred didn't make empty threats. If he said he'd do it, he would.

She couldn't afford that. There would be no way off Christ Colony—ships stopped there only rarely. At least on Kyristari, she would have a reasonable chance of freeing herself, either by escaping or simply talking De'Lar into turning her loose once she knew enough to make it on her own. Then she'd try to find a way to return home. She was damned if she was just going to take Jarred's word that another dimensional jump was impossible.

Celeste frowned. The problem with that plan was that it sounded as if it could take years. Unfortunately, it also seemed to be the only game in town. Which meant Jarred was right. She was going to have to go along with his game, much as it galled her.

She was going to have to learn to play sexsub.

Jarred watched his captive process her options—and find them not at all to her liking. He smiled darkly. Now she knew how he'd felt all these years.

Morosely, she forked up a bite of ambrosia snake, popped it into her mouth, and began to grimly chew. He knew the taste had hit her when her eyes widened and she focused her attention on her plate. "Hey, that's good!" Suddenly she looked up at him with narrow eyes. "It's not the snake, is it? . . . No, on the other hand, I don't think I want to know." She speared another bite and popped it into her mouth with a soft moan.

That tiny sound grabbed him by the dick like a demanding female hand. Jarred straightened in his seat, instantly hardening. *Damn,* he thought, fighting his lust as she worked her way through the snake, *I've had her twice today, in one way or another. I can't be hungry for her again.*

But as Celeste slowly slid a forkfull into her mouth, her tongue flicking out to capture a drop of creamy sauce that slipped from the tines, Jarred felt the heat intensify between his legs. She was so incredibly sensual . . .

He remembered how she'd writhed as he'd licked and sucked her glistening sex. How she'd ground fiercely up at him when he'd fucked her, her hard nipples teasing his chest, her skin so pale and soft and smooth against his own darker male flesh. Shifting in his seat, he surreptitiously reached under the table and adjusted the fit of his armor.

Suddenly an image flashed through his mind: Celeste, helplessly bound and twisting in pleasure as De'Lar took her with long thrusts.

Jarred frowned.

Given her beauty and intense sensuality, he had no doubt she'd soon become his friend's favorite sexsub. And despite her bitter protests, Jarred suspected it wouldn't be long before Celeste fell for the big Kyristari king. Beyond his obvious looks, De'Lar had the kind of slick charm women liked.

Jarred himself had never been any good at that kind of thing, never had a talent for coming up with smooth lines of pakshit. Not that he'd needed to. Women fell into his bed fast enough as it was.

Celeste's agile pink tongue licked the last of the ambrosia sauce from her fork. It was too damn easy to imagine her licking De'Lar's thick cock the same way.

Well, for the next two weeks at least, Celeste and that talented tongue belonged to him. And he was going to take advantage of every second he had them.

Rising from his seat, Jarred stalked around the table to catch his naked captive by the arm as she put down her fork. "Come on."

"What?" she asked, bewildered, as he pulled her to her feet. "And why are you looking so pissed all the sudden?"

"You said you wanted a bath," he reminded her, hustling her toward the door. "And I've got something else I want you to do with that mouth."

Celeste hurried down the corridor, intensely aware of Jarred's large hand engulfing her elbow, his powerful body at her back. She was still a bit sore from the last time he'd had her, yet she could sense waves of hot, angry lust pouring off him yet again. *High-handed 'borg creep.*

She could feel her body going wet between the thighs, readying for his use.

And that was what really ticked her off. No matter how angry she got at his arrogant belief that whatever he did to her was justified—despite the obvious injustice of it all—something in her responded to him. *Good God. Is he right? Am I some kind of sexual submissive?*

It was an appalling thought. She remembered the shame on Corinne's face the time Celeste had to come free her after her jerk ex-husband had left her tied to the bed. It was lucky she'd been able to reach the phone. Celeste hadn't found anything in the least erotic about that situation; she'd just wanted to beat in Dylan's smirking face.

So why was the idea of being dominated by Jarred so arousing?

God, she hoped Mykhayl didn't indulge *his* kinky tendencies with her sister. True, he had a romance hero's built-in decency, so he probably wouldn't hurt her intentionally, but he might not realize how fragile Corinne was until it was too late. Particularly given how furious he'd looked before he'd sent them here.

Jarred, on the other hand, didn't give a damn. He might be heroic, but he could also be ruthless as hell in pursuit of his goals. And at the moment, Celeste knew his primary goal was to drive her right out of her mind.

He hustled her through the door of his quarters. She caught no more than a glimpse of the furnishings she'd described in her books before he hauled her into the sprawling bathroom.

She'd always figured that anybody living alone in an interstellar vessel would want big rooms and lush decorations to keep from going nuts from boredom. The *Vengeance*'s head bore out that theory with a tub damn near big enough to swim laps in. Sunk into the floor and built more or less like a Jacuzzi, it dominated the oval room. Water poured into its broad, deep basin from a dozen nozzles. Evidently Jarred had used his computer implants to order the ship to fill it for him.

"Get in," he growled.

Celeste thought about telling him where to go, just on general principles . . . but she did want that bath. So, after a brief hesitation, she started down the steps that led down into the tub.

Deliciously warm currents frothed around her ankles, feeling so silken she forgot her outrage. With a sigh of raw pleasure, she descended until she could bend her knees and let herself sink to her chin in the hip-deep water. Around her, throbbing jets gently pummeled her body, cleansing it of any lingering stickiness.

Then she looked up and realized with a little skip of her heart that she was about to get sticky all over again. Jarred stared down at her with hot dark eyes as he leaned against a mirrored vanity. Popping the seals of his armored boots, he kicked his long legs free, then shucked out of his pants.

She licked her lips. "I don't want company."

"But I do." He turned to toss the pants through the bathroom door. "And since I'm the dominant, I get what I want. Unless you'd rather spend the rest of your life on Christ Colony in a semi-permanent state of pregnancy."

Celeste opened her mouth to growl a retort, only to forget what she'd been about to say as he turned, gorgeously nude. His cock jutted from his brawny torso in a display of male hunger that took her breath. Add long, muscled legs and a tight ass, and she had a view that made her hormones sit up and sing the Hallelujah chorus.

And given what she knew he could do to her . . .

Damn, Celeste thought. *He may be an arrogant jerk, but he is a hot arrogant jerk.*

To make matters even steamier, he was staring as if he wanted to eat her. Slowly. With a spoon. Licking off the whipped cream as he went.

As her nipples hardened helplessly at that particular image, Jarred descended the steps toward her. Celeste stood up so quickly, water sloshed. Crouching put her at eye-level with his cock, a view she found far too distracting to her peace of mind.

Groping for something to say that would hide her reaction to his animal sexuality, she gave him a challenging stare. "You wouldn't really abandon me with those religious lunatics, would you?"

He shrugged. "At least you'd be safe."

"Safe?" She glared, trying to work up a comfortable head of outrage. "Jarred, those guys consider criminal domestic violence a sacred duty. I don't want to spend the rest of my life as a punching bag for some self-appointed 'saint.' "

"Then you'd better concentrate on doing a damn good imitation of a Kyristari sexsub, because that's your only other option." He turned his massive back on her to fill his palms from a nozzle that poured liquid soap into them.

"It's a big galaxy, Jarred." Celeste eyed the muscled topography of his back and felt her heartbeat pick up speed. "There's got to be somewhere else I can go."

"Not if you don't want to get locked up as a vagrant." He turned and reached for her, liquid soap dripping from between his long fingers.

"Isn't there a school or something I could attend to learn whatever it is you think I need to learn?" She caught her breath as his soapy hands began to slowly stroke away the residue of his passion from her breasts and belly. His touch was slow and hypnotic, though gentleness was the last thing she would have expected after the way he'd hauled her in here.

"Probably, but if you think I'm paying for it, you can think again." Despite the brusque words, his low voice rasped with hunger. She looked up into his face, tracing the chiseled angles of cheekbones and chin, the sensual curve of his mouth, the line of his thick, dark brows over eyes that examined and possessed.

"I could—" Celeste broke off as his slick thumbs stroked her nipples. "I could pay you back."

His gaze flicked to her face with a hot interest that turned the offer into something far more erotic than she'd intended. "And how do you propose to do that?" He reached down a muscled arm and cupped her sex.

Celeste bit her lip as one long finger began to explore between her slick lips. "I could get a job."

"Doing what?" Jarred smiled tauntingly as he continued to explore.

She struggled to formulate a coherent answer. His wicked fingers made it impossible to think. "Writing. I'm sure storytelling hasn't changed any in four hundred years. I mean, we still read Shakespeare in my time . . ."

A second finger suddenly joined the first deep inside her sex. "And screw some other poor bastard in another universe? Don't you think you've got enough to pay for right here?" He drew out, then stroked inside again, thumbing her hard clit. "Though I'm getting some fascinating ideas about how to collect—"

"Jarred!" She writhed, but he flattened his other hand over her backside to hold her still.

"Mmm. You're really tight, Celeste," he purred, working his finger in and out in slow, suggestive strokes. "Though you may not stay that way if I have anything to say about it. And I do." His mouth twisted. "De'Lar may not find you so much fun after all."

Her eyes widened as she looked down at the broad shaft nudging her hip. He could actually make good on that threat.

"Luckily for you, I've got another orifice in mind right now." Reaching up, he wrapped a big fist in her hair and gently tugged her head down until her face was inches from his erection. "Suck my cock like a good sexsub, Celeste."

She hesitated as arousal quivered through her. Then, with a soft moan, she leaned forward and took him deep.

FOUR

The sensation of Celeste's silken mouth sliding up his shaft was so hot, so intense, Jarred had to bite back a moan. Tightening his grip on his fistful of her long blond curls, he watched in barely contained lust as more and more of his shaft disappeared between her soft lips. "Your knees," he growled, arousal deepening his voice into a rasp. "Get on your knees."

She obeyed, sinking deeper into the water, the movement sending a warm wave surging around his hips. Just as he'd intended, the position forced her to tilt her head so he could see more of her face as she suckled him. Green eyes met his, filled with an expression of voluptuous surrender. Jarred shuddered.

Her tongue laved the head of his shaft as her soft lips drew hard, sliding back and forth. Unable to resist, he made a slow, shallow thrust. It felt so incredible he began gently rocking his hips, savoring the sweet, raw eroticism of being serviced by the woman who'd tormented him for so long.

"Do you have any idea how many times I've imagined fucking your mouth?" he demanded, tightening his grip on her hair. "Dreamed of forcing you to your knees and taking you this way?" He shuddered and arched his hips. "Deeper, dammit."

As obedient as any wanton fantasy he'd ever had, she took his cock farther into slick paradise. He thought about making her swallow his come and had to bite back a moan.

Celeste had given her share of blowjobs over the years. Depending on her partner, the act had been a mildly pleasant chore at best; at worst, a tiring pain in the ass.

But kneeling at Jarred Varrain's feet and sucking his cock as he growled sensual orders at her was one of the hottest, kinkiest things she'd ever done.

Damn, maybe he's right, she thought, as she tried to work him deeper. *Maybe I am a sexsub.*

She didn't like that thought any better than she had the last time it had occurred to her.

He groaned in a deep, carnal rumble that made her sex grow creamy and swollen. Something about the sound reminded her of the way she'd begged him when he'd teased her with his cock.

She wondered suddenly if she could make *him* beg.

The idea was so irresistible she just had to try it. Seizing on every skill she'd ever learned, Celeste lifted off her knees, wrapped a hand around one of the tight cheeks of his ass, and swallowed every inch of him she possibly could.

Jarred's knees almost buckled as Celeste suddenly took him down her throat in a breathtaking rush of wet pleasure. She withdrew, then plunged him deep again, milking his shaft with ruthless skill. The sensation was so indescribably good he knew he wouldn't last more than a moment.

But just as he could feel the pressure building, she backed off. One slender hand wrapped around the base of his shaft and began to firmly stroke as the other caressed his balls. All the while, her tongue played loving court to his cock's sensitive head.

Over the next ten minutes, Jarred balanced on the sharp edge of a blazing orgasm as Celeste played him with lips and tongue and fingers—sucking, fondling, even nibbling gently. Then without warning, she'd deep throat him again.

Straining for the orgasm she never quite let him have, he didn't notice the submission in her eyes had been replaced by calculation.

The sensations she created were so intense he forgot his hunger for revenge, forgot his drive to dominate. All he knew was the sight of her kneeling at his feet, plunging him deeper into pleasure every time she took him into her mouth. Celeste, the woman he'd dreamed of for so long, his obsession and his fantasy . . .

Jarred felt the burning wave of his orgasm begin its roll up from his balls. He threw back his head, gasping. But just before his climax hit, she paused, denying him that last hot stroke he needed.

"God, Celeste, please . . ." he groaned. "Don't stop."

She swallowed his shaft to the balls in a single hot swoop that kicked him over the edge. Arching his back, he came in rolling jets of fire, one hand fisted in her hair. He roared in pleasure and triumph.

When it was finally over, he let himself sink back in the water to float bonelessly in the glowing aftermath.

"Jarred?" she asked, her voice a silken purr.

He opened his dazed eyes to see her wearing a taunting grin. "This time I made *you* beg," Celeste said.

* * *

All right, she thought half an hour later, *that was not the smartest thing I've ever said.*

She was flat on her back on a fluidmat bed, her wrists crossed on the pillow over her head, her thighs spread wide.

Completely unable to move.

After she'd made her little announcement, Jarred had gotten out of the tub and dragged her into his quarters, where he'd dug a cerebral control headband out of a drawer and snapped it into place around her forehead. The band had instantly emitted a field that blocked her brain's commands to her muscles; she would have collapsed into a heap if he hadn't caught her.

Without a word, he'd carried her into Garr's old cabin, where he'd arranged her limp body on the bed. The whole time, his face had looked as if it had been cast from frozen steel. His utter lack of expression spoke of rage far more eloquently than any ranting threats he could have made.

He'd scared the living hell out of her.

Straightening, he'd looked down at her. "I assume you know what else I can do with that band?"

Her fear was so complete she couldn't have answered even if she hadn't been paralyzed. Still, he must have read something in her eyes that pleased him. Giving her a rather sinister smile, he'd gently turned her head on the pillow to face a sculpture of a woman sitting in an inset wall niche. Naked and bound, the little figure seemed to writhe in voluptuous invitation. "Unless you want to spend the rest of your life on Christ Colony being punished for the sins of Eve, you'd better follow that example." Then he'd walked out.

Note to self, Celeste thought now. *Do not screw with Jarred.*

Restlessly she tried to roll over, only to find once again that her body wouldn't obey. Hell, she couldn't even move her eyes; they were focused on that stupid statue. She supposed she was lucky he let her blink.

Between the cerebral band and his computer implants, Jarred could manipulate her body like a puppet, and there was nothing she could do about it. Worse, he could use the band to broadcast sensory illusions into her brain, rather like the virtual reality glasses some game designers had been playing with back in her own time.

He'd once used a cerebral band on an enemy of his after slipping it onto the man in his sleep. Jarred had suspected his foe was the spymaster for a mole inside the Stellar Compact government, but he hadn't been able to prove it. The band gave him that proof by making the spymaster's brain see Jarred as the man suspected of being the mole. The spymaster awoke, thought he was talking to the traitor, and discussed the details of the next information exchange with Jarred. Both the spymaster and the mole had ended up in a Stellar Compact prison.

Jarred could use the band the same way on Celeste, creating any illusion he damn well wanted. And since none of it was real, he could get pretty nasty without hurting her.

But would he actually use the band to torture her, as he'd implied? She couldn't believe he'd go that far. True, he'd been pretty pissed off . . .

No, he was just trying to unnerve her.

Maybe.

Helplessly, she stared at the silver sexsub statue. *Damn,* she thought absently, *that's lewd.* The thing writhed in simulated ecstasy in its niche, all tits and legs and ass as it morphed into different obscene positions. It was so damn tacky, no wonder Garr had bought it. It had probably appealed to his warped sense of humor.

And Jarred wanted her to act like that? *Dream on, you big 'borg jerk.*

She again tried to look away from the pornographic figure, but her eyes stubbornly refused to obey. Her nose began to itch. Automatically, she tried to reach up and scratch it, but her hand wouldn't move, either.

Suddenly it hit Celeste all over again that she was totally paralyzed. What if she needed to go to the bathroom? What if they were attacked by a Zyris slave ship? What if a chunk of space debris got past the shields and hit the outer bulkhead? She'd be sucked helplessly into space, unable to even grab onto anything to save herself.

Okay, now you're losing it, Celeste told herself, trying to regain control of her skidding imagination. Damn Jarred anyway for doing this to her. The son of a bitch. She should have bitten off his dick instead of sucking it.

Rage rose in her, hot and searing. She stared bitterly at the twisting figure, watching it silently beg any male in the vicinity to fuck it. That's what Jarred wanted her to become.

Damn him, damn him damn him DAMN HIM DAMN HIM **DAMN HIM** *DAMN HIM* . . .

The statue took off out of its niche like a rocket and shot across the room. A series of soft thuds announced its impact on the carpet.

Jolted out of her frenzy of helpless rage, Celeste stared at the now-empty niche in shock. *Did I do that? No, I couldn't have. Unless . . .*

She knew telekinesis was possible in this universe; Jarred had fought a telekinetic assassin once, and Garr had been both precognitive and telepathic. Of course, she'd never had any such abilities herself—unless Jarred was right, and she'd somehow made everything happen here.

Oh, God. Maybe she really *had* killed Garr.

What if Jarred came in and saw the statue lying all the way across the room? He'd know she'd thrown it with something other than her paralyzed hands. What would he do?

Celeste was deeply certain she didn't want to find out. She had to put the statue back. But how? She couldn't see it. Hell, she couldn't even turn her head to look. Maybe if she pictured the thing in her mind. That's how Garr had always performed his psychic feats in her books . . .

Staring hard at the niche, Celeste remembered how it had looked sitting there twisting in lewd invitation. As if she was someone else, she imagined watching herself lying in the bed while the statue rose slowly off the floor and floated through the air.

She stared at the niche with such ferocious concentration, a headache took up a slow, deep throb behind her eyes. Sweat broke out on her forehead.

But nothing else happened.

Dammit, she thought, *I did it before. I can do it again. Concentrate!*

With a silent snarl, she focused all her energy on the image of the statue, on willing it to lift from the floor and levitate back to its niche.

Nothing.

Wait. She . . . felt . . . something. A sense of weight. And was that movement in the corner of her vision?

Celeste tried to turn her head, forgetting that her body couldn't obey. Her paralysis startled her so badly her concentration broke. She thought she glimpsed something fall.

Thud.

She wanted to scream. She'd been doing it! She'd almost had it!

Okay, okay, calm down. Try again.

Focusing her energies again, she reached out to the statue. This time she definitely felt something, as if she'd lifted it in one hand. Her skull was banging like a kettle drum now, but she ignored the pain. She was going to do this, by God!

A flash of silver rose in her peripheral vision. This time Celeste didn't let it break her concentration, instead focusing everything she had on guiding the statue back to its niche.

Wavering, it advanced slowly into her field of vision, still writhing enthusiastically. Her headache rang like the Anvil Chorus. She stared hard at the niche. The statue glided into it . . .

And promptly collapsed on its side. Blast it to hell, she'd put the thing down on its head.

"Celeste?"

Oh, God. Jarred was coming down the corridor. She had to right the statue before he walked in. Frantically, Celeste sent out a burst of energy so intense she could almost feel the burn on her skin. The statue flipped upright just as he walked in the door.

Fortunately, he wouldn't have been able to see the movement inside the wall niche. At least, she hoped not. Barely breathing, Celeste watched from the corner of one eye as he moved to stand over her. He frowned, staring down at her face. "Are you all right? You're sweating."

Feeling him release his control over her speech, she ground out, "I have a headache, and I need to go to the bathroom."

Both were the utter truth, as she knew his sensors would tell him. His frown deepened. Her muscles jerked as the band suddenly freed her. Celeste popped out of bed and raced for the room's attached head as if shot from a cannon.

She barely made it to the toilet before she began throwing up.

*   *   *

Jarred listened to his prisoner violently expelling the contents of her stomach and fought a twinge of guilt. He could sympathize. In the past, an enemy or two had used his computer to paralyze him. And he'd hated it. At least with chains, you still had some ability to move, but paralysis turned your body into a cage of flesh. Both experiences had given him such a roaring case of claustrophobia he never used the band himself except with prisoners he couldn't control any other way.

Which, of course, hadn't been the case with Celeste. He'd simply lost his temper. It had been so galling to realize he'd begged her for release after he'd sworn she'd be the one begging *him*.

But even as furious as he'd been, when he'd seen the panic in her green eyes, he'd almost taken the band off. It had been all he could do to walk out the door and leave her like that.

After he'd gone to his quarters, he'd found himself lying awake, straining to hear any sound, any indication that she might be suffering. That mysterious thud had given him the excuse he'd needed to check on her.

How his enemies would laugh. The implacable Jarred Varrain, gone too soft to take even minor revenge on the woman who had tortured him for a decade.

Garr had warned him.

His friend had known about Celeste, of course. Whenever Jarred's consciousness was snatched into limbo, his body fell into a coma, something that was pretty damn hard to miss.

In fact, it had been Garr who'd helped him figure out what was happening, though they'd both found the whole thing pretty hard to believe. His friend had been a powerful telepath—brain to Varrain's considerable brawn—but even Garr had never heard of anyone with the raw psychic strength to influence events in another universe.

But every time Jarred had returned from his involuntary dimensional jaunts raging that one day he'd make Celeste pay, Garr gave him a maddening grin. "You won't be able to touch a hair on her little blond head, my 'borg friend. You've always had a soft spot for women, and you know it. You spent too many years trying to win the approval of your bitch of a mother."

Garr had known him far too well.

Jarred was considering going into the head after Celeste when she staggered out, faintly green, a sheen of sweat on her face. A quick sensor scan told him she was still suffering from a vicious headache. "I'll get you something for that," he told her grudgingly, and stalked out.

A moment later he was back to press a small drug patch onto her forehead. The lines of pain between her eyes relaxed almost instantly as the patch did its job. "Thanks. Damn, that's better than Tylenol," she said with a sigh, collapsing on the bed.

Having no idea what Tylenol was—and frankly not caring—he gruffly told her to get some sleep.

Celeste's eyes widened as she realized he wasn't going to paralyze her again. Jarred turned and walked out before she had a chance to comment. If she was inclined to gloat about his weakness, he didn't want to know about it. He really didn't want his temper to push him into doing something he'd regret.

Like kissing her.

Celeste stared at Jarred's retreating back in wonder. Mercy was not a word she generally associated with him, yet somehow he'd sensed she couldn't take another second of paralysis. On the other hand, he hadn't removed the control band, either. That was troubling, given the thing's powers.

Well, she wasn't going to worry about it any more tonight. She needed some sleep. Her little psychic experiment had drained the energy right out of her.

With a weary sigh, she crawled onto the fluidmat bed, curled up on her side, and closed her eyes.

A moment later Celeste opened them again to stare at the sex-sub statue. It lifted a few inches off the shelf, then settled gently back down.

With a satisfied smile, she let her lids close again. In seconds, she was asleep.

FIVE

Celeste jerked awake to the sounds of an exotic, high-pitched screech. And froze.

She wasn't in Garr's bedroom anymore. Actually, she had no idea *where* the hell she was. It definitely wasn't the ship.

The fluidmat bed she had gone to sleep on had been replaced by a nest of curling, feathery—things. Leaves? Flowers? She couldn't tell which, but they felt soft and sensuous against her skin, and their scent was sweetly exotic.

She was, of course, naked. Jarred seemed to prefer her that way.

Cautiously Celeste lifted her head and glanced around. She lay in a clearing ringed with tall, alien vegetation in unearthly pastel shades. The light had a bluish tinge, as though dusk was falling. Two moons hung overhead, one white, the other faintly pink.

What had happened? How had she gotten here? She didn't remember leaving the *Vengeance* . . .

The control band. Of course. He'd never taken it off her. Jarred could easily create an illusion like this with his computer, then use the band to feed it into her mind. If that were the case, she was still on the ship, probably lying in Garr's cabin while her captor spun this virtual planet around her.

But why?

Stupid question, she thought dryly. Knowing him, it probably had something to do with sex—and some plot to both dominate her and drive her nuts.

So where was he?

Celeste rolled out of her nest and rose to her feet. She took a wary look around, but if a hulking cyborg stud lurked in the fluffy bushes, she didn't see him.

Well, she could sit tight or go looking for him. And since this was the first time in hours she'd been free to move around—even if it was only in virtual reality—she wasn't inclined to stay put.

Celeste set off, moving toward the nearest stand of the alien tree-things. She thought she could hear a musical patter coming from that direction, like a stream chuckling over rocks. She decided to investigate.

Besides, she figured she should take advantage of the opportunity to stretch her legs before Jarred got around to tying her up again.

The air was full of strange sounds she suspected were animals or birds, or at least the alien equivalent thereof. Chirps and squeaks and cries, like the soundtrack for a Tarzan movie. She wondered what kind of critter produced those noises, and hoped that whatever it was didn't have a taste for science fiction novelists. Glancing around curiously as she stepped between the "trees," she tried to spot the source of the racket.

It was much darker in here than it had been out in the clearing.

Celeste felt the hair rise on the back of her neck. Just exactly what did Jarred have in mind for this little simulation of his? *Here's hoping he never saw* Friday the 13th . . .

For a moment she considered retreating back into the clearing where the light was better, but she discarded that idea. It would soon be just as dark out there, and besides, she had no intention of letting the big jerk know he'd spooked her.

The sound of the stream got louder, and she peered through the vegetation ahead. Something shimmered like moonlight shining on something reflective. She lengthened her stride as the alien forest around her grew darker.

Where the hell was Jarred? If he was about to jump out from behind a tree at her, she swore to God she'd deck him.

A dense screen of feathery bushes rose in front of her, blocking her way. She pushed through them, shivering a little as the long, fern-like branches brushed her thighs and belly. She thought for a moment of her bare feet, which back home would have been stabbed by a dozen rocks and sticks by now. She was definitely not in Kansas anymore.

Not that she'd ever been to Kansas in the first place.

Finally Celeste forced her way clear of the oddly amorous plants into another clearing. Night had fallen with unnatural speed. Luckily the twin moons cast enough light to see by, despite the distracting double shadows they threw.

For a moment, she simply stood there, letting her eyes adjust. She stood on the edge of a small oblong pool at the base of a rocky cliff; the chuckling sound she'd heard was the sound of a pretty waterfall tumbling down the rocks like a fall of silver coins. Celeste looked up, her eyes automatically tracking up the rock face, following the path of the water as it bounced from stone to stone . . .

At the top, the figure of a man stood on the cliff's edge, silhouetted against the star-flecked sky. She couldn't make out the details—just the outline of broad shoulders and narrow hips and long, long legs. For just an instant, she thought she saw a flash of red light, as though his eyes glowed.

"There you are," Celeste whispered. Every last drop of spit dried from her mouth.

Teeth flashed white in the moonlight in what might have been a grin—were those *fangs?*—just before the figure flung himself off the edge of the cliff. Her heart jammed into her throat as she watched the leanly muscled body plummet toward the pool below. *Damn,* she thought, forgetting for an instant that the whole thing was an illusion. *I hope that's deep enough.*

He hit the water with barely a splash and disappeared. She licked her lips and stared at the spot, waiting for him to surface. Everything had gone quiet, as if even the alien beasties sensed there was a predator among them.

Nothing.

Where the hell has he gone . . . ?

A dark head suddenly appeared from under the water, shattering the pattern of bright reflection on the pool's surface. Twin red lights that were definitely eyes glittered from the shadowed face.

"Run," Jarred said in a growling rumble.

Celeste whirled on her heel and obeyed, completely spooked. And, much as she hated to admit it, aroused.

She barely felt the slap of alien ferns against her breasts and thighs as she catapulted through the bushes like a hare one bounce ahead of a wolf. Back on Earth, she would have been lucky not to run face-first into a tree, but Celeste wasn't worried about that here. In this virtual world of Jarred's, she wouldn't do any slapstick pratfalls. That wasn't the point.

The point was running. And getting caught.

It was the thought of what would come after the "getting caught" part that made her nipples harden to stiff points as she ran. She had a humiliating suspicion that she was going wet between her thighs again.

Had she really seen fangs? What the hell was he planning?

Celeste threw a quick glance over her shoulder—and almost swallowed her tongue as she saw him bearing down on her, all hungry masculinity barely a leap behind. She squeaked and darted around a tree. His snarl of frustration lifted the hair on the back of her neck as his reaching hand missed. He spun like a puma to shoot after her. Celeste scrambled around a clump of brush, feeling like something small and edible.

Which was no doubt exactly how he saw her.

She zigged left, zagged right, and jumped a half-seen stump— just as something slammed into the back of her knees. She yelped as bushes and sky and alien trees cartwheeled around her. Then an impact jarred the breath out of her—hard, but not as hard as it could have been. Jarred had wrapped himself around her to absorb most of the force as they struck the ground.

Before Celeste could do more than realize she'd damn well better escape, he rolled her beneath him. And suddenly she was once again covered by a blanket of muscled masculinity in a very dangerous mood.

Panicking, she flailed at him. She could have saved herself the effort. An instant later, both her wrists were encircled in a huge hand as Jarred's hips settled neatly between her thighs. She bucked under him, but only succeeded in grinding her crotch against his impressive hard-on. "Get off!"

He laughed, white teeth flashing. They looked perfectly human, but Celeste peered at them, unnerved. "I don't think so," he told her in a low wolf rumble. "I caught you, and now . . ."

"You'll what?" she challenged. "Eat me?"

He lifted off her just slightly and deliberately scanned her body. Glancing down, she saw her own breasts, gleaming white in the moonlight and quivering with her panting breaths. "Now that you mention it, you do look . . . appetizing."

Jarred lowered his head to capture one stiff nipple in his mouth. Celeste quivered helplessly, hoping those fangs she'd seen were just an effect he'd thrown in to spook her and not something he was planning to use in this little VR simulation of his.

But all he subjected her to was several searing moments of hot pleasure as he suckled her sensitive flesh. When he finally lifted his head again, the tight pink point felt wet and aching in the cool evening air.

Jarred propped his chin on her chest and smiled. "My sensors tell me you're a little spooked, goddess. That writer's imagination must be working overtime." Reaching down with his free hand, he stroked a finger into her wet core. She caught her breath.

"Wondering what wicked things I've got in mind?" He flicked his tongue over her nipple again, rolling his hips suggestively against hers. "With you wearing that control band, I can make you see anything, experience anything."

She swallowed. "Jarred . . ."

"Mmmmm." He shifted until his thick shaft nestled between the soft, damp lips of her vulva. "Definitely nervous. I wonder, goddess—have *you* ever wondered what it would be like to do it with someone who isn't quite"—his voice dropped and roughened into a low, animal growl—"human?"

Celeste's heart leaped into her throat.

Suddenly the moonlight blazed full into Jarred's face as if someone had switched on a spotlight. The hair on his head began to lengthen with impossible speed, like one of those stop-motion nature films of grass growing. At the same time, his goatee spread across his face and down his throat to meet the ruff on his chest. It, too, expanded as she watched, rolling along his body in a wave of velvet fur.

Until every inch of Jarred was covered in a rich pelt of inky silk that was as short and soft as a cat's.

Gaping in shock, Celeste looked up to meet eyes that glowed like the Terminator's. His grin displayed a set of inch-long fangs curving from upper and lower jaws. With a squawk of absolute terror, she went wild, flailing and writhing as she fought to free herself from the two-hundred-pound werewolf who held her. Grinning, he let her go.

Without taking time to question what he was up to, Celeste twisted in his arms, clawed for purchase in the dirt, and shot out from under him. She hadn't even made it all the way to her feet when he pounced, flattening her like a mouse under a cat's paw.

"Mmmm. Dinner," that rumbling almost-Jarred voice said in her ear.

"This isn't funny, you bastard!" she yelled, squirming desperately.

"No, but I'm enjoying it anyway." He grabbed her wrists, gathered them in on hand, and pinned them to the ground over her head. His muscled body covered in all that silken fur felt both sensuous and menacing against her naked back.

Acutely aware of her helplessness in the face of his superhuman strength, Celeste bit her lip. "What are you going to do?"

"What do you think?" he purred, rolling his hips against her bare ass. The only part of him that wasn't covered in fur nudged her butt with rapacious heat.

"Raping me won't prove I'm a sexsub."

"I'm not going to rape you." He reached under her body with his free hand to discover a tight, pebbled nipple. "I don't have to." Wickedly, he brushed the hard little peak with his thumb, back and forth, sending a sweet bloom of desire through her body. That fur-covered palm squeezed and stroked as his big body rubbed seductively across hers—her back, her rump, the length of her legs. The sensation of his short, silky pelt caressing her bare skin was impossibly decadent, impossibly erotic. She heard a low pleasure moan and realized it was her own.

"That's it," he murmured. His long hair brushed the side of her face as he leaned close. "Relax. You know I'm not going to hurt you." He laughed, low and suggestive. "Not unless you want me to, anyway."

He shifted, lifting his weight off her so he could pull her up onto her knees. She bit her lip and whimpered as she felt his long shaft angle against her bottom.

One velvet hand reached between her thighs. A strong finger stroked her tender lips, slid between them, burrowed deep enough to make her back arch. "My, you *are* creamy," he purred.

She actually heard a soft, liquid sound as he thrust that finger in and out. He added a second, stretching her a little more, forcing her to imagine the deep strokes of the broad cock she could feel pressing against her backside.

A pointed tongue flicked across the sensitive lobe of her ear, startling another moan out of her. "You do realize you're mine now?" he said. "Completely at my mercy. And I think"—he licked the straining cord of her throat—"you like it that way." She closed her eyes and whimpered.

Which was when she felt the press of four sharp points against her jugular as he closed his fangs in an almost-bite. She gasped in arousal, knowing at some gut level that he wouldn't hurt her. Threaten, yes. Dominate, yes. And God knew he was perfectly willing to scare the hell out of her. Yet despite it all, she sensed she could trust him.

Whether he wanted to be trustworthy or not.

Abruptly he released her captive wrists. "Get on your hands and knees," he ordered hoarsely. "I want to fuck you from behind."

"Oh," she whispered. An erotic shiver stole over her skin. "All right." Swallowing, she leaned forward to brace her palms on the soft, rich soil as she pulled her knees under her.

"Lower," Jarred ordered. "On your elbows, ass in the air. I'm going to take you deep."

At his words, it seemed a liquid fist clenched inside her. Celeste bent her forearms until her hard nipples brushed the feathery fern bed beneath her. Without being told, she spread her knees even farther apart to open herself completely for his cock.

God, she was hot. Maybe hotter than she'd ever been in her life.

He moved to cover her. Something thick and round and silken brushed the passion-swollen lips of her vulva. Bracing a brawny furred arm beside her head, he set his shaft against her opening. And began to slide inside. Slowly.

The position made him feel even bigger than he had before. It seemed to take him forever to impale her on that endless cock, a delicious eternity of gliding slick flesh that opened and stretched. All the while, he made a rough, crooning sound in her ear as he relentlessly stuffed her full.

"I'll never get tired of fucking you," he whispered, his voice hot and hoarse. "There's just something about being inside you, feeling you all tight and liquid . . ." He drove in a shallow thrust that made her gasp. "And helpless. God, I love it when you're helpless."

With a low growl, he began to rut in a series of hard, ruthless digs that tore a gasp of pleasure-pain from her lips. Instinctively, she tried to jerk out from under him, but his massive hands slapped down and pinned her wrists beside her head, keeping her there while he rode her.

Her knees slid out from under her. Jarred followed her down, covering her completely, not even missing a stroke as he forced her legs farther apart. With an animal snarl, he settled down to ream her without mercy.

Celeste moaned, overwhelmed by the sensation of being covered in silky fur and male muscle as his rock-hard cock plunged in and out of her wet sex.

God, it felt so good.

She lifted her hips. He took the hint and released one wrist so he could reach around and finger her clit with every demanding stroke. Heat gathered in a burning ball deep in her belly, a building climax jolting closer to detonation each time he rammed himself home.

"Mine," Jarred snarled. "You're mine, and you'll always be mine no matter how many times De'Lar fucks you. Say it!"

Bracing herself against his next powerful thrust, she opened her mouth only to discover herself unable to form words.

"Say it!" He slammed deep.

"Yours!" she cried, the word popping free as her orgasm went off like a bomb in a wave of heat and mindless pleasure. "I'm yours!"

"Yes!" He arched his back, lodging his cock halfway to her throat, roaring as he came.

The world ripped apart with the force of his climax in an explosion of light.

The next thing Celeste knew, she was staring at the headboard of Garr's bed with Jarred's body draped heavily over hers. Disoriented, she stared at the powerful hand gripping her wrists. It was covered in smooth tanned skin instead of silken black fur.

She realized she and Jarred occupied the exact same position as they had in the VR illusion. Had she really run from him, or had that been an illusion, too?

One thing was certain: the cock deep inside her was definitely real. So was the powerful body covering hers like a hard, sweaty blanket, and the ache deep inside her where he'd fucked her without mercy.

Suddenly she remembered the way he'd demanded she acknowledge his possession. That had been real, too.

The implication was stunning. *Jarred was jealous of De'Lar.*

Which was nuts. He was the one who'd decided to give her to the Kyristari king. But what did it mean? Despite everything, was he beginning to care for her?

And why did that idea send such joy surging through her?

Jarred lay draped over Celeste, his softened cock still buried in her tight little sex. He felt completely wrung out—and oddly euphoric.

Damn, that had been the best sex he'd ever had in his life. He didn't think he'd ever been hotter. Chasing Celeste, capturing her, dominating and *taking* her . . . God, he'd never experienced anything more erotic.

And he wasn't quite sure why.

As he lay still, listening to her thudding heartbeat settle as his own decreased its frantic pounding, Jarred frowned. He'd dommed other women in scenes even more kinky—punishing Ayla with De'Lar's help came to mind—but none of them had ever had quite this much raw sexual intensity.

But then, none of the women had been Celeste.

Before Jarred could consider the implications of that idea in any detail, she stirred and murmured sleepily under him. He realized he must be getting heavy. With a regretful sigh, he rolled off of her onto his back.

Automatically, he reached out and drew her against him to nestle her head in the curve between his shoulder and chest. She fit perfectly, her blond curls tickling his cheek. Sighing, she relaxed into him.

He felt as if all his muscles had turned to softened butter—a sure mark of good sex if ever there was one. Suddenly a thought penetrated his haze of post-coital bliss: *Why is it so much better with her?*

And why does it feel so damn good to hold her now?

Now *that* was an unnerving thought. He could accept being hot and horny after wanting her for ten years—naturally it would be good after all that. But damn it, what was he doing cuddling her?

Galvanized, Jarred caught Celeste by one shoulder and gently pushed, intent on disentangling himself from her warm, fragrant weight. She jerked her head up off his chest, jolted from her doze. "Wha . . . ?"

"Go back to sleep," he said gruffly, sliding out of the bed.

Jarred looked down at her. For just an instant, her pretty green eyes blinked at him, wounded. Then her lashes lowered. Without another word, she rolled over and gave him her back. He hesitated, staring at the slim, lovely line of her naked spine as she curled around herself. He'd hurt her.

It shouldn't matter. Not after everything she'd done to him. Not after Garr. He turned on a bare heel and walked out, knowing it did matter. Entirely too damn much.

SIX

Two weeks later

Celeste floated cross-legged six inches above Garr's bed, her hands resting on her knees, her ears straining to detect any hint of movement from Jarred. She couldn't afford to let him catch her.

A blizzard of small objects orbited her like electrons around an atomic nucleus—the sexsub statue, a couple of styluses, five or six book chips, several kitschy knickknacks from Garr's collection. Levitating all that plus her own body wasn't easy; her gritty eyes burned from lack of sleep and she had her habitual telekinetic migraine. But that was better than feeling hurt over Jarred's equally habitual post-sex desertion—he always left after he finished with her—and it was certainly better than sleeping.

She didn't like sleeping anymore. Or at least, not until she'd exhausted herself too much to dream.

Celeste could never quite remember the nightmares she'd begun having two weeks ago, soon after Jarred dommed her in the were-wolf fantasy. No matter how she strained, she could never recall more of those dreams than an impression of blood and fear and horrible grief.

Just enough, in other words, to scare the hell out of her.

With a grim frown, Celeste flicked a finger and sent the sexsub statue flying at top speed toward the bulkhead. It slammed into the cushioning force field she'd erected and stuck like a dart in peanut butter.

As her entourage of knickknacks continued to orbit, she floated in the air and contemplated the trapped figure with weary satis-faction. Not bad. She was getting pretty damn powerful.

Maybe too powerful. Frown deepening, she massaged her aching temples. Garr had once had nightmares like hers. That wasn't a comforting comparison, because he'd been precognitive as well as telepathic. He'd had some particularly chilling dreams the week before he died.

What if, besides being telekinetic, she was a precog, too? What if those dreams she couldn't quite remember foretold a nightmar-ish future?

Boy, that sucked. What was the point of having precognitive dreams if you couldn't remember them well enough to do some-thing about the future they foretold? Celeste shuddered and pulled the sexsub statue from the force field with a telekinetic jerk. Sigh-ing, she sent it back into orbit.

Her migraine was taking on a particularly demanding thump. Taking a silent poll of her aching thighs and gritty eyes, she tried to determine whether it was safe to put everything down and go to sleep.

Not yet.

At least Jarred was doing his bit to tire her out, whether he knew it or not. Over the past two weeks, he'd conducted a determined assault on her senses, evidently designed to drive home his dominance in the most elemental way possible.

Damn, the man was creative. He could have made a fortune writing erotica, judging from the kinky scenarios he plunged her into every night. Sometimes he used the control band to create VR illusions, sometimes he put her in the rack—she'd named it Brutus—and sometimes he mixed and matched the two.

He was a wicked pirate captain having his way with a pretty captive, or a lusty knight interrogating the lady of a captured castle. He was a slaveholder or a spymaster or a thief who slid through her bedroom window with more than the silver on his mind. Sometimes he was fiercely dominant, others as silkily seductive as any of Corinne's romance heroes.

And sometimes he got a sudden hot gleam in his eye, and the next thing she knew his massive cock was buried deep inside her as he rode her like a stallion mounting a mare. Though Celeste would never admit it, those were the times she liked best, because it seemed he had no other motive than simple need.

She liked being needed by him.

It was at those times that the aftermath was the sweetest. She would lie in his powerful arms, listening to his heartbeat slow, savoring the feeling of his body against hers, sweat-damp and strong. Sometimes she thought she felt his lips move against her forehead in a kiss that was far more tender than those he gave her when he was intent on dominance and seduction. It almost felt as if he cared for her.

At least until he got up and walked out.

Idiot, Celeste thought, and sent the sexsub statue zooming toward her reflection in the mirror screen over the bureau. She stopped it just before it hit and stared glumly at her reflection. She looked distinctly haggard these days.

Why the hell would he feel anything for you? Look at every-thing he is, and look at what you are.

Despite his streak of darkness, Jarred was essentially a hero—brilliant, handsome, and brave. Not to mention driven by a powerful sense of justice. She, on the other hand, was nobody's idea of a romantic heroine. True, she was reasonably smart, but she was certainly nowhere in Jarred's league. Neither was she particularly courageous; at times she was downright lazy, and she was, at best, only passably pretty.

No, if there seemed to be something more than lust between them, it was only because Jarred was lonely. Garr had been his only real friend, his sounding board and his balance, providing perspective and humor when he'd become consumed by his various obsessions.

At least until Celeste had killed Garr off.

Given the powers she was developing, she was beginning to suspect more and more that she really was responsible for the death of Jarred's best friend. Maybe she deserved to spend a year or two as a sex slave.

Glumly, Celeste sent her collection of toys spinning in the opposite direction. One way or another this interlude was about to end. They would arrive at Kyristari in two days.

And she'd never see him again.

She felt her eyes fill. Her butt hit the mattress as her powerfield collapsed, and she bounced once. A series of soft thumps announced the impact of her toys as they rained down on the bed around her, released from her telekinetic grip.

She was in love with him, of course.

She supposed it had been inevitable. After all, she'd been in love with him even before she knew he existed. With a sob, Celeste lay back on the bed, then jerked up, wincing, when she felt something hard under her spine.

Craning her neck to look down at it, she saw it was the sexsub statue. Naturally. Celeste sent it back to its niche, almost dropping it before it got there.

Damn. She knew that little bobble meant she'd about exhausted her powers. Resigned, she got out of bed, gathered the rest of her odds and ends, and wearily began putting them away.

As for the tears rolling down her cheeks, she ignored those.

Jarred looked down at Celeste as she lay curled up in Garr's old bed. She slept, but not peacefully. But then, she never seemed to sleep peacefully anymore. Her eyes flicked back and forth behind her closed lids, and that pretty face was pulled into a mask of fear. She whimpered again with that heartbreaking note that had drawn him from his own bed. "No!" she muttered. "No, don't . . . Jarred!"

He wondered what she dreamed he was doing to her. Did she honestly believe she was in danger from him? All he'd ever done was make love to her. Ruthlessly, true, but she'd also found pleasure in everything they'd done. He'd made sure of that.

So why had she begun looking so strained lately, so haunted? His sensors told him she was exhausted—though he could have gathered that from the shadows darkening the skin beneath her eyes.

And why did he care? He was doing all this for revenge, after all. Evidence that she was suffering should be welcome. Yet it wasn't.

Brooding, he watched as she made another soft, distressed sound and twisted uneasily on the mattress. Her pretty breasts bounced, pale and bare. He'd expected to relish every moment of his conquest of her, but he hadn't. Oh, the sex was incredible—he'd never had better. Yet a kind of discontent nagged at him, and he didn't know why.

To make matters worse, they were only two days out from Kyristari, and he wasn't tired of her yet. He'd expected to have had his fill by now. Expected to have reduced her to a state of helpless sexual submission. Yet even when Celeste yielded to him, she never quite surrendered. There remained some part of her that eluded him, no matter how thoroughly he pleasured her, no matter how many times he made her scream out her climax.

That wasn't good enough. He wanted all of her. And he had the ugly suspicion that even after he gave her to De'Lar, that need would still haunt him—and so would she.

Dammit, he'd been haunted by Celeste Carson long enough. The point of this entire revenge plot was to get her out of his system, but it seemed he'd only succeeded in embedding her more deeply.

Frowning, Jarred rolled his head on his shoulders, trying to work out the knots he could feel gathering in his spine. God, he was tired. He really should go back to bed. And yet, there was something profoundly unsatisfying about lying there alone. He wanted her next to him. And he didn't like *that* at all. You'd think he was one of Corinne's ridiculous romance heroes, mooning after his true love.

What pakshit.

A gasp of terror jolted Jarred out of his preoccupation. He looked down at Celeste just as her eyes flew wide. She screamed in absolute terror and catapulted from the bed like a woman who'd found a devil in it.

"Celeste!" Jarred caught her slim shoulders, stopping her in mid-lunge. Green eyes enormous, she battered his chest with small fists, wailing hopelessly. Her face was twisted in an expression of such black horror, pity stabbed his heart. "It's all right!" he called over her screams, trying to keep his voice even and calm. "Celeste, you're fine! You're just having a nightmare."

"She killed Jarred!" she cried, swatting his imprisoning forearms with her small fists. "He's dead!"

She's still asleep, he realized. "Darlin', I'm fine. Nobody killed me. It was just a bad dream."

At the sound of his voice, she stopped struggling and stared up at him with a heart-rending expression of hope. "Jarred?"

"Right here, sweetheart." But even as he spoke to her, he could tell from her vague, vulnerable expression that she was still asleep.

She collapsed into his arms with a muffled sob. "I thought you were dead."

"Not me." He cradled her, touched by her very real distress. "You know it would take a direct hit from a star cruiser to take me out."

Celeste burrowed her head into his chest with a whimper of relief. For a moment he let himself stand there enjoying her warm femininity. It felt oddly satisfying to hold her like that without the need to prove a point or take revenge or dominate her.

When she began to lean more heavily against him, he realized reluctantly that she was sliding deeper into sleep. He bent to sweep her up into his arms, then put her down on the bed again. She immediately curled into a small, silken ball, all blond curls and soft skin. He turned to leave the room.

"Glad you're not dead," she said in a slurred voice that spoke of a mind deeply asleep. "Love you."

Jarred's eyes widened as he stopped in mid-step. He turned to look down at her. "What did you say?"

But her only reply was a soft, breathy snore.

He stood looking down at her for a long moment. Then he bent, eased her over on the mattress, and slipped under the covers next to her. Wrapping his arms around her, he drew her close and let his own eyes slip closed.

If I left her alone, she'd only have another nightmare, he told himself. *This way we'll both get some sleep.* It had nothing to do with her semi-conscious admission. Which he didn't believe anyway.

He drifted to sleep listening to her deep, slow breathing. Neither of them woke again for the rest of the night.

When Jarred did finally wake again, she was draped over his chest, boneless as a scarf. He lifted his head and twisted his neck so he could look down into her face.

Still sleeping.

Frowning, he studied her porcelain-delicate features framed by that mass of tangled blond curls. She looked pale, and the shadows under her eyes seemed to have deepened. Even in sleep, a line of worry creased her brows. He remembered all the ways he'd taken her and felt a twinge of guilt. He evidently hadn't allowed her enough rest.

Love you.

Had she meant it?

Some small, unworthy part of his mind thought that would be a fine revenge—to make the woman who had tormented him fall helplessly in love, then walk off and leave her. But the rest of him . . .

The rest felt a bloom of something soft and warm whenever he remembered those drowsy words.

She was asleep, Jarred told himself. *She didn't mean it.* How could she? If anyone knew him, Celeste Carson did. She knew what he was capable of, had recorded every dark thought he'd had for a decade. Hell, he'd kidnapped and sexually tormented her for the past two weeks. Why in the name of the Galactic Gods would she fall in love with him? She'd been ready to kill him off fourteen days ago.

And yet . . .

And yet sometimes there was something in her eyes when she looked at him. A tenderness. A poignant need tinged with hope-lessness, as though she knew she'd never have whatever it was she wanted from him.

Freedom, Jarred told himself firmly. *She wants her freedom. She just wants to go home, and she thinks I can take her there.*

She shifted and murmured something he couldn't make out. He felt one of her lush breasts move against his chest as she sighed.

Jarred lifted one hand and put it in the delicate valley between her shoulders. Under his palm, he could feel each bump in her vul-nerable spine. She felt so fragile, so delicate. He drew in a deep breath, inhaling the scent of her hair. She'd put something on it that smelled of starlillies. A faint smile curved his lips as he won-dered if she even knew what a starlilly was.

The smile faded as he remembered they would arrive at Kyris-tari tomorrow. There'd be no more time with her—no more lis-tening to her cry out in passion, no more watching her face when she came. Those pleasures would belong to De'Lar.

God, he hated that thought.

Maybe she'd fail the sexsub test. No, no such luck. After the sensor readings he'd recorded, Jarred knew she'd score well into the submissive range. And then he'd have no choice except to re-turn to his empty ship and try to ignore the lingering scent of starlillies . . .

The idea of giving her up grated. The obsession was far from gone, despite a collection of memories that would give him a hard-on for weeks. *Probably years,* suggested a traitorous little voice in the back of his mind.

Hell, Jarred suspected he'd still be remembering his nights with Celeste when he was a lonely, broken-down old 'borg boring the young agents with ancient stories. He could almost hear their mocking laughter now. *You're a lying sonuvabitch, Pops. Or else dumber than deckplate, if you had a woman like that and gave her away.*

Would Celeste remember those nights with him as fondly? Probably not. Being tied up and screwed by some rutting 'borg was not the kind of memory a woman would cherish. Anyway, she'd probably fall in love with De'Lar and forget him completely.

Jarred set his jaw, his eyes narrowing. *Like hell.* At least once, he was going to make sure he'd haunt her as thoroughly as she'd always haunted him.

Celeste woke to Jarred's kiss. His mouth moved on hers in a deep and voluptuous possession of tongue and lips and teeth. He felt deliciously hard and strong, one big hand holding her chin. She sighed helplessly, her senses filled with him.

In a few hours, he would take her to De'Lar and she would never see him again.

The thought pumped desperation into her hunger. This might be the last time she ever touched him, ever kissed him. This might be the last time she felt that powerful body under her fingers. She wanted to store every sensation, every touch and kiss for the long, chill years ahead.

With a muffled moan, she lifted a hand to the side of his face. His beard felt like raw silk against her fingers. She stroked him, savoring each hair, exploring the haughty rise of his cheekbones, the line of his temple. Fisting her fingers in his hair, she dragged him down until she could deepen her contact with that impossibly seductive mouth.

He made a low, approving sound against her lips and pressed a chain of nibbling kisses down to the rise of her chin, then followed the curve of her jaw to find the taut, sensitive cord of her throat. His teeth closed in a gently wicked bite that sent a tingling starburst of pleasure up and down her spine. She felt her nipples harden.

His hands grew busy, stroking and touching. The line of her collarbone, the curve of her shoulder, the sensitive hollow at the bend of her elbow. A thumb stroked the fine-grained skin of her wrist. Her hand curved up in a silent plea, and he shifted his own to twine his fingers with hers. Palm stroked palm, exchanging a silent message of need and approval.

Jarred shifted his weight to cover her more completely, kissing his way back up her throat to her ear. "God, you feel so good," he said, his voice sounding less silken than usual. Not so much the polished seducer as a man in the grip of something powerful. "How the hell am I going to give you up?"

"Don't," she whimpered as he hungrily sucked and nibbled at the ear he'd whispered into. "Don't give me to De'Lar. Keep me."

"I can't."

You mean you won't. But she didn't say it, didn't want to risk losing this last glorious opportunity to touch him, to pretend he loved her.

It felt as though he did. The hands that roamed and stroked seemed impossibly tender as they lingered over hip and thigh and breast, teasing warmth and arousal from sensitive flesh. She wrapped both legs around his hips and arched her back to bring her sex in tighter contact with his. Digging her nails into his strong back, she bit her lip to keep from telling him how much she loved him. Either he wouldn't want to hear it, or he'd gloat. This moment might be all she'd ever have, and she didn't want to ruin it.

He pulled out of her arms. Instinctively, she tried to hold on, but she was no match for his strength. He didn't go far, though, just settled back onto his heels and scooped her bottom into his big hands. Lifting her hips, he angled them upward and draped her calves over his muscled forearms.

Celeste rose onto her elbows to watch as he took his shaft in one hand and presented it to her opening. Slowly, he began to press inside, his dark eyes locked hungrily on her face. She closed her eyes, afraid the hopeless love she felt would show.

"Look at me," he said, in a tone so vulnerable she automatically obeyed. To her surprise, she saw something almost tortured in his black eyes as he slid to his full length in her wet, tight sex. He leaned closer, catching one of her knees to prop it on his shoulder. The position allowed him to penetrate even farther than he ever had before.

Jarred began to thrust, rolling his hips slowly, deeply. One hand sought her breast to caress and tease as the other busied itself with her clit. Long, silken swirls of sensation spun through her body with each movement of his fingers, each stroke of his cock. All the while, those dark eyes watched her face with a kind of tender absorption unlike anything he'd shown her before. Returning that hot chocolate stare, she wondered at his metamorphosis from ruthless dominant to gentle lover.

Until the heat he built grew so fierce she could think of nothing except how delicious it was. She could feel her orgasm building, tightening deep muscles, preparing to burst free.

Throwing her head back, she gave herself up to it.

Jarred watched Celeste come, felt her strong muscles milking his shaft as those beautiful green eyes widened, her soft pink mouth forming an O of pleasure. She cried out. "Tell me it's true," he growled, barely aware of what he said. "Tell me you love me." He circled his hips deliberately as he stroked his thumb over the hard, engorged button of her clit.

"God, Jarred!" She convulsed and gave him what he wanted. "I love you!"

He came in a hot, roiling flood, pouring himself into her slick heated body with a roar.

Oh, God. She'd told him.

Celeste lay under his hot weight, feeling a horrible sense of vulnerability. He'd either gloat now or pretend she'd said nothing. He'd ruin it.

Jarred lifted his head and met her eyes, and she blurted the first thing that entered her head. "Well, what did you expect? I made you up. Of course I'd fall in love with you."

Instantly his face closed, and it occurred to her, far too late, that his expression hadn't been what she'd expected. There'd been something else there, something . . . what? "You didn't make me up," he gritted, and rolled off her onto his back.

Oh, hell. Might as well go on the offensive. "You seem to think I'm responsible for everything else that's ever happened to you."

Jarred shot her a sardonic look. "Believe it or not, I did exist before you ever wrote those books."

"How do you know?" she shot back. "Maybe you only *think* you existed."

"Now you're getting delusions of grandeur."

"You're the one that keeps calling me 'goddess.' "

"That's 'goddess' with a little 'g,' not the 'and-on-the-seventh-day-She-rested-G'."

She snorted. "I *wish* it had taken me only seven days to write one of those books."

"You know, you're working awfully hard to change the subject." He shot her a coolly perceptive look. "Why are you trying so hard to distract me?"

"I didn't want to give you the traditional male opportunity to ruin the moment."

His mouth curled into a faint, mocking smile. "Particularly when you could do such a good job of that on your own."

Celeste rolled out of bed. "Yeah, well, now that my work here is done, I'm going to take a shower."

Before she could take another step, he was in front of her, one big hand on her shoulder. "Not so fast. I want to . . ."

He stood with a whip in one big hand, saying something angry to De'Lar. Beside them, a naked blond woman lay on a bed, bound hand and foot. She turned her head to look up at them, and Celeste recognized herself.

Suddenly feminine hands appeared in her field of view, gestured. Snaking bolts of electric energy flashed toward Jarred's dark head . . .

As he stared into Celeste's eyes in irritation, all the blood abruptly drained from her face. Her body jerked backwards, spine arching into a bow as her mouth shaped a silent scream of agony and terror. Only his cyborg reflexes allowed him to catch her before she hit the deck. "Celeste!" he bellowed, barely aware of what he said.

As Jarred wrapped both arms around her and lowered her the rest of the way to the floor, she went into convulsions, her body lashing like an electrified doll, her eyes rolling back in her head until only the whites showed. Terror poured over him, cold and brutal as a hailstorm. *God, I can't lose her! Not her, too . . .*

He scanned her desperately as he tried to control her writhing body. The electrical activity in her brain was going wild, almost like an epileptic seizure, but more . . . organized than that. It reminded him of the precognitive visions Garr used to have, but it was far more violent.

What the hell was happening to her?

Just as he was about to snatch her up and run for sickbay, her eyes rolled down and focused on his face. "NO!" she screamed, and grabbed at his shoulders with desperate strength. "She's going to kill you!"

She's back. Relief poured over him, but he had to find out what the hell had just happened. He snatched her off the floor and rose, headed for the door.

"What are you . . . ?" Celeste looked around, dazed, trying to focus on her surroundings. "Where are you taking me? No, you've got to listen! I've got to tell you . . ."

"I'm getting you to sickbay," he gritted without breaking step. God, he'd never been more terrified in his entire life than he'd been when she collapsed. "I want to run you through the sensors there. I damn well am going to find out what just happened."

"Jarred . . ."

"One minute you're giving me a hard time, the next you're having a seizure." He strode down the hall with her in long, determined strides. "I shouldn't have ignored those fucking migraines you've been having . . ."

"It was a vision, Jarred." When he looked down at her, startled, he saw she'd closed her eyes, teeth gritted. Her color was bad, almost gray. "Put me down. We need to talk."

"Not until I check you out." The sickbay doors opened and he carried her inside to lay her in the treatment tube. "Cerebral strokes can produce effects people mistake for . . ."

"It's not a mistake, Jarred." He looked up to see a handheld wound sealer floating through the air toward his face. "I have powers."

For a long moment he stared at the sealer as it hung in the air. Then, slowly, he turned to look down at her. Telekinesis was one of the rarest of the psychic powers—and one of the most potentially deadly. The closest he'd ever come to death had been at the hands of a telekinetic. "How long have you been doing that?"

Celeste licked her lips and sat up. She tried to swing out of the treatment tube, but frowned in irritation as she realized its walls were too high. As Jarred watched, she floated off the tube bed, levitated over the side, and swung her feet down to the deck.

He stared at her. That kind of power—and the skill to use it—did not develop overnight. She must have been honing it for days. Which meant she'd hidden it from him. *I've been falling in love with her, and she's been sneaking around behind my back.*

She must have read the rage growing inside him, because her eyes widened. "Uh . . ."

"How long?" he snarled.

She bit her lip. "A couple of weeks."

"What else can you do?" God, he was an idiot. She'd spent a decade fucking with him, and now she was going to start doing it again. He should have killed her when he'd had the chance. He should kill her now.

But he couldn't, because the little bitch had made him fall in love with her. He couldn't touch a hair on that pretty little head—assuming she'd let him.

They always did this to him. Every last one of them. His mother. Ayla. They made him love them, and then they betrayed him.

Then they inflicted the greatest betrayal of all: they left him alone, bleeding and devastated.

Jesus, he just hoped she wasn't a telepath, too. He couldn't stand to let her know how completely she'd broken him.

"I can't really do all that much." The little idiot didn't realize how much power she had over him—in every sense—because she was staring at him as if she was afraid he'd beat her. He should have found her fear comforting, but it only pissed him off even more. *How could she believe I'd hurt her?* She twisted her fingers together and hunched her shoulders. "Just precognition and telekinesis."

"Considering you just picked up fifty-two kilos and floated it around, that's more than enough." *Quit looking at me like that, dammit.*

She took a deep breath and straightened her shoulders as if gathering her courage. "The precog is the important part. Jarred, you've got to listen to me. If we go to Kyristari, somebody's going to try to kill you."

He looked at her coldly. "Are they going to succeed?"

"They can't if we don't go there."

"Is that a threat?"

She gaped at him. "What?"

"I mean are you saying you'll make sure I die if I take you to Kyristari?"

Celeste recoiled. "What? No! I'm just telling you what I saw. It was a *vision*. There was a woman. She . . . did something. I'm not sure what. There were lighting bolts or something and . . ."

"A vision, or a plotline? Because if it's a plotline, I'm dead regardless." He was dying now. "You always make sure your plots happen."

"Jarred, *I'm not doing this*." She looked desperate now, afraid.

As if he could hurt her. "I did not plot this. Remember? Before you and Mykh showed up, I was blocked. I . . ."

"So I owe my continued existence to a case of writer's block. Nice. I think I'd better drop you off at Kyristari before you start feeling inspired." He turned and started out of the room.

She hurried after him to grab him by one shoulder. Even through his armored jacket, her touch seemed to burn. "Jarred, please, listen to me! You're in danger! She's going to try to kill you!"

He looked back at her. "What do you care? You were going to cash my chips, remember?"

Celeste looked at him as if he'd slapped her. Her lower lip trembled. "I care because I love you, Jarred." She pulled herself to her full height. "And if you go to Kyristari, you'll be in danger."

He turned away. "I'll be a lot safer once I leave you there."

SEVEN

Celeste sat staring fixedly out the window of the skycab as the Kyristari capital flashed by below. Normally she would have been enthralled by the futuristic city with its soaring, graceful architecture, surrounded by air transports that swooped between the buildings like swallows. Unfortunately, a knotted stomach and pounding temples put her in no mood for sightseeing.

Jarred sat in the seat facing her, his eyes as cold and hard as iced black steel. If he cared that he'd never see her again, it didn't show on his face. He hadn't spoken to her since he'd walked out of sickbay.

At first her nerves had stretched drum-tight, waiting for him to pounce on her in one of those humiliating, deliciously erotic displays of dominance. But he hadn't touched her. Hell, he'd even given her clothes for the first time in two weeks.

The black shipsuit Jarred had ordered the computer to create was so damn ugly, he'd obviously intended it as a statement of indifference. Celeste could only conclude he'd designed the whisper-thin silk shift she wore now for De'Lar's pleasure, not his.

Though she would have died rather than admit it, that rejection hurt. She didn't want to lose the last chance she might ever have to make love to Jarred—to pretend, however briefly, that he loved her. But it seemed he had no intention of allowing her even that illusionary solace.

Celeste wanted two things now: to get out of this without letting him see her cry, and to make sure the assassin didn't succeed in killing him. She was terrified that in his icy rage, Jarred wouldn't protect himself. He'd even warned her not to mention the vision or her abilities to De'Lar, a piece of deliberate stupidity if ever she'd heard of one.

"If you scare him off," he'd growled as they'd stepped down the ship's gangplank, "I swear to God I'm taking you to Christ Colony."

She couldn't believe he meant it. Those lunatics would probably stone her as a witch the first time she had a vision. But looking at his implacable face, she'd decided not to push it.

Now Celeste felt the bottom drop out of her stomach as the air-cab began to descend toward a sprawling collection of iridescent spires she realized must be the palace. Swallowing hard, she considered throwing up on Jarred's boots. *That should shock the icy look right off his face.*

"Just let me off," she gritted through teeth set against her rising gorge. "Don't go in with me. I'll find my own way."

He submerged her in a frigid stare. "You expect me to believe you'll just deliver yourself to De'Lar? I don't think so."

"But the assassin . . ."

"Did you actually see her kill me?"

Celeste frowned, trying to remember those nightmarish images.

She considered lying, but Jarred's sensors were better than a polygraph. "No. I saw her hands, I saw the energy bolts, I felt . . ."

"Who was it?"

"I don't know," she said, for what must have been the hundredth time. "I never saw her face." Frowning, Celeste nibbled on the tip of a nail. "But we both know Ayla is the logical suspect. I have no idea how she'd manage to throw energy bolts, but it has to be her. She was a spy for the Rekan. She probably still is—and they want you dead for what you did to General K'charit." She snorted. "They seem to take a dim view of people spacing their commanders."

At those words, hell blazed up in Jarred's eyes. She knew he was remembering Garr's bloody corpse. "I take an even dimmer view of people killing my friends."

Celeste gave him her best steady stare. "So do I."

Jarred shrugged his broad shoulders and looked away. "Throttle down, goddess. People try to murder me a couple of times a month. If I were that easy, we wouldn't be having this conversation."

She stretched her legs out in front of her and crossed them deliberately at the ankles. "You know, if I really was responsible for all the nasty stuff that's happened to you, has it ever occurred to you I might also have stacked the deck to keep you alive?"

He shifted his gaze to the toes of his armored boots. "All the time."

Anger stirred beneath her despair. "So maybe you should keep me and my telekinetic powers around, instead of handing me over to the first pervert that comes along."

"De'Lar is a dominant, not a pervert. In any case, I was an agent for the Stellar Compact for five years before you ever wrote a word." He smiled dismissively. "I imagine I can struggle along without you."

"Not if you get killed in the next ten minutes. Dammit, Jarred . . ."

"Drop it." His expression was so menacing, she badly wanted to obey.

Then she remembered the lightning-bolt-tossing assassin. "Why are you being so stupidly stubborn? Look, I swear to you, I will present myself to De'Lar and start sucking his dick the minute we land . . ."

He reached into his jacket and pulled out a control band. "If you won't shut your mouth, I can do it for you."

Celeste snapped her teeth shut. She knew she couldn't risk him paralyzing her again. She had to be ready when the assassin struck; she was damned if she'd stand by and watch some bitch murder the man she loved without doing something about it.

Assuming I don't kill him myself . . .

If looks were ion blasts, he'd be a smoking crater in the seat.

But then, Jarred wasn't particularly thrilled with the situation, either. The thought of surrendering Celeste to De'Lar made him burn with a sullen fury almost as intense as his dread of returning to that empty ship.

She'd sunk her claws in deep, all right.

Which was why he didn't dare keep her, though he could think of a dozen very good excuses to do so. She was right about those powers of hers making her invaluable; the Stellar Compact would probably be more than happy to hire her on as his partner.

But she still couldn't be trusted. She had too much power over him, in every sense. It wouldn't take her long to take advantage of his weakness.

Just like Ayla—and his mother.

All right, dammit, that's just absurd, he told himself firmly. Celeste wasn't Ayla, and she certainly wasn't Jamme Varrain. He had no idea why his mind kept digging at those old scars.

For God's sake, he'd been twelve when Jamme had enrolled him in the Stellar Compact's Enforcement Academy and left him without another word. Twenty years should have been more than enough time for *that* wound to heal.

Hell, it had been fifteen years since he'd graduated and gone looking for her, only to discover she'd been killed fighting the Rekan the year before. Truthfully, he'd expected to hear Jamme had died much earlier, since she'd never replied to even one of his com messages.

Which wasn't surprising. Jarred had known from the time he was very young that his mother hated him because he reminded her of his rapist father. He hadn't been surprised when Jamme had abandoned him the minute her sense of honor allowed it. He was lucky she hadn't aborted her pregnancy in the first place. She probably would have, if she hadn't enjoyed playing martyr so much.

None of which had a damn thing to do with Celeste. The point was, he needed to get her settled with De'Lar and get the hell away before she dug any deeper into his soul than she already had.

The skycab jolted as it landed, snapping him out of his revere. He shot a quick look at Celeste. She was too pale, her eyes darting as she scanned the palace grounds for his would-be assassin.

"Calm down," Jarred told her gruffly, trying not to be touched by her visible concern. "My sensors aren't picking up anybody who reads as though they'd like to kill me."

"Then your sensors are on the blink," Celeste muttered, as the cab's door popped open. "Because *I'd* like to kill you."

Actually, according to his sensors she was on the verge of crying, but he knew better than to make that observation aloud. He swung from the cab and turned to give her a hand, but she'd already scrambled out, flashing a mouth-watering length of tanned thigh. She turned to watch as the cab lumbered skyward with a whoosh of heated air, banked, and accelerated away like a big blue egg with jets.

"Jarred Varrain?"

He turned as Celeste jumped and spun around. *Nervous as a minxlin surrounded by a pack of bloodwolves*, Jarred thought, slanting a glance at her. She barely relaxed when she saw it was only De'Lar's assistant who walked toward them across the landing pad. Skinny and pompous though he was, she still looked him over as if he might be hiding an ion pistol in those iridescent court robes .

"Greetings, Gel'ka'far." Jarred gave him a civil nod.

The bureaucrat sketched a curt bow in return. "His majesty is expecting you. If you'll follow me . . ." Pivoting on a peacock-blue high-heeled boot, he hurried away, glancing impatiently over his shoulder to make sure they were following.

Jarred strode after Gel'ka'far, his own boots scraping on the landing pad's rough surface. Celeste crowded his heels. He noticed her hands were knotted into fists of anxiety. "You could have at least worn your helmet," she hissed.

"I am not wearing battle gear to visit an old friend. My usual armor is enough."

"But . . ."

He sighed. "Look, I'm scanning. If anybody shows up with any kind of energy weapon, I'll know it."

She growled something that sounded like, "Pigheaded 'borg," then subsided to eye everything and everyone they passed with such paranoia he started feeling jumpy himself.

Jarred frowned suddenly, eyes focusing on the whisper of silk that barely veiled her pretty pink nipples and the gleaming thatch between her thighs. It was a sexsub's standard costume, but if somebody started shooting at him, it would provide her with no protection at all. *Dammit, I should have thought of that earlier. I could have issued her some body armor of her own . . .* Too late now. He'd just have to make sure he got the killer before the killer got them.

Jarred widened the perimeter of his scan, but his computer still could detect no sign of any energy weapons beyond those De'Lar's guards carried. Could the Kyristari king have a traitor in his service?

The hair rose on the back of his neck as an even more chilling thought occurred to him: could De'Lar himself have sold out?

Celeste padded along the palace corridor at Jarred's heels, her nerves strung so tight she was surprised she wasn't humming like a tuning fork. She had to be ready to generate a protective field around him when the assassin started throwing lightning bolts, but she wasn't sure she was strong enough to block that much power.

Distraction from that sickening worry came in the form of a man walking down the corridor. He wore the blue and green of the palace guard—and a particularly nasty, speculative smirk as he stared at her. She gave him a what's-your-problem glare before she tracked his gaze back to her own gown. Pink nipples thrust against its sheer bodice.

She winced. *Oh, right, Jarred dressed me like a sexsub.* Not only did the silk shift put every detail of her anatomy on display, it was like wearing a sign around her neck that said, "Tie me up and do me."

The guard's taunting grin widened until his eyes flicked to Jarred. Whatever he saw on the big 'borg's face wiped the smile right off his own.

As he started to hurry past, Celeste positioned an invisible force field right in front of his shins. With a yelp, he tripped and went sprawling.

While the guard scrambled, cursing, to his feet, Jarred turned to lift a dark brow at her. She widened her eyes in mock innocence. For a moment she thought he was going to laugh, but instead he focused his gaze on their guide's narrow back and kept going.

The humor of the moment faded all too soon, leaving Celeste to spiral back into worry. She tried to focus on the elegant sweep of the palace's architecture, on the soaring niches with their animated statues of De'Lar's ancestors, on the glowing marble tiles beneath her sandaled feet.

Her obsessed mind foiled her efforts with a low background chant, *He's going to leave me—if they don't kill him first. He's going to leave me . . .*

Dammit, stop that, she told herself, clenching her fists. *Watch for the assassin. All that matters is making sure Jarred survives this.*

Just ahead, two men armed with ion pistols snapped to attention at their approach. Between them, the massive double doors they guarded swung slowly, majestically open. Her stomach clenched as De'Lar's obnoxious little assistant led them inside.

Oh, hell. Celeste looked warily around at the chamber with its high, soaring walls. Stepping close to her lover, she dropped her voice to a murmur. "Heads up, Jarred—I saw this in my vision. This is where the assassin's going to attack."

And there was Ayla, spy turned sexsub, curled in sensuous femininity on a bed big enough to sleep the entire New York Jets football team. Her dark eyes focused with hungry interest on Jarred.

Celeste considered slamming her into the nearest wall just on general principle.

Before she could yield to temptation, De'Lar stepped through another door. "Ah, there you are. I see you made it after all. Burned out your obsession yet, Jarred?" Fluid as a cat, he padded toward them, his attention focused with predatory intensity on Celeste's face.

She shifted uneasily, acutely aware of her all too visible nipples as he moved to stand in front of her. Damn, he was big. He wore another one of those flowing robes, this one in peacock blue embroidered in gold. It hung open over a very nice chest, plated in thick, lean muscle and swirled with golden hair. Skin-tight black trousers hugged his long, long legs before they tucked into shiny knee-high black boots.

He was, if anything, even better looking than Jarred, with the kind of perfectly sculpted male beauty of a GQ model—broad cheekbones sharp enough to grate cheese, a square chin set with a deep cleft, a thin nose, and the kind of full mouth that seemed designed for oral sex. Add to that a fall of golden hair that lay across his broad shoulders like a mantle, and you had any girl's sex fantasy come to life.

Yet staring up into those golden eyes, Celeste felt only a kind of profound despair. Handsome as he was, she didn't want him. She wanted dark, tormented, arrogant Jarred, sadistic streak and all. *Well, you're not going to get him,* she told herself grimly. *The most you can hope for is to get him out of here alive.*

She shifted her attention to Ayla, who was wearing a sexsub shift that revealed pouting brown nipples and long legs, but no weapon of mass destruction. Where the hell was she hiding it?

"I must admit, Jarred, you were right," De'Lar said. Celeste jumped as a big hand suddenly closed over her breast, thumb casually flicking her nipple. Fighting panic, she stared up into the Kyristari king's face as he slid his other arm around her waist and drew her close. "Judging from the sensor readings you sent me, she is deliciously responsive."

She shot a look at Jarred just in time to see fury blaze in his eyes before his expression smoothed into an icy mask.

If he hated so much seeing another man fondle her, why the hell was he giving her away? She glared at him and mouthed silently, "Pigheaded 'borg jerk."

"So you'll accept her as a sexsub?" Jarred sounded as indifferent as a teenager asking, "Do you want fries with that?" Celeste considered slugging him.

"Not quite—yet." De'Lar looked down at her breast, where her nipple remained stubbornly soft despite his skillful ministrations. "I would like to try her myself first. It's been my experience that some women only respond to one man."

The muscles in Jarred's powerful shoulders bunched under his jacket. "As you wish." Despite the tension in his big body, he sounded bored. "I'll leave you alone, then. You can call me aboard the *Vengeance* once you've made your decision."

No. Celeste bit her lip. *Don't leave me here with him!* Then her gaze fell on Ayla, still curled like a sullen snake on De'Lar's bed. "Sounds like a good plan to me," she managed, her mouth dry as dust.

What would the king do to her? He'd had some pretty kinky tastes in that story she'd written . . .

Jarred turned, but before he could start toward the door De'Lar said, "Wouldn't you rather share her with me?"

He stopped dead, but he didn't look around. "I thought the point was to see how she'll respond to *you*."

"True, but she doesn't know me." The Kyristari king smiled at him slowly and teased her captive nipple again. "You could help . . . ease the transition."

Celeste frowned. What the hell was he up to? She couldn't think of anything more miserable than screwing a stranger with the man she loved in the same bed . . .

She straightened convulsively. *De'Lar's testing Jarred to see if he can really stand to give me up.*

And she'd be more than willing to go along with it—if it wasn't for Ayla and her lightning bolts. "I really don't think that's a good idea . . ."

"And I really don't care," De'Lar told her coolly. "I'm not interested in you for your opinions. Jarred?"

He shrugged. "Certainly."

"Can we at least send Ayla out?" Glancing at her sullen enemy, Celeste improvised a quick excuse. "She's killing the mood."

De'Lar considered the request, then waved a regal hand. "You're excused, Ayla."

The former spy shot Celeste a glare seething with raw, jealous fury, then rolled from the bed and flounced out. Watching her stalk through double doors that thankfully sealed behind her, Celeste relaxed fractionally. If anybody was the assassin from her vision, it was Ayla.

She just had to make sure the little bitch didn't slip back in while they were . . . occupied.

But when Celeste pulled her attention from those closed doors, she found she faced a more immediate challenge: two very big men eyeing her with intensely predatory sexual interest. She swallowed, meeting Jarred's burning black stare. Where the hell had all that ravenous need been when they'd been alone on the *Vengeance* the last couple of days?

"Just like a man," she muttered under her breath. "Only wants me when somebody else is interested."

Jarred knew he should turn around and walk out the door right now. Hell, if Celeste was right, an assassin would soon take a shot at him. If that wasn't a reason to ignore his insistent dick, he didn't know what was.

And yet, he also knew when he left this room, he would never see her again. Never touch her satin skin, never taste that maddening mouth. Never drive to the balls into her wet, snug heat. Never hear her laugh or swear or purr at him in that velvet voice of hers.

Staring into Celeste's anxious green eyes, he realized he wouldn't be able to leave if an entire battalion of Rekan berserkers was about to break down the door. He had to have her again, even if it meant sharing her with De'Lar.

Then why are you giving her up, you idiot? a voice whispered in the back of his mind.

Because she's too dangerous to keep.

He was the first to reach for her.

One of Jarred's hands caught her wrist in a grip like tender iron. He spun her around and hustled her toward the bed as he unsealed his jacket with his free hand. De'Lar moved after them, letting his robe slither off massive shoulders. When Jarred released her to finish stripping, the king picked Celeste up and tossed her onto the bed.

She sprawled where she'd landed, half-afraid to move as the two men undressed with impatient jerks that shouted of lust spinning out of control. Dazed, she looked from one powerful male body to the other. De'Lar was the taller of the two, his lean body dusted with golden hair that thickened around his long, elegant cock. Jarred, by contrast, was broader, more powerfully built, his shoulders a bit wider, his chest roped with heavy muscle and pelted in dark hair.

And his cock was so erect it tilted upward, flushed dark with arousal, its thickness sending a hot quiver through her body as she remembered what it felt like digging so hard and deep into her.

Seeing the direction of her widened gaze, he wrapped a big hand around the base of his shaft and cupped his balls tauntingly. When she licked her lips, the grin faded from his lips. He released himself and reached out to wrap a big fist into the fabric of her shift. One tug ripped it from cleavage to hem. "I want her bound," he growled, his eyes flicking from her nipples to the thatch between her thighs.

De'Lar smiled slowly. "I think we can manage that."

So they tied her up. And not in the quick, offhand way Jarred had secured her wrists before. No, they took their time as they wrapped her in the thin silk cords, touching and stroking and tasting as they worked until she felt like a fly at the mercy of two amorous spiders. They bound her arms to her side and her ankles to her thighs, circled her breasts in loops of silk, even tied both her hard nipples, stringing a single thread between the two. Periodically, one man or the other would pluck the string, sending vibrations of heat radiating from the hard peaks.

Then, once she felt even more utterly immobilized than she'd been by Jarred's control band, they lay down on either side of her to play.

Hot mouths sucked and big hands stroked as she lay on the bed, sandwiched helplessly between two powerful males apparently intent on driving her out of her mind.

Both men were intensely skilled lovers, but their styles were sharply different. De'Lar was a calculating seducer who watched her every reaction, gauging her responses and adjusting his actions accordingly, his hands floating across her bare skin with wicked skill.

Jarred simply devoured her.

He buried his face between her thighs and plunged his tongue deep into her wet core in ruthless licks. Even as he drove her to madness with his mouth, he watched her face hungrily—not like a man trying to seduce a woman, but as though he desperately wanted to memorize her expression.

Shivering, she shifted her gaze from his hot stare to De'Lar's. Lazily sampling one nipple with slow strokes of his tongue, he brushed his thumb repeatedly across the other, each flick vibrating something deep inside her.

Suspended, dizzy, Celeste looked into the Kyristari king's handsome face. *He's going to be my lover,* she thought. *And he'll be good at it. But I won't fall in love with him.* The thought made her feel oddly empty.

Suddenly a big, dark hand came up and brushed De'Lar's aside. Jarred's strong fingers began plucking the nipple the king had been fondling. The little peak hardened deliciously between his wicked fingertips as he squeezed and rotated it. Whimpering in pleasure, Celeste barely noticed the assessing stare De'Lar shot him.

"She's creaming well," the Kyristari king commented. "I think she's ready to fuck. Up for a little double penetration, Jarred?"

Her eyes widened as she remembered what they'd done to Ayla. Suddenly an idea which had seemed so erotic in fantasy became highly intimidating in reality. Particularly when the reality in question would have shamed a Clydesdale. "I've . . . uh . . . never done"—her voice spiraled into a squeak—"*that.*"

"What?" De'Lar lifted a brow at her and gave Jarred an incredulous smirk. "You've had her two weeks and haven't gotten around to sodomizing her?"

A high flush started to mount Jarred's cheekbones only to fade an instant later, probably because he'd had his computer put a stop to it. "I was occupied with other pleasures." He sounded amazingly stiff for a man whose lips shone with a woman's sexual cream.

De'Lar's grin broadened nastily. "In that case, I'll let you do the honors."

Oh boy. Feeling her eyes widen, Celeste knew her panic showed. As big as he was, it would hurt. A lot. What was it he'd said about doing the same thing to Ayla? *"My sensors told me being impaled on my cock was painful for her, but I also knew she was so hot, she burned. Besides, after everything she'd done to me, I really didn't mind making her suffer."*

Ohboy.

Celeste stared at him like a rabbit fascinated by a snake.

A snake that was getting bigger by the moment. There'd been a time he'd fantasized about doing just what De'Lar had suggested. In fact, he'd originally planned to impale Celeste's tight little ass as one of his first acts of revenge.

But somehow he'd never gotten around to it.

This would be his last chance. He let himself imagine the moment and felt his cock jerk in lust. Her snug anus would grip him deliciously as he forced himself inside her with slow, deep thrusts. He could almost hear her soft, helpless moans . . .

Jarred frowned. He didn't want her final memory of him tainted with pain. True, he knew he could probably coax her into enjoying it before he was finished—he'd done it before, not least with Ayla.

But Celeste wasn't Ayla. She wasn't like any of the women he'd dominated in the past.

Jarred looked away from her pleading gaze, only to find himself unable to meet De'Lar's too knowing eyes, either. "I find I'm not in the mood to initiate a virgin tonight. I'll leave that pleasure for you."

The Kyristari king looked down at her. Celeste licked her lips nervously. Something hot and predatory swam through De'Lar's golden eyes.

Jarred felt jealousy flare up in his soul, burning through him until he had to fight the urge to plant his fist in his friend's face. The king glanced up at that moment, and Jarred knew his own expression had given away his rage. De'Lar's mouth took on a rueful twist. "Some other time. I think I'd rather test her talent at cocksucking."

He threw himself down on the mound of pillows at the head of the bed, then grabbed Celeste by one shoulder and flipped her onto her belly across his lap. Wrapping a big hand in her long blond hair, he dragged her head down over his cock. She immediately began to suck, submissive as any sexsub ever born.

Jarred watched her full lips close around De'Lar's thick shaft. Her long lashes drifted down to veil her green eyes, and her cheeks hollowed as she began servicing the king. He remembered how that sweet mouth had felt on his own dick. Heat spun into his balls and he gritted his teeth in rage.

The way they had her bound ankles to thighs forced her to kneel with her legs under her and her rounded backside thrust high. He could see her lusciously spread lips and tightly puckered anus, and he thought about giving her a buggering she would never forget. He moved up behind her, taking his big cock in hand . . .

De'Lar threw his blond head back and moaned. "God, the little bitch knows how to suck . . ."

Jarred snarled and set the ruddy rounded head of his erection against her tiny rosette. She flinched and made a smothered sound.

"Goddammit." Dropping his aim, he drove into her wet pussy

in one long, ruthless stroke. Celeste moaned helplessly around De'Lar's shaft, a sound of pleasure and desperate welcome. He worked deeper until he covered her completely as she lay with her head in the king's lap. Bracing one hand on the mattress, he used the other to pull her long hair aside to expose one delicate white ear. Slowly, he began to shaft her, sinking in and out in her tight, creamy heat as he bent close. "No matter how many times he fucks you," he whispered hoarsely, "you're never going to forget me."

Celeste had never felt so utterly stuffed, helpless and conquered. De'Lar ground his hips upward so his shaft shuttled in and out of her mouth while Jarred rammed her cunt, merciless as a bull in rut. Being the focus of all that virile male lust was both ferociously uncomfortable and the most arousing experience she'd ever had.

Jarred released her hair to reach under her body and between her thighs until he found the engorged bead of her clit. Skillfully, he began to stroke and circle. The pleasure of his demanding touch combined with the strong digs of his cock sent fireworks bursting behind her eyes. She whimpered in pleasure.

"By the gods!" De'Lar arched his hips, driving his cock halfway down her throat. His come exploded into her mouth in a bitter, salty flood. She swallowed it down and felt her own climax gathering under Jarred's seductive fingers and pumping cock. He tightened his grip, dragging her a fraction closer so he could reach just a little deeper. His hips circled against her ass . . .

And she screamed around her mouthful of cock as an orgasm hit her like a ball of flame. "God!" Jarred roared in her ear, and convulsed against her, coming in long, hot jets deep in her sex.

*   *   *

Celeste lay on the bed, bound and helpless, the taste of come in the back of her throat, her bottom sticky with it, savoring the feel of Jarred's deliciously sweaty weight draped over her back.

Then De'Lar stirred. "Well," he said, in a voice that was chill and dismissive, "I must confess I'm disappointed."

She gaped up at him as he pulled free of her mouth, kicked one leg over her head, and rose to his feet.

"What?" Jarred demanded in her ear, lifting off her body. She blinked, feeling suddenly cold, and craned her head around as he rose from her.

The king had bent to rummage in a chest that stood beside the bed. He lifted out something slim and black that swung and clicked.

It was a cat o'nine tails. Each of the whips' nine braided lashes was tipped with a small black weight.

"What are you doing with that?" Jarred demanded.

"She let me come too soon," De'Lar said coldly, straightening to step toward the bed. "If she's going to join my cloister, she needs to learn that I will not tolerate a lack of discipline in my sexsubs."

Oh, hell! Celeste thought, staring at the big man in shock as he moved to stand over her. *I knew he was kinky, but nobody said anything about vicious . . .*

EIGHT

Jarred stared at De'Lar in shock. If he had a best friend since Garr's death, it was the Kyristari king. Yet now the big man stalked Celeste with an expression of cold, brutal pleasure—a sadist's anticipation of inflicting pain on a bound and helpless woman.

Jarred's bound and helpless woman.

He was so stunned, he could only stare. He'd seen De'Lar spank his sexsubs as part of love play, but only if he knew they enjoyed it. Certainly never to inflict the kind of pain that whip promised. *This has to be some kind of joke.*

"I have high standards for my women," the king growled at Celeste as her lovely eyes rounded in panic. "And you're going to learn to meet them."

"What the hell do you think you're doing?" Jarred demanded, incredulous.

De'Lar gave him a cold smile. "She needs to learn her place— and I'm going to thoroughly enjoy putting her in it."

"But I didn't do anything!" Celeste wailed, squirming in her bonds in a way that drew the king's attention like a hungry cat spotting a trapped mouse.

"That, my dear, is not the point," he said, his eyes gleaming with cruel anticipation. "The point is my pleasure. And it would give me a great deal of pleasure to put a dozen stripes on that lovely white ass."

Friend or not, king or not, Jarred knew he was going to pound De'Lar's head in if he touched Celeste. Instinctively, he coiled into a fighting crouch. By God, he'd take on the king and every guard in this palace if he had to. "Your pleasure is about to have a higher price than you're prepared to pay," he snarled.

Dammit, how could he have misread the man so completely?

De'Lar gave him an astonished look, shaking out the cat with a flick of his wrist. "May I remind you that you handed her over to me to do with as I please? Anyway, I'd think you'd be eager to see her striped. She's the bane of your existence, remember?" He drew back the whip and started to bring it down on Celeste's flinching, helplessly proffered backside. "This is your chance to see her properly punished."

Jarred's hand flashed out and locked around the king's wrist. The weighted lashes snapped around and slashed across his face, but he scarcely noticed the hot pain. "I haven't given her to you," he snarled, snatching the whip from De'Lar's hand. "Which means she's not yours." He bared his teeth and gritted out every word: *"She's mine, I love her, and I will rip out your fucking throat before I let you touch her."*

De'Lar drew himself to his considerable height and glared. "Well, hell," he said. "I've been telling you that for two weeks."

Poised to attack the king, it took Jarred several seconds to process what he'd said. His muscles loosened in sheer relief that his friend wasn't the sadist he'd pretended.

Followed almost immediately by anger. "You tricked me! You never intended to whip her."

He sniffed. "Do I usually whip my subs for making me come? Frankly, I'm offended you were fooled."

"Dammit, De'Lar, I was about to beat in your face! I was ready to take on you and the entire palace guard. Do you know what I'm capable of doing to an ordinary human? I could have hurt someone over that stupid stunt!"

"And what does that tell you?"

Jarred stopped in mid-rant, his eyes falling on Celeste. She still lay tied up in that ridiculously arousing bundle, but there was an expression of incredulous joy on her face.

Oh God, he realized, *I just admitted I love her.*

Jarred's first instinct was to take it all back. Yes, she made him hotter than any woman he'd ever known. Yes, he got hard just looking at those amazing breasts and long, muscled legs. He'd have to be an idiot not to admire the courage she'd displayed in facing him down, even when she'd thought he was going to kill her. And it was no surprise that he loved sparring with her—her wicked intelligence and sharp wit made her a delight to argue with, or even just to talk to. But that didn't mean . . .

Damn, he thought, dazed. *I really have fallen in love with her.*

". . . obvious, not that I could have taken her into my cloister anyway," De'Lar was saying. "That girl is no more a sexsub than I am. If you'd bothered to use your sensors instead of probing her cunt for her tonsils, you'd have realized she was only responding to you. Computer, replay 2030.23 to 2110 . . ." A three-dimensional holographic display popped into being over the bed, its screen splitting to show an amazingly lewd image of Jarred and De'Lar tying Celeste up. Beside the image, a colored line bounced. "She finds me mildly attractive, but when you touch her . . ."

The recorded Jarred caressed her nipple and the readout leaped like a scalded starhopper. The king looked down at Celeste, who was still staring at Jarred with a stunned look on her face. "Frankly, darling, I'm wounded. What does that big psychopath have that I don't?"

"Severe trust issues," she muttered. "Which have something to do with his mother."

"They usually do. You'd be better off staying with me."

"Probably." Visibly gathering her courage, she choked out, "But I'm not in love with you."

Jarred stared at her, his mind spinning images of taking her back to the ship, burying himself in her tight, creamy body whenever he wanted, arguing and laughing with her. Letting her heal the wounds in his soul he'd pretended to ignore.

Wounds . . .

An image flashed though his mind—Garr, lying in a blooded, broken heap, his blue eyes empty, his face so swollen from the beating that Jarred had been able to identify him only by sensor readings.

Oh, hell. He felt the hope leach from him, leaving him cold and empty. Indulging his need for her could cost her life, and that was one price he damn well had no intention of paying.

"No." He said the word through gritted teeth. "You're not manipulating me into this."

All the life drained from Celeste's eyes as her face went white with pain.

Jarred looked away from her wounded gaze, ignoring the stab

of guilt easily in the face of his panic. "She's not staying with me. I'll take her to Christ Colony if you won't accept her here."

"By all the Galactic Gods, Jarred, don't be more of an idiot than you already are!" De'Lar glared at him in disgust. "You may have saved my life from assassins twice now, but you are trying my patience! Do you seriously believe you'll be anything but miserable without this girl?"

"That's not the fucking point!" he snarled. "Do you know what I do for a living?"

De'Lar drew himself to his considerable height. "Watch your tongue, Varrain."

"Dammit, *Your Majesty,* I'm an agent of the Stellar Compact!" Jarred spat, clenching his fist around the whip he still held until his knuckles went white. "And *that* means I am regularly used for target practice by every criminal, assassin, and enemy agent who gets the urge. If she goes with me, she ends up in the crosshairs, too!"

"Yes," Celeste said, "but I'm not exactly helpless."

He whirled on her. *"Neither was Garr."*

She blinked in shock. "Oh."

"Yeah. Oh." He looked away, trying to force down the image of her lying broken and dead, just the way Garr had been.

De'Lar broke the thrumming silence. "To love," he said quietly, "is always to risk. She could also be killed in a aircab accident or contract Zvarian fever."

"Either of which would be better than being battered to shards of bone by a two-meter-tall reptilian sadist." Jarred closed his eyes. "Hell yes, De'Lar, I want to keep her with me. She fills something in me that's been empty for so damn long I'd never even noticed it until I kidnapped her. But I don't dare. It would be like sending her naked into a minefield." He opened his eyes and shot the king a savage look. "And damn you anyway for forcing me to realize how much I love her."

There was a hiss of flame and the stench of burning. He looked down just in time to see the charred ropes drop away from Celeste as she rolled off the bed.

"I repeat, I am not helpless," she said. "And I'm picking up new abilities all the time. I didn't even know I could do pyrokinesis until just now."

He glowered. "You're lucky you didn't burn yourself, you little idiot."

"Pyrokinesis?" Startled, the king stared at the burned ropes until his gaze turned speculative. He lifted a brow at Jarred. "Been holding out on me, my friend? What else can she do?"

"Not enough to keep her alive," Jarred growled.

"How do you know that?" Celeste demanded. "If my powers continue to develop—"

"You'll still be a liability! What happens when one of my enemies kidnaps you?" Lifting the cat o'nine tails, he shook it at her. "If one of *them* decides to use something like this, you can bet your sweet ass it won't be an empty threat . . ."

Before she could retort, a deafening boom hammered through the room. Automatically, Jarred spun toward the sound, dropping into a combat crouch as the floor shook under their feet, as breakables rattled and something smashed.

"Shit! What the hell was that?" De'Lar swore.

For a horrified instant, Jarred locked eyes with Celeste as the realization struck them both.

The assassin!

Before any of them could make a move, a round, glowing hole swirling with rainbow light popped into midair. Celeste blinked at it. It looked like the doorway she and Jarred had leaped through, but it was much, much bigger.

She knew in her gut that things were about to get nasty. Heart hammering, she reached inside herself for the psychic energy she would need to defend Jarred.

Something massive and scaly thrust its way through the opening. The shape was so alien it took her a moment to realize it was a long, fanged head. An instant later, an immense reptilian body followed, surging into the room in a mass of muscle and wings and long, whipping tail. Something fell over and smashed.

Gaping up at the massive creature, Celeste realized Mykhayl and Corinne sat astride its powerful back.

Good God, Celeste realized, stunned. *It's Khyber, the imperial dragon!*

She remembered Corinne's books. That's right, the great beast could fly between universes . . .

"A whip?" Corinne snarled, her cold gaze locked on the cat'o-nine-tails Jarred still held. Her eyes tracked to Celeste, whose eyes widened in horror as she remembered her own nudity—and realized the conclusion her sister was drawing from it. "You've been abusing her, haven't you, you prick? I knew it!"

Lifting one slim hand, Corinne gestured violently. A lightning bolt zapped right at his head.

Celeste reacted without thinking, throwing a force shield around Jarred with every desperate erg of power she had.

She barely got it formed in time. The bolt of magical energy sizzled into the shield, searing her mind as it found the psychic pathways she'd opened.

"Arrgh!" She instinctively diverted the magical attack, letting it zap harmlessly into the far wall. Chunks of scorched marble flew.

Celeste turned to try to reason with Corinne, but before she could open her mouth, Jarred plowed into her. "Get *down*, dammit!" Tumbling with her across the floor, he curled around her in a protective ball, shielding her body with his own—and making himself a prime target for the next energy bolt.

"Jarred, no! She'll . . ." she began, just as she heard her sister yell, "Shit, Celeste! Are you okay? I didn't mean to . . ."

Craning her neck, Celeste watched Corinne jump off the dragon's back. Instinctively, she sent a wave of psychic force at her sister to scoop her off the floor.

"Hey!" Corinne protested, but Celeste ignored the outraged cry and pinned her neatly against the wall. She wasn't taking any chances with the kind of power her sister had evidently acquired.

Corinne blinked down at the floor several feet below, looking as stunned as Celeste felt. "How did you *do* that . . . ?"

Before she could even attempt an answer, Jarred dove for his jacket, rolling to his feet with his ion pistol in one hand. "No!" Celeste gasped, leaping up to grab his shoulder.

With a roar of fury, Mykhayl vaulted from the dragon, drawing his great sword in one smooth, lethal gesture.

"Guards!" De'Lar bellowed, just as the double doors burst wide and a dozen armed troopers stormed in, weapons at ready.

This is about to turn into a goatfuck of epic proportions, Celeste realized, as Mykhayl and Jarred faced off and the guards trained their rifles on the largest target in the room—Khyber, the imperial dragon.

"ENOUGH!" The great beast's roar shook the room as its sapient golden gaze swept over them all. They instinctively froze like mice under a cat's glare. "I will do something exquisitely painful to the next mortal who makes a hostile gesture toward anyone else," the dragon said, sounding like a lethally fed-up Sean Connery. His massive head swung toward Celeste. "Put the queen down, wench."

She swallowed and lowered her sister carefully to the ground. "Queen? Corinne, what's going on? Why did you try to kill Jarred? Where did you get those powers?"

"Where did you get yours?" Corinne straightened her gown with a jerk and gave her a wounded look. "And why did you stop me? He was about to beat you with a whip!" She shot him a narrow-eyed, suspicious stare. "Have you done something to her, you psychopathic creep?"

Jarred glared back. "I was *not* going to beat her!" he snarled. "I took that whip away from him." He stabbed a finger toward De'Lar, who instinctually flinched.

"I wasn't going to beat her, either," the king said hastily, eying the dragon. "I was trying to make a point."

"They're telling the truth," Celeste said hastily as anger gathered on her sister's face.

"If you say so." Shooting Jarred another suspicious glare, Corinne turned toward her. "Look, we came to take you home. Back to Earth, or you can come with me to Mykhayl's universe. Whatever you want."

She blinked. "You're not going to Earth, too?"

"No." Corinne's gaze tracked toward Mykhayl. He met her eyes, a faint, hot smile curving his lips. "I've found somewhere I'd rather be."

"So you two . . ."

Corinne smiled. Mykhayl moved toward her, reaching out to take her hand and lift it to his lips for a kiss. The look that passed between them this time was more than carnal—it was tender.

It was love.

"We're married," her sister said, without looking away from the High King's eyes.

The passion between them was so strong it seemed to vibrate like the magic that had filled the room with their arrival. Celeste felt her heart twist in her chest. She'd never exchanged a look like that with Jarred.

Automatically she turned toward him. His face was cool with that utter lack of expression she knew so well and despised so much.

He'll never love me. Something fragile seemed to wither deep in her chest with the thought. *He's got too many fears, too much distrust. He's protected himself too well.*

It was time she stopped banging her head against the wall and went home. Back to what she could have—the career, the home, the life.

All so empty of him.

She wouldn't even have the solace of writing about him any more. She didn't dare. Not and risk that the plots she imagined might plunge him into some dark hell. Gathering her strength, she turned to Corinne. "I want to go home."

Jarred felt panic sink its fangs into his chest, sending streamers of ice through his veins. She was going to leave him, and he'd never see her again. Not even in limbo; he knew she'd never write about him again.

"I want to go home."

The words echoed in his head, setting off reverberations that seemed to shake his bones—until something in him rose up in revolt. "You are home."

She turned toward him, her brows flying up in astonishment.

Dammit, it was time to roll the dice and take a chance. Hell, he'd always been lucky. "This is your home. With me. And I'm not letting you leave."

Her eyes widened. "But . . . your enemies!"

"You can block lightning bolts. You can handle an alien reptile assassin or two." In two long strides he reached her and dragged her into his arms. The feeling of her long, lush nudity reminded him that neither of them wore a stitch. He didn't care.

Her small hands clamped with desperate strength around his forearms. "But you don't trust women."

"I don't trust myself." He pulled her close and hard. "But I'll learn."

"Took you long enough," Khyber said, his hot breath gusting over them. "I was beginning to wonder if the light would ever dawn."

"Wait a minute." Corinne's jaw dropped as her eyes widened with realization. "You did this, didn't you, you big iguana?"

Kyhber sniffed. "I have no idea what you're talking about."

"You lying lizard! The spell's right there! I can feel it. You linked us to Jarred's and Mykhayl's universes so we could sense what was going to happen . . ."

The dragon lowered his great head and peeled his lips back from fangs as long as her forearm. "Watch whom you address in that tone, mortal. I but served the Great Order, as I have since the birth of the Seven Kingdoms. You were fated to come to Mykhayl, just as this one was fated to come here. I merely set events in motion."

"And you neglected to disclose it?" Mykhayl demanded. "And if you planned this, why did you force me to deal with that greedy wizard to fetch them?"

"You needed to experience how to make magic that you might stop fearing its wielders."

Corinne snarled. "You overgrown gecko, you're the one who needs a lesson. I ought to . . ."

Celeste tuned her sister out, too intent on Jarred's hot black eyes to care. His mouth curved in a lush smile just before he lowered his head and took her lips in a sizzling kiss that made her knees weak.

Naked, wrapped in one another, they were barely aware when Corinne broke off in mid-tirade to look at them. De'Lar grinned and started for the door, shepherding his guards ahead of him. Corinne, Mykhayl, and the dragon trailed after him, still arguing.

"Humans," Khyber grumbled, just before the door closed. "Can't live with them, can't eat them . . . Well, you can, of course, but the survivors kick up such a fuss about it afterwards . . ."

The double doors banged closed.

Jarred lifted his head at last. "Speaking of eating someone," he purred, and swept her into his arms.

Celeste gave him a wicked grin that burst into a giggle as he tossed her lightly onto the bed. He followed her down, wrapping her in strong, warm arms.

At first, it was enough just to lie against him, touch him, savor the sweet knowledge that he loved her, that he wanted to be with her.

But then his big hands began to move on her breasts, her bottom, her thighs. In contrast to his usual demanding lovemaking, his touch was so tender she felt tears start to her eyes.

"God," he breathed against her mouth, his lips silken on hers. "Do you know how beautiful you are?"

When he lifted his head, she met his gaze as he stared down at her. His eyes were so dark, so deep and so hungry she had the sensation of freefalling into them. His long, warm fingers stroked her breasts, tugged sweetly at her nipples as pleasure unfurled deep in her core. She felt her sex began to dew and heat. As if sensing that, he reached his free hand between her thighs to find her still slick from the last time he'd ridden her. His eyes drifted closed in pleasure, and he groaned in anticipation as he slid a forefinger deep into her snug, creamy core.

Celeste purred as she watched his animal pleasure in her. Reaching up, she stroked the high, arrogant line of a perfect male cheekbone, felt velvet skin under her fingers and the rough prickle of his beard. He stirred, and she felt something long and thick come to rest heavily against her hip. Licking her lips, she knew it was his cock.

Suddenly she had to touch him there. Had to. Had to feel the promise of his silken shaft filling her hands as it would soon fill her tight cunt. Reaching down, she captured him, and groaned at the sensation. Smooth and hard and eager.

"So good," she moaned. "You feel so good."

"So do you," he whispered roughly, and bent to kiss her again.

And so they touched and stroked, slowly at first, then more quickly as the hunger began to prowl in them. His mouth on her nipples, then between her thighs, licking, savoring the spill of cream that gathered with each flick of his tongue. Returning the favor, crouching naked astride his head while she slid his massive cock into her mouth. Being filled by him was wickedly erotic, especially when he began to gently rock his hips, slowly fucking her lips.

The heat built between them as each used hot skill to drive the other into deeper arousal. Until finally neither could take it any more, and they came together in a sudden frenzy.

Kneeling astride him, Celeste impaled herself on his cock and began to ride him hard. His big hands stroked her nipples and her clit as she leaned back, grabbed her ankles in both hands, and ground herself down on his cock with all her strength. She gloried in his rough growl of approval.

"Yeah," he rumbled. "That's it. All the way in, darlin'."

"Oh, God," she whimpered, eyes closed as she circled her hips. Her entire being was locked on the sensation of that massive shaft screwing deep as his clever fingers stroked clit and nipples. "You feel so damn good. I'm about to . . . oh! Oh, I can't . . ."

"Yeah, yeah, yeah!" The chant built into a shout, then a roar as he began driving upward at her, skewering her on that amazing cock of his until pleasure and pain dueled at the depth of his penetration.

Then pleasure won, and the orgasm crashed over her in a white hot wave. As she convulsed, she felt his seed pump deep and hot inside her.

Then everything else spun away.

It was much later as she lay across him, limp and sated, that she felt him stir. His arms tightened on her. "Marry me."

Celeste stiffened. Afraid to believe he'd actually said the words, she lifted her head and stared at him. "What?"

He met her gaze, calm and determined—and very, very possessive. "Marry me. I never want you to leave."

"But what about your job? The Rekan? You said . . ."

"We can take care of a lizard or two," Jarred said. "But I can't make it without you."

Slowly, she smiled. "You won't have to. I love you, Jarred Varrain."

"I love you, too, Celeste Carson."

EPILOGUE

The next day, Celeste walked the length of De'Lar's throne room in a shimmering white gown that was as much her sister's magic as anything else. Jarred watched her approach, his gaze hot and intent with anticipation. His black dress uniform with its silver piping looked almost austere in the sheer colorful splendor of the throne room. Yet somehow, the uniform only made him look more thoroughly male.

His dark, brooding presence was a stark contrast to his best man's regal majesty. An elegant green brocade tunic showcased Mykhayl's broad chest, while matching silken trousers tucked into his green boots.

De'Lar, for his part, wore elegant silk robes in peacock shades of iridescent blue. He held a book in one big hand, ready to perform the Stellar Compact marriage ceremony.

At Celeste's side, Corrine wore a simple silk sheath in a delicate shade of green that made the most of her coloring. She looked almost as delighted as Celeste felt as she took possession of her sister's spray of fireroses. Noticing Celeste's elegant train wasn't quite straight, Corrine gestured, rearranging it with a flick of her magic.

At last De'Lar began speaking the words of the wedding ceremony in those velvet, rolling tones of his. The throne room went completely silent, as the gathered members of the palace staff watched with rapt interest.

Celeste had eyes for no one but Jarred. She stared up into his handsome face, into the dark gaze that seemed to shine with the love he so obviously felt. A bubble of joy swelled in her heart, until she could barely breathe around it.

She grinned in sheer giddy delight as Jarred recited his vows with no hesitation. Somehow she managed to get through her own, ignoring her sister's happy sniffles.

"And now," De'Lar said, closing his book with a snap, "I present Jarred and Celeste Carson–Varrain, united this day in joy. You may kiss the . . ."

Jarred snatched Celeste into his arms before the last word was out of his friend's mouth. She moaned in delight, kissing him back with her entire soul.

Meanwhile, at the back of the room, Khyber coiled his big body, his fanged snout curling in a smug dragon smile.

It had all worked out precisely as he'd intended.